HENNING MANKELL

The White Lioness

Internationally acclaimed author Henning Mankell has written numerous Kurt Wallander mysteries. The books have been published in thirty-three countries and consistently top the bestseller lists in Europe, receiving major literary prizes (including the UK's Golden Dagger Award in 2000) and generating numerous international film and television adaptations. Born in a village in northern Sweden in 1948, Mankell divides his time between Sweden and Maputo, Mozambique, where he works as the director of Teatro Avenida.

D1188702

The White Lioness

The White Lioness

A MYSTERY

HENNING MANKELL

Translated from the Swedish by
Laurie Thompson

Vintage Crime/Black Lizard
Vintage Books
A Division of Random House, Inc.
New York

FIRST VINTAGE CRIME/BLACK LIZARD OPEN-MARKET EDITION,
MAY 2003

Library of Congress Cataloging-in-Publication Data
Mankell, Henning, 1948–.
The white lioness : a mystery / Henning Mankell ; translated from the Swedish by
Laurie Thompson.
[Vita lejoninnan. English]
p. cm.
Originally published: [Stockholm] : Ordfront, 1993.
I. Title
PT9876.23.A49 V5813 2003
839.73'74—dc21

Vintage Open-Market ISBN: 1-4000-3438-8

www.vintagebooks.com

Printed in the United States of America
10 9 8 7 6 5 4 3 2 1

The White Lioness

Prologue

In 1990 Nelson Mandela was released from Robben Island, where he had been a political prisoner for almost thirty years.

While the world rejoiced, many Afrikaners regarded the release of Nelson Mandela as an unspoken but signed and sealed declaration of war. President de Klerk became a hated traitor.

At the time of Mandela's release, a group of men met in absolute secrecy to take upon themselves responsibility for the future of the Afrikaners. They were ruthless men. At the same time, however, they regarded themselves as having a divine mission. They would never submit.

They met in secret and reached a decision. They would spark off a civil war which could end only one way: in a devastating bloodbath.

The
Woman
from Ystad

Chapter One

Louise Åkerblom, a real estate agent, left the Savings Bank in Skurup shortly after three o'clock in the afternoon on Friday, April 24. She paused for a moment on the sidewalk and sucked the fresh air into her lungs, figuring out what to do next. What she wanted most of all was to leave work right now and drive home to Ystad. She had promised a widow who called her that morning to stop by at a house the woman wanted to sell.

She tried to figure out how long it would take. An hour, maybe; hardly more. And she had to buy some bread. Her husband Robert usually baked all the bread they needed, but he hadn't managed to that week. She crossed over the square and turned off to the left where the bakery was. An old-fashioned bell tinkled as she opened the door. She was the only customer; later, the lady behind the counter would remember that Louise Åkerblom seemed to be in a good mood, and chatted about how nice it was that spring had arrived at last.

She bought some rye bread, and decided to surprise the family with napoleons for dessert. Then she returned to the bank, where her car was parked out back. On the way she met the young couple from Malmö to whom she had just sold a house. They had been at the bank tying up loose ends, paying the seller his money, signing the contract and the loan agreement. She was delighted for them, their joy at owning their own home. At the same time, she felt uneasy. Would they manage the mortgage and interest payments? Times were hard, and hardly anybody could feel secure in their work any more. What would happen if he lost his job? She had run a careful check on their finances. Unlike many other young people, they had not thoughtlessly run up credit card debts, and the young

3

housewife seemed to be the thrifty type. They would no doubt cope with buying their house. If not, she would see it advertised again soon enough. Maybe she or Robert would be the one to sell it. It wasn't unusual nowadays for her to sell the same house two or three times in the course of just a few years.

She unlocked the car and dialed the number of the Ystad office on the car phone. Robert had already gone home. She heard his voice on the answering machine informing callers that Åkerblom's Real Estate was closed for the weekend, but would reopen Monday morning at eight o' clock.

At first she was surprised to hear Robert had left so early. Then she remembered he was due to meet their accountant that afternoon. She left a message on the answering machine: "Hi there! I'm just going to take a look at a house at Krageholm. Then I'll be off to Ystad. It's a quarter after three. I'll be home by five." She replaced the car phone in its holder. Robert might go back to the office after his meeting with the accountant.

She pulled over a plastic folder lying on the seat, and took out the map she had drawn from the widow's description. The house was on a side road between Krageholm and Vollsjö. It would take her just over an hour to get there, look at the house and grounds, then drive back to Ystad.

Then she hesitated. It can wait, she thought. I'll take the coast road home and stop for a while and look at the sea instead. I've already sold one house today: that'll have to be enough.

She began humming a hymn, started the engine, and drove out of Skurup. When she came to the Trelleborg exit, though, she changed her mind once more. She wouldn't have time to look at the widow's house Monday or Tuesday. The lady might be disappointed, and turn to some other agency. They couldn't afford to let that happen. Times were hard enough as it was. The competition was getting stiffer and stiffer. Nobody could afford to pass up anything that came their way, unless it was completely impossible.

She sighed and turned off in the other direction. The coast road and the sea would have to wait. She kept glancing at the map. Next week she would buy a map holder so she didn't have to keep turning her head to check that she was on the right road. The widow's house shouldn't be all that hard to find even if she had never been on the road the lady described. She knew the district inside out. She and

Robert would have been running the real estate agency for ten years come next year.

That thought surprised her. Ten years already. Time had passed so quickly, all too quickly. During those ten years she had given birth to two children and worked diligently with Robert to establish the firm. When they started up, times were good; she could see that. Now, they would never have managed to break into the market. She ought to feel pleased. God had been good to her and her family. She would talk to Robert again and suggest they could afford to increase their contributions to Save the Children. He would be doubtful, of course; he worried about money more than she did. No doubt she could talk him into it, though. She usually did.

She suddenly realized she was on the wrong road, and braked. Thinking about the family and the past ten years had made her miss the first exit. She laughed to herself, shook her head, and looked around carefully before making a U-turn and retracing her steps.

Skåne is a beautiful place, she thought to herself. Pretty and open. Yet secretive as well. What seemed at first sight to be so flat could suddenly change and reveal deep hollows with houses and farms like isolated islands. She never ceased to be amazed by the changing nature of the landscape when she drove around to look at houses or show them to prospective buyers.

She pulled onto the shoulder after Erikslund to check the directions the widow had given. She was right. She took a left and could see the road to Krageholm ahead of her; it was beautiful. The terrain was hilly, and the road wriggled its way through the Krageholm forest where the lake lay glittering away beyond the deciduous woods to the left. She had often driven along that road, and never tired of it.

After some seven kilometers she started looking for the final turnoff. The widow had described it as a dirt road, ungraveled but easily negotiable. She slowed down when she saw it and turned right; according to the map, the house would be on the left-hand side in about a kilometer.

After three kilometers the road suddenly petered out, and she realized she must be wrong after all.

Just for a moment she was tempted to forget about the house and drive straight home instead. But she resisted the thought and went back to the Krageholm road. About five hundred meters further north she turned right again. There were no houses answering to the description here, either. She sighed, turned around, and decided to stop and ask the way. Shortly before, she had passed a house half hidden behind a clump of trees.

She stopped, switched off the engine and got out of the car. There was a fresh smell from the trees. She started walking towards the house, a white-painted, half-timbered, U-shaped building, the kind Skåne is full of. Only one of the wings was still standing, however. In the middle of the front yard was a well with a black-painted pump.

She hesitated, and stopped. The house seemed completely deserted. Maybe it was best to go home after all, and hope the widow wouldn't be upset.

I can always knock, she thought. That doesn't cost anything.

Before she came to the house, she passed a large, red-painted barn. She couldn't resist the temptation to peek in through the high, half-open doors.

She was surprised by what she saw. There were two cars in there. She was not well-versed in cars, but she couldn't help noticing that one was an extremely expensive Mercedes, and the other an equally valuable BMW.

There must be somebody in, then, she thought, and continued toward the whitewashed house. Somebody who's not short of cash.

She knocked at the door, but nothing happened. She knocked again, harder this time; still no answer. She tried to peek in through a window next to the door, but the drapes were drawn. She knocked a third time, before going to see if there was a back door.

Behind the house was an overgrown orchard. The apple trees had certainly not been pruned for twenty or thirty years. Some half-rotten garden furniture was standing under a pear tree. A magpie flapped its wings loudly and flew away. She couldn't find a door, and returned to the front of the house.

I'll knock just one more time, she thought. If nobody answers, I'll go back to Ystad. There'll be time to stop by the sea for a while before I need to start making dinner.

She hammered on the door.

Still no answer.

She could feel rather than hear that someone had come up behind her from the courtyard. She turned abruptly.

The man was about a meter away from her. He was motionless, looking straight at her. She saw he had a scar on his forehead.

She suddenly felt uneasy.

Where had he come from? Why hadn't she heard him? The courtyard was graveled. Had he crept up on her?

She took a step toward him and tried to sound normal.

"I hope I'm not intruding," she said. "I'm a real estate agent, and I'm lost. I just wanted to ask my way."

The man did not answer.

Maybe he's not Swedish, she thought. Maybe he couldn't understand what she was saying. There was something strange about his appearance that made her think he could be a foreigner.

She suddenly knew she had to get away. The motionless man and his cold eyes were scaring her.

"I won't disturb you any longer," she said. "Sorry to intrude."

She started to walk away but stopped in mid-stride. The motionless man had suddenly come to life. He took something out of his jacket pocket. At first she couldn't see what it was. Then she realized it was a pistol.

Slowly, he raised the gun and pointed it at her head.

Good God, she managed to think.

Good God, please help me. He's going to kill me.

Good God, help me.

It was a quarter to four in the afternoon of April 24, 1992.

Chapter Two

When Detective Chief Inspector Kurt Wallander arrived at the police station in Ystad on Monday morning, April 27, he was furious. He couldn't remember the last time he'd been in such a bad mood. His anger had even left its traces on his face, a band-aid on one cheek where he cut himself shaving.

He muttered a reply to colleagues who said good morning. When he got to his office, he slammed the door behind him, took the phone off its hook, and sat staring out the window.

Kurt Wallander was forty-four years old. He was considered a proficient cop, persistent and occasionally astute. That morning, though, he felt only anger and an increasingly bad temper. Sunday had been one of those days he would have preferred to forget all about.

One of the causes was his father, who lived alone in a house on the plain just outside Löderup. His relationship with his father had always been complicated. Things had gotten no better over the years as Kurt Wallander realized, with a growing feeling of annoyance, that he was becoming more and more like him. He tried to imagine himself at the same stage as his father, but this made him feel ill at ease. Would he also end up a sullen and unpredictable old man, capable of suddenly doing something absolutely crazy?

On Sunday afternoon Kurt Wallander had visited his father as usual. They played cards and drank coffee out on the veranda in the warm spring sunshine. Out of the blue his father announced his intention of getting married. Kurt Wallander thought at first he had misheard him.

"No," he said, "I'm not going to get married."

"I'm not talking about you," his father responded, "I'm talking about me."

Kurt Wallander stared at him in disbelief.

"You're almost eighty," he said. "You aren't getting married."

"I'm not dead yet," interrupted his father. "I'll do whatever I like. You'd be better off asking me who."

Kurt Wallander did as he was told.

"You ought to be able to work it out for yourself," said his father. "I thought cops were paid to draw conclusions?"

"But you don't know anybody your age, do you? You keep pretty much to yourself."

"I know one," said his father. "And anyway, who says you have to marry somebody your own age?"

Kurt Wallander suddenly realized there was only one possibility: Gertrud Anderson, the fifty-year-old woman who came to do the cleaning and wash his father's feet three times a week.

"Are you going to marry Gertrud?" he asked. "Have you thought of asking her if she wants to? There's thirty years between you. How do you think you're going to be able to live with another person? You've never been able to. Not even with my mother."

"I've grown better-tempered in my old age," replied his father mildly.

Kurt Wallander couldn't believe his ears. His father was going to get married? Better-tempered in his old age? Now, when he was more impossible than he'd ever been?

Then they had quarreled. It ended up with his father throwing his coffee cup into the tulip bed and locking himself in the shed where he used to paint his pictures with the same motif, repeated over and over again: sunset in an autumnal landscape, with or without a wood grouse in the foreground, depending on the taste of whoever commissioned it.

Kurt Wallander drove home much too fast. He had to put a stop to this crazy business. How on earth could Gertrud Anderson work for his father for a year and not see it was impossible to live with him?

He parked the car on Mariagatan in central Ystad where he lived, and made up his mind to call his sister Kristina in Stockholm right away. He would ask her to come to Skåne. Nobody could change his father's mind. But perhaps Gertrud Anderson could be made to see sense.

He never got around to calling his sister. When he got up to his apartment on the top floor, he could see the door had been broken open. A few minutes later it was clear the thieves had marched off with his brand-new stereo equipment, CD player, all his discs and records, the television, radio, clocks, and a camera. He slumped into a chair and just sat there for a long while, wondering what to do. In the end, he rang his workplace and asked to speak with one of the CID inspectors, Martinson, who he knew was on duty that Sunday.

He was kept waiting for ages before Martinson eventually came to the phone. Wallander guessed he'd been having coffee and chatting to some of the cops who were taking a rest from the big traffic operation they were mounting that weekend.

"Martinson here. How can I help you?"

"It's Wallander. You'd better get your ass over here."

"Where? To your office? I thought you were off today?"

"I'm at home. Get out here."

Martinson evidently realized it must be serious. He asked no more questions.

"OK," he said. "I'm on my way."

The rest of Sunday was spent doing a technical investigation of the apartment and writing a case report. Martinson, one of the younger cops Wallander worked with, was sometimes careless and impulsive. All the same, Wallander liked working with him, not least because he often proved to be surprisingly perceptive. When Martinson and the police technician had left, Wallander did a very provisional repair job on the door.

He spent most of the night lying awake, thinking about how he'd beat the shit out of the thieves if he ever laid hands on them. When he could no longer bear to torture himself thinking about the loss of all his discs, he lay there worrying about what to do with his father, feeling more and more resigned to it all.

At dawn he got up, brewed some coffee and looked for his home insurance documents. He sat at his kitchen table going through the papers, getting increasingly annoyed at the insurance company's incomprehensible jargon. In the end he flung the papers to one side and went to shave. When he cut himself, he considered calling the station and telling them he was sick, then going back to bed with the cover over his head. But the thought of being in his apartment without even being able to listen to a CD was too much for him.

Now it was half past seven in the morning and he was sitting in his office with the door closed. With a groan, he forced himself to become a policeman again, and replaced the phone.

It rang immediately. It was Ebba, the receptionist.

"Sorry to hear about the burglary," she said. "Did they really take all your records?"

"They left me a few 78s. I thought I might listen to them tonight. If I can get hold of a wind-up gramophone."

"It's awful."

"That's the way it goes. What do you want?"

"There's a man out here who insists on talking to you."

"What about?"

"About some missing person or other."

Wallander looked at the stack of case notes on his desk.

"Can't Svedberg look after him?"

"Svedberg's out hunting."

"He's what?"

"I don't quite know what to call it. He's out looking for a young bull that broke out of a field at Marsvinsholm. It's running around on the E14 freeway, playing havoc with the traffic."

"Surely the traffic cops can deal with that? Why should one of our men have to get involved?"

"It was Björk who sent Svedberg."

"Oh, my God!"

"Shall I send him in to you, then? The man who wants to report a missing person?"

Wallander nodded into the phone.

"All right," he said.

The knock on his door a few minutes later was so discreet, Wallander was not sure at first whether he'd heard anything at all. When he shouted "Come in," however, the door opened right away.

Wallander had always been convinced the first impression a person makes is crucial.

The man who entered Wallander's office was not at all conspicuous. Wallander guessed he was about thirty-five with a dark brown suit, close-cropped blond hair, and glasses.

Wallander immediately noticed something else as well.

The man was obviously worried. Wallander was clearly not the only one with a sleepless night behind him.

He got to his feet and offered his hand.

"Kurt Wallander. Detective Inspector Wallander."

"My name is Robert Åkerblom," said the man. "My wife has disappeared."

Wallander was surprised by the man's forthright statement.

"Let's start from the beginning," he said. "Please sit down. I'm afraid the chair's a bit old. The left armrest keeps dropping off. Don't worry about it."

The man sat down on the chair.

He suddenly started sobbing, heart-broken, desperate.

Wallander remained standing at his desk, at a loss. Then he decided to wait.

The man in the visitor's chair calmed down after a couple of minutes. He dried his eyes and blew his nose.

"I'm sorry," he said. "Something must have happened to Louise, though. She would never go away of her own accord."

"Cup of coffee?" asked Wallander. "Maybe we can get a pastry or something as well."

"No thank you," said Robert Åkerblom.

Wallander nodded and took a notebook out of one of the desk drawers. He used regular note pads he bought himself at the local bookstore, with his own money. He'd never managed to get around to coping with the flood of printed report forms the Central Police Authority used to overwhelm the force with. He'd occasionally thought of writing a letter to *Swedish Policeman* proposing that whoever drew up the forms should be presented with printed replies.

"You'd better start by giving me your personal details," said Wallander.

"My name's Robert Åkerblom," the man said. "I run Åkerblom's Real Estate with my wife."

Wallander nodded as he wrote. He knew the offices were close to the Saga cinema.

"We have two children," Robert Åkerblom went on, "ages four

and seven. Two girls. We live in a row house, 19 Åkarvägen. I was born in this town. My wife comes from Ronneby."

He broke off, took a photo out of his inside pocket, and put it on the desk in front of Wallander. It was a woman; she looked like any other woman. She was smiling at the photographer, and Wallander could see it was taken in a studio. He contemplated her face and decided it was somehow or other just right for Robert Åkerblom's wife.

"The photo was taken only three months ago," said Robert Åkerblom. "That's exactly what she looks like."

"And she's disappeared, has she?" asked Wallander.

"Last Friday she was at the Savings Bank in Skurup, clinching a property deal. Then she was going to look at a house somebody was putting on the market. I spent the afternoon with our accountant, at his office. I stopped in at the agency on my way home. She'd left a message on the answering machine saying she'd be home by five. She said it was a quarter after three when she called. That's the last we know."

Wallander frowned. It was Monday today. She'd already been away for three days. Three whole days, with two small children waiting for her at home.

Wallander felt instinctively that this was no ordinary disappearance. He knew that most people who went missing came back sooner or later, and that a natural explanation would gradually emerge. It was very common for people to go away for a few days or even a week, for instance, and forget to tell anybody. On the other hand, he also knew that relatively few women abandoned their children. That worried him.

He made a few notes on his pad.

"Do you still have the message she left on the answering machine?" he asked.

"Yes," said Robert Åkerblom. "I didn't think of bringing the cassette with me, though."

"That's OK, we'll sort that out later," said Wallander. "Was it clear where she was calling from?"

"She used the car phone."

Wallander put down his pen and contemplated the man on the visitor's chair. His anxiety gave the impression of being absolutely genuine.

"You can't think of why she might have had to go away?" Wallander asked.

"No."

"She can't be visiting friends?"

"No."

"Relatives?"

"No."

"There's no other possibility you can think of?"

"No."

"I hope you won't mind if I ask you some personal questions."

"We've never quarreled. If that's what you were wanting to know."

Wallander nodded.

"That was what I was going to ask," he said.

He started all over again.

"You say she disappeared last Friday afternoon. But you waited for three days before coming to us?"

"I was afraid," said Robert Åkerblom.

Wallander stared at him in surprise.

"Going to the police would be like accepting that something awful had happened," Robert Åkerblom went on. "That's why I didn't dare."

Wallander nodded slowly. He knew exactly what Robert Åkerblom meant.

"You've been out looking for her, of course," he went on.

Robert Åkerblom nodded.

"What other steps have you taken?" he asked, starting to make notes again.

"I've prayed to God," replied Robert Åkerblom, quite simply.

Wallander stopped writing.

"Prayed to God?"

"My family are Methodists. Yesterday, we joined the whole congregation and Pastor Tureson in praying that nothing unthinkable can have happened to Louise."

Wallander could feel something gnawing away in his stomach. He tried to conceal his disquiet from the man in the chair before him.

A mother with two children, member of a free church, he thought to himself. She wouldn't just disappear of her own accord.

Not unless she'd gone out of her mind. Or been possessed by religion. A mother of two children would hardly stroll out into the forest and take her own life. Such things do happen, but very rarely.

Wallander knew what was afoot.

Either there had been an accident, or Louise Åkerblom was the victim of a crime.

"Of course, you realize there might have been an accident," he said.

"I've called every hospital in Skåne," said Robert Åkerblom. "She hasn't been admitted anywhere. Besides, a hospital would have been in touch with me if anything had happened. Louise always had her ID card on her."

"What make of car did she drive?" asked Wallander.

"A Toyota Corolla. 1990 model. Dark blue. Registration number MHL 449."

Wallander wrote it all down.

Then he went back to the beginning again, methodically going through the details Robert Åkerblom knew about what his wife was doing that afternoon. They looked at maps, and Wallander could feel unease growing within him.

For God's sake, let's not have the murder of a woman on our plates, he thought. Anything but that.

Wallander put down his pen at a quarter to eleven.

"There's no reason to suppose that your wife won't be found safe and sound," he said, hoping his skepticism was not apparent. "But needless to say, we'll treat your report with the utmost seriousness."

Robert Åkerblom was slumped down on the chair. Wallander was afraid he might start bawling again. He suddenly felt incredibly sorry for him. He would have loved to console him. But how could he do that without showing how worried he really felt?

He got up from his chair.

"I'd like to listen to her telephone message," he said. "Then I'll drive over to Skurup and call in at the bank. Have you got somebody to help out with the children?"

"I don't need any help," said Robert Åkerblom. "I can manage on my own. What do you think has happened to Louise, Inspector?"

"I don't think anything at all as yet," replied Wallander. "Except that she'll soon be back home again."

I'm lying, he thought.

I don't think that. I'm just hoping.

Wallander followed Robert Åkerblom back into town. As soon as he had listened to the message on the answering machine and gone through her desk drawers, he'd go back to the office and talk to Björk. Even if there were very clear procedures for how to go about looking for a missing person, Wallander wanted all available resources placed at his disposal right away. The disappearance of Louise Åkerblom indicated from the start that a crime had been committed.

Åkerblom's Real Estate was located in a former grocery store. Wallander recalled it from his first year in Ystad, when he'd arrived as a young cop from Malmö. There were a couple of desks, and some stands with photographs and descriptions of properties. There was a table with visitors' chairs where clients could delve into the details of the various properties they were interested in. On the wall were a couple of ordinance survey maps, covered in pins of various colors. There was a little kitchen behind the office itself.

They entered the back way, but even so, Wallander noticed the handwritten card taped to the front door: "Closed Today."

"Which is your desk?" asked Wallander.

Robert Åkerblom pointed. Wallander sat down at the other desk. It was empty, apart from a diary, a photo of their two daughters, a few files and a pen stand. Wallander had the impression it had recently been tidied up.

"Who does the cleaning?" he asked.

"We have a cleaner who comes in three times a week," Robert Åkerblom replied. "Mind you, we generally do the dusting and empty the wastebaskets every day ourselves."

Wallander nodded. Then he took a look around the office. The only thing that struck him as being odd was a little crucifix on the wall by the kitchen door.

Then he nodded at the answering machine.

"It'll come right away," said Robert Åkerblom. "It was the only message we had after three o'clock on Friday."

First impressions, was what Wallander was thinking. Listen carefully now.

Hi there! I'm just going to take a look at a house at Krageholm. Then I'll be off to Ystad. It's a quarter after three. I'll be home by five.

Cheerful, thought Wallander. She sounds happy and keen. Not threatened, not scared.

"One more time," said Wallander. "But first I want to hear what you yourself say on the tape. If you still have that?"

Robert Åkerblom nodded, rewound the cassette, and pressed a button.

Welcome to Åkerblom's Real Estate. Right now we're out on business. But we'll be open again as usual on Monday morning, eight o'clock. If you would like to leave a message or send a fax, please do so after the beep. Thank you for calling, and we look forward to hearing from you again.

Wallander could hear that Robert Åkerblom was not comfortable when confronted with the answering machine's microphone. His voice sounded slightly strained.

Then he turned his attention to Louise Åkerblom again, and asked her husband to wind the tape back time after time.

Wallander tried to listen for some message that might have been concealed behind the words. He had no idea what it might be. But he tried even so.

When he had heard the tape some ten times, he nodded to Robert Åkerblom, indicating that was enough.

"I'll have to take the cassette with me," he said. "We can amplify the sound at the station."

Robert Åkerblom took out the little cassette and handed it to Wallander.

"I'd like you to do something for me while I'm going through the drawers in her desk," said Wallander. "Write down everything she did or was going to do last Friday. Who she was due to meet, and where. Write down what route you think she would have taken as well. Note the times. And I want an exact description of where that house is, the one she was going to look at near Krageholm."

"I can't tell you that," said Robert Åkerblom.

Wallander looked at him in surprise.

"It was Louise who took the call from the lady who wanted to sell the house," explained Robert Åkerblom. "She drew a map for herself, and took it with her. She wouldn't be putting all the details into a file until today. If we'd taken on the house either she or I would have gone back there to take a photograph."

Wallander thought for a moment.

"In other words, at the moment Louise is the only one who knows where the house is," he said.

Robert Åkerblom nodded.

"When would the lady who called get in touch again?" Wallander went on.

"Some time today," said Robert Åkerblom. "That's why Louise wanted to try and see the house on Friday."

"It's important that you're here when she calls," said Wallander. "Say that your wife has taken a look at the house, but unfortunately she's sick today. Ask for a description of how to get there again, and take her telephone number. As soon as she's been in touch, give me a call."

Robert Åkerblom nodded to show he'd understood. Then he sat down to write out the details Wallander wanted.

Wallander opened the desk drawers one at a time. He found nothing that seemed significant. None of the drawers appeared to be recently emptied. He lifted the green blotting pad, and found a recipe for hamburgers, torn from a magazine. Then he contemplated the photo of the two daughters.

He got up and went out into the kitchen. Hanging on one of the walls was a calendar and a sampler with a quotation from the Bible. A small jar of coffee was on one of the shelves, unopened. On another were several kinds of tea. He opened the refrigerator. A liter of milk and some margarine.

He thought about her voice, and what she'd said on the telephone. He was sure the car had been stationary when she made the call. Her voice was steady. It would not have been if she had been concentrating on driving at the same time. Later, when they amplified the sound at the station, he was proven right. Besides, Louise Åkerblom was sure to be a careful, law-abiding citizen who would not risk her life nor anybody else's by using the car phone while driving.

If the times she mentioned are right, she'll be in Skurup, thought Wallander. She'll have concluded her business at the bank and be about to set off for Krageholm. But she wants to call her husband first. She's pleased that everything went well at the bank. Moreover it's Friday afternoon, and she's finished work for the day. It's nice weather. She has every reason to feel happy.

Wallander went back and sat down at her desk once more, leafing through the desk diary. Robert Åkerblom handed him a sheet of paper with the details Wallander had asked for.

"I have just one more question for the moment," said Wallander. "It isn't really a question. But it is important. What kind of a person is Louise?"

He was very careful to use the present tense, as if nothing had happened. In his own mind, however, Louise Åkerblom was already someone who no longer existed.

"Everybody likes her," said Robert Åkerblom straightforwardly. "She's even-tempered, laughs a lot, finds it easy to talk to people. Actually, she finds it hard to do business. Anything to do with money or complicated negotiations, she hands over to me. She's easily moved. And upset. She's troubled by other people's suffering."

"Does she have any special idiosyncrasies?" asked Wallander.

"Idiosyncrasies?"

"We all have our peculiarities," said Wallander.

Robert Åkerblom thought for a moment.

"I can't think of anything," he said eventually.

Wallander nodded and got to his feet. It was already a quarter to twelve. He wanted to have a word with Björk before his boss went home for lunch.

"I'll be in touch later this afternoon," he said. "Try not to worry too much. See if you can think of anything you've forgotten. Something I ought to know about."

"What happened, do you think?" asked Robert Åkerblom as they shook hands.

"Probably nothing at all," said Wallander. "There's bound to be a natural explanation."

Wallander got hold of Björk just as he was about to leave. He was looking harassed, as usual. Wallander imagined a chief constable's job wasn't something to feel envious about.

"Sorry to hear about the burglary," said Björk, trying to look sympathetic. "Let's hope the newspapers don't get hold of this one. It wouldn't look good, a detective inspector's home being broken into. We have a high percentage of unsolved cases. The Swedish police force is pretty low on the international league tables."

"That's the way it goes," said Wallander. "I need to talk to you about something."

They were standing in the corridor outside Björk's office.

"It can't wait till after lunch," he added.

Björk nodded, and they went back into the office.

Wallander put his cards on the table. He reported in detail his meeting with Robert Åkerblom.

"A mother of two, religious," said Björk when Wallander had finished. "Missing since Friday. Doesn't sound good."

"No," said Wallander. "It doesn't sound good at all."

Björk eyed him shrewdly.

"You think there's been a crime?"

Wallander shrugged.

"I don't really know what I think," he said. "But this isn't a straightforward missing persons case. I'm sure about that. That's why we ought to mobilize the right resources from the start. Not just the usual wait-and-see tactics."

Björk nodded.

"I agree," he said. "Who do you want? Don't forget we're understaffed as long as Hanson's away. He managed to pick just the wrong moment to break his leg."

"Martinson and Svedberg," replied Wallander. "By the way, did Svedberg find that young bull that was careening around the E14?"

"A farmer got it with a lasso in the end," said Björk glumly. "Svedberg twisted his ankle when he tumbled into a ditch. But he's still at work."

Wallander stood up.

"I'll drive out to Skurup now," he said. "Let's get together at half past four and sort out what we know. We'd better start looking for her car right away."

He put a piece of paper on Björk's desk.

"Toyota Corolla," said Björk. "I'll see to that."

Wallander drove from Ystad to Skurup. He needed some time to think, and chose the coastal route.

A wind was picking up. Jagged clouds were racing across the sky. He could see a ferry from Poland on its way into the harbor.

When he got as far as Mossby Beach, he drove down to the deserted parking lot and stopped by the boarded-up hamburger stand. He stayed in the car, thinking about the previous year when a rubber dinghy had drifted into land just here, with two dead men in it. He thought about Baiba Liepa, the woman he'd met in Riga. Interesting that he hadn't managed to forget her, despite his best efforts.

A year ago, and he was still thinking about her all the time.

A murdered woman was the last thing he needed right now.

What he needed was peace and quiet.

He thought about his father getting married. About the burglary and all the music he'd lost. It felt as if someone had robbed him of an important part of his life.

He thought about his daughter, Linda, at college in Stockholm. He had the feeling he was losing touch with her.

It was too much, all at once.

He got out of the car, zipped up his jacket and walked down to the beach. The air was chilly, and he felt cold.

He went over in his mind what Robert Åkerblom had said, tried various theories yet again. Could there be a natural explanation, despite everything? Could she have committed suicide? He thought of her voice on the telephone. Her eagerness.

Shortly before one Wallander left the beach and continued his way towards Skurup.

He couldn't shake the conclusion he had come to: Louise Åkerblom was dead.

Chapter Three

Kurt Wallander had a recurring daydream he suspected he shared with a lot of other people: that he'd pulled off the ultimate bank robbery and astounded the world. He wondered about how much money was generally kept at a normal-sized bank. Less than you might think? But more than enough? He didn't know precisely how he'd go about it, yet the fantasy kept recurring.

He grinned to himself at the thought. But the grin quickly faded with his guilty conscience.

He was convinced they would never find Louise Åkerblom alive. He had no evidence; there was no crime scene, no victim. And yet he knew.

He couldn't get the photo of the two girls out of his mind.

How do you explain what it's not possible to explain, he wondered. How will Robert Åkerblom be able to go on praying to his God in the future, the God who's left him and two kids so cruelly in the lurch?

Kurt Wallander wandered around the Savings Bank at Skurup, waiting for the assistant manager who had helped Louise Åkerblom with the property deal the previous Friday to come back from the dentist. When Wallander had arrived at the bank a quarter of an hour earlier, he had talked with the manager, Gustav Halldén, whom he had met once before. He also asked Halldén to keep any information confidential.

"After all, we're not sure if anything serious has happened," Wallander explained.

"I get it," said Halldén. "You just think something may have happened."

Wallander nodded. That's exactly how it was. How could you

possibly be sure just where the boundary was between thinking and knowing?

His train of thought was interrupted by somebody addressing him.

"I believe you wanted to talk to me," said a man with a fuzzy voice behind him.

Wallander turned round.

"Are you Moberg, the assistant manager?"

The man nodded. He was young, surprisingly young according to Wallander's idea of how old an assistant manager should be. But there was something else that immediately attracted his attention.

One of the man's cheeks was noticeably swollen.

"I still have some trouble speaking," sputtered Moberg.

Wallander couldn't understand what the man was saying.

"We'd better wait," Moberg said. "Shouldn't we wait until the injection has worn off?"

"Let's try anyway," said Wallander. "I'm short on time, I'm afraid. If it doesn't hurt too much when you talk."

Moberg shook his head and led the way into a small conference room at the back.

"This is exactly where we were," explained the assistant manager. "You're sitting in Louise Åkerblom's chair. Halldén said you wanted to talk about her. Has she disappeared?"

"She's been reported missing," said Wallander. "I expect she's just visiting relatives and forgot to tell them at home."

He could see from Moberg's swollen face that he regarded Wallander's reservations with great skepticism. Fair enough, thought Wallander. If you're missing, you're missing. You can't be half-way missing.

"What was it you want to know?" asked the assistant manager, pouring a glass of water from the carafe on the table and gulping it down.

"What happened last Friday afternoon," said Wallander. "In detail. Exact time, what she said, what she did. I also want the name of the parties buying and selling the house, in case I need to contact them later. Had you met Louise Åkerblom before?"

"I met her several times," answered Moberg. "We were involved in four property deals together."

"Tell me about last Friday."

The assistant manager took out his diary from the inside pocket of his jacket.

"The meeting had been set for a quarter after two," he said. "Louise Åkerblom turned up a couple of minutes early. We exchanged a few words about the weather."

"Did she seem tense or worried?" asked Wallander.

Moberg thought for a moment before answering.

"No," he said. "On the contrary, she seemed happy. Before, I always thought she was uptight, but not on Friday."

Wallander nodded, encouraging him to go on.

"The clients arrived, a young couple called Nilson. And the seller, representing the estate of somebody who'd died in Sövde. We sat down here and went through the whole procedure. There was nothing unusual. All the documents were in order. The deeds, the mortgage bond, the loan forms, the draft. It didn't take long. Then we broke up. I expect we all wished one another a pleasant weekend, but I can't remember that."

"Was Louise Åkerblom in a hurry?" asked Wallander.

The assistant manager thought it over again.

"Could be," he said. "Maybe she was. I'm not sure. But there is something I'm quite certain about."

"What?"

"She didn't go straight to her car."

Moberg pointed at the window, which looked out over a little parking lot.

"Those lots are for the bank's customers," the assistant manager went on. "I saw her park there when she arrived. It was a quarter of an hour after she'd left the bank before she drove off. I was still in here, on the telephone. That's how I could see everything. I think she had a bag in her hand when she got to the car. As well as her briefcase."

"A bag?" asked Wallander. "What did it look like?"

Moberg shrugged his shoulders. Wallander could see the injection was wearing off.

"What does a bag look like?" said the assistant manager. "I think it was a paper bag. Not plastic."

"And then she drove off?"

"Before that she made a call from her car phone."

To her husband, thought Wallander. Everything fits in so far.

"It was just after three," Moberg went on. "I had another meeting at three-thirty, and needed to prepare myself. My own call dragged on a bit."

"Could you see when she drove off?"

"I'd already gone back to my office by then."

"So the last you saw of her was when she was using the car phone."

Moberg nodded.

"What make of car was it?"

"I'm not so up on cars," said the assistant manager. "But it was black. Dark blue, perhaps."

Wallander shut his notebook.

"If you think of anything else, let me know right away," he said. "Any little thing could be important."

Wallander left the bank after noting down the name and telephone numbers of both the seller and the buyer. He used the front entrance, and paused in the square.

A paper bag, he thought to himself. That sounds like a bakery. He remembered there was a bakery on the street running parallel to the railroad. He crossed over the square then turned off to the left.

The girl behind the counter had been working all day Friday, but she didn't recognize Louise Åkerblom from the photo Wallander showed her.

"There is another bakery," said the girl.

"Whereabouts?"

The girl explained, and Wallander could see it was just as close to the bank as the one where he was now. He thanked her, and left. He made his way to the bakery on the other side of the square. An elderly lady asked him what he wanted as he entered the shop. Wallander showed her the photograph and explained who he was.

"I wonder if you recognize her?" he asked. "She might have been here shopping shortly after three o'clock last Friday."

The woman went to fetch her eyeglasses in order to study the photo more carefully.

"Has something happened?" she asked, curious to know. "Who is she?"

"Just tell me if you recognize her," said Wallander gently.

The woman nodded.

"I remember her," she said. "I think she bought some pastries. Yes, I remember quite clearly. Napoleons. And a loaf of bread."

Wallander thought for a moment.

"How many pastries?" he asked.

"Four. I remember I was going to put them in a carton, but she said a bag would be OK. She seemed to be in a hurry."

Wallander nodded.

"Did you see where she went after she left?"

"No. There were other customers waiting to be served."

"Thank you," said Wallander. "You've been a great help."

"What happened?" the woman asked.

"Nothing," said Wallander. "Just routine."

He left the store and walked back to the rear of the bank where Louise Åkerblom had parked her car.

Thus far but no further, he thought. This is where we lose track. She sets out from here to see a house, but we still don't know where it is. After she'd left a message on the answering machine. She's in a good mood, she has pastries in a paper bag, and she's due home at five o'clock.

He looked at his watch. Three minutes to three. Exactly three days since Louise Åkerblom was standing on this very spot.

Wallander walked to his car, which was parked in front of the bank, put in a music cassette, one of the few he had left after the break-in, and tried to summarize where he'd gotten so far. Placido Domingo's voice filled the car as he thought about the four pastries, one for each member of the Åkerblom family. Then he wondered if they said grace before eating pastries as well. He wondered what it felt like to believe in a god.

An idea occurred to him at the same time. He had time for one more interview before they were gathering at the station to talk things through.

What had Robert Åkerblom said?

Pastor Tureson?

Wallander started the engine and drove off towards Ystad. When he came out onto the E14, he was only just within the speed limit. He called Ebba at the station switchboard, asked her to get hold of Pastor Tureson and tell him Wallander wanted to speak to him right away. Just before he got to Ystad, Ebba called him back. Pastor

Tureson was in the Methodist chapel and would be pleased to see him.

"It'll do you no harm to go to church now and again," said Ebba.

Wallander thought about the nights he'd spent with Baiba Liepa in a church in Riga the previous year. But he said nothing. Even if he wanted to, he had no time to think about her just now.

Pastor Tureson was an elderly man, tall and well built, with a mop of white hair. Wallander could feel the strength in his grip when they shook hands.

The inside of the chapel was simple. Wallander did not feel the oppression that often affected him when he went into a church. They sat down on wooden chairs by the altar.

"I called Robert a couple of hours ago," said Pastor Tureson. "Poor man, he was beside himself. Have you found her yet?"

"No," said Wallander.

"I don't understand what can have happened. Louise wasn't the type to get herself into dangerous situations."

"Sometimes you can't avoid it," said Wallander.

"What do you mean by that?"

"There are two kinds of dangerous situations. One is the kind you get yourself into. The other just sucks you in. That's not quite the same thing."

Pastor Tureson threw up his hands in acknowledgment. He seemed genuinely worried, and his sympathy with the husband and their children appeared to be real.

"Tell me about her," said Wallander. "What was she like? Had you known her long? What sort of a family were the Åkerbloms?"

Pastor Tureson stared at Wallander, a serious expression on his face.

"You ask questions as though it were all over," he said.

"It's just a bad habit of mine," said Wallander apologetically. "Of course I mean you should tell me what she *is* like."

"I've been pastor in this parish for five years," he began. "As you can probably hear, I'm originally from Göteborg. The Åkerbloms have been members of my congregation the whole time I've been here. They both come from Methodist families, and they met through the chapel. Now they're bringing up their daughters in the true religion. Robert and Louise are good people. Hard-working, thrifty, generous. It's hard to describe them any other way. In fact, it's hard not to talk about them as a couple. Members of the congregation are shattered by her disappearance. I could feel that at our prayer meeting yesterday."

The perfect family. Not a single crack in the façade, thought Wallander. I could talk to a thousand different people, and they would all say the same thing. Louise Åkerblom doesn't have a single weakness. Not one. The only odd thing about her is that she has disappeared.

Something doesn't add up. Nothing adds up.

"Something on your mind, Inspector?" asked Pastor Tureson.

"I was thinking about weakness," said Wallander. "Isn't that one of the basic features of all religions? That God will help us to overcome our weaknesses?"

"Absolutely."

"But it seems to me like Louise Åkerblom didn't have any weaknesses. The picture I'm getting of her is so perfect, I start getting suspicious. Do such utterly good people really exist?"

"That's the kind of person Louise is," said Pastor Tureson.

"You mean she's almost angelic?"

"Not quite," said Pastor Tureson. "I remember one time when she was making coffee for a social evening the chapel had organized. She burnt herself. I happened to hear that she actually swore."

Wallander tried going back to the beginning and starting again.

"There's no chance she and her husband were fighting?" he asked.

"None at all," replied Pastor Tureson.

"No other man?"

"Of course not. I hope that isn't a question you'll put to Robert."

"Could she have felt some kind of religious doubt?"

"I regard that as being out of the question. I'd have known about it."

"Was there any reason why she might have committed suicide?"

"No."

"Could she have gone out of her mind?"

"Why ever should she? She's a perfectly stable character."

"Most people have their secrets," said Wallander after a moment's silence. "Can you imagine that Louise Åkerblom might have had some secret she couldn't share with anybody, not even her husband?"

Pastor Tureson shook his head.

"Of course everybody has secrets," he said. "Often very murky secrets. All the same, I'm convinced Louise didn't have any that could lead her to abandon her family and cause all this worry."

Wallander had no more questions.

It doesn't add up, he thought again. There's something in this picture of perfection that simply doesn't add up.

He got to his feet and thanked Pastor Tureson.

"I'll be talking with other members of your congregation," he said. "If she doesn't turn up, that is."

"She'll have to turn up," said Pastor Tureson. "There's no other possibility."

It was five minutes past four when Wallander left the Methodist chapel. It had started raining, and he shivered in the wind. He sat in the car for a while, feeling tired. It was as if he couldn't cope with the thought that two little girls had lost their mother.

At half past four they were all gathered in Björk's office at the police station. Martinson was slumped back on the sofa; Svedberg leaned against a wall. As usual he was scratching his bald head, as if searching absentmindedly for the hair he had lost. Wallander sat on a wooden chair. Björk was leaning over his desk, engrossed in a telephone conversation. At last he put down the receiver and told Ebba they were not to be disturbed for the next half-hour. Unless it was Robert Åkerblom.

"Where are we?" asked Björk. "Where shall we start?"

"We've gotten nowhere," replied Wallander.

"I've filled in Svedberg and Martinson," Björk went on. "We've put out a search for her car. All the usual routines for missing person cases we consider to be serious."

"Not *consider* to be serious," said Wallander. "They *are* serious. If there had been an accident, we'd have heard about it by now. But we haven't. That means we're dealing with a crime. I'm convinced she's dead."

Martinson started to ask a question, but Wallander interrupted and summarized what he'd been doing that afternoon. He had to get his colleagues to see what he had realized. A person like Louise Åkerblom wouldn't voluntarily abandon her family.

Somebody or something must have forced her to fail to turn up at home at five o'clock, as she had promised on the telephone.

"It sounds nasty, no doubt about that," said Björk when Wallander had finished.

"Real estate agent, free church member, family," said Martinson. "Maybe it all got too much for her? She buys the pastries, drives off home. Then all of a sudden she turns around and heads for Copenhagen instead."

"We have to find the car," said Svedberg. "Without that, we won't get anywhere."

"First of all we have to find the house she was going to see," Wallander pointed out. "Hasn't Robert Åkerblom called yet?"

No one had heard from him.

"If she really did go to see that house somewhere near Krageholm, we ought to be able to follow her tracks until we find her, or until the tracks come to an end."

"Peters and Norén have been combing the side roads around Krageholm," said Björk. "No Toyota Corolla. They did find a stolen truck, though."

Wallander took the cassette from the answering machine out of his pocket. With some considerable difficulty they eventually managed to find a machine to play it. They all stood around the desk, listening to Louise Åkerblom's voice.

"We have to analyze the tape," said Wallander. "I can't imagine what the technical guys could possibly find. But still."

"One thing is clear," said Martinson. "When she left her message she wasn't threatened or pressured, scared or worried, desperate or unhappy."

"Which means something must have happened," said Wallander. "Between three and five. Somewhere in the area of Skurup, Krageholm, Ystad. Just over three days ago."

"How was she dressed?" asked Björk.

Wallander suddenly realized he'd forgotten to ask her husband this most basic question. He admitted as much.

"I still think there could be a natural explanation," said Martinson thoughtfully. "It's like you say yourself, Kurt. She's not the type to disappear of her own free will. But in spite of everything, assault

3 1

and murder are still pretty rare. I think we should go about it in the usual way. Let's not get hysterical."

"I'm not hysterical," said Wallander, realizing he was getting mad. "I know what I think, though, and I think certain conclusions speak for themselves."

Björk was just about to intervene when the telephone rang.

"I said we shouldn't be disturbed," said Björk.

Wallander quickly put his hand over the receiver.

"It could be Robert Åkerblom," he said. "Maybe it's best if I talk to him?"

He picked up the phone and gave his name.

"Robert Åkerblom here. Have you found Louise?"

"No," said Wallander. "Not yet."

"The widow just called," said Robert Åkerblom. "I have a map. I'm going there myself to take a look."

Wallander thought for a moment.

"I'll take you there," he said. "That'll probably be best. I'll come right away. Can you make a few copies of the map? Five will do."

"OK," said Robert Åkerblom.

Wallander thought how truly religious people were usually law-abiding and compliant with authority. Yet nobody could have stopped Robert Åkerblom from going out on his own to look for his wife.

Wallander slammed down the receiver.

"We have a map now," he said. "We'll take two cars to start with. Robert Åkerblom wants to come along. He can ride with me."

"Shouldn't we take a few patrol cars?" wondered Martinson.

"We'd have to drive as a column if we did that," said Wallander. "Let's take a look at the map first, and draw up a plan. Then we can send out everything we've got."

"Call me if anything happens," said Björk. "Here or at home."

Wallander almost ran down the corridor. He was in a hurry. He had to know if the track just petered out. Or if Louise Åkerblom was out there somewhere.

They took the map Robert Åkerblom had sketched in accordance with what he'd heard and spread it out over the hood of Wallander's car. Svedberg had dried it first with his handkerchief, as it had rained earlier that afternoon.

"E14," said Svedberg, "As far as the exit for Katslösa and Lake Kade. Take a left to Knickarp, then a right, then left again, and look for a dirt road."

"Wait a minute," said Wallander. "If you'd been in Skurup, which road would you have taken then?"

There were lots of possibilities. After some discussion Wallander turned to Robert Åkerblom.

"What do you think?" he asked.

"I think Louise would have taken a minor road," he said without hesitation. "She didn't like all the traffic on the E14. I think she'd have gone via Svaneholm and Brodda."

"Even if she was in a hurry? If she had to be home by five o'clock?"

"Even then," said Robert Åkerblom.

"You take that road," said Wallander to Martinson and Svedberg. "We'll go straight to the house. We can use the car phone if we need to."

They drove out of Ystad. Wallander let Martinson and Svedberg pass, since they had the longest distance to travel. Robert Åkerblom sat staring straight ahead. Wallander kept glancing at him. He was rubbing his hands anxiously, as if he couldn't make up his mind whether or not to clasp them together.

Wallander could feel Åkerbom's tension. What would they find?

He braked as they approached the exit for Lake Kade, let a truck pass, and recalled how he had driven along the same road one morning two years before, when an old farmer and his wife had been beaten to death in a remote farmhouse. He shuddered at the memory, and thought as he so often did of his colleague Rydberg, who died last year. Every time Wallander was faced with an investigation out of the ordinary, he missed the experience and advice of his elder colleague.

What's going on in this country of ours, he thought to himself. Where have all the old-fashioned thieves and con men gone? Where does all this senseless violence come from?

The map was lying by the gearshift.

"Are we going the right way?" he asked, in order to break the silence in the car.

33

"Yes," said Robert Åkerblom, without taking his eyes off the road. "We should take a left just over the top of this next hill."

They drove into Krageholm Forest. The lake was on the left, shimmering through the trees. Wallander slowed down, and they started looking out for the turnoff.

It was Robert Åkerblom who saw it first. Wallander had already driven past. He reversed and came to a halt.

"You stay in the car," he said. "I'll go look around."

The actual turnoff into the dirt road was almost completely overgrown. Wallander got down on one knee and could make out faint traces of car tires. He could feel Robert Åkerblom's eyes on the back of his neck.

He went back to the car and called Martinson and Svedberg. They'd just got as far as Skurup.

"We're at the start of the dirt road," said Wallander. "Be careful when you turn in. Don't spoil the tire marks."

"Roger," said Svedberg. "We're on our way now."

Wallander turned carefully into the track, avoiding the tire marks.

Two cars, he thought. Or the same one going in and coming back.

They shuddered along the muddy and badly maintained road. It was supposed to be a kilometer to the house that was up for sale. To his surprise, Wallander saw on the map that the house was called Solitude.

After three kilometers the track petered out. Robert Åkerblom stared uncomprehendingly at the map and at Wallander.

"Wrong road," said Wallander. "We couldn't have avoided seeing the house. It's right by the roadside. Let's go back."

When they emerged onto the main road, they drove slowly forward and came to the next turnoff some five hundred meters further on. Wallander repeated his investigation. Unlike the previous road, this one had lots of tire tracks, one over the other. The road also gave the impression of being better maintained and more often used.

But they could not find the right house here, either. They caught a glimpse of a farmhouse through the trees, but they kept going as it didn't seem anything like the description they had. Wallander stopped after four kilometers.

"Do you have Mrs. Wallin's number?" he inquired. "I have the distinct impression she has a very poor sense of direction."

Robert Åkerblom nodded and took a little telephone book from his inside pocket. Wallander noticed there was a bookmark shaped like an angel between the pages.

"Call her," said Wallander. "Explain that you're lost. Ask her to give you the directions again."

The phone rang for some time before the widow answered.

It turned out that Mrs. Wallin was by no means sure how many kilometers it was to the turnoff.

"Ask her for some other landmark," said Wallander. "There must be something we can use to get our bearings. If not, we'll have to send a car and bring her here."

Wallander let Robert Åkerblom talk to Mrs Wallin without switching the phone over to the loudspeaker.

"An oak tree struck by lightning," said Robert Åkerblom. "We turn off just before we get to the tree."

They drove on, and after two more kilometers saw the oak. There was also a turnoff to the right. Wallander called the other car, and explained how to find it. Then he investigated for the third time, looking for tire tracks. To his surprise he found nothing at all to suggest any vehicle had used this road for some time. That wasn't necessarily significant. The tracks could have been washed away by rain. Nevertheless, he felt something approaching disappointment.

The house was situated where it ought to have been, by the roadside just one kilometer in. They stopped and got out of the car. It had started raining, and the wind was blowing in gusts.

Suddenly Robert Åkerblom set off running towards the house, yelling out his wife's name in a shrill voice. Wallander stayed by the car. It all happened so quickly, he was taken completely by surprise. When Robert Åkerblom disappeared behind the house, he ran after him.

No car, he thought as he went. No car, and no Louise Åkerblom.

He caught up with Robert Åkerblom just as he was about to throw a broken brick through a window at the back of the house. Wallander grabbed his arm.

"It's no good," said Wallander.

"She may be in there," yelled Robert Åkerblom.

"You said she didn't have any keys to the house," Wallander

3 5

pointed out. "Drop that brick so that we can look for a door that's been forced. But I can tell you now she's not there."

Robert Åkerblom suddenly collapsed in a heap.

"Where is she?" he asked. "What's happened?"

Wallander felt a lump in his throat. He had no idea what to say.

Then he took Robert Åkerblom by the arm and helped him to his feet.

"No point in sitting here and making yourself ill," he said. "Let's look around."

There was no door that had been forced. They peeked in through undraped windows and saw only empty rooms. They had just concluded there was nothing else to see when Martinson and Svedberg turned into the drive.

"Nothing," said Wallander. At the same time, he put his finger to his lips, discreetly, so that Robert Åkerblom couldn't see.

He didn't want Svedberg and Martinson to start asking questions.

He didn't want to have to say Louise Åkerblom probably never got as far as the house.

"We have nothing to report either," said Martinson. "No car, nothing."

Wallander looked at his watch. Ten past six. He turned to Robert Åkerblom and tried to smile.

"I think the most useful thing you can do now is to go back home to the girls," he said. "Svedberg here will drive you home. We'll make a systematic search. Try not to worry. We'll find her all right."

"She's dead," said Robert Åkerblom in a low voice. "She's dead, and she'll never come back."

The three policemen stood in silence.

"No," said Wallander eventually. "There's no reason to think it's as bad as that. Svedberg will drive you home now. I promise to get in touch later on."

Svedberg drove off.

"Now we can start searching for real," said Wallander resolutely. He could feel the unease growing inside him all the time.

They sat in his car. Wallander called Björk and asked for all available personnel with cars to be sent to the split oak. At the same time Martinson started planning how best to go through all the roads in a circle around the house with a fine-tooth comb, as quickly and efficiently as possible. Wallander asked Björk to make sure they got suitable maps.

"We'll keep looking until it gets dark," said Wallander. "We start again at dawn tomorrow, if we don't find anything tonight. You can get in touch with the army as well. Then we'll have to consider a line search."

"Dogs," said Martinson. "We need dogs tonight, right now."

Björk promised to come along in person and take over responsibility.

Martinson and Wallander looked at each other.

"Summary," said Wallander. "What do you think?"

"She never came here," said Martinson. "She could have been close by, or a long way away. I don't know what can have happened. But we have to find the car. We're doing the right thing, starting the search here. Somebody must have seen it, surely. We'll have to start knocking on doors. Björk will have to hold a press conference tomorrow. We have to let it be known we regard the disappearance as serious."

"What can have happened?" wondered Wallander.

"Something we'd rather not think about," said Martinson.

The rain started drumming against the car windows and roof.

"Hell," said Wallander.

"Yes," said Martinson. "Exactly."

Shortly before midnight the policemen, tired and drenched, reassembled on the gravel in front of the house Louise Åkerblom had probably never seen. They'd found no trace of the dark blue car, still less of Louise Åkerblom. The most remarkable thing they found was two elk carcasses. And a police car almost crashed with a Mercedes racing along one of the dirt roads at high speed as they were on their way to the meeting.

Björk thanked everybody for their efforts. He had already agreed with Wallander that the weary cops could be sent home and told the search would begin again at six the next morning.

Wallander was the last to leave and head for Ystad. He had called Robert Åkerblom on his car telephone, and told them they regretted they had nothing new to report. Although it was late, Robert Åkerblom expressed the wish that Wallander should come and see him at their house, where he was alone with the daughters.

Before Wallander started the engine he called his sister in Stockholm. He knew she stayed up late at night. He told her their father was planning to marry his home aide. To Wallander's astonishment, she burst out laughing. But to his relief, she promised to come down to Skåne at the beginning of May.

Wallander replaced the telephone in its holder and set off for Ystad. Rain squalls hammered against the windshield.

He found his way to Robert Åkerblom's home. It was a row house like a thousand other houses. The light was still on downstairs.

Before getting out of the car he leaned back in his seat and closed his eyes.

She never got that far, he thought.

What happened on the way?

There's something about this disappearance that doesn't add up. I don't get it.

Chapter Four

The clock beside Kurt Wallander's bed rang at a quarter to five.

He groaned, and put the pillow over his face.

I get far too little sleep, he thought dejectedly. Why can't I be one of those cops who put everything to do with work aside as soon as they get home?

He stayed in bed, and turned his mind back to his short visit at Robert Åkerblom's house the night before. It had been pure torture to look into his distraught eyes and tell him they hadn't managed to find his wife. Kurt Wallander had gotten out of the house just as quickly as he could, and he felt ill as he drove back home. Then he'd lain awake until a quarter to three, despite feeling tired out, more or less exhausted.

We've got to find her, he thought. Now. Soon. Dead or alive. We've just got to find her.

He had arranged with Robert Åkerblom to get back in touch the next morning, as soon as the search had begun again. Wallander realized he would have to go through Louise Åkerblom's personal belongings, in order to find out what she was really like. Somewhere in the back of Wallander's mind was the nagging thought that there was something highly peculiar about her disappearance. There were peculiar circumstances every time a person went missing; but there was something in this case that was different from anything he had experienced before. He wanted to know what it was.

Wallander forced himself to get out of bed, switched on the coffee machine, and went to turn on the radio. He cursed when he remembered the burglary, and it occurred to him that nobody would have time to worry about that investigation, given the new circumstances.

He took a shower, got dressed, and had his coffee. The weather did not exactly improve his temper. It was pouring, and the wind was up. It was the worst weather imaginable for a line search. All day long the fields and coppices around Krageholm would be full of exhausted, irritable cops, dogs with their tails between their legs, and angry conscripts from the local regiment. Still, that was Björk's problem. His job was to go through Louise Åkerblom's belongings.

He got into his car and drove out to the shattered oak. Björk was pacing impatiently up and down the verge.

"What awful weather," he said "Why does it always have to rain when we're out looking for somebody?"

"Hmm," said Wallander. "It's odd."

"I've talked to the Lieutenant-Colonel: his name's Hernberg," said Björk. "He's sending two busloads of conscripts, at seven o'clock. I think we might as well start right away. Martinson's done all the spadework."

Wallander nodded appreciatively. Martinson was good when it came to line searches.

"I thought we'd call a press conference for ten o'clock," said Björk. "It would help if you could be there. We'll have to have a photo of her by then."

Wallander gave him the one he had in his inside pocket. Björk contemplated Louise Åkerblom's picture.

"Nice girl," he said. "I hope we find her alive. Is it a good likeness?"

"Her husband thinks it is."

Björk put the photo into a plastic wallet he carried in one of his raincoat pockets.

"I'm going to their house," said Wallander. "I think I can be of more use there."

Björk nodded. As Wallander made to walk over to his car, Björk grabbed him by the shoulder.

"What do you think?" he asked. "Is she dead? Is there some crime behind all this?"

"It can hardly be anything else," said Wallander. "Unless she's been hurt and is lying in agony somewhere or other. But I don't think so."

"It doesn't look good," said Björk. "Not good at all."

Wallander drove back to Ystad. The gray sea was looking very choppy.

When he entered the house in Åkarvägen, two little girls stood staring at him, wide-eyed.

"I've told them you're a cop," said Robert Åkerblom. "They know Mom's lost, and you're looking for her."

Wallander nodded and tried to smile, despite the lump that came into his throat.

"My name's Kurt," he said. "What's yours?"

"Maria and Magdalena," answered the girls, one after another.

"Those are lovely names," said Wallander. "I've got a daughter named Linda."

"They're going to be at my sister's today," said Robert Åkerblom. "She'll be here shortly to pick them up. Can I offer you a cup of tea?"

"Yes, please," said Wallander.

He hung up his overcoat, removed his shoes, and went into the kitchen. The two girls were standing in the doorway, watching him.

Where shall I start? wondered Wallander. Will he understand that I have to open every drawer, and go through every one of her papers?

The two girls were picked up, and Wallander finished his tea.

"We have a press conference at ten o'clock," he said. "That means we shall have to make your wife's name public, and ask for anybody who might have seen her to come forward. As you will realize, that implies something else. We can no longer exclude the possibility that a crime might have been committed."

Wallander had foreseen the risk that Robert Åkerblom might go to pieces and start weeping. But the pale, hollow-eyed man, immaculately dressed in suit and tie, seemed to be in control of himself this morning.

"We have to go on believing there's a natural explanation in spite of everything," said Wallander. "But we can no longer exclude anything at all."

"I understand," said Robert Åkerblom. "I've been clear about that all the time."

Wallander pushed his teacup to one side, said thank you, and got to his feet.

"Have you thought of anything else we ought to know about?" he asked.

"No," said Robert Åkerblom. "It's a complete mystery."

"Let's go through the house together," said Wallander. "Then I hope you will understand I have to look through all her clothes, drawers, everything that could give us a clue."

"She keeps everything in orderly fashion," said Robert Åkerblom.

They started upstairs, and worked their way down to the basement and the garage. Wallander noticed that Louise Åkerblom was extremely fond of pastel shades. Nowhere was there a dark drape or table cloth to be seen. The house exuded *joie de vivre*. The furniture was a mixture of old and new. Even when he was drinking his tea, he noticed how well the kitchen was equipped with machines and devices. Obviously, their everyday life was not restricted by excessive puritanism.

"I'll have to drive down to the office for a while," said Robert Åkerblom when they had finished their tour of the house. "I take it I can leave you here on your own."

"No problem," said Wallander. "I'll save my questions till you get back. Or I'll give you a call. In any case, I have to leave for the station shortly before ten, for the press conference."

"I'll be back before then," said Robert Åkerblom.

When Wallander was on his own, he started his methodical search of the house. He opened all the cupboards and drawers in the kitchen, examined the refrigerator and the freezer.

One thing intrigued him. In a cupboard under the sink was a well-stocked supply of liquor. That didn't fit in with the impression he had of the Åkerblom family.

He continued with the living room, without finding anything of note. Then he went upstairs. He ignored the girls' room. He searched the bathroom first, reading the labels on bottles from the pharmacist and noting some of Louise Åkerblom's medications in his pocket book. He stood on the bathroom scales, and made a face when he saw how much he weighed. Then he moved on to the bedroom. He always felt uncomfortable going through a woman's clothes, like somebody was watching him without his knowing it. He went through all the pouches and cardboard boxes in the wardrobes. Then he came to the chest of drawers where she kept her underwear. He found nothing that surprised him, nothing that told him anything he didn't know already. When he was through, he sat down on the edge of the bed and looked around the room.

Nothing, he thought. Absolutely nothing.

He sighed, and moved on to the next room, which was furnished as a study. He sat at the desk, opening drawer after drawer. He immersed himself in photo albums and bundles of letters. He didn't come across a single photograph in which Louise Åkerblom was not smiling or laughing.

He replaced everything carefully, closed the drawer, and tried the next one. Tax returns and insurance documents, school reports and conveyancing deeds, nothing that struck him as odd.

It was only when he opened the bottom drawer in the last of the chests that he was surprised. At first he thought it contained nothing but plain white writing paper. When he felt the bottom of the drawer, however, his fingers came into contact with a metal object. He took it out and sat there, frowning.

It was a pair of handcuffs. Not toy handcuffs; real ones. Made in England.

He put them on the desk in front of him.

They don't have to be significant, he thought. But they were well hidden. And I suspect Robert Åkerblom would have taken them away, if he knew they were there.

He closed the drawer and put the handcuffs in his pocket.

Then he went down to the basement rooms and the garage. On a shelf over a little workbench he found a few neatly made balsawood model airplanes. He pictured Robert Åkerblom in his mind's eye. Maybe he'd once dreamed of becoming a pilot?

The telephone started ringing in the background. He hurried to answer it right away.

It was nine o'clock by this time.

"Could I speak with Inspector Wallander?" It was Martinson's voice.

"Speaking," said Wallander.

"You'd better get out here," said Martinson. "Right away."

4 3

Wallander could feel his heart beating faster.

"Have you found her?" he asked.

"No," said Martinson. "Not her, and not the car either. But there's a house on fire not far away. Or to be more accurate, the house exploded. I thought there might be a link."

"I'm on my way," said Wallander.

He scribbled a note for Robert Åkerblom and left it on the kitchen table.

On the way to Krageholm he tried to work out the implications of what Martinson had said. A house had exploded? What house?

He overtook three large trucks in succession. The rain was now so heavy the wipers could only keep the windshield partially clear.

Just before he reached the shattered oak tree, the rain eased a little and he could see a column of black smoke rising above the trees. A police car was waiting for him by the oak. One of the cops inside indicated he should turn off. As they swung in from the main road, Wallander noted the road was one of those he'd taken in error the previous day, the one with the most tire ruts.

There was something else about that road, but he couldn't put his finger on what it was right now.

When he got to the scene of the fire, he recognized the house. It was to the left, and hardly visible from the road. The firefighters were already hard at work. Wallander got out of his car, and was immediately hit by the heat from the fire. Martinson was striding towards him.

"People?" asked Wallander.

"None," said Martinson. "Not as far as we know. In any case, it's impossible to go inside. The heat is terrific. The house has been empty for over a year since the owner died. One of the local farmers told me the background. Whoever was dealing with the estate couldn't make up his mind whether to rent it or sell it."

"Let's hear it," said Wallander, eying the enormous clouds of smoke.

"I was out on the main road," said Martinson. "One of the army search lines had gotten into a bit of a mess. Then there was this sudden bang. It sounded like a bomb going off. At first I thought an airplane had crashed. Then I saw the smoke. It took me five minutes at most to get here. Everything was in flames. Not just the house, but the barn as well."

Wallander tried to think.

"A bomb," he said. "Could it have been a gas leak?"

Martinson shook his head.

"Not even twenty canisters of propane could have made an explosion like that," he said. "Fruit trees in the back have snapped off. Or been blown up by the roots. It must have been set up."

"The whole area is crawling with cops and soldiers," said Wallander. "An odd time to choose for arson."

"Exactly what I thought," said Martinson. "That's why I thought right away there could be a connection."

"Any ideas?" asked Wallander.

"No," said Martinson. "None at all."

"Find out who owns the house," said Wallander. "Who's responsible for the estate. I agree with you, this seems to be more than just a coincidence. Where's Björk?"

"He already left for the station, to get ready for the press conference," said Martinson. "You know how nervous he always gets when he has to face journalists who never write what he says. But he knows what's happened. Svedberg's been speaking to him. He knows you're here as well."

"I'll have a closer look at this when they've put the fire out," said Wallander. "But it would be a good idea for you to detail some guys to run a fine-tooth comb over this area."

"Looking for Louise Åkerblom?" asked Martinson.

"For the car in the first place," replied Wallander.

Martinson went off to talk to the farmer. Wallander stayed put, staring at the raging fire.

If there is a connection, what is it? he wondered. A woman goes missing and a house explodes. Right under the noses of guys doing an intensive search.

He looked at his watch. Ten to ten. He beckoned to one of the firemen.

"When will I be able to start rooting around in there?" he asked.

"It's burning pretty fast," said the firefighter. "By this afternoon you should be able to get close to the house in any case."

"Good," said Wallander. "It seems to have been a hell of a bang," he went on.

"That wasn't started with a match," said the fireman. "I wouldn't be surprised if a hundred kilos of dynamite went off."

Wallander drove back towards Ystad. He called Ebba in reception and asked her to tell Björk he was on his way.

Then he suddenly remembered what it was he'd forgotten. The previous evening one of the patrol car crews reported they'd nearly been hit by a Mercedes speeding down one of the dirt roads. Wallander was pretty sure it was the very track where the house had exploded.

Too many coincidences, he thought. Soon we'll have to find something that makes it all start to add up.

Björk was pacing up and down restlessly in the reception area at the police station when Wallander got there.

"I'll never get used to press conferences," he said. "What's all this about a fire that Svedberg called to inform me about? He expressed himself very oddly, I must say. He said the house and barn had exploded. What did he mean by that? What house was he talking about?"

"Svedberg's description was probably accurate," said Wallander. "It can hardly have anything to do with the press conference on the disappearance of Louise Åkerblom, though, so I suggest we talk about it later. The guys out there might have more information by then, anyway."

Björk nodded.

"Let's keep this simple," he said. "A brief and straightforward reference to her being missing, hand out the photos, appeal to the general public. You can deal with questions about how the investigation is going."

"The investigation isn't really going at all," said Wallander. "If only we'd traced her car. But we've got nothing."

"You'd better make something up," said Björk. "Police who claim they have nothing to tell reporters are fair game. Never forget that."

The press conference took just over half an hour. In addition to the local papers and local radio, the local reps for the *Express* and *Today* had shown up. Nobody from the Stockholm papers, though. They won't arrive until we've found her, thought Wallander. Assuming she's dead.

Björk opened the press conference and announced that a woman was missing in circumstances the police considered to be serious. He described the woman and her car, and distributed photographs.

Then he invited questions, nodded towards Wallander, and sat down. Wallander mounted the little dais and waited.

"What do you think has happened?" asked the reporter from the local radio station. Wallander had never seen him before. The local radio station always seemed to be changing personnel.

"We don't think anything," answered Wallander. "But the circumstances suggest we should be taking the disappearance of Louise Åkerblom seriously."

"Tell us about the circumstances, then," suggested the local reporter.

Wallander waded in.

"We must be clear about the fact that most people in this country who go missing in one way or another turn up again sooner or later. Two times out of three there is a totally natural explanation. One of the most common is forgetfulness. Just occasionally there are signs to suggest there could be another explanation. Then we treat the disappearance very seriously."

Björk raised his hand.

"Which is not to say, of course, that the police don't take all cases of missing persons very seriously," he explained.

Oh my God, thought Wallander.

The man from the *Express*, a young guy with a red beard, raised his hand and spoke up.

"Can't you be a bit more precise?" he said. "You're not excluding the possibility that a crime may have been committed. Why aren't you? I also think it's not clear where she disappeared, and who was the last to see her."

Wallander nodded. The journalist was right. Björk had been vague on several important counts.

"She left the Savings Bank in Skurup just after three last Friday afternoon," he said. "An employee at the bank saw her start her car and drive off around a quarter past three. We can be quite sure about the time. Nobody saw her after that. Moreover we are quite sure she took one of two possible routes. Either the E14 towards Ystad, or she might have driven past Slimminge and Rögla towards the Krageholm district. As you heard, Louise Åkerblom is a real estate agent. She might have gone to see a house that was being put up for sale. Or she might have driven straight home. We're not sure what she decided to do."

"Which house?" asked one of the local press reporters.

"I can't answer that question for reasons connected with the investigation," replied Wallander.

The press conference died out of its own accord. The local radio reporter interviewed Björk. Wallander talked to one of the local press reporters in the corridor outside. When he was alone, he fixed himself a cup of coffee, went into his office and called the scene of the fire. He got hold of Svedberg, who told him that Martinson had already diverted a group of searchers to concentrate on the area around the burning house.

"I've never seen a fire like this one," said Svedberg. "There won't be a single roof beam left when it's over."

"I'll be out there this afternoon," said Wallander. "I'm going out to Robert Åkerblom's place again. Call me there if anything develops."

"We'll call you," said Svedberg. "What did the press have to say?"

"Nothing worth commenting on," said Wallander, putting the phone down.

That moment Björk knocked on his door.

"That went pretty well," he said. "No dirty tricks, just reasonable questions. Let's just hope they write what we want them to."

"We'll have to detail a few extra people to man the phones tomorrow," said Wallander, not bothering to comment on his assessment of the press conference. "When a religious mother of two disappears, I'm afraid lots of folk who've seen nothing at all will be calling in. Giving the police the benefit of their blessing and prayers. Quite apart from those we hope might really have something useful to tell us."

"Assuming we don't find her during the course of today," said Björk.

"I don't believe that, and neither do you," said Wallander.

Then he told the story of the remarkable fire. The explosion. Björk listened with a worried look on his face.

"What does all this mean?" he asked.

Wallander stretched out his arms.

"I don't know. I'm going back to see Robert Åkerblom now, though. Find out what else he's got to say."

Björk stood in the door.

"We'll have a debriefing in my office at five o'clock," he said.

Just as Wallander was about to leave his office, he remembered he'd forgotten to ask Svedberg to do something for him. He called the scene of the fire once more.

"Do you remember how a police car nearly crashed into a Mercedes last night?" he asked.

"I have a vague memory," said Svedberg.

"Find out all you can about the incident," Wallander went on. "I have a strong suspicion that Mercedes has something to do with the fire. I'm not quite so sure whether it has anything to do with Louise Åkerblom."

"Roger," said Svedberg. "Anything else?"

"We have a meeting here at five o'clock," said Wallander, replacing the receiver.

A quarter of an hour later he was back in Robert Åkerblom's kitchen. He sat down on the same chair he'd occupied a few hours earlier, and had another cup of tea.

"Sometimes you get called out on some sudden emergency," said Wallander. "There's been a major fire incident. But it's under control now."

"I understand," said Robert Åkerblom politely. "I'm sure it's not easy, being a cop."

Wallander observed the man opposite him at the table. At the same time, he could feel the handcuffs in his trouser pocket. He wasn't looking forward to the interrogation he was about to launch.

"I have a few questions," he said. "We can talk just as easily here as anywhere else."

"Of course," said Robert Åkerblom. "Ask as many questions as you like."

Wallander noticed he was irritated by the gentle and yet unmistakably admonishing tone in Robert Åkerblom's voice.

"I'm not sure about the first question," said Wallander. "Does your wife have any medical problems?"

The man looked at him in surprise.

"No," he said. "What are you getting at?"

"It just occurred to me she might have heard she was suffering from some serious illness. Has she been to the doctor lately?"

"No. And if she'd been ill, she'd have told me."

"There are some serious illnesses people are sometimes hesitant to talk about," said Wallander. "Or at least, they need a few days to gather together their thoughts and emotions. It's often the case that the sick person is the one who has to console whoever it is he or she tells."

Robert Åkerblom thought for a moment before answering.

"I'm sure that's not the case here," he said.

Wallander nodded and went on.

"Did she have a drinking problem?" he asked.

Robert Åkerblom winced.

"How can you ask such a question?" he said after a moment's silence. "Neither of us so much as touches a drop of alcohol."

"Nevertheless the cupboard under the sink is full of liquor," said Wallander.

"We have nothing against other people drinking," said Robert Åkerblom. "Within reason, of course. We sometimes have guests. Even a little real estate agency like ours occasionally needs to entertain its clients."

Wallander nodded. He had no reason to question the response. He took the handcuffs out of his pocket and put them on the table. He kept his eye on Robert Åkerblom's reaction the whole time.

It was exactly what he had expected. Incomprehension.

"Are you arresting me?" he asked.

"No," said Wallander. "But I found these handcuffs in the bottom drawer to the left of the desk, under a stack of writing paper, in your study upstairs."

"Handcuffs," said Robert Åkerblom. "I've never seen them before."

"As it can hardly have been one of your daughters who put them there, we'll have to assume it was your wife," said Wallander.

"I just don't get it," said Robert Åkerblom.

Suddenly Wallander knew the man across the kitchen table was lying. A barely noticeable shift in his voice, a sudden insecurity in his eyes. But enough for Wallander to register it.

"Could anybody else have put them there?" he went on.

"I don't know," said Robert Åkerblom. "The only visitors we have are from the chapel. Apart from clients. And they never go upstairs."

"Nobody else at all?"

"Our parents. A few relatives. The kids' friends."

"That's quite a lot of people," said Wallander.

"I don't get it," said Robert Åkerblom again.

Maybe you don't understand how you could have forgotten to take them away, thought Wallander. Just for now the question is, what do they mean?

For the first time Wallander asked himself whether Robert Åkerblom could have killed his own wife. But he dismissed it. The handcuffs and the lie were not enough to overturn everything Wallander had already established.

"Are you certain you can't explain these handcuffs?" asked Wallander once again. "Perhaps I should point out it's not against the law to keep a pair of handcuffs in your home. You don't need a license. On the other hand, of course, you can't just keep people locked up however you like."

"Do you think I'm not telling you the truth?" asked Robert Åkerblom.

"I don't think anything," said Wallander. "I just want to know why these handcuffs were hidden away in a desk drawer."

"I've already said I don't understand how they could have gotten into the house."

Wallander nodded. He didn't think it was necessary to press him any further. Not yet, at least. But Wallander was sure he was lying. Could it be that the marriage concealed a perverted and possibly dramatic sex life? Could that in its turn explain why Louise Åkerblom had disappeared?

Wallander slid his teacup to one side, indicating that the conversation was over. He put the handcuffs back in his pocket, wrapped inside a handkerchief. A technical analysis might be able to reveal more about what they'd been used for.

"That's all for the time being," said Wallander, getting to his feet. "I'll be in touch just as soon as I have anything to report. You'd better be ready for a bit of a fuss tonight, when the evening papers come out and the local radio has broadcast its piece. We'll have to hope it all helps us, of course."

Robert Åkerblom nodded without replying.

Wallander shook hands and went out to his car. The weather was changing. It was drizzling and the wind had eased off. Wallander drove down to Fridolf's Café near the coach station for a coffee and a couple of sandwiches. It was half past twelve by the time he was back behind the wheel and on his way out to the scene of the fire. He parked, clambered over the barriers, and observed that both the house and the barn were already smoking ruins. It was too early yet for the police techies to start their investigation. Wallander approached the seat of the fire and had a word with the man in charge, Peter Edler, whom he knew well.

"We're soaking it in water," he said. "Not much else we can do. Is it arson?"

"I've no idea," said Wallander. "Have you seen Svedberg or Martinson?"

"I think they've gone for something to eat," said Edler. "In Rydsgård. And Lieutenant-Colonel Hernberg has taken his soaking wet recruits to their barracks. They'll be back, though."

Wallander nodded, and left the fire chief.

A policeman with a dog was standing a few meters away. He was eating a sandwich, and the dog was scratching away at the sooty, wet gravel with one paw.

Suddenly the dog started howling. The cop tugged impatiently at the leash a couple of times, then looked to see what the dog was digging for.

Then Wallander saw him draw back with a start and drop his sandwich.

Wallander couldn't help being curious, and walked over towards them.

"What's the dog found?" he asked.

The cop turned round to face Wallander. He was white as a sheet, and trembling.

Wallander hurried over and bent down.

In the mud before him was a finger.

A black finger. Not a thumb, and not a little finger. But a human finger.

Wallander felt ill.

He told the dog handler to get in touch with Svedberg and Martinson right away.

"Get them here immediately," he said. "Even if they're halfway through their meal. There's an empty plastic bag in the back seat of my car. Get it."

The cop did as he was told.

What's going on? thought Wallander. A black finger. A black man's finger. Cut off. In the middle of Skåne.

When the cop returned with the plastic bag, Wallander made a temporary cover to protect the finger from the rain. The rumor had spread, and several firefighters gathered around the find.

"We must start looking for the remains of bodies among the ashes," said Wallander to the fire chief. "God knows what's been going on here."

"A finger," said Peter Edler incredulously.

Twenty minutes later Svedberg and Martinson arrived, and came running up to the spot. They stared at the black finger uncomprehendingly.

Neither had anything to say.

In the end, it was Wallander who broke the silence.

"One thing's for sure at least," he said. "This isn't one of Louise Åkerblom's fingers."

Chapter Five

They gathered at five o'clock in one of the conference rooms at the police station. Wallander could not remember a more silent meeting.

In the middle of the table, on a plastic cloth, was the black finger.

He could see that Björk had angled his chair so he couldn't see it.

Everyone else stared at the finger. Nobody said a word.

After a while, an ambulance arrived from the hospital and removed the severed remnant. Once it was gone, Svedberg went to get a tray of coffee cups, and Björk commenced proceedings.

"Just for once, I'm speechless," was his opening gambit. "Can any of you suggest a plausible explanation?"

Nobody responded. It was a pointless question.

"Wallander," said Björk, trying another angle, "could you perhaps give us a summary of where we've gotten so far?"

"It won't be easy," said Wallander, "but I'll give it a shot. The rest of you can fill in the gaps."

He opened his notebook and leafed through.

"Louise Åkerblom went missing almost exactly four days ago," he began. "To be more precise, ninety-eight hours ago. Nobody's seen her since, as far as we know. While we were looking for her, and not least for her car, a house exploded just where we think she might be found. We now know the occupant is deceased, and the house was up for sale. The representative of the estate is a lawyer who lives in Värnamo. He's at a loss to explain what has happened. The house has been empty for more than a year. The beneficiaries have not yet been able to decide whether to sell or to keep it in the family, and rent it. It's not impossible that some of the heirs might buy out the rest. The lawyer's name is Holmgren, and we've asked our colleagues in Värnamo to discuss the matter with him. At the very least, we want the names and addresses of the rest of the beneficiaries."

He took a slurp of coffee before proceeding.

"The fire broke out at nine o'clock," he said. "The evidence suggests some form of powerful explosive was used, with a timing device. There is absolutely no reason to suppose the fire was started by any other, natural causes. Holmgren was quite certain there were no propane canisters in the house, for instance. The whole house was rewired just last year. While the fire was being fought, one of our police dogs sniffed out a human finger some twenty-five meters from the blaze. It's an index finger or middle finger from a left hand. In all probability, it belonged to a man. A black man. Our technical guys have run a fine-tooth comb over whatever parts of the heart of the fire and the surrounding area are accessible, but they've found nothing more. We've run an intensive line search over the whole area, and found nothing at all. No sign of the car, no sign of Louise Åkerblom. A house has blown up, and we've found a finger belonging to a black man. That's about it."

Björk made a face.

"What do the medics have to say?" he asked.

"Maria Lestadius from the hospital was here," said Svedberg. "She says we should get onto the forensic lab right away. She claims she's not competent to read fingers."

Björk squirmed on his chair.

"Say that again," he said. " 'Read fingers'?"

"That's the way she put it." Svedberg seemed resigned. It was a well-known peculiarity of Björk's, picking on inessentials.

Björk thumped the table almost absentmindedly.

"This is awful," he said. "To put it bluntly, we don't know anything at all. Hasn't Robert Åkerblom been able to give us any pointers?"

Wallander made up his mind on the spot to say nothing about the handcuffs, not for now. He was afraid that might take them in directions that were of less than immediate significance. Besides, he was not convinced the handcuffs had any direct connection with her disappearance.

"Nothing at all," he said. "I think the Åkerbloms were the happiest family in the whole of Sweden."

"Might she have gone over the top, from a religious point of view?" asked Björk. "We're always reading about those crazy sects."

"You can hardly call the Methodists a 'crazy sect'," said Wallander. "It's one of our oldest free churches. I have to admit I'm not sure just what they stand for."

"We'll have to look into that," said Björk. "What do you think we should do now?"

"Let's hope for what tomorrow might bring," said Martinson. "We might get some calls."

"I've already got personnel to man the telephones," said Björk. "Anything else we should be doing?"

"Let's face it," said Wallander, "we have nothing to go on. We have a finger. That means that somewhere or other, there's a black man missing a finger on his left hand. That means in turn he needs help from a doctor or a hospital. If he hasn't shown up already, he will do sooner or later. We can't exclude the possibility that he might contact the police. Nobody cuts his own fingers off. Well, not very often. In other words, somebody has subjected him to torture. Needless to say, it's possible he might have fled the country already."

"Fingerprints," said Svedberg. "I don't know how many Africans there are in this country, legally or illegally, but there's a chance we might be able to trace a print in our files. We can send out a request to Interpol as well. To my knowledge a lot of African states have been building up advanced criminal files these last few years. There was an article about it in *Swedish Policeman* magazine a month or two ago. I agree with Kurt. Even if we can't see any connection between Louise Åkerblom and this finger, we have to assume there might be one."

"Shall we give this to the newspapers?" Björk wondered. "The cops are looking for the owner of a finger. That should get a headline or two, anyway."

"Why not?" said Wallander. "We've got nothing to lose."

"I'll think about it," said Björk. "Let's wait a bit. I agree every hospital in the country should be alerted, though. Surely the medics have a duty to inform the police if they suspect an injury has been caused by a criminal action?"

"They're also bound by confidentiality," said Svedberg. "But of course the hospitals should be contacted. Health centers, too. Does anybody know how many medical practitioners we have in this country?"

Nobody knew.

"Ask Ebba to find out," said Wallander.

It took her ten minutes to call the secretary of the Swedish Medical Association.

"There are just over twenty-five thousand doctors in Sweden," said Wallander, when she had reported to the conference room.

They gaped in astonishment.

Twenty-five thousand doctors.

"Where are they all when we need 'em?" wondered Martinson.

Björk was starting to get impatient.

"Is this getting us anywhere?" he asked. "If not, we've all got plenty to do. We'll have another meeting tomorrow morning at eight."

"I'll see to the hospital business," said Martinson.

They had just collected their papers and got to their feet when the telephone rang. Martinson and Wallander were already out in the corridor when Björk called them back.

"Breakthrough!" he said, his face flushed. "They think they've found the car. It was Norén on the phone. Some farmer showed up at the fire and asked the police if they were interested in something he'd found in a pond a few kilometers away. Out towards Sjöbo, I think he said. Norén drove to the spot and saw a radio antenna sticking out of the mud. The farmer, whose name is Antonson, was sure the car wasn't there a week ago."

"Right, let's get the hell out of here," said Wallander. "We've got to get that car up tonight. We can't wait until tomorrow. We'll have to find searchlights and a crane."

"I hope there's nobody in the car," said Svedberg.

"That's exactly what we're going to find out," said Wallander. "Come on."

The pond was difficult to get to, close to a thicket, to the north of Krageholm on the way to Sjöbo. It took the police three hours to get searchlights and a mobile crane on site, and it was half past nine before they had managed to attach a cable to the car. Then Wallander contrived to slip and fall halfway into the pond. He borrowed overalls from Norén, who had a spare in his car. But he hardly noticed he was wet and starting to feel cold. All his attention was concentrated on the car.

He was both tense and uncomfortable. He hoped it was the right car. But he was afraid Louise Åkerblom might be found inside it.

"One thing's for sure, in any case," said Svedberg. "This was no accident. The car was driven into the mud so that it wouldn't be seen. Probably in the middle of the night. Whoever did it couldn't see the aerial sticking up."

Wallander nodded. Svedberg was right.

The cable slowly tightened. The mobile crane strained against its stanchions and started to pull.

The rear end slowly came into view.

Wallander looked at Svedberg, who was an expert on cars.

"Is it the right one?" he asked.

"Hang on a bit," said Svedberg, "I can't see yet."

Then the cable came loose. The car vanished back into the mud. They had to start all over again.

Half an hour later, the crane started pulling once more.

Wallander kept looking from the slowly emerging car to Svedberg, and back again.

Suddenly, Svedberg nodded.

"That's the one. It's a Toyota Corolla. No doubt about it."

Wallander aimed one of the searchlights. Now they could see the car was dark blue.

The car slowly emerged from the pond. The crane stopped. Svedberg looked at Wallander. They walked over and looked in, one at each side.

The car was empty.

Wallander opened the trunk.

Nothing.

"The car's empty," he told Björk.

"She could still be in the pond," said Svedberg.

Wallander nodded. The pond was about a hundred meters in circumference, but the aerial had been visible, so it couldn't be very deep.

"We need some divers," he said to Björk. "Now, right away."

"A diver wouldn't be able to see anything, it's too dark," said Björk. "We'd better wait till the morning."

"They only need to wade along the bottom," said Wallander. "Dragging grappling irons between them. I don't want to wait till tomorrow."

Björk gave in. He went over to one of the police cars and made a call. Meanwhile Svedberg had opened the driver's door and poked around with a torch. He carefully worked loose the soaking wet car telephone.

"The last number called is usually registered," he said. "She might have made some other call, as well as the one to the answering machine at the office."

"Good," said Wallander. "Good thinking, Svedberg."

While they were waiting for the divers, they made a preliminary search of the car. Wallander found a paper bag in the back seat, with soggy pastries.

Everything fits in so far, he thought. But then what happened? On the road? Who did you meet, Louise Åkerblom? Somebody you'd arranged to see?

Or somebody else? Somebody who wanted to meet you, without your knowing about it?

"No purse," said Svedberg. "No brief case. Nothing in the glove compartment apart from the log book and insurance documents. And a copy of the New Testament."

"Look for a handwritten map," said Wallander.

Svedberg did not find one.

Wallander walked slowly around the car. It was undamaged. Louise Åkerblom had not been involved in an accident.

They sat in one of the patrol cars, drinking coffee from a thermos. It had stopped raining, and there was barely a cloud in the sky.

"Is she in the pond?" wondered Svedberg.

"I don't know," said Wallander. "Could be."

Two young divers arrived in one of the fire brigade's emergency vehicles. Wallander and Svedberg shook hands—they had met them before.

"What are we looking for?" asked one of the divers.

60

"Maybe a body," said Wallander. "Maybe a briefcase, or a purse. Maybe something else we don't know about."

The divers made their preparations, then waded out into the dirty, stagnant water, holding a line with grappling irons between them.

The cops watched in silence.

Martinson showed up just as the divers had completed their first drag.

"It's the right car, I see," said Martinson.

"She could be in the pond," said Wallander.

The divers were conscientious. One of them would occasionally stop and pull at the grappling iron. A collection of various objects was starting to build up on the shore. A broken sled, parts of a threshing attachment, some rotten tree branches, a rubber boot.

It was past midnight. Still no sign of Louise Åkerblom.

"There's nothing more in there," said one of the divers. "We can try again tomorrow, if you think it would be worth it."

"No point," said Wallander. "She's not there."

They exchanged a few brief pleasantries, then drove off to their respective homes.

Wallander had a beer and a couple of crusty rolls when he got back. He was so exhausted, he couldn't think straight. He didn't bother to get undressed, just lay down on the bed with a blanket over him.

By seven-thirty on Wednesday morning, April 29, Wallander was back at the police station.

A thought had struck him while he was in the car. He looked up Pastor Tureson's telephone number. Tureson himself answered. Wallander apologized for calling so early, then asked if they could meet some time that day.

"Is it about anything in particular?" asked Tureson.

"No," replied Wallander. "I've just had a few thoughts that raise a few questions I'd like answering. You never know what might be important."

"I heard the radio reports," said Tureson. "And I've read the papers. Is there anything new?"

"She's still missing," said Wallander. "I can't say very much about how the investigation is proceeding, for technical reasons."

"I understand," said Tureson. "Forgive me for asking. I am worried about Louise's disappearance, though, naturally."

They agreed to meet at eleven o'clock, at the Methodist chapel.

Wallander put the phone down, and went in to Björk's office. Svedberg was already sitting there, yawning, and Martinson was on Björk's phone. Björk was drumming his fingers impatiently on the desk. Martinson replaced the receiver, making a face.

"The tipoffs have started coming in," he said. "There doesn't seem to be anything worthwhile yet. Somebody called to say he was absolutely certain he had seen Louise Åkerblom at Las Palmas airport last Thursday. The day before she vanished, that is."

"Let's get started," said Björk, interrupting him.

The chief constable had obviously slept badly. He seemed tired and irritated.

"Let's continue where we left off yesterday," said Wallander. "The car will have to be gone over thoroughly, and the telephone tipoffs dealt with as they come in. I intend to drive out to the scene of the fire again, to see what the technicians have come up with. The finger is on its way to forensics. The question is, shall we let the media know about that or not?"

"Let's do it," said Björk without hesitation. "Martinson can help me write a press release. I guess there'll be an uproar once the editorial staff get hold of that."

"It would be better if Svedberg took care of it," said Martinson. "I'm busy contacting twenty-five thousand Swedish doctors. Plus an endless list of health centers and emergency clinics. That takes time."

"OK," said Björk. "I'll get onto that lawyer in Värnamo. We'll meet again this afternoon, unless something happens."

Wallander went out to his car. It looked like it would be a nice day in Skåne. He paused and filled his lungs with fresh air. For the first time that year, he had the feeling spring was on its way.

When he got to the burned-out house, there were two surprises in store for him.

The police technicians had done some fruitful work early that morning. He was met by Sven Nyberg, who had only joined the Ystad force a few months ago. He had been working in Malmö, but did not hesitate to move to Ystad when the opportunity arose. Wallander had not had very much to do with him as yet, but the reputation that preceded him suggested he was a skillful investigator at the scene of the crime. Wallander had discovered for himself that he was also brusque and hard to make contact with.

"I think you ought to look at a couple of things," said Nyberg.

They walked over to a little rain shelter that had been rigged up over four posts.

Some twisted bits of metal were lying on a sheet of plastic.

"A bomb?" Wallander asked.

"No," said Nyberg. "We've found no trace of a bomb so far. But this is at least as interesting. You're looking at some bits from a big radio installation."

Wallander stared at him aghast.

"A combined transmitter and receiver," said Nyberg. "I can't tell you what type or what make it is, but it's definitely an installation for radio buffs. You might well think it's a bit odd to find something like this in a deserted house. Especially one that's been blown up."

Wallander nodded.

"You're right," he said. "I want to know more about this."

Nyberg picked up another piece of metal from the plastic sheet.

"This is at least as interesting," he said. "Can you see what it is?"

Wallander thought it looked like a pistol butt.

"A gun," he said.

Nyberg nodded.

"A pistol," he said. "There was presumably a live magazine in place when the house blew up. The pistol was smashed to bits when the magazine exploded, due either to the fire or the pressure waves. I also have a suspicion this is a pretty unusual model. The butt is extended, as you can see. It's certainly not a Luger or a Beretta."

"What is it, then?" asked Wallander.

"Too early to say," said Nyberg. "But I'll let you know as soon as we find out."

Nyberg filled his pipe and lit up.

"What do you think about this little lot?" he asked.

Wallander shook his head.

"I don't think I've ever been so confused," he answered, honestly. "I can't find any links. All I know is I'm looking for a missing woman, and all the time I keep coming across the strangest things. A severed finger, parts of a powerful radio transmitter, unusual weapons. Maybe it's precisely these unusual features I should use as a starting point? Something I haven't come across before in all my police experience?"

"Patience," said Nyberg. "We'll establish the links sooner or later, no doubt."

Nyberg went back to his meticulous piecing together of the jigsaw. Wallander wandered around for a while, trying yet again to summarize everything to his own satisfaction. In the end he gave up.

He got into his car and called the station.

"Have we had many tipoffs?" he asked Ebba.

"The calls are coming in non-stop," she replied. "Svedberg stopped by a couple of minutes ago, and said some of the people offering information seemed reliable and interesting. That's all I know."

Wallander gave her the number of the Methodist chapel, and made up his mind to do another thorough search of Louise Åkerblom's desk at the office, when he'd finished talking to the minister. He had a guilty conscience for not having followed up his first cursory search.

He drove back to Ystad. As he had plenty of time before he was due to meet Tureson, he parked at the Square and went into the radio store. Without wasting much time thinking about it, he signed up for a credit purchase of a new hi-fi installation. Then he drove home to Mariagatan and set it up. He'd bought a CD of Puccini's *Turandot*. He put it on, lay back on the sofa, and tried to think of Baiba Liepa. But instead, Louise Åkerblom's face kept filling his mind.

He woke with a start and looked at his watch. He cursed when he realized he ought to have been at the chapel ten minutes ago.

Pastor Tureson was waiting for him in a back room, a sort of storeroom and office combined. Tapestries with various Bible quotations

64

were hanging on the walls. A coffee machine stood on a window ledge.

"Sorry I'm late," said Wallander.

"I'm well aware you police have a lot to do," said Tureson.

Wallander sat down on a chair and took out his notebook. Tureson offered him a cup of coffee, but he declined.

"I'm trying to build up an image of just what Louise Åkerblom is really like," he began. "Everything I've found out so far seems to indicate just one thing: Louise Åkerblom was a woman completely at peace with herself who would never voluntarily leave her husband and her children."

"That's the Louise Åkerblom we all know," said Tureson.

"At the same time, that makes me suspicious," said Wallander.

"Suspicious?"

Tureson looked puzzled.

"I just cannot believe that such perfect individuals exist," Wallander explained. "Everybody has his or her secrets. The question is: what are Louise Åkerblom's? I take it for granted she hasn't vanished voluntarily because she hasn't been able to cope with her own good fortune."

"You'd get the same answers from every single member of our church, Inspector," said Tureson.

Afterwards, Wallander could never manage to put his finger on just what had happened; but there was something in Tureson's response that made him sit up and take notice. It was as if the minister were defending Louise Åkerblom's image, even though it was not being questioned, apart from the general points Wallander was making. Or was there something else he was defending?

Wallander rapidly shifted his position and put a question that had seemed less important previously.

"Tell me about your congregation," he said. "Why does one choose to become a member of the Methodist church?"

"Our faith and our interpretation of the Bible stand out as being right," came Tureson's reply.

"Is that justified?" Wallander wondered.

"In my opinion and that of my congregation it is," said Pastor Tureson. "Needless to say, members of other denominations would disagree. That's only natural."

"Is there anybody in your congregation who doesn't like Louise

Åkerblom?" asked Wallander, and immediately got the impression the man opposite was hesitating just a fraction too long before replying.

"I can't imagine there would be," said Pastor Tureson.

There it is again, thought Wallander. Something evasive, something not quite straightforward about his answer.

"Why don't I believe you?" he asked.

"But you should, Inspector," said Tureson. "I know my congregation."

Wallander suddenly felt tired. He could see he would have to put his questions rather differently if he was going to succeed in throwing the minister off balance. A full frontal attack it would have to be.

"I know that Louise Åkerblom has enemies in your congregation," he said. "Never mind how I know. But I'd like to hear your views."

Tureson stared hard at him for some time before replying.

"Not enemies," he said. "But it is true that one of our members had an unfortunate relationship with her."

He got up and went over to a window.

"I've been wavering," said Pastor Tureson. "I almost called you last night, in fact. But I didn't. I mean, everybody hopes Louise will come back to us. That everything will turn out to have a natural explanation. All the same, I've been getting more and more worried. I have to admit that."

He returned to his chair.

"I also have responsibilities to all the other members of my church," he said. "I don't want to have to put anybody in a bad light, to make an accusation that later proves to be completely wrong."

"This conversation is not an official interrogation," said Wallander. "Whatever you say will go no further. I'm not taking minutes."

"I don't know how to put it," said Pastor Tureson.

"Tell it as it is," said Wallander. "That's generally the simplest way."

"Two years ago, our church welcomed a new member," Tureson began. "He was an engineer on one of the Poland ferries, and he started coming to our services. He was divorced, thirty-five, friendly and considerate. He soon became well liked and much appreciated by other church members. About a year ago, though, Louise Åkerblom asked to speak to me. She was very insistent that her husband Robert shouldn't know anything about it. We sat here in this room, and she told me that the new member of our congregation had started pestering her with declarations of love. He was sending her letters, stalking her, calling her. She tried to put him off as nicely as she could, but he persisted and the situation was becoming intolerable. Louise asked me to have a word with him. I did so, and suddenly he seemed to change into an altogether different person. He fell into a terrible rage, claimed that Louise had let him down, and that he knew I was the one having a bad influence on her. He claimed she was actually in love with him, and wanted to leave her husband. It was totally absurd. He stopped coming to our meetings, he gave up his job on the ferry, and we thought he'd disappeared for good. I simply told the rest of the congregation that he'd moved away from town, and was too shy to say goodbye. It was a great relief for Louise, of course. But then about three months ago, it all started again. One evening Louise noticed him standing on the street outside their house. It was a terrible shock for her, naturally. He started pestering her with declarations of love all over again. I have to admit, Inspector Wallander, that we actually considered calling in the police. Now, of course, I'm sorry we didn't. It might just have been a coincidence, naturally. But I begin to wonder more and more as the days pass."

At last, thought Wallander. Now I have something to get my teeth into. Even if I don't understand what's going on regarding black fingers, blown-up radio stations and rare pistols. Now I have something to get my teeth into.

"What's the man called?" he asked.

"Stig Gustafson."

"Any idea of his address?"

"No. I've got his social security number, though. He fixed the church's heating system on one occasion, and we paid him."

Tureson went over to a desk and leafed through a file.

"570503-0470," he said.

Wallander closed his notebook.

"You were right to tell me about this," he said. "I'd have found out about it sooner or later, anyway. This way, we save time."

"She's dead, isn't she?" Tureson suddenly exclaimed.

"I don't know," said Wallander. "To be absolutely honest with you, I just don't know the answer to that question."

Wallander shook hands with the minister and left the church. It was a quarter past twelve.

Now, he thought, at last I have something to go on.

He almost ran to his car and drove straight to the station. He hurried up to his office in order to summon his colleagues to a meeting. Just as he was sitting down at his desk, the phone rang. It was Nyberg, who was still rummaging through the ashes.

"Found something new?" asked Wallander.

"No," said Nyberg. "But I've just realized what the make on the handgun is. The one we found the butt of."

"I'm writing it down," said Wallander, taking out his notebook.

"I was right when I said it was an unusual pistol," Nyberg went on. "I doubt if there are many of them in this country."

"So much the better," said Wallander, "Makes it easier to trace."

"It's a 9mm Astra Constable," said Nyberg. "I saw one at a gun show in Frankfurt once upon a time. I've got a pretty good memory for guns."

"Where is it made?" asked Wallander.

"That's what so odd about it," said Nyberg. "As far as I know, it's only manufactured legally in one country."

"Which?"

"South Africa."

Wallander put his pen down.

"South Africa?"

"Yes."

"Why's that?"

"I can't tell you why a particular gun is popular in one country but not in another. It just is."

"Damn it. South Africa?"

"There's no denying it gives us a link to that finger we found."

"What's a South African pistol doing in this country?"

"That's your job to find out," said Nyberg.

"OK," said Wallander. "It's good that you called me right away. We'll talk about this again later."

"I just thought you'd want to know," said Nyberg, and hung up.

Wallander got out of his chair and went over to the window.

A couple of minutes later, he'd made up his mind.

They'd give priority to finding Louise Åkerblom and checking out Stig Gustafson. Everything else would have to take a back seat for the time being.

This is as far as we've gotten, thought Wallander. This is as far as we've gotten, a hundred and seventeen hours after Louise Åkerblom disappeared.

He picked up the telephone.

Suddenly he didn't feel the slightest bit tired.

Chapter Six

Peter Hanson was a thief.

He was not a particularly successful criminal, but he usually managed to execute the assignments allocated to him by his employer and customer, a fence in Malmö by the name of Morell.

That very day, the morning of Walpurgis Eve, April 30, Morell's stock was at a pretty low ebb with Hanson. He planned to take the day off, like everyone else, and maybe treat himself to a trip to Copenhagen. Late the previous night, however, Morell called to say he had an urgent job for Peter Hanson.

"I want you to get hold of four water pumps," Morell said. "The old-fashioned sort. The kind you can see outside every cottage in the countryside."

"Surely it can wait until after the holiday," Peter Hanson objected. He was already asleep when Morell called, and he did not like being woken up.

"It can't wait," said Morell. "There's a guy who lives in Spain, and he's driving there the day after tomorrow. He wants those pumps in the car with him. He sells them to other Swedish residents down there. They are sentimental, and pay good money to have old Swedish water pumps outside their haciendas."

"How the hell am I going to get hold of four water pumps?" Peter Hanson asked. "Have you forgotten it's a holiday? Every summer cottage will be occupied tomorrow."

"That's your problem," Morell replied. "Start early enough and you'll manage it."

Then he turned threatening.

"If you don't, I'll be forced to go through my papers and work out how much your brother owes me," he said.

Peter Hanson slammed down the phone. He knew Morell would take that as a positive reply. As he had been woken up and would not be able to get to sleep again for ages, he got dressed and drove down to town from Rosengård, where he lived. He went into a bar and ordered a beer.

Peter Hanson had a brother called Jan-Olof. He was Peter Hanson's big misfortune in life. Jan-Olof played the ponies at Jägersro, at the Tote, and occasionally also at other trotting tracks up and down the country. He did a lot of betting, and he did it badly. He lost more than he could afford, and ended up in Morell's hands. As he could not provide any guarantees, Peter Hanson had been forced to step in as a living guarantee.

Morell was first and foremost a fence. In recent years, however, he had realized that, like all other businessmen, he would have to make up his mind how to develop his future activities. Either he would have to specialize and concentrate on a smaller field, or he could broaden his base. He chose the latter.

Although he had a big network of customers who could give very precise information about the goods they ordered, he decided to go in for loan-sharking as well. That way, he figured he could increase his turnover considerably.

Morell was just turned fifty. After twenty years in the fraud business, he had changed course and since the end of the 1970s had built up a successful receiving empire across southern Sweden. He had about thirty thieves and drivers on his secret payroll, and every week truckloads of stolen goods would be transported to his warehouse in the Malmö free port, ready for moving on to foreign importers. He collected stereos, televisions, and mobile telephones from Småland. Caravans of stolen cars came rolling up from Halland and were passed on to expectant buyers in Poland and, nowadays, the former East Germany. He could see an important new market ready to be opened up in the Baltic states, and he had already delivered a few luxury cars to Czechoslovakia as well. Peter Hanson was one of the least important cogs in his organization. Morell was still doubtful about how good he was, and used him mostly for the occasional one-off deal. Four water pumps was an ideal assignment for him.

That was why Peter Morell was sitting cursing in his car on the morning of Walpurgis Eve. Morell had ruined his holiday. He was also worried about the assignment he had taken on. There were too many people on the move for him to be confident of working undisturbed.

Peter Hanson was born in Hörby, and knew Skåne inside out. There was not the tiniest of side roads in this part of the country he had not been on, and his memory was good. He had been working for Morell for four years now, ever since he was nineteen. He sometimes thought about all the things he had loaded into his rusty old van. He once rustled two young bulls. Orders for pigs were common around Christmas time. Several times he had acquired a few tombstones, and wondered what kind of a sick person ordered those. He had carried off front doors while the house owner was asleep upstairs, and dismantled a church spire with the assistance of a crane operator brought in for the purpose. Water pumps were nothing unusual. But it was an unfortunate choice of day.

He decided to start in the area to the east of Sturup airport. He banished all thought of Österlen. Every single second home would be occupied today.

If he was going to make it, he'd have to concentrate on the area between Sturup, Hörby, and Ystad. There were quite a few empty houses around there, and with luck he might be able to work undisturbed.

Just beyond Krageholm, on a little dirt road winding through the woods and eventually hitting the main road at Sövde, he found his first pump. The house had almost collapsed, and was well hidden from view. The pump was rusty, but intact. He started working it loose from the wooden base with a crowbar, but the wood was rotten. He dropped the crowbar and tugged at the pump, easing it away from the boards over the well itself. He began to think that maybe it wouldn't be impossible to find four pumps for Morell after all. Three more deserted houses, and he could be back in Malmö by early afternoon. It was still only ten past eight. Maybe he would be able to nip over to Copenhagen that evening after all.

Then he broke loose the rusty pump.

As a result, the wooden boards crumbled and fell away.

He glanced down into the well.

There was something down there in the darkness. Something light yellow.

He realized to his horror that it was a human head with blond hair.

There was a woman lying there.

A corpse doubled up, twisted, deformed.

He dropped the pump and ran away. He drove off at a crazy speed, getting away from the deserted house as fast as possible. After a few kilometers, just before he got to Sövde, he braked, opened the car door, and threw up.

Then he tried to think. He knew he had not imagined it all. There was a woman down the well.

A woman lying in a well must have been murdered, he thought.

Then it occurred to him he'd left his fingerprints on the water pump he'd broken off.

His fingerprints were in the files.

Morell, he thought, all confused. Morell's the man to sort this one out.

He drove through Sövde, far too fast, then took a left southwards towards Ystad. He would drive back to Malmö and let Morell see to everything. The guy leaving for Spain would have to go without his pumps.

Just before he got to the turnoff for the Ystad garbage dump, his journey came to an end. He went into a skid as he tried to light a cigarette with his shaking hands, and could only partially correct it. The van crashed into a fence, smashed through a row of mailboxes, and came to a stop. Peter Hanson was wearing a seat belt, which prevented him from shooting through the windshield. Even so, the crash dazed him, and he remained in his seat, in shock.

A man mowing his lawn had seen what happened. He first ran over the road to make sure nobody had been badly injured, then he hurried back to his house, called the police, and stood by the car to make sure the man behind the wheel did not try to run away. He must be drunk, he assumed. Why else would he lose control on a stretch of straight road?

A quarter of an hour later, a patrol car arrived from Ystad. Peters and Norén, two of the most experienced cops in the district, had taken the call. Once they had established that no one was injured, Peters started directing traffic past the scene of the accident, while Norén sat beside Peter Hanson in the back of the police car, to try and find out what happened. Norén made him blow into the booze bag, but the result was negative. The man seemed very confused, and not in the least interested in explaining how the accident happened. Norén was starting to think the man was mentally deranged. He was talking disjointedly about water pumps, a fence in Malmö, and an empty house with a well.

"There's a woman in the well," he said.

"Oh, yes," said Norén. "A woman in a well?"

"She was dead," mumbled Hanson.

Norén suddenly started to feel uneasy. What was the man trying to say? That he'd found a dead woman in a well at a deserted house?

Norén told the man to stay in the car. Then he hurried out into the road where Peters was keeping the traffic moving and waving on curious drivers who slowed down and showed signs of stopping.

"He claims he's found a dead woman in a well," said Norén. "With blond hair."

Peters dropped his arms to his side.

"Louise Åkerblom?"

"I don't know. I don't even know if it's true."

"Get hold of Wallander," said Peters. "Right away."

The mood among the detectives in the Ystad police station this Walpurgis Eve morning was expectant. They had gathered in the conference room at eight, and Björk rushed through the business. He had other things besides a missing woman to think about on a day like this. It was traditionally one of the most unruly days in the whole year, and there was a lot to do in preparation for the fun and games they could expect that evening and into the night.

The whole meeting was devoted to Stig Gustafson. Wallander had set his troops looking for the former marine engineer all Thursday afternoon and evening. When he reported on his conversation with Pastor Tureson, everybody thought they were on the threshold of a breakthrough. They also realized that the severed finger and the blown-up house would have to wait. Martinson had even been of the view that it was pure coincidence after all. That there simply was no connection between the incidents.

"This kind of thing has happened before," he said. "We've raided an illegal home distillery, and found an Aladdin's cave in a neighbor's house when we stopped to ask the way."

By Friday morning they still had not succeeded in finding out where Stig Gustafson lived.

"We have to crack this today," said Wallander. "Maybe we won't find him. But if we get his address, we can establish whether he's gone off in a hurry."

At that very moment, the telephone rang. Björk grabbed the receiver, listened briefly, then handed it to Wallander.

"It's Norén," he said. "He's at a car accident somewhere outside of town."

"Somebody else can take it," said Wallander, annoyed.

He took the receiver nevertheless, and listened to what Norén had to say. Martinson and Svedberg were well acquainted with Wallander's reactions and adept at picking up the slightest change in his mood, and they could see right away that the call was important.

Wallander replaced the receiver slowly, and looked at his colleagues.

"Norén's at the junction with the road leading to the garbage dump," he said. "There's been a minor car accident. They have a guy who claims he's found a dead woman stuffed down a well."

They waited anxiously to hear what Wallander had to say next.

"If I understood it rightly," said Wallander, "this well is less than five kilometers from the property Louise Åkerblom was going to inspect. And even closer to the pond where we found her car."

There was a moment's silence. Then they all got to their feet at the same time.

"Do you want a full-scale call-out right away?" asked Björk.

"No," said Wallander. "We've got to get it confirmed first. Norén warned us not to get overexcited. He thought the man seemed very confused."

"So would I have been," said Svedberg. "If I'd first of all found a dead woman in a well, then driven off the road."

"Exactly what I was thinking," said Wallander.

They left Ystad in patrol cars. Wallander had Svedberg with him, while Martinson had a car to himself. When they got to the northern exit road, Wallander switched on the siren. Svedberg stared at him in surprise.

"There's hardly any traffic," he said.

"Even so," said Wallander.

They stopped at the turnoff to the garbage dump, put the ashen Peter Hanson in the back seat, and followed his directions.

"It wasn't me," he said, over and over again.

"Who did what?" asked Wallander.

"I didn't kill her," he said.

"What were you doing there, then?" asked Wallander.

"I was only going to steal the pump."

Wallander and Svedberg exchanged glances.

"Morell called late last night and ordered four water pumps," muttered Hanson. "But I didn't kill her."

Wallander was lost. The penny suddenly dropped for Svedberg, and he explained.

"I think I get it," he said. "There is a notorious fence in Malmö called Morell. He's notorious because our colleagues in town have never been able to pin anything onto him."

"Water pumps?" Wallander was suspicious.

"Antique value," said Svedberg.

They drove into the yard in front of the deserted house. Wallander had time to register that it looked like a nice day for the holiday. There wasn't a cloud in the sky, not a puff of wind, and it must be at least 60 degrees, even though it was only nine o'clock.

He contemplated the well and the broken-off pump lying beside it. Then he took a deep breath, went up to the well, and looked down.

Martinson and Svedberg were waiting in the background, with Peter Hanson.

Wallander could see right away that it was Louise Åkerblom.

Even in death, there was a fixed smile on her face.

He suddenly felt very ill. He turned away quickly and sat on his haunches.

Martinson and Svedberg approached the well. Both of them jerked back violently.

"Damn," said Martinson.

Wallander swallowed and forced himself to breath deeply. He thought of Louise Åkerblom's daughters. And of Robert Åkerblom. He wondered how they would be able to keep on believing in a good and all-powerful God when their mother and wife had been murdered and shoved down a well.

He stood up and went back to the well.

"It's her," he said. "No doubt about it."

Martinson ran to his car, called Björk, and requested a full-scale emergency call-out. They would need the fire brigade to get Louise Åkerblom's body out of the well. Wallander sat down with Peter Hanson on the dilapidated veranda, and listened to his story. He occasionally asked questions, and nodded when Peter Hanson answered. He could tell already that Hanson was telling the truth. In fact, the police had reason to be grateful that he had set out that morning to steal old water pumps. If he hadn't, it could have been a very long time before they found Louise Åkerblom.

"Take down his personal details," said Wallander to Svedberg, when he had finished talking to Peter Hanson. "Then let him go. But make sure that Morell guy backs up his story."

Svedberg nodded.

"Who's the prosecutor on duty?" Wallander wondered.

"I think Björk said it was Per Åkeson," replied Svedberg.

"Get hold of him," said Wallander. "Tell him we've found her. And that it's murder. I'll give him a report later this afternoon."

"What do we do about Stig Gustafson?" asked Svedberg.

"You'll have to keep on hunting him by yourself for the time being," said Wallander. "I want Martinson to be here when we get her up and make the first examination."

"I'll be only too glad to miss that," said Svedberg.

He drove off in one of the cars.

Wallander took a few more deep breaths before approaching the well once more.

He did not want to be on his own when he informed Robert Åkerblom where they found his wife.

It took two hours to get Louise Åkerblom's corpse out of the well. The ones who did the work were the same two young firemen who had dragged the pond two days before, when her car had been found. They pulled her up using a rescue harness, and put the body in an investigation tent that had been raised alongside the well. As they were pulling up the body, it became clear to Wallander how she died. She had been shot in the forehead. Once again he was struck by the thought that nothing in this investigation was straightforward. He still had not met Stig Gustafson, if he really was the one who killed her. But would he have shot her from the front? There was something that didn't add up.

He asked Martinson for his first reaction.

"A bullet straight into the forehead," said Martinson. "That doesn't make me think of uncontrolled passion and unhappy love. It makes me think of a cold-blooded execution."

"Exactly what I was thinking," said Wallander.

The firemen pumped the water out of the well. Then they went down again, and when they came back up they had with them Louise Åkerblom's purse, her briefcase, and one of her shoes. The other was still on her foot. The water was pumped into a hastily constructed plastic pool. Martinson found nothing else of interest when they filtered it.

The firemen went back one more time to the bottom of the well. They shone powerful lamps all around, but found nothing apart from a cat's skeleton.

The doctor looked pale when she emerged from the tent.

"It's terrible," she said to Wallander.

"Yeah," he replied. "We know the most important thing, namely that she was shot. I want the pathologists in Malmö to find out two things for me right away: first the bullet, second a report on any other injuries which might suggest she had been beaten or held prisoner. Anything you can find. And of course, whether she's been subjected to sexual assault."

"The bullet's still in her head," said the doctor. "I can't see any exit hole."

"One other thing," said Wallander. "I want her wrists and ankles examined. I want to know if there is any sign of her having been put in handcuffs."

"Handcuffs?"

"That's right," said Wallander. "Handcuffs."

Björk had been staying in the background while they worked to lift the corpse out of the well. Once the body had been placed on a stretcher and driven off to the hospital in an ambulance, he took Wallander aside.

"We have to inform her husband," he said.

"We," thought Wallander. You mean, I'll have to do it.

"I'll take Pastor Tureson with me," he said.

"You'll have to try and find out how long it will take him to inform all her close relatives," Björk continued. "I'm very much afraid we won't be able to keep this quiet for very long. And then, I really don't understand how you could just let that thief go. He can run to some evening tabloid or other and earn himself a fortune if he spills the beans on this story."

Wallander was irritated by Björk's niggling tone. On the other hand, he had to admit that there was a very real risk.

"Yes," he said. "That was stupid. My fault."

"I thought it was Svedberg who let him go," said Björk.

"It was Svedberg," said Wallander. "But it's my responsibility in any case."

"Please don't get angry with me for saying this," said Björk.

Wallander shrugged.

"I'm angry at whoever did this to Louise Åkerblom," he said. "And to her daughters. And to her husband."

They put the house out of bounds, and the investigation continued. Wallander got into his car and called Pastor Tureson. He answered more or less right away. Wallander explained what had happened. Pastor Tureson was silent for quite some time before answering. He promised to wait for Wallander outside the church.

"Will he break down?" asked Wallander.

"He has faith in God," said Pastor Tureson.

We'll see about that, thought Wallander. We'll see if that's enough.

But he said nothing.

Pastor Tureson was standing on the street, his head bowed.

Wallander found it difficult to gather his thoughts as he drove into town. There was nothing he found more difficult than informing relatives that someone in their family had suddenly died. There was no real difference whether the death was caused by an accident, a suicide, or a violent crime. No matter how hard he tried to express himself carefully and considerately, his words were cruelty itself. It had occurred to him that he was the ultimate herald of tragedy. He remembered what Rydberg, his friend and colleague, had said a few months before he died. *There will never be an appropriate way for a cop to tell somebody a sudden death has occurred. That's why we have to do it ourselves, and never delegate it to anybody else. We're probably more resilient than the others—we've seen more of what nobody ought ever to see.*

On the way into town he had also been aware of that persistent feeling that something was completely wrong, absolutely incomprehensible; the whole investigation was totally misguided, and some explanation or other must soon come to light. He would ask Martinson and Svedberg straight up if they felt the same as he did. Was there a link between that severed black finger and Louise Åkerblom's disappearance and eventual death? Or was it just a combination of unpredictable coincidences?

It occurred to him that there might also be a third possibility: that somebody had intentionally created the confusion.

But why had this death taken place so suddenly, he asked himself. The only motive we have been able to find so far is unrequited love. But it is a pretty big step from there to accusations of murder. Not to mention being so cold-blooded that the car was hidden in one place while the body was found somewhere else.

Maybe we haven't found a single stone worth turning over, he thought. What do we do if we find Stig Gustafson is not worth following up?

He thought of the handcuffs. Of Louise Åkerblom's constant smile. Of the happy family that no longer existed.

But was it the image that had collapsed? Or was it the reality?

Pastor Tureson got into the car. He had tears in his eyes. Wallander immediately felt a lump in his throat.

"Well, she's dead," said Wallander. "We've found her at the site of an empty house some way outside of Ystad. I can't tell you any more just now."

"How did she die?"

Wallander thought for a moment before replying.

"She was shot," he said.

"I have one more question," said Pastor Tureson. "Apart from wanting to know who could have carried out such a crazy act. Did she suffer a lot before she died?"

"I don't know yet," said Wallander. "But even if I did know, I would tell her husband that death came very quickly, and hence painlessly."

They stopped outside the house. On the way to the Methodist church Wallander had stopped off at the station and taken his own car. He did not want to turn up in a police car.

Robert Åkerblom answered almost as soon as they rang the doorbell. He's seen us, thought Wallander. The moment a car brakes in the street outside, he runs over to the nearest window to see who it is.

He ushered them into the living room. Wallander listened to see if there was any noise. The two girls did not appear to be home.

"I'm afraid I have to tell you your wife is dead," Wallander began. "We've found her at an abandoned house some way outside of town. She was murdered."

Robert Åkerblom stared at him, his face motionless. It seemed he was waiting for more.

"I very much regret this, " said Wallander. "But the best I can do is to tell you exactly how it is. I'm afraid I shall also have to ask you to identify the body. But that can wait. It doesn't need to be done today. And it would be all right if Pastor Tureson were to do it."

Robert Åkerblom kept on staring at him.

"Are your daughters at home?" asked Wallander, cautiously. "This must be awful for them."

He turned to Pastor Tureson, appealing for help.

"We'll do all we can to help," said Tureson.

"Thank you for letting me know," said Robert Åkerblom all of a sudden. "All this uncertainty has been so difficult to bear."

"I am really sorry things have turned out so badly," said Wallander. "All of us on the case were hoping there would have been some natural explanation."

"Who?" said Robert Åkerblom.

"We don't know," said Wallander. "But we shall not rest until we do know."

"You'll never know," said Robert Åkerblom.

Wallander looked at him inquiringly.

"Why do you think that?" he said.

"Nobody could have wanted to kill Louise," said Robert Åkerblom. "So how could you possibly find whoever is guilty?"

Wallander did not know what to say. Robert Åkerblom had put his finger on their biggest problem.

A few minutes later he stood up. Pastor Tureson accompanied him into the hall.

"You have a few hours in which to contact all the closest relatives," said Wallander. "Call me if you can't locate them. We can't keep this secret for ever."

"I hear what you're saying," said Pastor Tureson.

Then he lowered his voice.

"Stig Gustafson?" he asked.

"We're still looking," said Wallander. "We don't know if it is him."

"Have you any other leads?" asked Pastor Tureson.

"Could be," said Wallander, "but I'm afraid I can't answer that either."

"For technical reasons?"

"Exactly."

Wallander could see Pastor Tureson had one more question.

"Well," he said. "Fire away!"

Pastor Tureson lowered his voice so far that Wallander could hardly hear what he was saying.

"Rape?" he asked.

"We don't know yet," said Wallander. "But of course, that's not an impossibility."

Wallander felt a strange mixture of hunger and uneasiness when he left the Åkerbloms' house. He stopped on the Österleden highway and forced down a hamburger. He couldn't remember when he had

8 3

last eaten. Then he hurried along to the police station. When he got there he was met by Svedberg, who informed him that Björk had been forced to improvise a press conference at short notice. As he knew Wallander was busy informing relatives of Louise Åkerblom's death and he didn't want to disturb him, he had enlisted the help of Martinson.

"Can you guess how the news leaked out?" he asked.

"Yes," said Wallander. "Peter Hanson?"

"Wrong! Try again!"

"One of us?"

"Not this time. It was Morell. He saw the chance to squeeze some money from one of the evening papers if he tipped them off. He's obviously a real bastard. At least the guys in Malmö have something to pin on him now. Ordering somebody to steal four water pumps is a criminal offense."

"He'll only get probation," said Wallander.

They went to the canteen and poured a mug of coffee each.

"How did Robert Åkerblom take it?" asked Svedberg.

"I don't know," said Wallander. "It must feel like half your life has been taken away. No one can imagine what it's like unless they've been through something similar themselves. I can't. All I can say just now is that we'll have to have a meeting as soon as the press conference is over. I'll be in my office till then, writing a summary."

"I thought I could try and put together an overview of the tipoffs we've had," said Svedberg. "Somebody might have seen Louise Åkerblom on Friday with a man who could be Stig Gustafson."

"Do that," said Wallander. "And let us have all you know about the man."

The press conference dragged on and on, eventually ending after an hour and a half. By then Wallander had tried to compose a summary under various headings and draw up a plan for the next phase of the investigation.

Björk and Martinson were totally exhausted when they came to the conference room.

"Now I understand how you usually feel," said Martinson, flopping down into a chair. "The only thing they didn't ask about was the color of her underwear."

Wallander reacted immediately.

"That was unnecessary," he said.

Martinson opened his arms wide in apology.

"I'll try and give you a summary," said Wallander. "We know how it all started, so I'll jump over that bit. Anyway, we've found Louise Åkerblom. She's been murdered, shot through the forehead. My guess is she was shot at close range. But we'll know for sure later. We don't know if she was subjected to sexual assault. Nor do we know if she was ill-treated or held prisoner. We don't know where she was killed, either. Nor when. But we can be sure she was dead when she was put down that well. We've also found her car. It's essential we get a preliminary report from the hospital as soon as possible. Not least as to whether there was a sexual assault. Then we can start checking up on known criminals who might have done it."

Wallander took a slurp of coffee before continuing.

"As for motive and murderer, we only have one track to follow so far," he went on. "The engineer Stig Gustafson, who's been persecuting her and pestering her with hopeless declarations of love. We still haven't found him. You know more about that, Svedberg. You can also give us a summary of the tipoffs we've had. Further complications in this investigation are the severed black finger and the house that blew up. Things have been made no easier by the fact that Nyberg found the remains of an advanced radio transmitter in the ashes, and the butt of a handgun used mainly in South Africa, if I understood him properly. In one sense the finger and the pistol are linked by that fact. Not that it helps much. We still don't know if the two incidents are connected."

Wallander was through, and looked at Svedberg, who was leafing through the stack of papers he was constantly fiddling with.

"I'll start with the tipoffs," he said. "I'm thinking of writing a book one of these days called *People Who Want to Help the Police*. It'll make me a rich man. As usual we've had curses, blessings, confessions, dreams, hallucinations, and the occasional sensible tip. As far as I can see, though, there's only one of immediate interest. The warden of the Rydsgård estate is quite certain he saw Louise Åkerblom driving past last Friday afternoon. The time is about right. That means we know which route she took. Apart from that there's very little of interest. Now we know, of course, it's often a day or two before the best tipoffs come in. They come from sensible people who hesitate before getting in touch. As for Stig Gustafson, we haven't managed to discover where he's moved to. But he's supposed to have an unmarried female relative in Malmö. Unfortunately we don't know her first name. The Malmö telephone directory is full of Gustafsons, of course. Stacks and stacks of them. We'll just have to get down to it and divide the list between us. That's all I have to say."

Wallander sat in silence for a moment. Björk looked expectantly at him.

"Let's concentrate our efforts," said Wallander at length. "We have to find Stig Gustafson, that's the first priority. If the only lead we have is that relative in Malmö, then that's the one we'll have to follow up. Everybody in this station who's capable of picking up a phone will have to help. I'll join in and assist with the telephoning, as soon as I've dealt with the hospital."

Then he turned to Björk.

"We'd better keep going all evening," he said. "It's essential."

Björk nodded in agreement.

"Do that," he said. "I'll be around if anything important happens."

Svedberg began organizing the hunt for marine engineer Stig Gustafson's relative in Malmö, while Wallander went back to his office. Before calling the hospital, he dialed his father's number. It was a long time before he answered. He assumed his father had been in his studio, painting. Wallander could hear right away that he was in a bad mood.

"Hi! It's me," he said.

"Who's me?" asked his father.

"You know full well who it is," said Wallander.

"I've forgotten what your voice sounds like," said his father.

Wallander gritted his teeth and resisted the temptation to slam down the receiver.

"I'm busy," he said. "I've just found a dead woman in a well. A woman who was murdered. I won't be able to get out to your place today. I hope you'll understand."

To his astonishment his father suddenly sounded friendly.

"I can see you can't do that," he said. "It sounds unpleasant."

8 6

"It is," said Wallander. "I just want to wish you a pleasant evening. And I'll try and come out tomorrow."

"Only if you get time," said his father. "I can't go on talking any longer right now."

"Why not?"

"I'm expecting a visitor."

Wallander could hear he'd been cut off. He was left sitting there with the receiver in his hand.

A visitor, he thought. So Gertrud Anderson goes around to see him even when she's not working?

He shook his head for a long time.

I must make time to go and see him soon, he thought. It would be a complete disaster if he married her.

He got up and went in to Svedberg. He collected a list of names and telephone numbers, returned to his office, and dialed the first on the list. At the same time he remembered he had to contact the on-duty prosecutor at some point during the afternoon.

Four o'clock came and they still hadn't traced Stig Gustafson's relative.

At half past four Wallander called Per Åkeson at home. He reported on what had happened so far, and announced that they could now concentrate on tracking down Stig Gustafson. The prosecutor had no objections. He asked Wallander to let him know if anything developed during the evening.

At a quarter past five, Wallander fetched his third list of names from Svedberg. Still no luck. Wallander groaned at the thought of it being Walpurgis Eve. A lot of people were out. They had gone away for the holiday.

Nobody answered the first two numbers he called. The third was to an elderly lady who was quite sure there was no one called Stig in her family.

Wallander opened the window, and could feel a headache coming on. Then he went back to the phone and dialed the fourth number. He let it go on ringing for quite a while, and was just about to replace the receiver when somebody answered. He could hear it was a young woman on the other end. He explained who he was and what he wanted to know.

"Sure," said the young woman, whose name was Monica. "I

have a half-brother called Stig. He's a marine engineer. Has something happened to him?"

Wallander could feel all his exhaustion and dissatisfaction falling away at a stroke.

"No," he said. "But we'd like to get in touch with him as soon as possible. Do you know where he lives?"

"Of course I know where he lives," she said. "In Lomma. But he's not at home."

"Where is he, then?"

"He's in Las Palmas. He'll be back home tomorrow, though. He's due to land at Copenhagen at ten o'clock tomorrow morning. I think he's on a Spies package."

"Excellent," said Wallander. "I'd be grateful if you could give me his address and phone number."

She told him what he wanted to know, he apologized for disturbing her evening, and hung up. Then he rushed into Svedberg's office, collecting Martinson on the way. No one knew where Björk was.

"We'll go to Malmö ourselves," said Wallander. "Our colleagues in town can assist. Run a check at the passport control on everybody disembarking from the various ferries. Björk will have to fix that."

"Did she say how long he'd been away?" asked Martinson. "If he had a week's vacation, that would mean he'd left last Saturday."

They looked at one another. The significance of Martinson's point was obvious.

"I think you should go home now," said Wallander. "At least some of us ought to have had a good night's sleep before tomorrow. Let's meet here at eight tomorrow morning. Then we'll drive to Malmö."

Martinson and Svedberg went home. Wallander talked to Björk, who promised to call his counterpart in Malmö and arrange things according to Wallander's wishes.

At a quarter past six Wallander called the hospital. The doctor was only able to give vague answers.

"There are no visible injuries on the body," she said. "No bruises, no fractures. Superficially, it doesn't look as though there was any sexual assault. I'll have to come back to that, though. I can't see any marks on her wrists or ankles."

"That's fine," said Wallander. "Thanks. I'll be in touch again tomorrow."

Then he left the police station.

He drove out to Kåseberga and sat for a while on the cliff top, staring out to sea.

He was back home soon after nine.

Chapter Seven

At dawn, just before he woke up, Kurt Wallander had a dream. He had discovered that one of his hands was black.

He had not put on a black glove. It was his skin that had grown darker until his hand was like an African's.

In his dream Wallander wavered between reactions of horror and satisfaction. Rydberg, his former colleague who had been dead for nearly two years, looked disapprovingly at the hand. He asked Wallander why only one of them was black.

"Something will have to happen tomorrow as well," Wallander replied in his dream.

When he woke up and recalled the dream, he lay in bed wondering about the reply he gave Rydberg. What did he mean, in fact?

Then he got up and looked out the window. The first of May in Skåne this year was cloud-free and sunny, but very windy. It was six o'clock.

Although he had only slept for two hours, he did not feel tired. That morning they would get an answer to the question of whether Stig Gustafson had an alibi for Friday afternoon the previous week, when Louise Åkerblom had most probably been murdered.

If we can solve the crime today already, it will have been surprisingly simple, he thought. The first few days we had nothing to go on. Then everything started to happen very quickly. A criminal investigation seldom follows everyday rhythms. It has its own life, its own energy. The clocks of a criminal investigation distort time, making it stand still, or race forward. No one can know in advance.

They met at eight o'clock in the conference room, and Wallander set the ball rolling.

"There's no need for us to interfere in what the Danish police are doing," he began. "If what his half-sister says is to be believed, Stig Gustafson will land on a Scanair flight to Copenhagen at ten o'clock. You can check that, Svedberg. Then he has three possible ways of getting to Malmö. The ferry to Limhamn, the hydrofoil, or the SAS hovercraft. We'll be keeping an eye on all three."

"An old marine engineer will probably take the big ferry," said Martinson.

"He might have had enough of boats," objected Wallander. "We'll have two men at each spot. He's to be taken firmly and informed of the reasons. A certain amount of caution would no doubt be appropriate. Then we'll bring him here. I thought I would start talking to him."

"Two men seem on the low side," said Björk. "Shouldn't we have a patrol car in the background, at least?"

Wallander went along with that.

"I've talked to our colleagues in Malmö," Björk went on. "We'll get all the help we need. You can decide for yourselves what signal the immigration people should give you when he shows up."

Wallander looked at his watch.

"If that's all, we'd better get going," said Wallander. "It's best if we get to Malmö in good time."

"The flight could be delayed by up to twenty-four hours," said Svedberg. "Wait until I've checked."

Fifteen minutes later, he informed them the plane from Las Palmas was expected at Kastrup at twenty minutes past nine.

"It's already taken off," said Svedberg. "And they have a tail-wind."

They drove to Malmö immediately, talked to their colleagues there, and divided up the assignments. Wallander allocated himself to the hovercraft terminal, along with a rookie cop named Engman, who was wet behind the ears. He had come in place of a cop named Näslund, with whom Wallander had worked for many years. He was from the island of Gotland, and couldn't wait for an assignment back home. When a vacancy occurred in the Visby force, he did not hesitate to go for it. Wallander missed him at times, especially his unfailing good humor. Martinson and a colleague were taking care of Limhamn, and Svedberg was keeping an eye on the hydrofoils. They were in touch by walkie-talkie. Everything was set by half past nine. Wallander managed to arrange for coffee to be delivered to himself and the trainee by colleagues at the terminal.

"This is the first murderer I've ever hunted," said Engman.

"We don't know if he's our man," said Wallander. "In this country a man is innocent until he's proven guilty. Never forget that."

He was uncomfortable about the critical tone of his voice. He thought he'd better make up for it by saying something kind. But he couldn't think of anything.

At half past ten Svedberg and his colleague made an undramatic arrest at the hydrofoil terminal. Stig Gustafson was a small man, thin, balding, sunburnt after his holiday.

Svedberg explained how he was suspected of murder, put the cuffs on him and announced he was being taken to Ystad.

"I don't know what you're talking about," said Stig Gustafson. "Why do I have to be handcuffed? Why are you taking me to Ystad? Who am I supposed to have murdered?"

Svedberg noted that he seemed genuinely surprised. The thought suddenly struck him that marine engineer Gustafson might be innocent.

At ten minutes to twelve Wallander was sitting opposite Gustafson in an interview room at the Ystad police station. By that time he had already informed the prosecutor, Per Åkeson, of the arrest.

He started by asking if Stig Gustafson would like a cup of coffee.

"No," he said. "I want to go home. And I want to know why I'm here."

"I want to talk to you," said Wallander, "and the answers I get will decide whether or not you can go home."

He started from the beginning. Wrote down Gustafson's personal details, noted that his middle name was Emil, and that he was born in Landskrona. The man was obviously nervous, and Wallander could see he was sweating at the roots of his hair. But that did not necessarily mean anything. Police phobia is just as real as snake phobia.

Then the real interrogation started. Wallander came straight to the point, intrigued to find out what sort of a reaction he would get.

"You are here to answer questions about a brutal murder," he said. "The murder of Louise Åkerblom."

Wallander saw the man stiffen. Had he not counted on the body being found so soon? wondered Wallander. Or is he genuinely surprised?

"Louise Åkerblom disappeared last Friday," he continued. "Her body was found a few days ago. She was probably murdered during the latter part of Friday. What have you to say to that?"

"Is it the Louise Åkerblom I know?" asked Stig Gustafson.

Wallander could see he was scared now.

"Yes," he said. "The one you got to know through the Methodists."

"Has she been murdered?"

"Yes."

"That's terrible!"

Wallander immediately began to feel a gnawing sensation in his stomach, and knew something was wrong, absolutely damned wrong. Stig Gustafson's shocked astonishment gave the impression of being completely genuine. Mind you, Wallander knew from his own experience there were perpetrators of the most horrific crimes you could think of who nevertheless had the ability to appear innocent in the most convincing way possible.

All the same, he could feel that gnawing sensation.

Had they been following a trail that was cold from the start?

"I want to know what you were doing last Friday," said Wallander. "Start by telling me about the afternoon."

The answer he got surprised him.

"I was with the police," said Stig Gustafson.

"The police?"

"Yes. The cops in Malmö. I was flying to Las Palmas the next day. And I'd suddenly realized my passport had run out. I was at the station in Malmö, getting a new passport. The office was already closed by the time I got there, but they were nice and helped me anyway. I got my passport at four o'clock."

Deep down Wallander knew from that moment on that Stig

Gustafson was out of the picture. Even so, he didn't seem to want to let go. He had a pressing need to solve this murder as soon as humanly possible. Anyway, it would have been dereliction of duty to allow the interrogation to be governed by his feelings.

"I parked at Central Station," added Gustafson. "Then I went to the bar for a beer."

"Is there anybody who can prove you were in the bar shortly after four o'clock last Friday?" asked Wallander.

Stig Gustafson considered for a moment.

"I don't know," he said eventually. "I was sitting on my own. Maybe one of the bartenders will remember me? I very rarely go to the bar, though. I'm not exactly a regular customer."

"How long were you there?" asked Wallander.

"An hour, maybe. No longer."

"Until about half past five? Is that right?"

"I suppose so. I'd planned to go to the liquor store before they closed."

"Which one?"

"The one behind the NK department store. I don't know the name of the street."

"And you went there?"

"I just bought a few beers."

"Can anybody prove you were there?"

Stig Gustafson shook his head.

"The man who served me had a red beard," he said. "But I might still have the receipt. There's the date on those receipts, isn't there?"

"Go on," said Wallander, nodding.

"Then I collected the car," said Stig Gustafson. "I was going to buy a suitcase at the B&W discount warehouse, out at Jägersro."

"Is there anybody there who might recognize you?"

"I didn't buy a suitcase," said Stig Gustafson. "They were too expensive. I thought I could manage with my old one. It was a disappointment."

"What did you do next?"

"I had a hamburger at the McDonald's out there. But the servers are only kids. I don't suppose they'll remember anything at all."

"Young people often have good memories," said Wallander,

thinking of a young bank teller who had been extremely helpful in an investigation some years ago.

"I've just remembered something else," said Stig Gustafson suddenly. "Something that happened while I was at the bar."

"Go on."

"I went down to the rest room. I stood there talking to a guy for a couple of minutes. He was complaining that there weren't any paper towels to dry your hands on. He was a bit drunk. Not too much. He said his name was Forsgård and he ran a garden center at Höör."

Wallander made a note.

"We'll follow that one up," he said. "If we go back to McDonald's at Jägersro, the time would have been about half past six, right?"

"That's probably about right," said Stig Gustafson.

"What did you do next?"

"I went to Nisse's to play cards."

"Who's Nisse?"

"An old carpenter I used to have as a shipmate for many years. His name's Nisse Strömgren. Lives on Föreningsgatan. We play cards now and then. A game we learned in the Middle East. It's pretty complicated. But fun once you know it. You have to collect jacks."

"How long were you there?"

"It was probably near midnight by the time I went home. A bit too late, as I was going to have to get up so early. The bus was due to leave at six from Central Station. The bus to Kastrup, that is."

Wallander nodded. Stig Gustafson has an alibi, he thought. If what he says is true. And if Louise Åkerblom really was killed last Friday.

Right now there were not enough grounds to arrest Stig Gustafson. The prosecutor would never agree to it.

It's not him, thought Wallander. If I start pressing him on his persecution of Louise Åkerblom, we'll get nowhere.

He stood up.

"Wait here," he said and left the room.

They gathered in the conference room and listened gloomily to Wallander's account.

"We'll check up on what he said," said Wallander. "But to be honest, I no longer think he's our man. This was a blind alley."

"I think you're jumping the gun," objected Björk. "We don't even know for sure she really did die on Friday afternoon. Stig Gustafson could in fact have driven from Lomma to Krageholm after leaving his card-playing pal."

"That hardly seems likely," said Wallander. "What could have kept Louise Åkerblom out until that time? Don't forget she left a message on her answering machine to say she'd be home by five. We've got to believe that. Something happened before five o'clock."

Nobody spoke.

Wallander looked around.

"I'll have to talk to the prosecutor," he said. "If nobody has anything to say, I'm going to let Stig Gustafson go."

Nobody had any objection.

Wallander walked over to the other end of the police station, where the prosecution authorities had their offices. He was admitted to Per Åkeson and gave him a report of the interrogation. Every time Wallander visited his office, he was struck by the astonishing disorder all around him. Papers were stacked up haphazardly on desks and chairs; the garbage bin was overflowing. But Per Åkeson was a skillful prosecutor. Moreover, no one had ever accused him of losing a single paper of significance.

"We can't hold him," he said when Wallander had finished. "I take it you can check his alibi pretty quickly?"

"Yes," said Wallander. "To tell you the truth, I don't think he did it."

"Do you have any other leads?"

"It's all very vague," said Wallander. "We wondered if he might have hired somebody else to kill her. We'll make a thorough check this afternoon before we go any further. But we have no other individual to go after. We'll have to keep going on a broad basis for the time being. I'll be in touch."

Per Åkeson nodded, and stared at Wallander, frowning.

"How much sleep are you getting?" he asked. "Or rather, how little? Have you seen yourself in a mirror? You look terrible!"

"That's nothing compared to how I feel," said Wallander, getting to his feet.

He went back down the corridor, opened the door to the interview room, and went in.

"We'll arrange transport to take you to Lomma," he said. "But you can bet we'll be in touch again."

"Am I free?" asked Gustafson.

"You've never been anything else," said Wallander. "Being interrogated isn't the same as being accused."

"I didn't kill her," said Stig Gustafson. "I can't understand how you could think such a thing."

"Really?" said Wallander. "Even though you've been chasing after her on and off?"

Wallander saw a shadow of unease flit over Stig Gustafson's face.

Just so he knows we know, thought Wallander.

He accompanied Stig Gustafson out to reception, and arranged for him to be taken home.

I won't be seeing him again, he thought. We can write him off.

After an hour for lunch, they reassembled in the conference room. Wallander had been home for a few sandwiches in his kitchen.

"Where are all the honest thieves nowadays?" asked Martinson with a sigh. "This case seems to have come out of a storybook. All we have is a dead woman from a low-church sect, dumped in a well. And a severed black finger."

"I agree with you," said Wallander. "But we can't get away from that finger, no matter how much we'd like to."

"There are too many loose ends flying around out of control," said Svedberg, scratching his bald head in irritation. "We have to collect together everything we have. And we must do it now. Otherwise we'll never get anywhere."

Wallander could detect in Svedberg's words indirect criticism of the way he was leading the investigation. But he had to concede even now that it was not totally unjustified. There was always a danger of concentrating too soon on a single line of investigation. Svedberg's imagery reflected all too accurately the confusion he felt.

"You're right," said Wallander. "Let's see how far we've come. Louise Åkerblom is murdered. We don't know exactly where and we don't know who did it. But we do know roughly when. Not far from where we found her, a house that had been standing empty explodes. In the ruins of the fire, Nyberg finds parts of an advanced radio transmitter and the charred remains of a pistol butt. The pistol is manufactured in South Africa. In addition, we find a severed black finger in the yard outside the house. Then somebody tries to hide Louise Åkerblom's car in a pond. It's pure coincidence we find it as quickly as we do. The same applies to her body. We also know she was shot in the middle of her forehead, and the whole setup gives the impression of an execution. I called the hospital before we started this meeting. There are no signs of sexual assault. She was just shot."

"We have to get all this sorted out," said Martinson. "We have to find more evidence. About the finger, the radio transmitter, the handgun. That lawyer in Värnamo who was looking after the house has to be contacted immediately. There must obviously have been somebody in the house."

"We'll sort out who does what before we close the meeting," said Wallander. "I just have two more thoughts I'd like to put forward."

"We'll kick off with them," said Björk.

"Who could possibly have wanted to shoot Louise Åkerblom?" said Wallander. "A rapist would have been a possibility. But she was evidently not raped, according to preliminary medical reports. There are no signs of her being beaten up or held prisoner. She has no enemies. That all makes me wonder if the whole business could have been a mistake. She was killed instead of somebody else. The other possibility is that she happened to witness something she ought not to have seen or heard."

"The house could fit in there," said Martinson. "It wasn't far from the property she was due to look over. Something has definitely been going on in that house. She might have seen something, and been shot. Peters and Norén went to the house she was going to examine. The one that belongs to a widow by the name of Wallin. They both said it was easy to go astray on the way there."

Wallander nodded.

"Go on," he said.

"There's not much more to say," said Martinson. "For some reason or other, a finger gets cut off. Unless that happened when the house blew up. But it doesn't look that way. An explosion like that turns a man into pulp. The finger was whole, apart from having been cut off."

"I don't know much about South Africa," said Svedberg. "Except that it's a racist country with lots of violence. Sweden has no diplomatic relations with South Africa. We don't even play tennis or do business with them. Not officially, at least. What I can't understand for the life of me is why something from South Africa should end up in Sweden. You'd think Sweden would be the last place to be involved."

"Maybe that's exactly why," muttered Martinson.

Wallander homed in on Martinson's comment immediately.

"What do you mean?" he asked.

"Nothing," said Martinson. "I just think we have to start thinking in a completely different way if we're going to get anywhere with this case."

"I agree entirely," said Björk, interrupting the exchange. "I want a written report on this business from every one of you by tomorrow. Let's see if a little quiet contemplation might get us somewhere."

They divided up the assignments among themselves. Wallander took over the lawyer in Värnamo from Björk, who was going to concentrate on producing a preliminary report on examinations of the finger.

Wallander punched in the number to the lawyer's office, and asked to speak to Mr. Holmgren on urgent business. There was such a long delay before Holmgren answered that Wallander grew annoyed.

"It's about the property you are looking after in Skåne," he said. "The house that burned down."

"Completely inexplicable," said Holmgren. "But I have checked to make sure the insurance policy arranged by the late owner covers the incident. Do the police have any explanation for what happened?"

"No," said Wallander. "But we're working on it. I have some questions I need to ask you on the telephone."

"I hope this won't take long," said the lawyer. "I'm very busy."

"If you can't take the questions by telephone, the police in Värnamo will have to take you down to the station," said Wallander, ignoring the fact that he sounded brusque.

There was a pause before the lawyer responded.

"OK, fire away. I'm listening."

"We're still waiting for a fax with the names and addresses of the joint heirs to the estate."

"I'll make sure that's sent."

"Then I wonder who is directly responsible for the property."

"I am. I'm not sure what you mean by the question."

"A house needs attention occasionally. Roof tiles need replacing, mice keeping under control. Do you do that as well?"

"One of the beneficiaries of the estate lives in Vollsjö. He usually looks after the house. His name is Alfred Hanson."

Wallander noted his address and telephone number.

"So the house has been empty for a year?"

"For more than a year. There's been some disagreement as to whether it should be sold or not."

"In other words, nobody's been living in the house?"

"Of course not."

"Are you quite sure?"

"I don't understand what you're getting at. The house has been boarded up. Alfred Hanson has been calling me at regular intervals to report that all is in order."

"When did he call last?"

"How on earth am I supposed to remember that?"

"I don't know. But I'd like an answer to my question."

"Some time around New Year's, I believe. But I can't swear to it. Why is that important?"

"Everything is important for the moment. But thank you for the information."

Wallander hung up, opened his telephone directory, and checked Alfred Hanson's address. Then he got up, grabbed his jacket and left the office.

"I'm off to Vollsjö," he said as he passed the door to Martinson's office. "There's something odd about the house that blew up."

"I think there's something odd about everything," said Martinson. "I was just talking to Nyberg before you came, by the way. He maintains that radio transmitter could well have been made in Russia."

"Russia?"

"That's what he said. Don't ask me."

"Another country," said Wallander. "Sweden, South Africa, Russia. Where's it all going to end?"

Just over half an hour later, he drove up to the house where Alfred Hanson supposedly lived. It was a relatively modern house, very much different from the original building. Some German shepherds started barking frenziedly as Wallander got out of his car. It was half past four by now, and he was feeling hungry.

A man in his forties opened the door and came out onto the steps in his stocking feet. His hair was in a mess, and as Wallander approached he could smell strong liquor.

"Alfred Hanson?" he enquired.

The man nodded.

"I'm from the police in Ystad," said Wallander.

"Oh, hell!" said the man even before Wallander had given his name.

"Excuse me?"

"Who's squealed? Is it that shit Bengtson?"

Wallander thought rapidly before saying anything.

"I can't comment on that," he said. "The police protect all their informers."

"It's gotta be Bengtson," said the man. "Am I under arrest?"

"We can talk about that," said Wallander.

The man let Wallander into the kitchen. He immediately detected the faint but unmistakable smell of fusel oil. Something clicked. Alfred Hanson was running an illegal still, and thought Wallander had come to arrest him.

The man had flopped down on a kitchen chair and was scratching his head.

"Just my luck," he sighed.

"We'll talk about the moonshine later," said Wallander. "There's something else I want to talk about."

"What?"

"The property that burned down."

"I know nothing about that," said the man.

Wallander noticed immediately that he was worried.

"You know nothing about what?"

The man lit a crumpled cigarette with trembling fingers.

"I'm really a paint sprayer," said the man. "But I can't face starting work at seven o'clock every morning. So I thought I might as well rent out that little shack, if anybody was interested. I mean, I want to sell the thing. But the family's making such a damned fuss."

"Who was interested?"

"Some guy from Stockholm. He'd been driving around the area, looking for something suitable. Then he found this house, and liked the location. I'm still wondering how he managed to trace it to me."

"What was his name?"

"He said he was called Nordström. I took that with a pinch of salt, though."

"Why?"

"He spoke good Swedish, but he had a foreign accent. You show me a goddamned foreigner called Nordström!"

"But he wanted to rent the house?"

"Yeah. And he paid well. I was gonna get ten thousand kronor a month. You don't turn your nose up at a deal like that. It wasn't doing anybody any harm, I thought. I get a bit of a reward in return for looking after the house. No need for the heirs or Holmgren in Värnamo to know anything about it."

"How long was he going to rent the house?"

"He came at the beginning of April. Said he wanted it till the end of May."

"Did he say what he was going to use it for?"

"For people who wanted to be left in peace to do some painting."

"Painting?"

Wallander thought of his father.

"Artists, that is. And he offered cash up front. Damn right I was going to take it."

"When did you meet him next?"

"Never."

"Never?"

"It was a sort of unspoken condition. That I should keep my nose out of it. And I did. He got the keys, and that was that."

"Have you got the keys back?"

"No. He was going to mail them to me."

"And you have no address?"

"No."

"Can you describe him?"

"He was extremely fat."

"Anything else?"

"How the hell do you describe a fat guy? He was balding, red-faced and fat. And when I say fat, do I mean fat! He was like a barrel."

Wallander nodded.

"Have you any of the money left?" he asked, thinking of possible fingerprints.

"Not an öre. That's why I started distilling again."

"If you stop that as of today, I won't take you in to Ystad," said Wallander.

Alfred Hanson could hardly believe his ears.

"I mean what I say," said Wallander. "But I'll check up that you really have stopped. And you must pour away everything you've made already."

The man was sitting open-mouthed at the kitchen table when Wallander left.

Dereliction of duty, he thought. But I haven't time to bother with moonshiners just now.

He drove back to Ystad. Without really knowing why, he turned into the parking lot by Krageholm Lake. He got out of the car and walked down to the water's edge.

There was something about this investigation, about the death of Louise Åkerblom, that scared him. As if the whole thing had barely started yet.

I'm scared, he thought. It's like that black finger were pointing straight at me. I'm in the middle of something I can't understand.

He sat down on a rock, even though it was damp. Suddenly his weariness and depression threatened to overwhelm him.

He gazed out over the lake, thinking there was a fundamental similarity between this case he was up to his neck in and the feelings he had inside. He seemed to have as little control over himself as he had chance of solving the case. With a sigh even he thought was pathetic, he decided he was as much at sea with his own life as he was with the search for Louise Åkerblom's murderer.

"Where do I go from here?" he said aloud to himself. "I don't want anything to do with ruthless killers with no respect for life. I don't want to get involved in a kind of violence that will be incomprehensible to me as long as I live. Maybe the next generation of cops in this country will have a different kind of experience and have a different view of their work. But it's too late for me. I'll never be any different than what I am. A pretty good cop in a medium-sized Swedish police district."

He stood up and watched a magpie launching itself from a treetop.

All questions remain unanswered in the end, he thought. I devote my life to trying to catch and then put away crooks who are guilty of various crimes. Sometimes I succeed, often I don't. But when I eventually pass away one of these days, I'll have failed in the biggest investigation of all. Life will still be an insoluble riddle.

I want to see my daughter, he thought. I miss her so much at times, it hurts. I have to catch a black man missing a finger, especially if he's the one who killed Louise Åkerblom. I have a question for him I need an answer to: why did you kill her?

I must follow up on Stig Gustafson, not let him slide out of the picture too soon, even though I'm already convinced he's innocent.

He walked back to his car.

The fear and repugnance would not go away. The finger was still pointing.

The
Man from
Transkei

Chapter Eight

Y ou could hardly see the man squatting in the shadow of the wrecked car. He did not move a muscle, and his black face was indistinguishable from the dark bodywork.

He had chosen his hiding place carefully. He had been waiting since early afternoon, and now the sun was beginning to sink beyond the dusty silhouette of the suburban ghetto that was Soweto. The dry, red earth glowed in the setting sun. It was April 8, 1992.

He had traveled a long way to get to the meeting place on time. The white man who sought him out had said he would have to set off early. For security reasons they preferred not to give him a precise pickup time. All he as told was that it would be shortly after sunset.

Only twenty-six hours had passed since the man who introduced himself as Stewart stood outside his home in Ntibane. When he heard the knock at the door, he thought at first it was the police in Umtata. Seldom a month went by without a visit from them. As soon as a bank robbery or a murder took place, there would be an investigator from the Umtata homicide squad at his door. Sometimes they would take him in to town for questioning, but usually they accepted his alibi, even if it was no more than that he'd been drunk in one of the local bars.

When he emerged from the corrugated iron shack that was his home, he did not recognize the man standing in the bright sunlight claiming to be Stewart.

Victor Mabasha could see right away the man was lying. He could have been called anything at all, but not Stewart. Although he spoke English, Victor could hear from his pronunciation that he was of Afrikaner origin. And *boere* just weren't called Stewart.

It was afternoon when the man showed up. Victor Mabasha was asleep in bed when the knock came. He made no attempt to hurry as he got up, put on a pair of pants, and opened the door. He was getting used to nobody wanting him for any thing important anymore. It was usually somebody he owed money to. Or somebody stupid enough to think he could borrow money from him. Unless it was the cops. But they didn't knock. They hammered on the door. Or forced it open.

The man claiming to be Stewart was about fifty. He wore an ill-fitting suit and was sweating profusely. His car was parked under a baoba tree on the other side of the road. Victor noticed the plates were from Transvaal. He wondered briefly why he had come so far, all the way to Transkei province, in order to meet him.

The man did not ask to come in. He just handed over an envelope and said somebody wanted to see him on important business on the outskirts of Soweto the following day.

"All you need to know is in the letter," he said.

A few half-naked children were playing with a buckled hubcap just outside the hut. Victor yelled at them to go away. They disappeared immediately.

"Who?" asked Victor.

He mistrusted all white men. But most of all he mistrusted white men who lied so badly, and made things worse by thinking he would be satisfied with an envelope.

"I can't tell you that," said Stewart.

"There's always somebody wanting to see me," said Victor. "Question is, do I want to see him?"

"It's all in the envelope," Stewart repeated.

Victor held out his hand and took the thick, brown envelope. He could feel right away there was a thick bundle of bills in there. That was both reassuring and worrisome. He needed money. But he did not know why he was being given it. That made him uneasy. He had no desire to get involved in something he knew too little about.

Stewart wiped his face and bald head with a soaking wet handkerchief.

"There's a map," he said. "The meeting place is marked. It's close to Soweto. You haven't forgotten the layout there?"

"Everything changes," said Victor. "I know what Soweto looked like eight years ago, but I have no idea what it looks like today."

"It's not in Soweto itself," said Stewart. "The pickup point is on a feeder road to the Johannesburg freeway. Nothing has changed out there. You'll have to leave early tomorrow morning if you're going to make it in time."

"Who wants to see me?" Victor asked again.

"He prefers not to give his name," said Stewart. "You'll meet him tomorrow."

Victor shook his head slowly and handed back the envelope.

"I want a name," he repeated. "If I don't get a name, I won't be at the pickup point on time. I won't ever be there."

The man hesitated. Victor stared fixedly at him. After a long pause, Stewart seemed to realize that Victor meant what he said. He looked around. The kids had gone away. It was about fifty meters to Victor's nearest neighbors, who lived in a corrugated iron shack just as dilapidated as his own. A woman was pounding corn in the swirling dust outside the front door. A few goats searched for blades of grass in the parched red earth.

"Jan Kleyn," he said in a low voice. "Jan Kleyn wants to see you. Forget I ever said that. But you've got to be on time."

Then he turned and went back to his car. Victor stood watching him disappear in a cloud of dust. He was driving far too fast. Victor thought that was typical of a white man who felt insecure and exposed when he entered a black township. For Stewart it was like entering enemy territory. And it was.

He grinned at the thought.

White men were scared men.

Then he wondered how Jan Kleyn could stoop so low as to use a messenger like that.

Or might it be another lie from Stewart? Maybe it wasn't Jan Kleyn who sent him? Maybe it was somebody else?

The kids playing with the hubcap were back again. He went back into his hut, lit the kerosene lamp, sat down on the rickety bed, and slowly slit open the envelope.

From force of habit he opened it from the bottom up. Letter-bombers nearly always placed their detonators at the top of the envelope. Few people expecting a bomb through the mail opened their letters the normal way.

The envelope contained a map, carefully drawn by hand in black India ink. A red cross marked the meeting place. He could see it in his mind's eye. It would be impossible to go wrong. Apart from the map there was a bundle of red fifty-rand bills in the envelope. Without counting, Victor knew there were five thousand rand.

That was all. There was no message saying why Jan Kleyn wanted to see him.

Victor put the envelope on the mud floor and stretched out on the bed. The blanket smelled moldy. An invisible mosquito buzzed around his face. He turned his head and contemplated the kerosene lamp.

Jan Kleyn, he thought. Jan Kleyn wants to see me. It's been two years since the last time. And he said then he never wanted anything to do with me again. But now he wants to see me. Why?

He sat up on the bed and looked at his wristwatch. If he was going to be in Soweto the next day, he'd have to take the bus from Umtata this evening. Stewart was wrong. He couldn't wait until tomorrow morning. It was nearly nine hundred kilometers to Johannesburg.

He had no decisions to make. Having accepted the money, he would have to go. He had no desire to owe Jan Kleyn five thousand rand. That would be tantamount to signing his own death warrant. He knew Jan Kleyn well enough to be aware that nobody who crossed him ever got away with it.

He took out a bag tucked under the bed. As he did not know how long he was going to be away, or what Jan Kleyn wanted him to do, he just packed a few shirts, underpants and a pair of sturdy shoes. If the assignment was going to be a long one, he would have to buy whatever clothes he needed. Then he carefully detached the back of of the bed frame. His two knives were coated in grease and wrapped in plastic. He wiped away the grease and took off his shirt. He took down the specially made knife belt from a hook in the ceiling and buckled it around his waist, noting with satisfaction that he could still use the same hole. Although he had spent several months until his money ran out drinking beer, he had not put on weight. He was still in good shape, even though he would soon be thirty-one.

He put the two knives in their sheaths, after checking the edges with his finger tips. He needed only to press slightly to draw blood. Then he removed another part of the bed frame and produced his pistol: that, too, was greased with coconut fat and wrapped in plastic. He sat on the bed and cleaned the gun meticulously. It was a 9mm Parabellum. He loaded the magazine with special ammunition that could only be obtained from an unlicensed arms dealer in Ravenmore. He wrapped two spare magazines inside one of his shirts in the bag. Then he strapped on his shoulder holster and inserted the pistol. Now he was ready to meet Jan Kleyn.

Shortly afterwards he left the shack. He locked it with the rusty padlock, and started walking to the bus stop a few kilometers down the road to Umtata.

He screwed up his eyes and gazed at the red sun rapidly setting over Soweto, remembering the last time he was there eight years ago. A local businessman had given him five hundred rand to shoot a competitor. As usual, he took all conceivable precautions and drew up a detailed plan. But it all went wrong from the very start. A police patrol happened to be passing by, and he fled Soweto as fast as his feet could take him. He had not been back since.

The African dusk was short. Suddenly, he was surrounded by darkness. In the distance he could hear the roar of traffic on the freeway headed for Cape Town and, in the other direction, Port Elizabeth. A police siren was wailing in the far distance, and it occurred to him that Jan Kleyn must have a very special reason for contacting him of all people. There are lots of assassins ready to shoot anyone you like for a thousand rand. But Jan Kleyn had paid him five thousand rand in advance, and that could not be only because he was considered the best and most cold-blooded professional killer in all of South Africa.

His thoughts were interrupted by the sound of a car peeling off from the freeway. Soon afterwards, he could see headlights approaching. He moved further back into the shadows, and drew his pistol. He released the catch with a flourish.

The car came to a halt where the exit road petered out. The headlights lit up the dusty bushes and wrecked car. Victor Mabasha waited in the shadows. He was on tenterhooks now.

A man got out of the car. Victor could see right away that it was not Jan Kleyn. He had not really expected to see him anyway. Jan Kleyn sent others to summon the people he wanted to talk to.

Victor slipped cautiously around the wreck and worked his way in a circle behind the man. The car had stopped exactly where he thought it would, and he had practiced the flanking movement to be sure of doing it silently.

He stopped just behind the man, and pressed the pistol against his temple. The man started.

"Where's Jan Kleyn?" asked Victor Mabasha.

The man turned his head carefully.

"I'll take you to him," the man replied. Victor Mabasha could hear he was scared.

"Where is he exactly?" asked Victor Mabasha.

"On a farm near Pretoria. In Hammanskraal."

Victor knew right away this was not a setup. He had done business with Jan Kleyn once before in Hammanskraal. He put his pistol back into its holster.

"We'd better get going, then," he said. "It's a hundred kilometers to Hammanskraal."

He sat in the back seat. The man at the wheel was silent. The lights of Johannesburg appeared as they drove past on the freeway to the north of the city.

Every time he found himself in the vicinity of Johannesburg he could feel the raging hatred he had always felt welling up inside him. It was like a wild animal constantly following him around, constantly appearing and reminding him of things he would rather forget.

Victor Mabasha had grown up in Johannesburg. His father was a miner, rarely at home. For many years he worked in the diamond mines at Kimberley, and later in the mines to the north-east of Johannesburg, in Verwoerdburg. At the age of forty-two, his lungs collapsed. Victor Mabasha could still remember the horrific rattling noise his father made as he struggled to breathe during the last year of his life, a look of terror in his eyes. During those years his mother tried to keep the house going and take care of the nine children. They lived in a slum, and Victor remembered his childhood as one long, drawn-out, and seemingly endless humiliation. He rebelled against it all from an early age, but his protest was misguided and confused. He joined a gang of young thieves, was arrested, and beaten up in a prison cell by white cops. That merely increased his bitterness, and he returned to the streets and a life of crime. Unlike many of his comrades, he went his own way when it came to surviving the humiliation. Instead of joining the black awareness movement that was slowly forming, he went the opposite way. Although it was white oppression that had ruined his life, he decided the only way to get by was to remain on good terms with the whites. He started off by thieving for white fences, in return for their protection. Then one day, shortly after his twentieth birthday, he was promised twelve hundred rand to kill a black politician who had insulted a white store owner. Victor never hesitated. This was final proof that he sided with the whites. His revenge would always be that they did not understand how deep his contempt for them was. They thought he was a simple *kaffir* who knew how blacks should behave in South Africa. But deep down, he hated the whites and that was why he ran their errands.

Sometimes he read in the newspapers how one of his former companions had been hanged or given a long prison sentence. He could feel sorry for what had happened to them, but he never doubted that he had chosen the right way to survive and maybe in the end start to build a life for himself outside the slums.

When he was twenty-two, he met Jan Kleyn for the first time. Although they were the same age, Kleyn treated him with superior contempt.

Jan Kleyn was a fanatic. Victor Mabasha knew he hated the blacks and thought they were animals to be controlled by the whites. Kleyn had joined the fascist Afrikaner Resistance Movement at an early age, and in just a few years reached a leading position. But he was no politician; he worked in the background, and did so from a post he held in BOSS, the South African intelligence service. His biggest asset was his ruthlessness. As far as he was concerned, there was no difference between shooting a black and killing a rat.

Victor Mabasha both hated and admired Jan Kleyn. Kleyn's absolute conviction that the Afrikaners were a chosen people and his utter ruthlessness combined with a total disregard for death impressed him. He always seemed to have his thoughts and emotions under control. Victor Mabasha tried in vain to find a weakness in Jan Kleyn. There was no such thing.

On two occasions he carried out murders for Jan Kleyn. He performed satisfactorily. Jan Kleyn was pleased. But although they met regularly at that time, Jan Kleyn had never so much as shaken his hand.

The lights from Johannesburg faded slowly behind them. Traffic on the freeway to Pretoria thinned out. Victor Mabasha leaned back in his seat and closed his eyes. He would soon discover what had changed Jan Kleyn's decision that they should never meet again. Against his will, he could feel his own excitement building. Jan Kleyn would never have sent for him unless it was a matter of great importance.

The house was on a hill about ten kilometers outside Hammansk-raal. It was surrounded by high fences, and German shepherds roaming loose ensured that no unauthorized persons gained entry.

That evening two men were sitting in a room full of hunting trophies, waiting for Victor Mabasha. The drapes were drawn, and the servants had been sent home. The two men were sitting on either side of a table covered by a green felt cloth. They were drinking whiskey and talking in low voices, as if there might have been someone listening despite all the precautions.

One of the men was Jan Kleyn. He was extremely thin, as if recovering from a serious illness. His face was angular, resembling a bird on the lookout. He had gray eyes, thin blond hair, and was wearing a dark suit, white shirt, and necktie. When he spoke, his voice was hoarse, and his way of expressing himself restrained, almost slow.

The other man was his opposite. Franz Malan was tall and fat. His belly hung over his waistband, his face was red and blotchy, and he was sweating copiously. To all outward appearances they were an ill-matched couple, waiting for Victor Mabasha to arrive that evening in April, 1992.

Jan Kleyn glanced at his wristwatch.

"Another half hour and he'll be here," he said.

"I hope you're right," said Franz Malan.

Jan Kleyn started back, as if somebody had suddenly pointed a gun at him.

"Am I ever wrong?" he asked. He was still talking in a low voice. But his threatening tone was unmistakable.

Franz Malan looked at him thoughtfully.

"Not yet," he said. "It was just a thought."

"You're thinking the wrong thoughts," said Jan Kleyn. "You're wasting your time worrying unnecessarily. Everything will go according to plan."

"I hope so," said Franz Malan. "My superiors would put a price on my head if anything went wrong."

Jan Kleyn smiled at him.

"I would commit suicide," he said. "But I have no intention of dying. When we have recovered all we have lost during the last few years, I will withdraw. But not until then."

Jan Kleyn had enjoyed an astonishing career. His uncompromising hatred of everyone who wanted to put a stop to apartheid policies in South Africa was well known, or notorious, depending on one's point of view. Many dismissed him as the biggest madman in the Afrikaner Resistance Movement. But those who knew him were well aware he was a cold, calculating man whose ruthlessness never pushed him into rash actions. He described himself as a "political surgeon," whose job was to remove tumors constantly threatening the healthy body of South Afrikanerdom. Few people knew he was one of the BOSS's most efficient employees.

Franz Malan had been working more than ten years for the South African army, which had its own intelligence section. He had previously been an officer in the field, and led secret operations in Southern Rhodesia and Mozambique. When he suffered a heart attack at the age of forty-four, his military career came to an end. But his views and his abilities led to his being redeployed immediately in the security service. His assignments were varied, ranging from planting car bombs in the vehicles of opponents of apartheid to the organization of terrorist attacks on ANC meetings and their delegates. He was also a member of the Afrikaner Resistance Movement. But like Jan Kleyn, his role was behind the scenes. They had worked out a plan together, which was to be realized that very evening with the arrival of Victor Mabasha. They had been discussing what had to be done for many days and nights. Eventually, they reached an agreement. They put their plan before the secret society that was never known as anything other than the Committee.

It was the Committee that gave them their current assignment.

It all started when Nelson Mandela was released from the prison cell he had occupied on Robben Island for nearly thirty years. As far as Jan Kleyn, Franz Malan, and all other right-thinking *boere** were concerned, the act was a declaration of war. President de Klerk had betrayed his own people, the whites of South Africa. The apartheid system would collapse unless something drastic was done. A number of highly placed *boere*, among them Jan Kleyn and Franz Malan, realized that free elections would inevitably lead to black majority rule. That would be a catastrophe, doomsday for the right of the chosen people to rule South Africa as they saw fit. They discussed many different courses of action before finally deciding what needed to be done.

The decision had been made four months earlier. They met in this very house, which was owned by the South African army and used for conferences and meetings that required privacy. Officially neither BOSS nor the military had any links with secret societies. Their loyalty was formally bound to the sitting government and the South African constitution. But the reality was quite different. Just as when the Broederbond was at its peak, Jan Kleyn and Franz Malan had contacts throughout South African society. The operation they had planned on behalf of The Committee and were now ready to set in motion was based in the high command of the South African army, the Inkatha movement that opposed the ANC, and among well-placed businessmen and bank officials.

They had been sitting in the same room as they found themselves in now, at the table with the green cloth, when Jan Kleyn suddenly said:

"Who is the single most important person in South Africa today?"

It did not take Franz Malan long to realize to whom Jan Kleyn was referring.

"Try a little thought experiment," Jan Kleyn went on. "Imagine him dead. Not from natural causes. That would only turn him into a martyr. No, imagine him assassinated."

"There would be uproar in the black townships on a scale far beyond what we could have imagined so far. General strikes, chaos. The rest of the world would isolate us even more."

boere: descendants of one of the first waves of immigration to South Africa by homeless Dutch Huguenots in the 1680s.

"Think further. Let's suppose it could be proved he was mur- dered by a black man."

"That would increase the confusion. Inkatha and the ANC would go for each other in an all-out war. We could sit watching with our arms crossed while they annihilated each other with their machetes and axes and spears."

"Right. But think one step further. That the man who murdered him was a member of the ANC."

"The movement would collapse in chaos. The crown princes would slit each others' throats."

Jan Kleyn nodded enthusiastically.

"Right. Think further!"

Franz Malan pondered for a moment before responding.

"In the end no doubt the blacks would turn on the whites. And since the black political movement would be on the brink of total collapse and anarchy by this point, we'd be forced to send in the police and the army. The result would be a brief civil war. With a little careful planning we should be able to eliminate every black of significance. Whether the rest of the world liked it or not, it would be forced to accept that it was the blacks who started the war."

Jan Kleyn nodded.

Franz Malan gazed expectantly at the man opposite him.

"Are you serious about this?" he asked slowly.

Jan Kleyn looked at him in surprise.

"Serious?"

"That we should actually kill him?"

"Of course I'm serious about it. The man will be liquidated before next summer. I'm thinking of calling it Operation Spriengboek."

"Why?"

"Everything has to have a name. Have you ever shot an antelope? If you hit it in the right spot, it jumps into the air before it dies. That's the jump I'm going to offer to the greatest enemy we have."

They sat up until dawn. Franz Malan could not help admiring the meticulous way in which Jan Kleyn had thought the whole thing through. The plan was daring without taking unnecessary risks. When they walked out onto the veranda at dawn to stretch their legs, Franz Malan voiced one last objection.

"Your plan is excellent," he said. "I can see only one possible snag. You are relying on Victor Mabasha not letting us down. You are forgetting he comes from the Zulu tribe. They are reminiscent of the *boere* in some respects. Their uttermost loyalty is given to themselves and the ancestors they worship. That means you are placing an enormous amount of faith in a black man. You know they can never feel the same loyalty we do. Presumably you are right. He will become a rich man. Richer than he could ever have dreamed of. But still, the plan means we are relying on a black man."

"You can have my answer right away," said Jan Kleyn. "I don't trust anybody at all. Not completely, at least. I trust you. But I'm aware that everybody has a weak point somewhere or other. I replace this lack of trust by being extra cautious. That naturally applies to Victor Mabasha as well."

"The only person you trust is yourself," said Franz Malan.

"Yes," said Jan Kleyn. "You'll never find the weak point you're speaking of in me. Of course Victor Mabasha will be under constant scrutiny. And I'll make sure he knows that. He'll get some special training by one of the world's leading experts on assassination. If he lets us down, he will know he can look forward to a slow and painful death so awful, he'd wish he'd never been born. Victor Mabasha knows the meaning of torture. He will understand what we expect of him."

A few hours later they separated and drove off in their different directions.

Four months later the plan was firmly established among a group of conspirators who had sworn a solemn oath of silence.

The plan was becoming a reality.

When the car came to a halt outside the house on the hill, Franz Malan tethered the dogs. Victor Mabasha, terrified of German shepherds, remained in the car until he was certain he would not be attacked. Jan Kleyn was on the veranda to receive him. Victor Mabasha could not resist the temptation to hold out his hand. But Jan Kleyn ignored it and asked instead how the journey had been.

"When you're sitting in a bus all night, you have time to think up any number of questions," Victor Mabasha replied.

"Excellent," said Jan Kleyn. "You'll get all the answers you need."

"Who decides that?" asked Victor Mabasha. "What I need or don't need to know?"

Before Jan Kleyn could reply, Franz Malan emerged from the shadows. He did not offer his hand either.

"Let's go inside," said Jan Kleyn. "We have a lot to talk about, and time is short."

"I'm Franz," said Franz Malan. "Put your hands up over your head."

Victor did not protest. It was one of the unwritten rules that you gave up your weapons before negotiations could begin. Franz Malan took his pistol and then examined the knives.

"They were made by an African armorer," said Victor Mabasha. "Excellent both for close combat and throwing."

They went inside and sat down at the table with the green felt cloth. The driver went to make coffee in the kitchen.

Victor Mabasha waited. He hoped the two men would not notice how tense he was.

"A million rand," said Jan Kleyn. "Let's start at the end just this once. I want you to bear in mind the whole time how much we're offering you for this job we want you to do for us."

"A million can be a lot or very little," said Victor Mabasha. "It depends on the circumstances. And who's 'we'?"

"Save your questions for later," said Jan Kleyn. "You know me, you know you can trust me. You can regard Franz, sitting opposite you, as an extension of my arm. You can trust him just as much as you can trust me."

Victor Mabasha nodded. He understood. The game had started. Everybody was assuring everybody else how reliable they were. In fact, nobody trusted anybody but themselves.

"We thought we'd ask you to do a little job for us," repeated Jan Kleyn, making it sound to Victor Mabasha's ears as though he was asking him to get a glass of water. "Who 'we' are in this context doesn't matter as far as you're concerned."

"A million rand," said Victor Mabasha. "Let's assume that's a lot of money. I take it you want me to kill somebody for you. A million is too much for such an assignment. So let's assume it's too little—what's the explanation?"

"How the hell can a million be too little?" asked Franz Malan in annoyance.

Jan Kleyn made a deprecatory gesture.

"Let's just say it's good money for an intense but brief assignment," he said.

"You want me to kill somebody," Victor Mabasha repeated.

Jan Kleyn looked at him for a long time before replying. Victor Mabasha suddenly felt as if a cold wind was blowing through the room.

"That's right," said Jan Kleyn slowly. "We want you to kill somebody."

"Who?"

"You'll find out when the time is ripe," said Jan Kleyn.

Victor Mabasha suddenly felt uneasy. It ought to be the obvious first move, giving him the most important piece of information. Who he would be aiming his gun at.

"This is a very special assignment," Jan Kleyn went on. "It will involve travel, perhaps a month of preparations, rehearsals, and extreme caution. Let me just say it's a man we want you to eliminate. An important man."

"A South African?" asked Victor Mabasha.

Jan Kleyn hesitated for a moment before replying.

"Yes," he said. "A South African."

Victor Mabasha tried to work out quickly who it could be. But there was a lot he did not know. And who was this fat, sweaty man sitting silently and hunched up in the shadows on the other side of the table? Victor Mabasha had a vague feeling he recognized him. Had he met him before? If so, in what connection? Had he seen his photograph in a newspaper? He searched his memory frantically, but in vain.

The driver put out some cups and saucers, and placed the coffeepot in the middle of the green cloth. Nobody said a word until he left the room and closed the door behind him.

"In about ten days we want you to leave South Africa," said Jan Kleyn. "You'll go straight back to Ntibane. Tell everybody you know there you're going to Botswana to work for an uncle who has an ironmonger's store in Gaborone. You'll be receiving a letter postmarked in Botswana, offering you a job. Show people this letter as often as you can. On April 15, in a week, you'll take the bus to Johannesburg. You'll be picked up at the bus station and spend the night in an apartment, where you'll meet me in order to receive your final instructions. The next day you'll fly to Europe, and then on to St. Petersburg. Your passport will say you're from Zimbabwe, and you'll have a new name. You can choose one yourself. When you get to St. Petersburg you'll be met at the airport. You'll take the train to Finland, and go from there to Sweden by boat. You'll stay in Sweden for a few weeks. You'll meet somebody there who'll give you your most important instructions. On a date as yet unfixed you'll return to South Africa. Once you're back here, I'll take over responsibility for the final phase. It'll be all over by the end of June at the latest. You can collect your money wherever you like in the world. You'll be paid an advance of 100,000 rand as soon as you've agreed to carry out this little assignment we have lined up for you."

Jan Kleyn stared intently at him in silence. Victor Mabasha wondered if his ears had deceived him. St. Petersburg? Finland? Sweden? He tried to conjure up a map of Europe in his mind's eye, but failed.

"I have just one question," he said after a while. "What's this all about?"

"It shows we are cautious and meticulous," said Jan Kleyn. "You ought to appreciate that, because it's a guarantee for your own safety."

"I can look after myself," said Victor Mabasha dismissively. "But let's start from the beginning. Who'll be meeting me in St. Petersburg?"

"As you may know, the Soviet Union has undergone big changes these last few years," said Jan Kleyn. "Changes we're all very pleased about. But on the other hand, it has meant that a lot of very efficient people are out of a job. Including officers in the secret police, the KGB. We get a constant stream of inquiries from these people, wondering if we're interested in their skills and experience. In many cases there's no limit to what they'll do in order to get a residence permit in our country."

"I'm not working with the KGB," said Victor Mabasha. "I don't work with anybody. I'll do whatever I have to do, and I'll do it alone."

"Quite right, too," said Jan Kleyn. "You'll be working on your own. But you'll get some very useful tips from our friends who'll be picking you up in St. Petersburg. They're very good."

"Why Sweden?"

Jan Kleyn took a sip of coffee.

"A good question, and a natural one to ask," he began. "In the first place, it's a diversionary measure. Even if nobody in this country who's not involved has any idea what's going on, it's a good idea to put out a few smoke screens. Sweden is a neutral, insignificant little country, and has always been very aggressively opposed to our social system. It would never occur to anybody that the lamb would hide away in the wolf's lair. Second, our friends in St. Petersburg have some good contacts in Sweden. It's very easy to get into the country because the border controls are pretty casual, if indeed there are any at all. Many of our Russian friends have already established themselves in Sweden, with false names and false papers. Third, we have some reliable friends who can arrange appropriate living quarters for us in Sweden. But most important of all, perhaps, is that you keep well away from South Africa. There are far too many people interested in knowing what a fellow like me is up to. A plan can be exposed."

Victor Mabasha shook his head.

"I have to know who it is I'm going to kill," he said.

"When the time is ripe," said Jan Kleyn. "Not before. Let me conclude by reminding you of a conversation we had nearly eight years ago. You said then that it's possible to kill anybody at all, provided you plan it properly. The bottom line is that nobody can get away. And now I'm waiting for your answer."

That was the moment it dawned on Victor Mabasha whom he was going to kill.

The thought sent him reeling. But it all fit. Jan Kleyn's irrational hatred of blacks, the increasing liberalization of South Africa.

An important man. They wanted him to shoot President de Klerk.

His first reaction was to say no. It would be taking too big a risk. How could he possibly get past all the bodyguards surrounding the president night and day? How could he possibly escape afterward? President de Klerk was a target for an assassin who was prepared to die in a suicide attack.

At the same time he could not deny he still believed what he had said to Jan Kleyn eight years ago. Nobody in the world was immune from a skilled assassin.

And a million rand. Mind-boggling. He couldn't refuse.

"Three hundred thousand in advance," he said. "I want it in a

London bank by the day after tomorrow at the latest. I want the right to refuse to go along with the final plan if I consider it to be too risky. In that case you would have the right to require me to work out an alternative. In those circumstances I'll take it on."

Jan Kleyn smiled.

"Excellent," he said. "I knew you would."

"I want my passport made out in the name of Ben Travis."

"Of course. A good name. Easy to remember."

There was a plastic file on the floor next to Jan Kleyn's chair. He took out a letter postmarked in Botswana and handed it over to Victor Mabasha.

"There's a bus to Johannesburg from Umtata at six in the morning on April 15. That's the one we want you to take."

Jan Kleyn and the man who said his name was Franz got to their feet.

"We'll take you back home by car," said Jan Kleyn. "As time is short, you'd better go tonight. You can sleep in the back seat."

Victor Mabasha nodded. He was in a hurry to get home. A week was not long for him to sort out all the things he needed to do. Such as finding out who this Franz really was.

Now his own safety was on the line. It needed all his concentration.

They parted on the veranda. This time Victor Mabasha did not hold out his hand. His weapons were returned, and he got into the back seat of the car.

President de Klerk, he thought. Nobody can escape. Not even you.

Jan Kleyn and Franz Malan remained on the veranda, watching the car lights disappear.

"I think you're right," said Franz Malan. "I think he'll do it."

"Of course he'll do it," Jan Kleyn replied. "Why do you think I chose the best?"

Franz Malan stared thoughtfully up at the stars.

"Do you think he realized who the target was?"

"I think he guessed it was de Klerk," said Jan Kleyn. "That would be the obvious person."

Franz Malan turned away from the stars and looked straight at Jan Kleyn.

"That was what you wanted him to do, wasn't it? Guess?"

"Of course," Jan Kleyn replied. "I never do anything by chance. And now I think we'd better go our separate ways. I have an important meeting in Bloemfontein tomorrow."

On April 17 Victor Mabasha flew to London under the name of Ben Travis. By then he knew who Franz Malan was. That had also convinced him the target was President de Klerk. In his suitcase he had a few books about de Klerk. He knew he would have to find out as much about him as possible.

The next day he flew to St. Petersburg. He was met there by a man called Konovalenko.

Two days later a ferry pulled into the docks at Stockholm. After a long car journey southwards, he came to a remote cottage late in the evening. The man driving the car spoke excellent English, even though he did have a Russian accent.

On Monday April 20 Victor Mabasha woke up at dawn. He went out into the yard to relieve himself. A mist lay motionless over the fields. He shivered in the chilly air.

Sweden, he thought. You are welcoming Ben Travis with fog, cold, and silence.

Chapter Nine

Foreign Minister Pik Botha was first to notice the snake.

It was almost midnight and most members of the South African government had said goodnight and withdrawn to their bungalows. The only ones left around the campfire were President de Klerk, Foreign Minister Botha, Home Secretary Vlok and his private secretary, plus a few of the security men handpicked by the president and his cabinet. They were all officers who had pledged special oaths of allegiance and secrecy to de Klerk personally. Further away, barely visible from the campfire, some black servants were hovering in the shadows.

It was a green mamba, and difficult to see as it lay motionless at the edge of the flickering light. The foreign minister would probably never have noticed it had he not bent forward to scratch his ankle. He started when he caught sight of the snake, then just sat motionless. He had learned early in life that a snake can only see and attack moving objects.

"There is a poisonous snake two meters away from my feet," he said in a low voice.

President de Klerk was deep in thought. He had adjusted his lounger so that he could stretch out in a semi-recumbent position. As usual he was sitting some distance away from his colleagues. It had struck him some time ago that his ministers never placed their chairs too close to him when they were gathered around the campfire, in order to show their respect. That suited him perfectly. President de Klerk was a man who often felt a burning necessity to be on his own.

The foreign secretary's words slowly sunk in and intruded into his thoughts. He turned to look at his foreign secretary's face in the light of the dancing flames.

"Did you say something?" he asked.

"There is a green poisonous snake by my feet," said Pik Botha once again. "I don't think I've ever seen such a big mamba."

President de Klerk sat up slowly in his chair. He hated snakes. He had an almost pathological fear of crawling animals in general. Back at the presidential residence, the servants knew they had to make a meticulous search of every nook and cranny every day for spiders, beetles, or any other insects. The same applied to those who cleaned the president's office, his cars, and the cabinet offices.

He slowly craned his neck and located the snake. He felt sick immediately.

"Kill it," he said.

The home secretary had fallen asleep in his lounger, and his private secretary was listening to music in his headphones. One of the bodyguards slowly drew a knife he had stuck in his belt, and struck at the snake with unerring accuracy. The mamba's head was severed from its body. The bodyguard picked up the snake's body, still thrashing from side to side, and flung it into the fire. To his horror de Klerk saw how the snake's head, still lying on the ground, was opening and closing its mouth, displaying its fangs. He felt even worse and was overcome by dizziness, as if about to faint. He leaned back quickly in his chair and closed his eyes.

A dead snake, he thought. But its body is still writhing away, and anyone not in the know would think it was still alive. That's just what it's like here, in my country, my South Africa. A lot of the old ways, things we thought were dead and buried, are still alive. We're not just fighting alongside and against the living, we've also got to fight those who insist on coming back to life to haunt us.

About every four months President de Klerk took his ministers and selected secretaries to a camp at Ons Hoop, just south of the border with Botswana. They generally stayed for a few days, and everything was done completely openly. Officially, the president and his cabinet gathered away from the public eye to consider important matters of various kinds. De Klerk had introduced this routine right from the start when he first came into office as head of state. Now he had been president for nearly four years, and he knew some of the government's most important decisions had been made in the informal atmosphere around the campfire at Ons Hoop. The camp had been built with government money, and de Klerk had no difficulty in justifying its existence. It seemed he and his assistants thought more liberal and perhaps also more daring thoughts while sitting around the campfire under the night sky, enjoying the scents of ancient Africa. De Klerk sometimes thought it was their Boer blood coming to the fore. Free men, always linked with nature, who could never quite get used to a modern era, to air-conditioned studies and cars with bulletproof windows. Here in Ons Hoop they could enjoy the mountains on the horizon, the endless plains, and not least a well-cooked *braai*. They could have their discussions without needing to feel hounded by time, and de Klerk thought it had produced results.

Pik Botha contemplated the snake being consumed by the fire. Then he turned his head and saw de Klerk was sitting with his eyes closed. He knew that meant the president wanted to be left alone. He shook the home secretary gently by the shoulder. Vlok woke up with a start. When they stood up, his secretary quickly switched off his music cassette and collected some papers that were lying under his chair.

Pik Botha hung back after the others had disappeared, escorted by a servant with a lamp. It sometimes happened that the president wanted to exchange a few words with his foreign secretary in confidence.

"I think I'll be going, then," said Pik Botha.

De Klerk opened his eyes and looked at him. That particular night he had nothing to discuss with Pik Botha.

"You do that," he said. "We need all the sleep we can get."

Pik Botha nodded, wished him good night, and left the president on his own.

Generally de Klerk would sit there alone for a while, thinking through the discussions that had taken place that day and evening. When they went out to the camp at Ons Hoop, it was to discuss overall political strategies, not routine government affairs. In the light of the campfire, they would talk about the future of South

Africa, never about anything else. It was here they had set up the strategy for how the country would change without the whites losing too much influence.

But on that night, April 27, 1992, de Klerk was waiting for a man he wanted to meet by himself, without even his foreign secretary, his most trusted colleague in the government, knowing about it. He nodded to one of the bodyguards, who disappeared immediately. When the guard returned a few minutes later, he had with him a man in his forties, dressed in a simple khaki suit. He greeted de Klerk and moved one of the loungers closer to the president. At the same time de Klerk gestured to the bodyguards that they should withdraw. He wanted them close by, but not within earshot.

There were four people de Klerk trusted in this life. First of all his wife. Then his foreign secretary Pik Botha. And there were two others. One of them was sitting right now in the chair beside him. His name was Pieter van Heerden, and he worked for the South African intelligence service, BOSS. But even more important than his work for the security of the republic was the fact that van Heerden played the role of special informer and messenger to de Klerk, bringing him news of the state of the nation. From Pieter van Heerden, de Klerk received regular reports about what was foremost in the minds of the military high command, the police, the other political parties, and the internal organizations of BOSS. If a military coup was being planned, if a conspiracy was under way, van Heerden would hear and inform the president immediately. Without van Heerden, de Klerk would be missing a pointer to the forces working against him. In his private life and in his work as an intelligence officer, van Heerden played the role of a man openly critical of President de Klerk. He performed skillfully, always well balanced, never exaggerated. No one would ever suspect him of being the president's personal messenger.

De Klerk was aware that by enlisting the aid of van Heerden, he was restricting the confidence he placed in his own cabinet. But he could see no other way of guaranteeing himself the information he considered essential to carry out the big changes South Africa needed to avoid a national catastrophe.

This was not least associated with the fourth person in whom de Klerk placed absolute trust.

Nelson Mandela.

The leader of ANC, the man who had been imprisoned for twenty-seven years on Robben Island off Cape Town, who had been incarcerated for life at the beginning of the 1960s for alleged but never proven acts of sabotage.

President de Klerk had few illusions. He could see that the only two people who together could prevent a civil war from breaking out and the inevitable bloodbath that would follow were himself and Nelson Mandela. Many a time he had prowled sleepless through the presidential palace at night, gazing out at the lights from the city of Pretoria, and thinking how the future of South Africa would depend on the compromise he and Nelson Mandela would hopefully be able to reach.

He could speak quite openly with Nelson Mandela. He knew that feeling was mutual. As human beings they were very different in character and temperament. Nelson Mandela was a truth-seeker of philosophical leanings, who used those qualities to achieve the decisiveness and practical drive he also possessed. President de Klerk lacked that philosophical dimension. He would head straight for a practical solution to every problem that cropped up. For him the future of the republic lay in changing political realities, and constant choices between what was possible to achieve and what was not. But between these two men with such different qualifications and experiences was a level of trust which could only be destroyed by open betrayal. That meant they never needed to disguise their differences of opinion, never needed to resort to unnecessary rhetoric when they were talking one on one. But it also meant they were fighting on two different fronts at the same time. The white population was split, and de Klerk knew everything would collapse if he could not manage to make progress bit by bit, by means of compromises that could be accepted by a majority of the white population. He would never manage to reach the ultra-conservative bastions. Nor would he ever convince the racist members of the officer class in the army and the police force. But he was forced to ensure they did not become too powerful.

President de Klerk knew Nelson Mandela had similar problems. The blacks were also split among themselves. Not least between the Inkatha movement, dominated by the Zulus, and the ANC. This meant they could come together in an understanding of each other's difficulties, but at the same time they need never deny the disunity that existed.

Van Heerden was a guarantee for the information de Klerk needed to have. He knew it was necessary to stay close to his friends, but to stay even closer to his enemies and their thoughts.

They normally met once a week in de Klerk's office, usually late on Saturday afternoons. But on this occasion, van Heerden had requested an urgent meeting. At first de Klerk had been unwilling to let him come to the camp. It would be difficult to meet him there without the rest of the government finding out. But van Heerden had been unusually persistent. The meeting could not be put off until de Klerk returned to Pretoria. At that point de Klerk had given way. He knew van Heerden was thoroughly cold-blooded and disciplined, and would never react impulsively; he realized he must have something extremely important about which to enlighten the president of the republic.

"We're alone now," said de Klerk. "Pik found a poisonous snake right by his feet just a few minutes ago. I wondered for a moment if it might have been fitted with a concealed radio transmitter."

Van Heerden smiled.

"We haven't yet started to use poisonous snakes as informers," he said. "Maybe we'll have to one of these days. Who knows?"

De Klerk looked at him searchingly. What was so important that it couldn't wait?

Van Heerden moistened his lips before starting to speak.

"A plot to assassinate you is currently at an intensive planning stage," he began. "There is absolutely no shadow of a doubt that this is a serious threat even now. To yourself, to government policy in general, and in the long run to the whole nation."

Van Heerden paused after his opening words. He was used to de Klerk firing questions at him. But on this occasion de Klerk did not say a word. He merely gazed attentively at van Heerden.

"I'm still short of information about many details of the plot," van Heerden went on. "But I'm aware of the main trend, and that's serious enough. The plotters have links with the military high command, and with extreme conservative circles, notably the Afrikaner Resistance Movement. But we must not forget that many conservatives, most of them in fact, are not members of political organizations. In addition there are signs that foreign terrorist experts, primarily from the KGB, are involved."

"There's no such thing as the KGB anymore," said de Klerk, interrupting him. "At least, not in the form we are familiar with."

"There are unemployed KGB officers, though," said van Heerden. "As I have told you before, Mr. President, we get lots of offers nowadays from former officers in the Soviet intelligence service, offering us their services for some future occasion."

De Klerk nodded.

"A conspiracy always has a hard core," he said after a while. "One or more people, usually very few, in the background, very much in the background, pulling the strings. Who are they?"

"I don't know," said van Heerden. "And that worries me. There's somebody in the military intelligence service called Franz Malan—you can be quite sure he's involved. He has been careless enough to store some material connected with the conspiracy in his computer files, without blocking them. I noticed it when I asked one of my trusted colleagues to run a routine check."

If only people knew, thought de Klerk. It's come to something when security service members spy on one another, hack their way into one another's computer files, suspect one another of permanent political disloyalty.

"Why just me?" asked de Klerk. "Why not Mandela as well?"

"It's too soon to say," said van Heerden. "But of course, it's not difficult to imagine what effect a successful assassination attempt on you would have in the current circumstances."

De Klerk raised his hand. Van Heerden did not need to spell it out. De Klerk could picture the resulting catastrophe very clearly.

"There is another detail which worries me," said van Heerden. "We naturally keep a constant watch on a number of known murderers, both black and white. People who are prepared to kill anybody at all if the contract is right. I think I'm right in claiming that our precautionary measures against possible attacks on politicians are quite efficient. Yesterday I received a report from the security police in Umtata saying that a certain Victor Mabasha paid a short visit to Johannesburg a few days ago. When he returned to Ntibane, he had a lot of cash with him."

De Klerk made a face.

"That sounds a bit circumstantial," he said.

"I'm not so sure about that," said van Heerden. "If I were planning to kill the president of this country, I would probably choose Victor Mabasha to do it."

De Klerk raised his eyebrows.

"Even if you were going to assassinate Nelson Mandela?"

"Even then."

"A black contract killer."

"He is very good."

De Klerk got up from his lounger and poked away at the fire, which was dying out. He did not have the strength just now to hear what constituted a good contract killer. He put a few branches on the fire, and stretched his back. His bald head glittered in the light from the fire, which flamed up once more. He looked up at the sky and contemplated the Southern Cross. He felt very tired. Nevertheless, he tried to come to terms with what van Heerden had said. He realized a conspiracy was more than plausible. He had thought many a time about being killed by an assassin, sent by furious white *boere* who were always accusing him of selling out and handing his country over to the blacks. Of course, he also wondered what would happen if Mandela were to die, irrespective of whether it was a natural or an unnatural death. Nelson Mandela was an old man. Even if he did have a strong constitution, he had spent nearly thirty years in jail.

De Klerk went back to his chair.

"Naturally, you'll have to concentrate on exposing this conspiracy," he said. "Use whatever means you like. Money is no problem at all. Get in touch with me at any time of day or night if something significant happens. For the moment, there are two measures that must be taken, or at least considered. One is perfectly obvious, of course: my guard will have to be intensified as discreetly as possible. I'm rather more doubtful about the other one."

Van Heerden suspected what the president had in mind. He waited for him to continue.

"Shall I tell him, or shan't I?" wondered de Klerk. "How will he react? Or should I wait until we know a bit more?"

Van Heerden knew de Klerk was not asking him for advice. The questions were directed towards himself. The answers would also be his own.

"I'll think about it," said de Klerk. "We live in the most beautiful country on earth. But there are monsters lurking in the shadows. I sometimes wish I could see into the future. I'd like to be able to. But to be honest, I don't know if I dare."

The meeting was over. Van Heerden disappeared into the shadows.

De Klerk sat staring into the fire. He was really too tired to make a decision. Should he inform Mandela of the conspiracy, or should he wait?

He remained seated by the fire, watching it slowly die down.

Eventually, he made up his mind.

He would not say anything to his friend just yet.

Chapter Ten

Victor Mabasha had been trying in vain to dismiss what happened as just a bad dream. The woman outside the house had never existed. Konovalenko, the man he was forced to hate, did not kill her. It was just a dream that a spirit, a *songoma*, had poisoned his mind with, to make him unsure, and possibly unable to carry out his assignment. It was the curse hanging over him because he was a black South African, he was aware of that. Not knowing who he was, or what he was allowed to be. A man who ruthlessly wallowed in violence one minute, and the next minute failed to understand how anybody could kill a fellow human being. He realized the spirits had set their singing hounds on him. They were watching over him, keeping tabs on him; they were his ultimate guardians, so vastly more watchful than Jan Kleyn could ever be. . . .

Everything had gone wrong from the very start. He instinctively disliked and mistrusted the man who met him at the airport outside St. Petersburg. There was something devious about him.

To make things worse, Anatoli Konovalenko was clearly racist. On several occasions Victor had come close to throttling him and telling him that he knew what Konovalenko was thinking: that Victor was just a *kaffir*, an inferior being.

But he didn't. He controlled himself. He had an assignment, and that had to come before anything else. The violence of his own reaction surprised him. He had been surrounded by racism his whole life. In his own way, he had learned to live with it. So why did he react like this to Konovalenko? Perhaps he could not accept being regarded as inferior by a white man who did not come from South Africa?

The journey from Johannesburg to London, and then on to St. Petersburg, had gone without a hitch. He sat awake on the night flight to London, looking out into the darkness. He occasionally thought he could see fires blazing away in the darkness far below. But he realized it was his imagination. It was not the first time he had left South Africa. He once liquidated an ANC representative in Lusaka, and on another occasion he had been in what was then Southern Rhodesia to take part in an assassination attempt on the revolutionary leader Joshua Nkomo. That was the only time he had failed. And that was when he decided he would only work alone in the future.

Yebo, yebo. Never again would he subordinate himself. As soon as he was ready to return to South Africa from this frozen Scandinavian land, Anatoli Konovalenko would be no more than an insignificant detail in the bad dream that his *songoma* had poisoned him with. Konovalenko was an insignificant puff of smoke that would be chased out of his body. The holy spirit hidden in the howls of the singing hounds would chase him away. His poisoned memory would never again need to worry about the arrogant Russian with gray, worn-down teeth.

Konovalenko was small and sturdy. He barely came up to Victor Mabasha's shoulders. (But there was nothing wrong with his head, something Victor had established right away.) It was not surprising, of course. Jan Kleyn would never be satisfied with anything less than the best on the market.

On the other hand, Victor could never have imagined how brutal Konovalenko was. Of course, he realized that an ex-officer in the upper echelons of the KGB whose specialty was liquidating infiltrators and deserters would have few scruples about killing people. But as far as Victor was concerned, unnecessary brutality was the sign of an amateur. A liquidation should be carried out *mningi checha,* quickly and without unnecessary suffering for the victim.

They left St. Petersburg the day after Victor arrived. The ferry to Sweden was so cold he spent the whole voyage in his cabin, wrapped up in blankets. Before their arrival in Stockholm Konovalenko gave him his new passport and instructions. To his astonishment he discovered he was now a Swedish citizen named Shalid.

"You used to be a stateless Eritrean exile," Konovalenko explained. "You came to Sweden at the end of the sixties, and were granted citizenship in 1978."

"Shouldn't I at least speak a few words of Swedish after more than twenty years?" Victor wondered.

"It'll be enough to be able to say thank you, *tack*," said Konovalenko. "No one will ask you anything."

Konovalenko was right.

To Victor's great surprise, the young Swedish passport officer had done no more than glance casually at his passport before returning it. Could it really be as simple as this to travel into and out of a country? He began to understand why the final preparations for his assignment were happening so far away from South Africa.

Even if he distrusted—no, positively disliked—the man who was to be his instructor, he could not help but be impressed by the invisible organization that seemed to cover everything that happened around him. A car was waiting for them at the docks in Stockholm. The keys were on the left rear wheel. As Konovalenko didn't know his way out of Stockholm, another car led them out as far as the southbound highway before disappearing. It seemed to Victor the world was being run by secret organizations and people like his *songoma*. The world was shaped and changed in the underworld. People like Jan Kleyn were mere messengers. Just where Victor fitted into this secret organization, he had no idea. He wasn't even sure if he wanted to know.

They traveled through the Swedish countryside. Here and there Victor glimpsed patches of snow through the conifer trees. Konovalenko did not drive especially fast, and said practically nothing as he drove. That suited Victor, as he was tired after the long journey. He kept falling asleep in the back seat, and immediately his spirit would start talking to him. The singing hound howled away in the darkness of his dreams, and when he opened his eyes he was not at all sure where he was. It was raining non-stop. Everything seemed clean and orderly. When they stopped for a meal, Victor had the feeling that nothing could ever go wrong in this country.

But there was something missing. Victor tried in vain to put his finger on it. The countryside they were traveling through filled him with a nostalgic longing.

The journey took all day.

"Where are we headed?" asked Victor after they had been in the car for over three hours. Konovalenko waited several minutes to reply.

"We're headed south," he said. "You'll see when we get there."

The evil dream of his *songoma* was still some way off. The woman had not yet entered the yard, and her skull had not yet been shattered by the bullet from Konovalenko's pistol. Victor Mabasha had no thoughts beyond doing what Jan Kleyn was paying him to do. Part of the assignment was to listen to what Konovalenko had to say to him. According to Victor Mabasha's imagination the spirits, both good and bad, had been left behind in South Africa, in the mountain caves near Ntibane. The spirits never left the country, never crossed borders.

They arrived at the remote house shortly before eight in the evening. Even in St. Petersburg Victor had noted with surprise that dusk and night were not the same as in Africa. It was light when it should have been dark, and dusk did not drop down over the earth like the heavy fist of night; it wafted down slowly like a leaf floating on an invisible breath of air.

They carried a few bags into the house and installed themselves in their separate bedrooms. Victor noticed the house was comfortably warm. That too must have been thanks to the perfectionism of the discreet organization. They must have assumed a black man would freeze to death in polar regions like this. And a man who is cold, like a man who is hungry or thirsty, would be unable to do or learn anything.

The ceilings were low. Victor could barely fit under the exposed roof beams. He wandered around the house and noticed a strange smell of furniture, carpets and wax polish. But the smell he missed most of all was that of an open fire.

Africa was a long way away. It occurred to him that making him feel the distance might be intentional. This is where the plan was to be tested, retested, and perfected. Nothing should be allowed to interfere; nothing should arouse thoughts of what might be in store later.

Konovalenko produced frozen meals from a big freezer. Victor realized he should check this out later to see how many portions were stored there; then he could figure out how long he was expected to stay in the house.

Konovalenko opened his bags and took out a bottle of Russian vodka. He offered Victor a glass as they sat at the dining table, but he declined; he always cut down on the booze when he was preparing for an assignment; just one beer a day, two at the most. But Konovalenko drank heavily and was clearly drunk even the first evening. This presented Victor with an obvious advantage. If he needed to, he could exploit Konovalenko's weakness for liquor.

The vodka loosened Konovalenko's tongue. He started talking about paradise lost, the KGB during the 1960s and 70s, when they held undisputed sway over the Soviet empire and no individual politician could feel sure the KGB did not have extensive files on their innermost secrets. Victor thought the KGB might have replaced the *songoma* in this Russian empire, where no citizen was allowed to believe in holy spirits except in great secrecy. It seemed to him that a society that attempted to put the gods to flight would be doomed. The *nkosis* know that in my homeland, and hence our gods have not been threatened by apartheid. They can live freely and have never been subjected to the pass laws; they have always been able to move around without being humiliated. If our holy spirits had been banished to remote prison islands, and our singing hounds chased out into the Kalahari Desert, not a single white man, woman or child would have survived in South Africa. All of them, Afrikaners as well as Englishmen, would have been annihilated long ago and their miserable skeletons buried in the red soil. In the old days, when his ancestors were still fighting openly against the white intruders, the Zulu warriors used to cut off their fallen victims' lower jaw. An *impi* returning from a victorious battle would bring with him these jawbones as trophies to adorn the temple entrances of their tribal chiefs. Now it was the gods who were on the front line against the whites, and they would never submit to defeat.

The first night in the strange house, Victor Mabasha enjoyed a dreamless sleep. He divested himself of the lingering aftereffects of his long journey, and when he woke at dawn he felt rested and restored. Somewhere in the background he could hear Konovalenko snoring. He got up, dressed, and gave the house a thorough search.

He did not know what he was looking for. Yet Jan Kleyn was always present: his watchful eye was always somewhere to be found.

In the attic, which surprisingly enough smelled vaguely of corn, reminiscent of sorghum, he found a sophisticated radio transmitter. Victor Mabasha was no expert on sophisticated electronics, but he had no doubt this equipment was capable of both transmitting and receiving messages from South Africa. He continued his search, and eventually found what he was looking for—in the form of a locked door at one end of the house. Behind that door was the reason he had undertaken this long journey.

He went outside and urinated in the yard. He had the impression his urine had never been so yellow. It must be the food, he thought. This strange, unspiced food. The long journey. And the spirits struggling in my dreams. Wherever I go, I take Africa with me.

There was a mist lying motionless over the countryside. He went around the house, and came upon a neglected orchard where he could recognize only a few of the trees. It was all very silent, and it seemed to him he might have been somewhere else—possibly even somewhere in Natal one morning in June.

He felt cold, and went back in the house. Konovalenko had woken up. He was making coffee in the kitchen, dressed in a red track suit. When he turned his back on Victor, he saw it had KGB embroidered on it.

The work started after breakfast. Konovalenko unlocked the door to the secret room. It was empty, apart from a table and a very bright ceiling light. In the middle of the table were a rifle and a pistol. Victor could see immediately that they were makes with which he was completely unfamiliar. His first impression was that the rifle looked awkward.

"This is one of our prize products," said Konovalenko. "Effective, but not exactly sleek. The starting point was a run-of-the-mill Remington 375 HH. But our KGB technicians refined the weapon until it reached a state of perfection. You can pick off whatever you like up to eight hundred meters. The only things to rival the laser sights are in the American army's most guarded secret weapons. Unfortunately, we were never able to use this masterpiece in any of our assignments. In other words, you have the honor of introducing it to the world."

Victor Mabasha approached the table and examined the rifle.

"Feel it," said Konovalenko. "From this moment on, you will be inseparable."

Victor Mabasha was surprised how light the rifle was. But when he raised it to his shoulder, it felt well balanced and stable.

"What type of ammunition?" he asked.

"Superplastic," said Konovalenko. "A specially prepared variation of the classical Spitzer prototype. The bullet will travel fast over a long distance. The pointed version is better at overcoming air resistance."

Victor Mabasha put the rifle on the table and picked up the pistol. It was a 9mm Glock Compact. He had read about this weapon in various magazines, but had never held one.

"I think standard ammunition will be OK in this case," said Konovalenko. "No point in overdoing things."

"I'll have to get used to the rifle," said Victor. "That'll take time if the range is going to be nearly a kilometer. But where can you find an eight-hundred-meter-long training range that's sufficiently private?"

"Here," said Konovalenko. "This house has been carefully chosen."

"By whom?"

"Those whose job it was," said Konovalenko.

Victor could hear that questions not triggered directly by what Konovalenko said annoyed him.

"There are no neighbors around here," Konovalenko went on. "And the wind blows all the time. Nobody will hear a thing. Let's go back to the living room and sit down. Before we start working I want to review the situation with you."

They sat opposite each other in two old, worn leather chairs.

"It's very simple," Konovalenko began. "First, and most important, this liquidation will be the most difficult of your career. Not only because there's a technical complication, the distance, but primarily because failure is simply not an option. You will have only one opportunity. Second, the final plan will be decided on very short notice. You won't have much time to get everything organized. There'll be no time for hesitation or contemplating various alternatives. The fact that you have been chosen doesn't only mean you are thought to be skillful and cold-blooded. You also work best on your own. In this case you'll be more alone than you've ever been. Nobody can help you, nobody will acknowledge you, nobody will support you. Third, there is a psychological dimension to this assignment which shouldn't be underestimated. You won't discover who your victim is until the very last moment. You will need to be totally cold-blooded. You already know the person to be liquidated is exceptionally important. That means you're devoting a lot of time to wondering who it can be. But you won't know until you've almost got your finger on the trigger."

Victor Mabasha was irritated by Konovalenko's denigrating tone. For a fleeting moment he wanted to tell him he already knew who the victim was. But he said nothing.

"I can tell you we had you in the KGB archives," said Konovalenko with a smile. "If my memory serves me right we had you down as a very useful lone wolf. Unfortunately we can no longer check that because all the archives have been destroyed or are in a state of chaos."

Konovalenko fell silent and seemed to be deep in thought about the proud secret service organization that no longer existed. But the silence didn't last long.

"We don't have much time," said Konovalenko. "That doesn't need to be a negative factor. It will force you to concentrate. The days will be divided between practical target practice with the rifle, psychological exercises, and working out the various possible liquidation scenarios. Moreover, I gather you are not used to driving. I'll be sending you out in a car for a few hours every day."

"They drive on the right in this country," said Victor Mabasha. "In South Africa we drive on the left."

"Exactly," said Konovalenko. "That should help sharpen your reflexes. Any questions?"

"Lots of questions," said Victor Mabasha. "But I realize I'll only get answers to a few of them."

"Quite right," said Konovalenko.

"How did Jan Kleyn get hold of you?" asked Victor Mabasha. "He hates communists. And as a KGB man, you were a communist. Maybe you still are, for all I know."

"You don't bite the hand that feeds you," said Konovalenko. "Being a member of a secret security service is a question of loyalty to those whose hands happen to be attached to the arms of the people in power. Of course you could find a few ideologically convinced communists in the KGB at any given time. But the vast majority were professionals who carried out the assignments given them."

"That doesn't explain your contact with Jan Kleyn."

"If you suddenly lose your job, you start looking for work," said Konovalenko. "Unless you prefer to shoot yourself. South Africa has always seemed to me and many of my colleagues a well-organized and disciplined country. Never mind all the uncertainty there now. I simply offered my services through channels that already existed between our respective intelligence agencies. Evidently, I had the qualifications to interest Jan Kleyn. We made a deal. I agreed to take care of you for a few days—for a price."

"How much?" wondered Victor Mabasha.

"No money," said Konovalenko. "But I get the possibility of immigrating to South Africa and certain guarantees regarding the possibility of work in the future."

Importing murderers, thought Victor Mabasha. But of course, that is a clever thing to do from Jan Kleyn's point of view. I might well have done the same myself.

"Any more questions?" asked Konovalenko.

"Later," Victor Mabasha replied. "I think it's better to come back to that another time."

Konovalenko jumped up from the leather chair surprisingly quickly.

"The mist has dispersed," he said. "The wind is up. I suggest we start getting acquainted with the rifle."

Victor Mabasha would recall the days that followed in the isolated house where the wind was always howling as a long-drawn-out wait for a catastrophe that was bound to happen. Yet when it actually came, it was not in the form he had expected. Everything ended up in complete chaos, and even when he was making his escape he still did not understand what had happened.

Superficially, the days appeared to be going according to plan. Victor Mabasha quickly mastered the rifle. He practiced shooting in prone, sitting, and standing positions in a field behind the house. There was a sandbank on the opposite side of the field on which

Konovalenko had set up various targets. Victor Mabasha shot at footballs, cardboard faces, an old suitcase, a radio set, saucepans, coffee trays, and other objects he couldn't even name. Every time he pulled the trigger, he was given a report on the outcome via a walkie-talkie, and made very slight, barely noticeable adjustments to the sights. Slowly, the rifle began to obey Victor's commands.

The days were divided into three parts, separated by meals prepared by Konovalenko. Victor Mabasha kept thinking Konovalenko knew exactly what he was doing, and was very good at passing on what he knew. Jan Kleyn had chosen the right man.

The feeling of imminent catastrophe came from another direction altogether.

It was Konovalenko's attitude towards him, the black contract killer. For as long as possible, Victor Mabasha tried to overlook the scornful tone of everything Konovalenko said, but in the end it was impossible. And when his Russian master drank far too much vodka at the end of the day, his contempt came out in the open. There were never any direct racial aspersions to give Victor Mabasha an excuse to react. But that only made things worse. Victor Mabasha felt he could not hold out much longer.

If things continued like this he would be forced to kill Konovalenko even though doing so would make the whole situation impossible.

When they were sitting in their leather armchairs for the psychological sessions, Victor Mabasha noticed Konovalenko assumed he was completely ignorant about the most basic human reactions. As a means of defusing his growing hatred, Victor decided to play the role he had been given. He pretended to be stupid, made the most irrelevant comments he could think of, and noted how delighted Konovalenko was to find his prejudices confirmed.

At night, the singing hounds howled in his ears. He sometimes woke up and imagined Konovalenko leaning over him with a gun in his hand. But there was never anybody there, in fact, and he would lie awake until dawn.

The only breathing space he had were the daily car rides. There were two cars in an outbuilding, one of which, a Mercedes, was meant for him. Konovalenko used the other car for trips, whose purpose he never alluded to.

Victor Mabasha drove around on minor roads, found his way to a town called Ystad and explored some roads along the coast. These trips helped him to hold out. One night he got out of bed and counted the portions of frozen food in the freezer: they would be spending another week in this isolated cottage.

I'll have to put up with it, he thought. Jan Kleyn expects me to do whatever I have to do for my million rand.

He assumed Konovalenko was in constant touch with South Africa, and that the transmissions were made while he was out in the car. He was also confident Konovalenko would send only good reports to Jan Kleyn.

But the feeling of approaching catastrophe would not go away. Every hour that passed brought him closer to the breaking point, to the moment when his nature would require him to kill Konovalenko. He knew he would be forced to do it so as not to offend his ancestors, and not to lose his self-respect.

But nothing happened as he had expected.

They were sitting in the leather chairs at about four in the afternoon, and Konovalenko was talking about the problems and opportunities associated with carrying out a liquidation from various kinds of rooftops.

Suddenly, he stiffened. At the same time, Victor Mabasha heard what he was reacting to. A car was approaching, and came to a halt.

They sat motionless, listening. A car door opened, then shut.

Konovalenko, who always carried his pistol, a simple Luger, tucked into one of his track-suit pockets, rose quickly to his feet and slipped the safety catch.

"Move out of the way so you can't be seen from the window," he said.

Victor Mabasha did as he was told. He crouched down by the open fire, out of sight from the window. Konovalenko carefully opened a door leading out into the overgrown orchard, closed it behind him, and disappeared.

He did not know how long he had been crouching behind the fire.

But he was still there when the pistol shot rang out like the crack of a whip.

He straightened up cautiously and looked out a window at Konovalenko bending over something at the front of the house. He went out.

There was a woman lying on her back on the damp gravel. Konovalenko had shot her through the head.

"Who is she?" asked Victor Mabasha.

"How should I know?" answered Konovalenko. "But she was alone in the car."

"What did she want?"

Konovalenko shrugged and replied as he closed the dead woman's eyes with his foot. Mud from the sole of his shoe stuck to her face.

"She asked for directions," he said. "She'd evidently taken a wrong turn."

Victor Mabasha could never decide whether it was the bits of mud from Konovalenko's shoe on the woman's face, or the fact that she had been killed just for asking directions that made him finally decide to kill Konovalenko.

Now he had one more reason: the man's unfettered brutality. Killing a woman for asking the way was something he would never be able to do. Nor could he close somebody's eyes by putting his foot into a dead person's face.

"You're crazy," he said.

Konovalenko raised his eyebrows in surprise.

"What else could I have done?"

"You could have said you didn't know where the road was that she was looking for."

Konovalenko put his pistol back in his pocket.

"You still don't understand," he said. "We don't exist. We'll be disappearing from here in a few days, and everything must be as if we had never been here."

"She was just asking directions," said Victor Mabasha again, and he could feel he was starting to sweat with excitement. "There has to be a reason for killing a human being."

"Get back in the house," said Konovalenko. "I'll take care of it."

He watched from the window as Konovalenko backed the woman's car up to the body and put it in the trunk before driving off.

He was back again in barely an hour. He came walking along the cart track, and there was no sign of her car.

"Where is she?" asked Victor Mabasha.

"Buried," said Konovalenko.

"And the car?"

"Also buried."

"That didn't take long."

Konovalenko put the coffeepot on the stove. He turned to Victor Mabasha with a smile.

"Something else for you to learn," he said. "No matter how well organized you are, the unexpected is always liable to happen. But that's precisely why such detailed planning is necessary. If you are well organized, you can improvise. If not, the unexpected merely causes chaos and confusion."

Konovalenko turned back to the coffeepot.

I'll kill him, thought Victor Mabasha. When all this is over, when we're ready to go our separate ways, I'll kill him. There's no going back now.

That night he could not sleep. He could hear Konovalenko snoring through the wall. Jan Kleyn will understand, he thought.

He is like me. He likes everything to be clean-cut and well planned. He hates brutality, hates senseless violence.

By my killing President de Klerk he wants to put an end to all the pointless killing in South Africa today.

A monster like Konovalenko must never be granted asylum in our country. A monster must never be given permission to enter paradise on earth.

Three days later Konovalenko announced they were ready to move on.

"I've taught you all I can," he said. "And you've mastered the rifle. You know how to think once you're told who will soon be featuring in your sights. You know how to think when you're planning the final details of the assassination. It's time for you to go back home."

"There's one thing I've been wondering," said Victor Mabasha. "How am I going to get the rifle to South Africa with me?"

"You won't be traveling together, of course," said Konovalenko, not bothering to disguise his contempt for what seemed to him such an idiotic question. "We'll use another method of transport. You don't need to know what."

"I have another question," Victor Mabasha went on. "The pistol. I haven't even had a test shot, not a single one."

"You don't need one," said Konovalenko. "That's for you. If you fail. It's a gun that can never be traced."

Wrong, thought Victor Mabasha. I'm never going to point that gun at my own head.

I'm going to use it on you.

That same evening Konovalenko got drunker than Victor Mabasha had ever seen him. He sat opposite him at the table, staring at him with bloodshot eyes.

What is he thinking about, Victor Mabasha asked himself. Has that man ever experienced love? If I were a woman, what would it be like to share a bed with him?

The thought made him uneasy. He pictured the dead woman in the yard in front of him.

"You have many faults," said Konovalenko, interrupting his train of thought, "but the biggest is that you are sentimental."

"Sentimental?"

He knew what it meant. But he was not sure just what significance Konovalenko was attaching to the word.

"You didn't like me shooting that woman," said Konovalenko. "These last few days you've been absentminded and you've been shooting very badly. I'll point out this weakness in my final report to Jan Kleyn. It worries me."

"It worries me even more to think that a man can be as brutal as you are," said Victor Mabasha.

Suddenly there was no turning back. He knew he was going to have to tell Konovalenko what he was thinking.

"You're dumber than I thought," said Konovalenko. "I guess that's the way black men are."

Victor Mabasha let the words sink into his consciousness. Then he rose slowly to his feet.

"I'm going to kill you," he said.

Konovalenko shook his head with a smile.

"No you're not," he said.

Victor Mabasha drew the pistol and aimed at Konovalenko.

"You shouldn't have killed her," he said. "You degraded both me and yourself."

He saw that Konovalenko was scared.

"You're crazy," he said. "You can't kill me."

"There's nothing I'm better at than doing what needs to be done," said Victor Mabasha. "Get up. Slowly. Hands up. Turn around."

Konovalenko did as he was told.

Victor Mabasha had just enough time to register that something was wrong before Konovalenko flung himself to one side with enormous speed. Victor Mabasha pulled the trigger, but the bullet hit a bookcase.

Where the knife came from he had no idea. But Konovalenko had it in his hand when he hurled himself at him. Their combined weight crushed a table beneath them. Victor Mabasha was strong, but so was Konovalenko. Victor Mabasha could see the knife being forced closer and closer to his face. Only when he managed to kick Konovalenko in the back did he loosen his grip. He had dropped the pistol. He thumped Konovalenko with his fist, but there was no reaction. Before he broke loose he suddenly felt a stinging sensation in his left hand. His whole arm went numb. But he managed to grab Konovalenko's half-empty bottle of vodka, turn around and smash it over his head. Konovalenko collapsed and stayed down.

At the same moment Victor Mabasha realized the index finger of his left hand had been sliced off and was hanging on to his hand by a thin piece of skin.

He staggered out of the house. He had no doubt he had smashed Konovalenko's skull. He looked at the blood pouring out of his hand. Then he gritted his teeth and tore off the scrap of skin. The finger dropped onto the gravel. He went back into the house, wrapped a dishcloth round his bleeding hand, flung some clothes into his suitcase and then looked around for the pistol. He shut the door behind him, started the Mercedes, and hurtled off after a racing start. He was driving far too fast for the narrow dirt road. At one point he narrowly avoided a collision with an oncoming car. Then he found his way out onto a bigger road and forced himself to slow down.

My finger, he thought. It's for you, *songoma*. Guide me home now. Jan Kleyn will understand. He is a clever *nkosi*. He knows he can trust me. I shall do what he wants me to do. Even if I don't use a rifle that can shoot over eight hundred meters. I shall do what he wants me to do and he'll give me a million rand. But I need your help now, *songoma*. That's why I have sacrificed my finger.

Konovalenko sat motionless in one of the leather chairs. His head was throbbing. If the vodka bottle had hit his head in front rather than from the side, he would have been dead. But he was still alive. Now and then he pressed a handkerchief filled with ice cubes against one temple. He forced himself to think clearly despite the pain. This was not the first time Konovalenko had found himself in a crisis.

After about an hour he had considered all the alternatives and knew what he was going to do. He looked at his watch. He could call South Africa twice a day and get in direct touch with Jan Kleyn. There were twenty minutes to go before the next transmission. He went into the kitchen and refilled his handkerchief with ice cubes.

Twenty minutes later he was in the attic, calling South Africa via the advanced radio transmitter. It took a few minutes before Jan Kleyn answered. They used no names when they talked to each other.

Konovalenko reported what had happened. *The cage was open and the bird has disappeared. It hasn't managed to learn how to sing.*

It was a while before Jan Kleyn realized what had happened. But once he had a clear picture of the situation, his response was unequivocal. *The bird must be caught. Another bird will be sent as a substitute. More information about this later. For the time being, everything goes back to square one.*

When the conversation was over, Konovalenko felt deeply satisfied. Jan Kleyn understood that Konovalenko had done what was expected of him.

"Try him out," Jan Kleyn had said when they met in Nairobi to plan Victor Mabasha's future. "Test his staying power, look for his weaknesses. We have to know if he really can hold out. There's too much at stake for anything to be left to chance. If he's not up to it, he'll have to be replaced."

Victor Mabasha was not up to it, thought Konovalenko. When the chips were down, behind that tough facade was no more than a confused, sentimental African.

Now it was Konovalenko's job to find and kill him. Then he would train Jan Kleyn's new candidate.

He realized that what he had to do next would not be all that easy. Victor Mabasha was wounded, and he would be acting irrationally. But Konovalenko had no doubt he would succeed. His staying power was legendary during his KGB days. He was a man who never gave up.

Konovalenko lay on the bed and slept for a few hours.

As dawn broke he packed his bag and carried it out to the BMW.

Before he locked the front door he primed the detonator to blow up the whole house. He set it for three hours. When the explosion came, he would be a long way away.

He drove off shortly after six. He would be in Stockholm by late afternoon.

There were two police cars by the junction of the E14. For a brief moment he was afraid Victor Mabasha had revealed both his own and Konovalenko's existence. But nobody in the cars reacted as he drove past.

Jan Kleyn called Franz Malan at home shortly before seven o'clock on Tuesday morning.

"We have to meet," he said curtly. "The Committee will have to meet as soon as possible."

"Has something happened?" asked Franz Malan.

"Yes," replied Jan Kleyn. "The first bird wasn't up to the job. We'll have to find another."

Chapter Eleven

The apartment was in a high-rise complex in Hallunda.

Konovalenko parked outside late in the evening of Tuesday, April 28. He took his time on the journey up from Skåne. Even though he liked driving fast and the powerful BMW invited high speeds, he was careful to stay within the speed limits. Just outside Jönköping he observed grimly how a number of motorists had been waved down at the side of the road by the cops. As several of them had overtaken him, he assumed they had been caught in a radar speed trap.

Konovalenko had no confidence at all in the Swedish police. He assumed the basic reason for this was his contempt for the open, democratic Swedish society. Konovalenko not only mistrusted democracy, he hated it. It had robbed him of a large part of his life. Even if it would take a very long time to introduce it—perhaps it would never be a reality—he left Leningrad the moment he realized the old, closed Soviet society was past saving. The final straw was the failed coup in the fall of 1991, when a number of leading military officers and Politburo members of the old school tried to restore the former hierarchical system. But when the failure was plain for all to see, Konovalenko immediately started planning his escape. He would never be able to live in a democracy, no matter what form it took. The uniform he had worn ever since he joined the KGB as a recruit in his twenties had become an outer skin as far as he was concerned. And he just could not shed his skin. What would be left if he did?

He was not the only one to think like that. In those last years, when the KGB was subjected to severe reforms and the Berlin wall collapsed, he and his colleagues were always discussing what the future would look like. It was one of the unwritten rules of the intelligence service that somebody would have to be held responsible when a totalitarian society started to crumble. Far too many citizens had been subjected to treatment by the KGB, far too many relatives were eager to extract vengeance for their missing or dead kin. Konovalenko had no desire to be hauled before the courts and treated like his former Stasi colleagues in the new Germany. He hung a map of the world on his office wall and studied it for hours. He was forced to grit his teeth and accept that he was not cut out for life in the late twentieth century. He found it hard to imagine himself living in one of the brutal but highly unstable dictatorships in South America. Nor did he have any confidence in the home-rule leaders who were still in power in some African states. On the other hand, he thought seriously about building a future in some fundamentalist Arab country. In some ways he was indifferent to the Islamic religion, and in other ways he hated it. But he knew the governments ran both open and secret police forces with far-reaching powers. In the end, though, he rejected this alternative as well. He thought he would never be able to handle the transformation to such a foreign culture, no matter which Islamic state he selected. Besides, he did not want to give up drinking vodka.

He had also considered offering his services to an international security company. But he lacked the necessary confidence; it was a world with which he was unfamiliar.

In the end, there was only one country he could contemplate. South Africa. He read whatever literature he could lay his hands on, but it was not easy to find much. Thanks to the authority still attached to KGB officers, he managed to track down and unlock a few literary and political poison cabinets. What he read confirmed his impression that South Africa would be a suitable place to build a future for himself. He was attracted by the racial discrimination, and could see how both the regular and secret police forces were well organized and wielded considerable influence.

He disliked people of color, especially blacks. As far as he was concerned, they were inferior beings, unpredictable, usually criminal. Whether such views constituted prejudice, he had no idea. He just decided that was the way things were. But he liked the thought of having domestics, servants, and gardeners.

Anatoli Konovalenko was married, but he was planning a new

life without Mira. He had grown tired of her years ago. She was probably just as tired of him. He never bothered to ask her. All they had left was a routine, lacking in substance, lacking in emotions. He compensated by indulging in regular affairs with women he met through his work.

Their two daughters were already living their own independent lives. No need to worry about them.

As the empire collapsed all around him, he thought he would be able to melt into oblivion. Anatoli Konovalenko would cease to exist. He would change his identity, and perhaps also his appearance. His wife would have to exist as best she could on the pension she would receive once he was declared dead.

Like most of his colleagues, Konovalenko had organized a series of emergency exits over the years through which he could escape if necessary from a crisis situation. He had built up a reserve of foreign currency, and had a variety of identities at his disposal in the form of passports and other documents. He also had a strong network of contacts in strategically important positions in Aeroflot, the customs authorities, and the foreign service. Anybody belonging to the *nomenklatura* was like a member of a secret society. They were there to help each other, and as a group could guarantee that their way of life would not give way beneath them. Or so they thought, until the unthinkable collapse actually happened.

Toward the end, just before he fled, everything happened very quickly. He contacted Jan Kleyn, who was a liaison officer for the KGB and the South African intelligence service. They had met when Konovalenko was visiting the Moscow station in Nairobi—his first trip to the African continent, in fact. Jan Kleyn made it very clear that Konovalenko's services could be useful to him and his country. He filled Konovalenko's head with visions of immigration and a comfortable future.

But that would take time. Konovalenko needed an intermediate port of call after leaving the Soviet Union. He decided on Sweden. Several colleagues had recommended it. Apart from the high standard of living, it was easy to cross the borders, and at least as easy to keep out of the public eye; to be completely anonymous, if that was what you wanted. There was also a growing colony of Russians, many of them criminals, organized into gangs, that had started to operate in Sweden. They were often the first of the rats to leave the sinking ship, rather than the last. Konovalenko knew he would be able to benefit from these people. The KGB had always had excellent relations with the Russian criminal classes. Now they could be mutually helpful even in exile.

He got out of the car, and noted that there were blotches on the face of even this country, which was supposed to be an ideal model. The gloomy housing estate reminded him of both Leningrad and Berlin. It looked like future decay was already built into the façades. And yet he could see that Vladimir Rykoff and his wife Tania had done the right thing when they settled in Hallunda. They could live here in the anonymity they desired.

That I desire, he thought, correcting himself.

When he first came to Sweden, he used Rykoff to help him settle in quickly. Rykoff had been living in Stockholm since the beginning of the eighties. He had shot a KGB colonel in Kiev by mistake and fled the country. Because he had a dark complexion and looked like an Arab, he traveled as a Persian refugee and was rapidly granted refugee status, even though he did not speak a word of Persian. When he eventually received Swedish citizenship, he took back his real name, Rykoff. He was only an Iranian when he dealt with the Swedish authorities. In order to support himself and his supposedly Iranian wife, he carried out a few simple bank robberies while he was still living in a refugee camp near Flen. This produced a fair amount of capital to start out with. It also occurred to him that he could earn money by setting up a settlement service for other Russian immigrants who were making their way to Sweden, more or less legally, in increasing numbers. His somewhat unorthodox travel agency soon became well known, and there were times when he had more people than he could really cope with. He had various representatives of the Swedish authorities on his payroll, including at times people in the immigration office, and it all helped to give the agency the reputation of being efficient and thorough. He was sometimes irritated by the fact that it was so hard to bribe Swedish civil servants. But he generally managed it eventually, if he was careful how he went about it. Rykoff had also established the much appreciated custom of providing all new arrivals with a genuine Russian dinner in his apartment at Hallunda.

It did not take Konovalenko long to grasp that behind the hard exterior, Rykoff was in fact a weak character and easily led. When

Konovalenko made a pass at his wife and she proved to be far from unwilling, he soon had Rykoff where he wanted him. Konovalenko arranged his life so that Rykoff did all the mundane legwork, all the boring routine assignments.

When Jan Kleyn contacted him and offered him the job of taking care of an African contract killer who was to carry out an important assassination in South Africa, it was Rykoff who saw to all the practical arrangements. It was Rykoff who rented the house in Skåne, fixed the cars, and brought in the food supply. He dealt with the forgers and the weapon Konovalenko managed to smuggle out of St. Petersburg.

Konovalenko knew Rykoff had another virtue.

He never hesitated to kill, if necessary.

Konovalenko locked the car, picked up his bag, and took the elevator up to the fifth floor. He had a key, but he rang the doorbell instead. The signal was simple, a sort of coded version of the "Internationale."

Tania opened the door. She stared at him in surprise when she saw no sign of Victor Mabasha.

"You're here already?" she said. "Where's the African?"

"Is Vladimir in?" asked Konovalenko, without bothering to answer.

He handed her his bag and stepped inside the apartment. It had four rooms and was furnished with expensive leather armchairs, a marble table, and the last word in hi-fi and video equipment. It was all very tasteless, and Konovalenko did not like living there. Right now, though, he had no alternative.

Vladimir emerged from the bedroom dressed in a silk robe. Unlike Tania, who was so slim, Vladimir Rykoff looked as if he'd been given an order to get fat—an order he'd been delighted to receive.

Tania prepared a simple meal and put a bottle of vodka on the table. Konovalenko told them as much as he thought they needed to know. But he said nothing about the woman he had been forced to kill.

The most important thing was that Victor Mabasha had suffered a mysterious breakdown. Now he was at large somewhere in Sweden, and had to be liquidated immediately.

"Why didn't you do it in Skåne?" asked Vladimir.

"There were certain difficulties," Konovalenko replied.

Neither Vladimir nor Tania asked any more questions.

While he was driving to Stockholm, Konovalenko had thought carefully about what had happened, and what needed to happen now. It dawned on him that Victor Mabasha had only one possibility of leaving the country.

He would have to find Konovalenko. Konovalenko was the one with the passports and tickets; he was the one who could supply him with money.

Victor Mabasha would most probably make his way to Stockholm. He was probably there already. Konovalenko and Rykoff would be ready to receive him.

Konovalenko drank a few glasses of vodka. But he was careful not to get drunk. Even if that was what he most wanted to do right now, he had an important job to do first.

He had to call Jan Kleyn on the Pretoria telephone number he was only allowed to use in extreme cases of necessity.

"Go into the bedroom," he said to Tania and Vladimir. "Close the door and switch the radio on. I have to make a telephone call, and I don't want to be disturbed."

He knew that both Tania and Vladimir would listen in if they had the chance and he wanted none of that. He needed to inform Jan Kleyn about the woman he had been forced to kill.

That would give him the perfect reason to imply that Victor Mabasha's breakdown was in fact something positive. It would be obvious that it was entirely thanks to Konovalenko that the man's weakness had been exposed before it was too late.

Killing the woman could also provide him with another benefit. It would be clear to Jan Kleyn, if he did not know already, that Konovalenko was absolutely ruthless.

When they were in Nairobi, that is the kind of person Jan Kleyn had said South Africa needed most of all right now.

White people with a disregard for death.

Konovalenko dialed the number he had memorized as soon as he was given it in Africa. During his many years as a KGB officer he had always tried to hone his powers of concentration and memory by memorizing telephone numbers.

He had to dial the string of numbers four times before they were picked up by the satellite over the equator and sent back to earth again.

Someone picked up the receiver in Pretoria.

Konovalenko recognized immediately the slow, hoarse voice.

He explained once again what had happened. As usual, he spoke in code. Victor Mabasha was the *entrepreneur*. He had prepared himself thoroughly while driving up to Stockholm, and Jan Kleyn did not interrupt him a single time with questions or requests for further explanations.

When Konovalenko was finished, there was silence.

He waited.

"We'll send you a new entrepreneur," said Jan Kleyn in the end. "The other one must be dismissed immediately, of course. We'll be in touch as soon as we know more about who his successor will be."

The conversation was over.

Konovalenko replaced the receiver and knew the call had turned out exactly as he hoped. Jan Kleyn interpreted events as a case of Konovalenko preventing a disastrous outcome of the planned assassination.

He could not resist sneaking up to the bedroom door and listening. It was silent, apart from the radio.

He sat down at the table and poured himself half a glass of vodka. Now he could afford to get drunk. Since he needed to be alone, he let the bedroom door stay closed.

He thought about escorting Tania to the room where he slept when in residence. All in good time.

Early the next morning, he rose carefully so as not to disturb Tania. Rykoff was already up, sitting in the kitchen over a cup of coffee. Konovalenko got a cup himself and sat down opposite him.

"Victor Mabasha has got to die," he said. "Sooner or later he'll come to Stockholm. I have a strong suspicion he's already here. I cut off one of his fingers before he disappeared. That means he'll have a bandage or a glove on his left hand. He'll probably go to the clubs in town where Africans generally gather. He has no other alternative if he's going to track me down. And so you can start spreading the word today that there's a contract out on Victor Mabasha. A hundred thousand kronor to anybody who can eliminate him. Go and see all your contacts, all the Russian criminals you know. Don't mention my name. Just say the person issuing the contract is OK."

"That's a lot of cash," said Vladimir.

"You leave that to me," said Konovalenko. "Just do as I say. There's nothing to stop you earning the money, in fact. Nor me, come to that."

Konovalenko would have nothing against putting a pistol to Victor Mabasha's head himself. But he knew that was hardly likely. Such good fortune would be too much to hope for.

"Tonight we can tour the clubs," he said. "By then the contract must have been issued so that everybody who ought to know about it has heard. I'd say you've plenty to do."

Vladimir nodded and got to his feet. Despite his flabbiness, Konovalenko knew he was most effective when the chips were down.

Half an hour later Vladimir left the apartment. Konovalenko stood at the window watching him in the parking lot down below, getting into a Volvo that looked to Konovalenko like a more recent model than the one he'd had before.

He's eating himself to death, thought Konovalenko. He gets his kicks from buying new cars. He'll die without having experienced the great pleasure of exceeding his own limitations. There's barely any difference between him and a cow chewing its cud.

Konovalenko also had an important job to do that day.

He had to raise a hundred thousand kronor. He knew it would have to be done by robbery. The only question was which bank to choose.

He went back to his bedroom and was momentarily tempted to creep back under the covers and wake Tania. But he resisted, and got dressed silently and quickly.

Shortly before ten he left the apartment in Hallunda.

There was a chill in the air, and it was raining.

He wondered for a moment where Victor Mabasha was.

* * *

At a quarter after two on Wednesday, April 29, Anatoli Konovalenko robbed the Commercial Bank in Akalla. The raid took two minutes. He raced out of the bank around the corner and jumped into his car for a quick getaway.

He figured he had gotten away with at least twice as much as he needed. If nothing else, he intended treating himself and Tania to a gourmet dinner once Victor Mabasha was out of the way.

The road he was on curved sharply to the right as he approached Ulvsundavägen. Suddenly he slammed his foot on the brakes. There were two police cars ahead of him, blocking the way. How had the police had time to set up a roadblock? It was only ten minutes at most since he left the bank and the alarm went off. And how could they have known he would choose this particular route?

Then he acted.

He slammed into reverse and heard the tires squealing. As he swung around he knocked over a trash can on the sidewalk and ripped the rear fender loose against a tree. Now there was no question of driving slowly anymore. All that mattered now was his escape.

He could hear the sirens behind him. He swore aloud to himself, and wondered one more time what could have happened. He also cursed the fact that he did not know his way around the district north of Sundbyberg. In fact, the escape routes he had to choose between would all have taken him onto a major highway leading to the city center. But he had no idea where he was, and could not figure out the best getaway.

He soon strayed into an industrial estate and found himself trapped on a one-way street. The police were still on his tail, even though he had stretched the distance between them by running two lights. He leaped out of the car, the plastic bag in one hand and his pistol in the other. When the first squad car screeched to a halt he took aim and shattered the windshield. He had no idea if he hit anybody, but now he had the advantage he needed. The cops would not chase him until they had called for reinforcements.

He scrambled rapidly over a fence and into an enclosure that could have been either a dump or a building site. But he was lucky. A car with a young couple had driven in from the other side. They were looking for some place off the beaten track where they could be alone. Konovalenko did not hesitate. He crept up on the car from behind and thrust the pistol through the window at the man's head.

"Quiet and do exactly what I say," he said in his broken Swedish. "Out of the car. Leave the keys."

The couple seemed completely confused. Konovalenko had no time to waste. He ripped open the door, dragged out the driver, leapt in behind the wheel, and looked at the girl in the seat next to him.

"Now I drive," he said. "You have exactly one second to decide if you come with me or no."

She screamed and flung herself out of the car. Konovalenko drove off. Now he was no longer in a hurry. Sirens were approaching from all directions, but his pursuers had no way of knowing he had already gotten himself a new escape car.

Did I kill anybody? he thought. I'll find out if I turn on the television tonight.

He left the car at the subway station in Duvbo and rode back to Hallunda. Neither Tania nor Vladimir were at home when he rang the doorbell. He let himself in with his own key, put the plastic bag on the dining table, and got out the vodka bottle. A few big gulps calmed him down. Everything had gone well. If he had wounded or even killed a policeman, that would naturally raise tensions throughout the city. But he could not see how that would put a stop to or even delay the liquidation of Victor Mabasha.

He checked the money; he had a total of 162,000 kronor.

At six o'clock he switched on the television to catch the early evening news. Only Tania was back home by then, in the kitchen preparing dinner.

The broadcast opened with the story Konovalenko was waiting for. To his astonishment, he found that the pistol shot intended to do no more than shatter the windshield had proven to be a master shot. The bullet hit one of the cops in the squad car right where his nose met his forehead, right between the eyes. He died instantly.

Then came a picture of the cop Konovalenko had killed: Klas Tengblad, twenty-six years old, married with two small kids.

The police had no clues beyond the fact that the killer had been alone, and was the same man who had robbed the Akalla branch of the Commercial Bank just a few minutes previously.

Konovalenko made a face and moved to switch off the television. Just then he noticed Tania in the doorway, watching him.

"The only good cop's a dead one," he said, punching the off button. "What's for dinner? I'm hungry."

Vladimir came home and sat down at the table just as Tania and Konovalenko were finishing their meal.

"A bank robbery," said Vladimir. "And a dead cop. A solitary killer speaking broken Swedish. The town won't exactly be clear of cops tonight."

"These things happen," said Konovalenko. "Have you finished spreading the word about the contract?"

"There's not a single hood in the underworld who won't know before midnight that there's a hundred thousand kronor to be earned," said Rykoff.

Tania gave him a plate with some food.

"Was it really necessary to shoot a cop, today of all days?" he asked.

"What makes you think it was me who shot him?" wondered Konovalenko.

Vladimir shrugged his shoulders.

"A masterly shot," he said. "A bank raid to raise the money for the Victor Mabasha contract. Foreign accent. It sounds pretty much like you."

"You're wrong if you think the shot was a direct hit," said Konovalenko. "It was pure luck. Or bad luck. Depends how you look at it. But to be on the safe side I think you'd better go in to town on your own tonight. Or take Tania with you."

"There are a few clubs in the south of the city where Africans generally hang out," said Vladimir. "I thought I'd start there."

At eight-thirty Tania and Vladimir drove back to town. Konovalenko showered, then settled down to watch television. Every news broadcast had long items on the dead cop. But there were no hard clues to follow up.

Of course not, thought Konovalenko. I don't leave a trail.

He had fallen asleep in his chair when the telephone rang. Just one signal. Then another ring, seven signals this time. When it rang for the third time Konovalenko lifted the receiver. He knew it was

Vladimir, using the code they had agreed on. The noise in the background suggested he was at a disco.

"Can you hear me?" Vladimir yelled.

"I can hear you," replied Konovalenko.

"I can hardly hear myself speak," he went on. "But I've got news."

"Has somebody seen Victor Mabasha here in Stockholm?" Konovalenko knew that must be why he was calling.

"Even better," said Vladimir. "He's in here right now."

Konovalenko took a deep breath.

"Has he seen you?"

"No. But he's on his guard."

"Is anybody with him?"

"He's on his own."

Konovalenko thought for a moment. It was twenty past eleven. What was the best thing to do?

"Give me your address," he said. "I'm on my way. Wait for me outside with a layout of the club. Especially where the emergency exits are."

"Will do," said Vladimir.

Konovalenko checked his pistol and slipped an extra magazine into his pocket. Then he went to his room and opened a plastic chest standing along one wall. He took out three tear gas canisters and two gas masks, which he put into the plastic carrier bag he had used earlier that afternoon for the money from the bank raid.

Finally he combed his hair carefully in front of the bathroom mirror. This was part of the ritual he always went through before setting out on an important assignment.

At a quarter to twelve he left the apartment in Hallunda and took a cab in to town. He asked to be taken to Östermalmstorg. He got out there, hailed another cab, and headed for Söder to the south.

The disco was at number 45. Konovalenko directed the driver to number 60. He got out and started walking back slowly the way he had come.

Suddenly Vladimir stepped out of the shadows.

"He's still there," he said. "Tania has gone home."

Konovalenko nodded slowly.

"Let's go get him, then," he said.

He asked Vladimir to describe the layout.

"Exactly where is he?" asked Konovalenko when he could picture it.

"At the bar," said Vladimir.

Konovalenko nodded.

A few minutes later, they donned the gas masks and cocked their guns.

Vladimir flung open the entrance and hurled the two astonished doormen to one side.

Then Konovalenko tossed in the tear gas.

Chapter Twelve

Give me the night, songoma. How shall I survive these nights full of light that prevents me from finding a hiding place? Why have you sent me to this strange land where people have been robbed of their darkness? I give you my severed finger, songoma. I sacrifice a part of my body so you can give me back my darkness in return. But you have forsaken me. I am all alone. As lonely as the antelope no longer capable of avoiding the cheetah hunting him down.

Victor Mabasha experienced his flight as a journey made in a dream-like, weightless state. His soul seemed to be traveling on its own, invisible, somewhere close by. He thought he could feel his own breath on his neck. In the Mercedes, whose leather seats reminded him of the distant smell of hides from skinned antelope, there was nothing but his body, and above all his aching hand. His finger was gone, but was there even so, like a homeless pain in a strange land.

From the very beginning of his wild flight he had tried to make himself control his thoughts, act sensibly. I am a *zulu*, he kept repeating to himself, like a mantra. I belong to the undefeated warrior race, I am one of the Sons of Heaven. My forefathers were always in the front line when the *impis* attacked. We defeated the whites long before they hounded the bush-men into the endless wildernesses where they soon succumbed. We defeated them before they claimed our land was theirs. We defeated them at the foot of Isandlwana and cut off their jawbones to adorn the *kraaler* of our kings. I am a *zulu*, one of my fingers is severed. But I can endure the pain and I have nine fingers left, as many as the jackal has lives.

* * *

When he could bear it no longer he turned off into the forest on the first little dirt track he saw, and came to a halt by a glistening lake. The water was so black, he at first thought it was oil. He sat there on a stone by the shore, unwound the bloodstained towel and forced himself to examine his hand. It was still bleeding. It seemed unfamiliar. The pain was more in his mind than where the severed finger had been.

How was it possible for Konovalenko to be faster than he was? His momentary hesitation had defeated him. He also realized his flight had been thoughtless. He had behaved like a bewildered child. His actions were unworthy, of himself and of Jan Kleyn. He should have stayed put, and searched through Konovalenko's baggage, looking for air tickets and money. But all he did was to grab a few clothes and the pistol. He couldn't even remember the route he had taken. There was no possibility of returning. He would never find his way back.

Weakness, he thought. I have never managed to overcome it, even though I have renounced all my loyalties, all the principles that possessed me as I grew up. I have been burdened with weakness as a punishment by my *songoma*. She has listened to the spirits and let the hounds sing my song, a song of the weakness I shall never be able to overcome.

The sun never seemed to rest in this strange land; it had already climbed over the horizon. A bird of prey rose from a treetop and flapped its way over the mirror-like lake.

First of all he must sleep. A few hours, no more. He knew he did not need much sleep. Afterward, his brain would be able to assist him once again.

At a time which seemed to him as far distant as the dim and distant past of his ancestors, his father, Okumana, the man who could make better spear tips than anyone else, had explained to him that there was always a way out of any situation, as long as one was alive. Death was the last hiding place. That was something to keep in reserve until there was no other way of avoiding an apparently insuperable threat. There were always escape routes that were not immediately obvious, and that was why humans, unlike animals, had a brain. In order to look inward, not outward. Inward, toward the secret places where the spirits of one's ancestors were waiting to act as a man's guide through life.

Who am I? he thought. A human being who has lost his identity is no longer a human being. He is an animal. That's what has happened to me. I started to kill people because I myself was dead. When I was a child and saw the signs, the accursed signs telling the blacks where they were allowed to go and what existed exclusively for the whites, I started to be diminished even then. A child should grow, grow bigger; but in my country a black child had to learn how to grow smaller and smaller. I saw my parents succumb to their own invisibility, their own accumulated bitterness. I was an obedient child and learned to be a nobody among nobodies. Apartheid was my real father. I learned what no one should need to learn. To live with falsehood, contempt, a lie elevated to the only truth in my country. A lie enforced by the police and laws, but above all by a flood of white water, a torrent of words about the natural differences between white and black, the superiority of white civilization. That superiority turned me into a murderer, *songoma*. And I can believe this is the ultimate consequence of learning to grow smaller and smaller as a child. For what has this apartheid, this falsified white superiority been but a systematic plundering of our souls? When our despair exploded in furious destruction, the whites failed to see the despair and hatred which is so boundlessly greater. All the things we have been carrying around inside us. It is inside myself I see my thoughts and feelings being split asunder as if with a sword. I can manage without one of my fingers. But how can I live without knowing who I am?

He came to with a start, and realized he had almost fallen asleep. In the borderlands of sleep, half dreaming, thoughts he had long since forgotten returned to him.

He remained on the stone by the lake for a long time.

The memories found their own way into his head. He had no need to summon them.

Summer, 1967. He had just passed his sixth birthday when he discovered a talent distinguishing him from the other children he used to play with in the dusty slum just outside Johannesburg. They had made a ball out of paper and string, and it suddenly dawned on him he had far more skill with it than any of his friends. He could work miracles with the ball, and it followed him like an obedient dog. This discovery led to his first great dream, which was to be crushed ruthlessly by the apartheid society held sacred. He would be the best rugby player in South Africa.

It brought him untold joy. He thought the spirits of his forefathers had been good to him. He filled a bottle with water from a tap and sacrificed it to the red earth.

One day that summer a white liquor dealer stopped his car in the dust where Victor and his friends were playing with the paper-and-string ball. The man behind the wheel sat for a long time watching the black boy with the phenomenal gifts of ball control.

On one occasion the ball rolled over to the car. Victor approached gingerly, bowed to the man and picked up the ball.

"If only you'd been born white," said the man. "I've never seen anybody handle a ball like you do. It's a pity you're black."

He watched an airplane sketching a white streak over the sky.

I don't remember the pain, he thought. But it must have existed, even then. Or did I simply not react because it was so ingrained into me as a six-year-old that injustice was the natural state of affairs? Ten years later, when he was sixteen, everything had changed.

June 1976. Soweto. More than fifteen thousand students were assembled outside Orlando West Junior Secondary School. He did not really belong there. He lived on the streets, lived the obscure but increasingly skillful, increasingly ruthless life of a thief. He was still only robbing blacks. But his eyes were already drawn to the white residential areas where it was possible to carry out big robberies. He was carried along by the tide of young people, and shared their fury over the decision that education would take place in future in the hated language of the Boers. He could still recall the young girl clenching her fist and yelling at the president, who was not present: "Vorster! You speak *zulu*, then we'll speak Afrikaans!" He was in turmoil. The drama of the situation as the police charged, beating people randomly with their *sjamboks*, did not affect him until he was beaten himself. He had taken part in the stone-throwing, and his ball skills had not deserted him. Nearly every throw hit home; he saw a policeman clutch at his cheek as blood poured out between his fingers, and he remembered the man in the car and his words spoken as he bent down to the red earth to pick up his paper ball. Then he was caught, and the lashes from the whips dug so deeply into his skin, the pain penetrated his inner self. He remembered one cop above all the others, a powerful red-faced man smelling of stale liquor. He had suddenly detected a gleam of fear in his eye. At that moment he realized he was the stronger, and from then on the white man's terror would always fill him with boundless contempt.

He was woken out of his reverie by a movement on the other side of the lake. It was a rowboat, he realized, slowly coming toward him. A man was rowing with lazy strokes. The sound from the oarlocks reached his ears despite the distance.

He got up from the stone, staggered in a sudden fit of dizziness, and knew he had to see a doctor. He had always had thin blood, and once he started bleeding, it went on for a long time. Moreover, he must find something to drink. He sat in the car, started the engine, and saw he had enough gas for an hour of travel at most.

When he came out onto the main road, he continued in the same direction as before.

It took him forty-five minutes to get to a little town called Älmhult. He tried to imagine how the name was pronounced. He stopped at a gas station. Konovalenko had given him money for gas earlier on. He had two hundred-kronor bills left, and knew how to operate the automatic dispenser. His injured hand was hindering him, and he could see it was attracting attention.

An elderly man offered to help him. Victor Mabasha could not understand what he said, but nodded and tried to smile. He used one of the hundred-kronor notes and saw it was only enough for just over three liters. But he needed something to eat and above all he needed to quench his thirst. He went into the gas station after mumbling his thanks to the man who helped him and drove the car away from the pump. He bought some bread and two large bottles of Coca-Cola. That left him with forty kronor. There was a map among various promotional offers on the counter, and he tried in vain to find Älmhult.

He went back to the car and bit off a large chunk of bread. He emptied a whole bottle of Coca-Cola before his thirst was quenched. He tried to make up his mind what to do. Where could he find a doctor or a hospital? But he had no money to pay for treatment anyway. The hospital staff would turn him away and refuse to treat him.

He knew what that meant. He would have to commit a robbery. The pistol in the glove compartment was his only way out.

He left the little town behind him and continued driving through the endless forest.

I hope I don't need to kill anyone, he thought. I don't want to kill anyone until I have completed my assignment, shooting de Klerk.

The first time I killed a human being, *songoma*, I was not alone. I still can't forget it, even if I have difficulty in remembering other people I have killed later. It was that morning in January, 1981, in the cemetery at Duduza. I can remember the cracked gravestones, *songoma*, I remember thinking I was walking over the roof of the abode of the dead. We were going to bury an old relative that morning; I think he was my father's cousin. There were other burials taking place elsewhere in the cemetery. Suddenly there was a disturbance somewhere: a funeral procession was breaking up. I saw a young girl running among the memorial stones, running like a hunted hind. She *was* being hunted. Somebody yelled that she was a white informant, a black girl working for the police. She was caught, she screamed; her despair was greater than anything I had ever seen before. But she was stabbed, clubbed, and lay between the graves, still alive. Then we started gathering dry sticks and clumps of grass we pulled up from between the gravestones. I say "we," because I was suddenly involved in what was happening. A black woman passing information to the police—what right had she to live? She begged for her life, but her body was soon covered in dry sticks and grass and we burned her alive as she lay there. She tried in vain to get away from the flames, but we held her down until her face turned black. She was the first human being I killed, *songoma*, and I have never forgotten her, for in killing her I also killed myself. Racial segregation had triumphed. I had become an animal, *songoma*. There was no turning back.

His hand started hurting again. Victor Mabasha tried to hold it completely still in order to reduce the pain. The sun was still very high in the sky, and he did not even bother to look at his watch. He still had a long time to sit in the car with his thoughts for company.

I have no idea where I am, he thought. I know I'm in Sweden. But that's all. Perhaps that's what the world is really like. No here nor there. Only a now.

Eventually the strange, barely noticeable dusk descended.

He loaded his pistol and tucked it into his belt.

He no longer had his knives. But then, he was determined not to kill anybody, if he could possibly avoid it.

He glanced at the gas gauge. Soon he would be forced to fill the tank. He needed to solve the cash problem—still, he hoped, without killing anyone.

A few kilometers farther on he came upon a little store open at night. He stopped, switched off the engine and waited until all the customers had gone. He released the safety catch on his pistol, got out of the car and went quickly inside. There was an elderly man behind the counter. Victor pointed at the cash register with his pistol. The man tried to say something but Victor fired a shot into the ceiling and pointed again. With trembling hands the man opened the cash drawer. Victor leaned forward, switched the pistol over to his injured hand, and grabbed all the cash he could see. Then he turned and hurried out of the store.

He didn't see the man collapse on the floor behind the counter. As he fell, he hit his head hard on the concrete floor. Afterwards, they would decide the thief had knocked him down.

The man behind the counter was already dead. His heart could not cope with the sudden shock.

As Victor hastened out of the store, his bandage caught in the door. He had no time to carefully extricate it, so he gritted his teeth against the pain and jerked his hand free.

Just then he noticed a girl standing outside, staring at him. She was about thirteen, and wide-eyed. She gaped at his bloodstained hand.

I'll have to kill her, he thought. There can't be any witnesses.

He drew his pistol and pointed it at her. But he couldn't bring himself to do it. He dropped his hand, raced back to the car and drove away.

He knew he would have the cops after him now. They would start looking for a black man with a mutilated hand. The girl he hadn't killed would start talking. He gave himself four hours at most before he would be forced to change cars.

He stopped at an unmanned gas station and filled his tank. He had noticed a signpost for Stockholm earlier on, and this time he made a point of remembering how to retrace his steps.

He suddenly felt very weary. Somewhere along the way he would have to stop and sleep.

He hoped he would manage to find another lake with still, black water.

He found one on the great plain, just south of Linköping. He had already changed cars by then. Near Huskvarna he turned into a motel and managed to crack the door lock and short-circuit the ignition of another Mercedes. He continued driving until his strength ran out. Shortly before Linköping he turned off onto a minor road, then onto a still smaller one, and eventually came to a lake stretched out before him. It was just turned midnight. He curled up on the back seat and fell asleep.

He awoke with a start just before five in the morning.

Outside the car he could hear a bird singing in a way he had never heard before.

Then he continued his journey northward.

Shortly before eleven in the morning he came to Stockholm.

It was Wednesday, April 29, the day before Walpurgis Eve, 1992.

Chapter Thirteen

Three masked men turned up just as dessert was being served. In the space of two minutes they fired 300 shots from their automatic weapons and disappeared into a waiting car.

Afterwards there was a brief moment of silence. Then came the screams from the wounded and shocked.

It had been the annual meeting of the venerable wine-tasting club in Durban. The dining committee had carefully considered security before deciding to hold the banquet after the meeting at the golf club restaurant in Pinetown, not far from Durban. So far Pinetown had escaped the violence now becoming increasingly common and widespread in Natal. Moreover, the restaurant manager had promised to increase security for the evening.

But the guards were struck down before they could raise the alarm. The fence surrounding the restaurant had been cut through with wire cutters. The attackers had also managed to throttle a German shepherd.

There were fifty people altogether in the restaurant when the three men burst in, guns in hand. All the members of the wine-tasting club were white. There were five black waiters, four men and a woman. The black chefs and kitchen hands fled the restaurant through the back door with the Portuguese master chef as soon as the shooting started.

When it was all over, nine people lay dead among the upturned tables and chairs, broken crockery, and fallen chandeliers. Seventeen were more or less seriously wounded, and all the rest were in shock, including an elderly lady who would die later from a heart attack.

More than two hundred bottles of red wine had been shot to

pieces. The police who arrived at the scene after the massacre had a hard time distinguishing blood from red wine.

Chief Inspector Samuel de Beer from the Durban homicide squad was one of the first to reach the restaurant. He had with him Inspector Harry Sibande, who was black. Although de Beer was a cop who made no attempt to conceal his racial prejudice, Harry Sibande had learnt to tolerate his contempt for blacks. This was due not least to the fact that Sibande realized long ago he was a much better cop than de Beer could ever be.

They surveyed the devastation, and watched the wounded being carried to the stream of ambulances bound for various Durban hospitals.

The badly shocked witnesses to whom they had access did not have much to say. There were three men, all of them masked. But their hands were black.

De Beer knew this was one of the most serious raids carried out by any of the black army factions in Natal so far this year. That evening, April 30, 1992, open civil war between blacks and whites in Natal had come a step closer.

De Beer called Intelligence in Pretoria immediately. They promised to send him assistance first thing in the morning. The army's special unit for political assassinations and terrorist actions would place an experienced investigator at his disposal.

President de Klerk was informed about the incident shortly before midnight. His Foreign Secretary, Pik Botha, called the presidential residence on the presidential hot line.

The Foreign Secretary could hear de Klerk was annoyed at being disturbed.

"Innocent people get murdered every day," he said. "What's so special about this incident?"

"The scale," the Foreign Secretary replied. "It's all too big, too crude, too brutal. There'll be a violent reaction within the party unless you make a very firm statement tomorrow morning. I'm convinced the ANC leadership, presumably Mandela himself, will condemn what's happened. It won't look good if you have nothing to say."

Botha was one of the few who had President de Klerk's ear. The president generally acted on advice he received from his Foreign Secretary.

"I'll do as you suggest," said de Klerk. "Put something together by tomorrow. See I get it by seven o'clock."

Later that evening another telephone conversation took place between Johannesburg and Pretoria concerning the Pinetown incident. A colonel in the army's special and extremely secret security service, Franz Malan, took a call from his colleague in BOSS, Jan Kleyn. Both of them had been informed of what happened a few hours earlier at the restaurant in Pinetown. Both reacted with dismay and disgust. They played their roles like the old hands they were. Both Jan Kleyn and Franz Malan were hovering in the background when the Pinetown massacre was planned. It was part of a strategy to raise the level of insecurity across the country. At the end of it all, the final link in a chain of increasingly frequent and serious attacks and murders, was the liquidation Victor Mabasha was to be responsible for.

Jan Kleyn called Franz Malan about an entirely different matter, however. He had discovered earlier in the day that someone had hacked into his private computer files at work. After a few hours of pondering and a process of elimination, he had figured out who it must be that was keeping them under scrutiny. He also realized the discovery was a threat to the vital operation they were currently planning.

They never used their names when they telephoned each other. They recognized each other's voices. If they ever got a bad line, they had a special code to identify themselves.

"We have to meet," said Jan Kleyn. "You know where I'm going tomorrow?"

"Yes," replied Franz Malan.

"Make sure you do the same," said Jan Kleyn.

Franz Malan had been told a captain by the name of Breytenbach would represent his own secret unit in the investigation of the massacre. But he also knew he only needed to call Breytenbach in order to ensure that he could take over himself. Malan had a special dispensation to alter any particular assignment he found advisable, without needing to consult his superiors.

"I'll be there," he said.

That was the end of the conversation. Franz Malan called Captain Breytenbach and announced that he would be flying over to Durban himself the next day. Then he wondered what could be bugging Jan Kleyn. He suspected it had something to do with the major operation. He just hoped their plans were not collapsing.

At four in the morning on the first of May, Jan Kleyn put Pretoria behind him. He skirted Johannesburg and was soon driving along the E3 freeway to Durban. He expected to get there by eight.

Jan Kleyn enjoyed driving. If he wanted, he could have had a helicopter take him to Durban. But the journey would have been over too quickly. Alone in the car, with the countryside flashing past, he would have time to reflect.

He stepped on the gas and thought the problems in Sweden would soon be solved. For some days he had been wondering if Konovalenko really was as skillful and cold-blooded as he had assumed. Had he made a mistake in employing him? He decided that was not the case. Konovalenko would do whatever was necessary. Victor Mabasha would soon be liquidated. Indeed, it might have happened already. A man called Sikosi Tsiki, number two on his original list, would take his place and Konovalenko would give him the same training Victor Mabasha had received.

The only thing that still struck Jan Kleyn as strange was the incident that brought on Victor Mabasha's breakdown. How could a man like him react so violently to the death of an insignificant Swedish woman? Had there been a weak point of sentimentality in him after all? In that case it was a good job they found out in time. If they hadn't, what might have happened when Victor Mabasha had his victim in sight?

He brushed all thoughts of Victor Mabasha to one side and returned instead to the surveillance he had been subjected to without his knowledge. There were no details in his computer files, no names, no places, nothing. But he was aware that a skillful intelligence officer could draw certain conclusions even so, not the least of which would be that an unusual and crucial political assassination was being planned.

It seemed to Jan Kleyn that in reality he had been lucky. He had discovered the penetration of his computer in time, and would be able to do something about it.

*   *   *

Colonel Franz Malan climbed aboard the helicopter waiting for him at the special army airfield near Johannesburg. It was a quarter past seven; he figured he'd be in Durban by about eight. He nodded to the pilots, fastened his seat belt, and contemplated the ground below as they took off. He was tired. The thought of what could be worrying Jan Kleyn had kept him awake until dawn.

He gazed thoughtfully at the African township they were flying over. He could see the decay, the slums, the smoke from the fires.

How could they defeat us? he wondered. All we need is to be stubborn and show them we mean business. It will cost a lot of blood, even white blood, as in Pinetown last night. But continued white rule in South Africa doesn't come for free. It requires sacrifices.

He leaned back, closed his eyes, and tried to sleep.

Soon he would find out what had been bugging Jan Kleyn.

They got to the cordoned-off restaurant in Pinetown within ten minutes of each other. They spent a little over an hour in the bloodstained rooms together with the local investigators, led by Inspector Samuel de Beer. It was clear to both Jan Kleyn and Franz Malan that the attackers had done a good job. They had expected the death toll to be higher than nine, but that was of minor importance. The massacre of the innocent wine-tasters had the expected effect. Blind fury and demands for revenge from the whites had already been forthcoming. Jan Kleyn heard both Nelson Mandela and President de Klerk independently condemning the incident on his car radio. De Klerk even threatened the perpetrators with violent revenge.

"Is there any trace of whoever carried out this crazy outrage?" wondered Jan Kleyn.

"Not yet," said Samuel de Beer. "We haven't even found anyone who saw the escape car."

"The best thing would be for the government to offer a reward right away," said Franz Malan. "I shall personally ask the Minister of Defense to propose that at the next cabinet meeting."

As he spoke there came the sound of a disturbance on the barricaded street outside, where a crowd of whites had gathered. Many of them were brandishing guns, and blacks who saw the crowd turned off and went another way. The restaurant door burst open and a white woman in her thirties barged in. She was highly excited, verging on the hysterical. When she saw Inspector Sibande, the only black man on the premises, she drew a pistol and fired a shot in his direction. Harry Sibande managed to fling himself to the ground and took refuge behind an upturned table. But the woman kept on going straight for the table, still shooting the pistol which she was holding stiffly in both hands. All the time she was screeching in Afrikaans that she would avenge her brother who had been killed the previous evening. She would not rest until every single *kaffir* had been wiped out.

Samuel de Beer grappled with her and disarmed her. Then he led her out to a waiting police car. Harry Sibande stood up behind the table. He was shaken. One of the bullets had gone through the table top and ripped the sleeve of his uniform.

Jan Kleyn and Franz Malan had observed the incident. It all happened very quickly, but both of them were thinking the same thing. The white woman's reaction was exactly what the previous night's massacre was intended to provoke. Only on a larger scale. Hatred should engulf the whole country in one giant wave.

De Beer returned, wiping sweat and blood from his face.

"You can't help but sympathize with her," he said.

Harry Sibande said nothing.

Jan Kleyn and Franz Malan promised to send all the assistance de Beer thought he needed. They concluded the conversation by assuring one another this terrorist outrage must and would be solved quickly. The they left the restaurant together in Jan Kleyn's car, and drove out of Pinetown. They went north along the N2 and turned off toward the sea at a sign for Umhlanga Rocks. Jan Kleyn pulled up at a little seafood restaurant right on the seafront. They could be undisturbed here. They ordered langouste and drank mineral water. Franz Malan took off his jacket and hung it up.

"According to my information, Inspector de Beer is an outstandingly incompetent detective," he said. "His *kaffir* colleague is supposed to be much brighter. Persistent as well."

"Yes, that's what I've heard," said Jan Kleyn. "The investigation will go around and around in meaningless circles until all the relatives have forgotten what happened."

He put his knife down and wiped his mouth with a napkin.

"Death is never pleasant," he went on. "Nobody causes a blood-bath unless it's really necessary. On the other hand, there are no winners, only losers. Nor are there any victors without sacrifices. I suppose I'm basically a very primitive Darwinist. Survival of the fittest. When a house is on fire, no one asks where the fire started before putting it out."

"What'll happen to the three men?" asked Franz Malan. "I don't remember seeing what was decided."

"Let's take a little walk when we've finished eating," said Jan Kleyn with a grin.

Franz Malan knew that was the nearest he would get to an answer for the time being. He knew Kleyn well enough to be aware it was a waste of time asking any more questions. He'd find out soon enough.

Over coffee Jan Kleyn started to explain why it had been so necessary for him to meet with Franz Malan.

"As you know, those of us who work undercover for various intelligence organizations live in accordance with several unwritten rules and assumptions," he began. "One of them is that we all keep an eye on everybody else. The trust we place in our colleagues is always limited. We all take our own measures to keep tabs on our personal security. Not least in order to make sure nobody trespasses too far into our own territory. We lay a minefield all around us, and we do so because everybody else does the same. In this way we strike a balance, and everybody can get on with his job. Unfortunately, I have discovered that somebody has been taking too great an interest in my computer files. Somebody has been given the job of checking me out. That assignment must have come from very high up."

Franz Malan turned pale.

"Have our plans been exposed?" he asked.

Jan Kleyn looked at him with eyes as cold as ice.

"Needless to say, I am not as careless as that," he said. "Nothing in my computer files can reveal the undertaking we have set ourselves, and that we are in the process of carrying out. There are no names, nothing. On the other hand, one can't get away from the fact that a sufficiently intelligent person could draw conclusions which might point him in the right direction. That makes it serious."

"It'll be difficult to find out who it is," said Franz Malan.

"Not at all," said Jan Kleyn. "I already know who it is."

Franz Malan stared at him in astonishment.

"I started to find my way forward by going backward," said Jan Kleyn. "That's often an excellent way of getting results. I asked myself where the assignment could have come from. It didn't take long to see that there are only two persons who can really be interested in finding out what I'm up to. The president and the foreign secretary."

Franz Malan opened his mouth in order to interject.

"Let me go on," said Jan Kleyn. "If you just think for a moment, you'll see that's obvious. There is a fear of conspiracy in this country, and rightly so. De Klerk has every reason to be afraid of some of the thinking current in some parts of the military high command. Similarly, he can't be sure of the automatic loyalty of those in charge of the state intelligence service. There's great uncertainty in South Africa today. Not everything can be calculated or taken for granted. That means there's no limit to the amount of information that needs to be collected. There's only one person in the cabinet the president can trust absolutely, and that is Foreign Secretary Botha. Once I'd got that far in my analysis, all I needed to do was to go through the list of feasible candidates for the post of secret messenger to the president. For reasons I don't need to go into, it soon boiled down to just one possibility. Pieter van Heerden."

Franz Malan knew who that was. He had met him on several occasions.

"Pieter van Heerden," said Jan Kleyn. "He has been the president's messenger boy. He's been sitting at the president's feet and exposed our most secret thoughts."

"I regard van Heerden as very intelligent," said Franz Malan.

Jan Kleyn nodded.

"Quite right," he said. "He's a very dangerous man. An enemy who deserves our respect. Unfortunately, he's on the sickly side."

Franz Malan raised an eyebrow.

"Sickly?"

"Some difficulties solve themselves," said Jan Kleyn. "I happen to know he's going into a private hospital in Johannesburg next week, for a minor operation. He has some prostate problems."

Jan Kleyn took a slurp of coffee.

"He'll never leave that hospital," he went on. "I'll take care of that myself. After all, it's me he was trying to get at. They were my computer files he hacked into."

They sat silently while a black waiter cleared the table.

"I've solved the problem myself," said Jan Kleyn when they were alone again. "But I wanted to tell you about it for one reason, and one reason only. You must also be very careful. In all probability there's someone peeking over your shoulder as well."

"It's good that I know," said Franz Malan. "I'll double-check my security procedures."

The waiter reappeared with the check, and Jan Kleyn paid.

"Let's take a little walk," said Jan Kleyn. "You had a question."

They walked along a cliff path in the direction of some steep precipices that gave the beach its name.

"Sikosi Tsiki leaves for Sweden Wednesday," said Jan Kleyn.

"You think he's the best?"

"He was number two on our list. I have every confidence in him."

"And Victor Mabasha?"

"Presumably he's dead by now. I'm expecting Konovalenko to get in touch tonight, or tomorrow at the latest."

"We've heard a rumor from Cape Town that there'll be a big meeting there on June 12," said Franz Malan. "I'm investigating to see whether that could be a suitable opportunity."

Jan Kleyn stopped.

"Yes," he said. "That could be an excellent time."

"I'll keep you informed," said Franz Malan.

Jan Kleyn stood on the brink of a precipice dropping straight down to the sea.

Franz Malan peeked down.

Far down below was a car wreck.

"The car has evidently not been traced yet," said Jan Kleyn. "When they discover it, they'll find three dead men. Black men aged about twenty-five. Somebody shot them and then pushed the car over the cliff."

Jan Kleyn pointed to a parking lot just behind them.

"The agreement was they'd get their money here," he said. "But they didn't, did they?"

They turned and retraced their steps.

Franz Malan did not bother to ask who had executed the three men responsible for the restaurant massacre. There were some things he would rather not know.

Shortly after one that afternoon Jan Kleyn dropped Franz Malan at an army camp near Durban. They shook hands and parted rapidly.

Jan Kleyn avoided the freeway back to Pretoria. He preferred to take roads with less traffic through Natal. He was in no hurry, and felt the need to assess how things stood. There was a lot at stake, for himself, for his fellow conspirators, and not least for all the white citizens of South Africa.

It also occurred to him that he was driving through Nelson Mandela's home territory. This is where he was born, this is where he was raised. Presumably he would also be brought back here when his life was over.

Jan Kleyn was sometimes scared by his own lack of feelings. He knew he was what was often called a fanatic. But he knew of no other life he would prefer to lead.

There were basically just two things that made him uneasy. One was the nightmares he sometimes had. In them he saw himself trapped in a world populated exclusively by black people. He could no longer speak. What came out of his mouth were words transformed into animal noises. He sounded like a laughing hyena.

The other was that nobody knew how much time they had been allotted.

It was not that he wanted to live forever. But he did want to live long enough to see white South Africans secure their threatened dominion.

Then he could die. But not before.

He stopped for dinner at a little restaurant in Witbank.

By then he had thought through the plan one more time, all the assumptions and all the pitfalls. He felt at ease. Everything would go according to plan. Maybe Franz Malan's idea about June 12 in Cape Town would be a good opportunity.

Just before nine that evening he turned into the drive leading to his big house on the outskirts of Pretoria.

His black night porter opened the gate for him.

The last thing he thought about before falling asleep was Victor Mabasha.

He already found it difficult to remember what he looked like.

Chapter Fourteen

Pieter van Heerden was depressed.

Feelings of uneasiness, of insidious fear, were nothing new to him. Moments of excitement and danger were a natural part of his work in the intelligence service. But it seemed he was more defenseless in the face of his unrest, now that he was in a hospital bed at Brenthurst Clinic, waiting to be operated on.

Brenthurst Clinic was a private hospital in the north Johannesburg suburb of Hillbrow. He could have chosen a much more expensive alternative, but Brenthurst suited him. It was famous for its high medical standards, the doctors' skills were tried and tested, and the level of care was beyond reproach. On the other hand, the wards were not luxuriously appointed. On the contrary, the whole building was rather shabby. Van Heerden was well off without being rich. But he did not like ostentation. On vacation, he avoided staying at luxury hotels, which just made him feel surrounded by that special kind of emptiness white South Africans seemed to wallow in. That was why he preferred not to have his operation in a hospital that treated the best-placed white citizens in the country.

Van Heerden was in a room on the second floor. He could hear someone laughing outside in the corridor. Shortly afterwards a tea cart rattled past. He looked out the window. A solitary pigeon was sitting on the roof of a house. Behind it the sky was the dark shade of blue he was so fond of. The brief African dusk would soon be over. His uneasiness increased as darkness rapidly drew in.

It was Monday, May 4. The next day, at eight in the morning, Doctor Plitt and Doctor Berkowitsch would perform the straightforward surgery that would hopefully cure the urinary problems he had been having. He was not worried about the operation. The doctors he saw during the day convinced him the operation was not dangerous. He had no reason to doubt them. A few days later he would be discharged, and after another week or so he would have forgotten all about it.

There was something else bugging him. It was partly to do with his illness. He was thirty-six years old, but afflicted with a physical complaint normally restricted almost exclusively to men in their sixties. He wondered if he were already burned out, if he had aged so prematurely and so dramatically. Working for BOSS was certainly demanding; that had been clear to him for a long time. Being the president's special secret messenger was another thing that increased the pressure he was always forced to live with. But he kept himself in good physical shape. He did not smoke, and he very seldom touched alcohol.

What made him uneasy, and was no doubt also an indirect cause of his illness, was the growing feeling that there was nothing he could do about the state his country was in.

Pieter van Heerden was an Afrikaner. He grew up in Kimberley, and had been surrounded since birth by all the Afrikaner traditions. His family's neighbors were *boere*, as were his schoolmates and his teachers. His father had worked for de Beers, the Afrikaner-owned company that controlled the production of diamonds in South Africa and, indeed, the world as a whole. His mother had assumed the traditional role of Boer housewife, subservient to her husband and dedicated to the task of raising their children and teaching them a fundamentally religious view of the order of things. She devoted all her time and all her energy to Pieter and his four siblings. Until he was twenty and in his second year at Stellenbosch University near Cape Town, he had never questioned the life he led. The very fact that he managed to persuade his father to let him attend that reputedly radical university was his first great triumph on the way to achieving independence. As he did not think he possessed any special talents and cherished no startling future ambitions, he envisioned a future career as a civil servant. He was not tempted to follow in his father's footsteps and devote his life to mining and the production of diamonds. He studied law and found it suited him, even if he did not distinguish himself at all.

The big change came when he was persuaded by a fellow student to visit a black township not far from Cape Town. In acknowledgement of the fact that times were changing, like it or not, some students were driven by curiosity to visit black suburbs. The radicalism claimed by the liberal students at Stellenbosch University had previously been no more than words. Now there was a change, and it was dramatic. For the first time they were forced to see things with their own eyes.

It was a shocking experience for van Heerden. He became aware of the wretched and humiliating circumstances in which the blacks lived. The contrast between the park-like neighborhoods where the whites lived and the black shanty towns was heartrending. He simply failed to understand how they could all be living in the same country. His visit to the black suburb sent his emotions into turmoil. He became introverted and withdrew from the company of his friends. Looking back long afterward, it seemed to him it was like unmasking a skillful fake. But this was not a painting on a wall with a false signature. The whole of his life so far had been a lie. Even his memories now seemed to him distorted and untrue. He had a black nanny as a child. One of his earliest and most secure childhood memories was the way she lifted him in her strong arms and clutched him to her breast. Now he could see she must have hated him. That meant it was not only the whites who were living in a false world. The same applied to the blacks who, in order to survive, were forced to conceal the hatred caused by the boundless injustice they constantly suffered. And this in a country that had belonged to them but had been stolen from them. The whole basis on which his life was built, with rights given by God, nature, and tradition, had proved to be a morass. His conception of the world, which he had never questioned, was founded on shameful injustice. And he discovered all this in the black township of Langa, situated as far away from exclusively white Cape Town as the architects of apartheid had considered appropriate.

This experience affected him more deeply than most of his friends. When he tried to discuss it, he realized that what had been a severe trauma for him was more like a sentimental experience for them. Whereas he thought he could see an impending apocalyptic catastrophe, his friends talked about organizing collections of cast-off clothing.

He took his final examinations without having come to terms with his experience. On one occasion, when he went home to Kimberley during a vacation, his father had a fit of rage when his son told him about his visit to the black township. It dawned on him that his thoughts were like himself—increasingly homeless.

After graduation he was offered a position in the Department of Justice in Pretoria. He accepted without hesitation. He had proved his worth after a year, and one day was asked whether he might like to consider working for the intelligence service. By that time he had learned to live with his trauma, as he had been unable to find any way of solving it. His split was reflected in his personality. He could play the part of the right-thinking and convinced Afrikaner who did and said what was expected of him; but deep down, the feeling of impending catastrophe was getting stronger. One day the illusion would collapse, and the blacks would take merciless revenge. There was no one he could talk to, and he lived a solitary, increasingly isolated existence.

He soon saw his work for BOSS had many advantages. Not least was the insight he was able to get into the political process of which the general public only had a vague or incomplete conception.

When Frederick de Klerk became president and made his public declaration to the effect that Nelson Mandela would be released and the ANC no longer banned, it seemed to him there might yet be a possibility of averting the catastrophe. The shame over what had happened previously would never pass; but nevertheless, could there perhaps be a future for South Africa after all?

Pieter van Heerden had immediately started to worship President de Klerk. He could understand those who branded him a traitor, but he did not share their views. As far as he was concerned, de Klerk was a savior. When he was picked to be the president's contact man, he felt something he recognized as pride. A mutual trust rapidly grew up between him and de Klerk. For the first time in his life van Heerden had the feeling he was doing something significant. By passing on to the president information which was sometimes not intended for his ears, van Heerden was helping those forces that wanted to create a new South Africa, free of racial oppression.

He thought about that as he lay in bed at the Brenthurst Clinic. Not until South Africa had been transformed, with Nelson Mandela as its first black president, would the uneasiness he always felt within him disappear.

The door opened and a black nurse entered. Her name was Marta.

"Dr. Plitt just called," she said. "He'll be here in about half an hour to give you a lumbar puncture."

Van Heerden looked at her in surprise.

"Lumbar puncture?" he asked. "Now?"

"I think it's odd as well," said Marta. "But he was quite specific. I was to tell you to lie on your left side right away. Best to do as you're told. The operation's tomorrow morning. Dr. Plitt's bound to know what he's doing."

Van Heerden nodded. He had every confidence in the young doctor. All the same, he couldn't help thinking it was an odd time to do a lumbar puncture.

Marta helped him to lie as he was supposed to.

"Dr. Plitt said you were to lie absolutely still. You shouldn't move at all."

"I'm a well-behaved patient," said van Heerden. "I do what the doctors tell me. I usually do what you tell me, too, don't I?"

"We don't have any problems with you," said Marta. "I'll see you tomorrow, after the operation. I'm off tonight."

She went out, and van Heerden thought about the bus journey of an hour or more she had ahead of her. He did not know where she lived, but assumed it was Soweto.

He had almost fallen asleep when he heard the door open. It was dark in the room; only his bedside lamp was on. He could see the doctor's reflection in the window pane as he entered the room.

"Good evening," said van Heerden, without moving.

"Good evening, Pieter van Heerden," he heard a voice reply.

It was not Dr. Plitt's voice. But he recognized it. It took a few seconds before it dawned on him who was standing behind him. He turned over in a flash.

Jan Kleyn knew the doctors at Brenthurst Clinic very seldom wore white coats when visiting patients. He knew everything he needed to know about the hospital routines. It had been very easy to set up a situation where he could pretend to be a doctor. The doctors often traded shifts. They didn't even need to work at the same hospital. Moreover, it was not unusual for doctors to visit their patients at odd times. That was especially true just before or after an operation. Once he had established when the nursing staff changed shifts, his plan was straightforward. He parked his car at the front of the hospital, walked through reception and showed the security guards an identity card issued by a transport firm often used by hospitals and laboratories.

"I'm here for an urgent blood sample," he said. "A patient on ward two."

"Do you know your way?" asked the guard.

"I've been there before," replied Jan Kleyn, pressing the elevator button.

That was absolutely true, in fact. He had been to the hospital the previous day, carrying a bag of fruit. He pretended to be visiting a patient on ward two. He knew exactly how to get there.

The corridor was empty, and he went straight to the room he knew van Heerden was in. At the far end of the corridor a night nurse was busy reading case records. He moved quietly and opened the door carefully.

When van Heerden turned around in terror, Jan Kleyn already had the silenced pistol in his right hand.

In his left hand was a jackal skin.

Jan Kleyn sometimes liked to make his presence felt by introducing a touch of the macabre. In this case, moreover, the jackal skin would act as a decoy, diverting the detectives who would arrive later to investigate the murder. An intelligence officer shot in a hospital would cause quite a stir in the Johannesburg homicide department. They would try to establish a link between the murder and the work Pieter van Heerden was doing. His links with President de Klerk would make it all the more imperative to solve the murder. Jan Kleyn had therefore decided to point the police in a direction that was bound to lead nowhere. Black criminals sometimes amused themselves by introducing some ritual element or other into their crimes. That was especially true in cases of robbery with violence. They were not content with smearing blood on the walls. The perpetrator often left some kind of symbol by the victim's side. A broken branch, or stones arranged in a certain pattern. Or an animal skin.

Kleyn had immediately thought of a jackal. As far as he was concerned, that was the role van Heerden had been playing: exploiting other people's abilities, other people's information, and passing them on in a way he should never have contemplated.

He observed van Heerden's horrified expression.

"The operation's been cancelled," said Jan Kleyn in a hoarse voice.

Then he threw the jackal skin over van Heerden's face and pumped three bullets into his head. A stain started to spread over the pillow. Kleyn put the pistol in his pocket and opened a drawer in the bedside table. He took van Heerden's wallet, and left the room. He managed to get away as unobtrusively as he came. Afterwards, the guards would be unable to give any clear description of the man who had robbed and killed van Heerden.

Robbery with violence was how the police classified the attack, which was eventually written off. But President de Klerk was not convinced. As far as he was concerned, van Heerden's death had been his last communiqué. There was no longer any doubt about it. The conspiracy was a fact.

Whoever was behind the plot meant business.

A Flock
of Sheep
in the Fog

Chapter Fifteen

On Monday, May 4, Kurt Wallander was ready to turn over responsibility for the investigation into Louise Åkerblom's death to one of his colleagues. It was not because he felt the fact they were getting nowhere reflected badly on his abilities as a policeman. It was down to something quite different. A feeling he had that was getting stronger and stronger. It was quite simply that he couldn't raise the effort anymore.

The investigation was completely stalled on Saturday and Sunday. It was the May Day holiday weekend, and people were away or unobtainable. It was practically impossible to get any response from the technical guys in Stockholm. The hunt for an unknown man who shot a young policeman in the capital was still going at full throttle.

The investigation into Louise Åkerblom's death was shrouded in silence. Björk had been struck down by a sudden severe attack of gallstones on Friday night and rushed to the hospital. Wallander visited him early on Saturday to receive instructions.

When he got back from the hospital, Wallander sat down with Martinson and Svedberg in the conference room at the station.

"Today and tomorrow Sweden is closed down," said Wallander. "The results of the various technical tests we're waiting for are not going to be here before Monday. That means we can use the next two days to go through the material we already have. I also think it would be a good idea for you, Martinson, to show your face at home and spend some time with your family. I suspect next week might be a bit busy. But let's keep our wits about us for a while this morning. I want us to go through the whole thing so far just one more time, right from the start. I also want you to answer a question, both of you."

He paused for a moment before continuing.

"I know this isn't in accordance with police procedures," he said, "but throughout this investigation I've had the feeling there's something funny going on. I can't put it any clearer than that. What I want to know is, have either of you had the same feeling? As if we were up against a crime that doesn't fit into the usual patterns?"

Wallander had expected a surprised reaction, possibly even skepticism. But Martinson and Svedberg shared his feeling.

"I've never seen anything quite like this," said Martinson. "Of course, I don't have as much experience as you, Kurt. But I have to admit I'm baffled by the whole business. First we try to catch somebody who's carried out the horrific murder of a woman. The deeper we dig, the harder it is to understand why she's been murdered. In the end we come back to the feeling that her death is just an incident on the periphery of something quite different, something bigger. I didn't get much sleep this last week. That's unusual for me."

Wallander nodded and looked at Svedberg.

"What can I say?" he began, scratching his bald head. "Martinson's already said it, better than I could put it. When I got home last night I made a list: *dead woman, well, black finger, blown-up house, radio transmitter, pistol, South Africa*. Then I sat staring at that list for over an hour, as if it were a rebus. It's like we can't grasp that there just don't seem to be any connections and contexts in this investigation. I don't think I've ever had such a feeling of wandering around in the dark as I do now."

"That's what I wanted to know," said Wallander. "I guess it's not insignificant that we all feel the same about this investigation. Nevertheless, let's see if we can manage to penetrate a bit of this darkness Svedberg is talking about."

They went through the investigation right from the beginning. It took them nearly three hours; afterward, they felt once again that they hadn't made any big mistakes, despite everything. But they also hadn't found any new clues.

"It's all very obscure, to say the least," said Wallander, summing up. "The only real clue we have is a black finger. We can also be pretty sure the man who lost his finger was not alone, assuming he's the one who did it. Alfred Hanson had rented the house to an

African. We know that for sure. But we've no idea who this man is who calls himself Nordström and paid ten thousand kronor up front. Nor do we know what the house was used for. When it comes to the connection between these people and Louise Åkerblom or the blown-up house, the radio transmitter, and the pistol, we only have vague and unsubstantiated theories. There's nothing so dangerous as investigations that invite guessing rather than logical thinking. The theory that seems most likely just now, despite everything, is that Louise Åkerblom happened to see something she shouldn't have seen. But what kind of people turn that into a reason for an execution? That's what we have to find out."

They sat around the table in silence, thinking over what he had said. A cleaning lady opened the door and peeked in.

"Not now," said Wallander.

She shut the door again.

"I think I'll spend the day going through the tipoffs we've had," said Svedberg. "If I need any help, I'll let you know. I'm hardly going to have time for anything else."

"It might be as well to sort out Stig Gustafson once and for all," said Martinson. "I can start by checking his alibi, in so far as that's possible on a day like today. If necessary I'll drive over to Malmö. But first I'll try and track down that flower seller Forsgård he claims to have met in the john."

"This is a murder investigation," said Wallander. "Track these people down even if they're in their vacation homes trying to get some peace and quiet."

They agreed to meet again at five to see where they were. Wallander got some coffee, went to his office and called Nyberg at home.

"You'll have my report on Monday," said Nyberg. "But you already know the most important parts."

"No," said Wallander. "I still don't know why the house burned down. I don't know the cause of the fire."

"Maybe you ought to talk to the chief fire officer about that," said Nyberg. "He might have a good explanation. We're not ready yet."

"I thought we were working together," said Wallander, irritated. "Us and the fire service. But maybe there've been some new instructions I don't know about?"

"We don't have an obvious explanation," said Nyberg.

"What do you think, then? What does the fire service think? What does Peter Edler think?"

"The explosion must have been so powerful that there's nothing left of the detonator. We've discussed the possibility of a series of explosions."

"No," said Wallander. "There was only one bang."

"I don't mean it quite like that," said Nyberg patiently. "You can plan ten explosions within a second if you're smart enough. We'd be talking about a chain with a tenth-of-a-second delay between each charge. But that increases the effect enormously. It has to do with the changed air pressure."

Wallander thought for a moment.

"We're not talking about a bunch of amateurs, then?" he said.

"No way."

"Can there be any other explanation for the fire?"

"Hardly."

Wallander glanced at his papers before going on.

"Can you say anything else about the radio transmitter?" he ventured. "There's a rumor that it was made in Russia."

"That's not just a rumor," said Nyberg. "I have had confirmation. I've had help from the army guys."

"What do you make of that?"

"No idea. The army is very interested to know how it got here. It's a mystery."

Wallander pressed ahead.

"The pistol butt?"

"Nothing new on that."

"Anything else?"

"Not really. The report isn't going to reveal anything surprising."

Wallander brought the call to a close. Then he did something he'd made up his mind to do during that morning's meeting. He dialed the number of police headquarters in Stockholm and asked to speak with Inspector Lovén. Wallander had met him the previous year, while investigating a raft carrying two bodies that were washed up at Mossby Beach. Although they only worked together for a few days, Wallander could see he was a good detective.

"Inspector Lovén isn't available at the moment," said the operator at HQ.

"This is Inspector Wallander, Ystad. I have an urgent message. It has to do with the policeman killed in Stockholm a few days ago."

"I'll see if I can find Inspector Lovén," said the operator.

"It's urgent," Wallander repeated.

It took Lovén exactly twelve minutes to call back.

"Wallander," he said. "I thought of you the other day when I read about the murder of that woman. How's it going?"

"Slowly," said Wallander. "How about you?"

"We'll get him," said Lovén. "We always get the guys who shoot one of ours sooner or later. You had something to tell us in that connection?"

"Could be," said Wallander. "It's just that the woman down here was shot through the head. Just like Tengblad. I think it would be a good idea to compare the bullets as soon as possible."

"Yeah," said Lovén. "Don't forget, this guy was shooting through a windshield. Must have been hard to make out a face on the other side. And it's a hell of a shot if you can get somebody in the middle of the forehead when they're in a moving car. But you're right, of course. We ought to check it out."

"Do you have a description of the guy?" asked Wallander.

The reply came without a pause.

"He stole a car from a young couple after the murder," said Lovén. "Unfortunately they were so scared they've only been able to give us very confused accounts of what he looked like."

"They didn't happen to hear him speak, did they?" Wallander wondered.

"That was the only thing they agreed on," said Lovén. "He had some sort of a foreign accent."

Wallander could feel his excitement growing. He told Lovén about his conversation with Alfred Hanson and about the man who had paid ten thousand kronor to rent an empty house out in the sticks.

"We'll obviously have to look into this," said Lovén when Wallander was through. "Even if it does sound odd."

"The whole business is very odd," said Wallander. "I could drive up to Stockholm on Monday. I suspect that's where my African is."

"Maybe he was mixed up in the tear gas attack on a discothèque in the Söder district of Stockholm," said Lovén.

Wallander vaguely remembered seeing something about that in the *Ystad Chronicle* the previous day.

"What attack was that?" he asked.

"Somebody threw some tear gas canisters into a club in Söder," said Lovén. "A discothèque with lots of Africans among the clientele. We've never had any trouble there before. But we have now. Somebody fired a few shots as well."

"Take good care of those bullets," said Wallander. "Let's take a close look at them as well."

"You think there's only one gun in this country?"

"No. But I'm looking for links. Unexpected links."

"I'll set things in motion here," said Lovén. "Thanks for calling. I'll tell the people running the investigation you'll be coming on Monday."

They assembled as agreed at five o'clock, and the meeting was very short. Martinson had managed to confirm so much of Stig Gustafson's alibi that he was well on the way to being excluded from the investigation. All the same, Wallander felt doubtful, without being quite sure why.

"Let's not let him go altogether," he said. "We'll go through all the evidence concerning him one more time."

Martinson stared at him in surprise.

"What exactly do you expect to find?" he asked.

Wallander shrugged.

"I don't know," he said. "I'm just worried about letting him go too soon."

Martinson was about to protest, but checked himself. He had great respect for Wallander's judgement and intuition.

Svedberg had worked his way through the stack of tips the police had received so far. There was nothing that obviously threw new light on either Louise Åkerblom's death or the blown-up house.

"You'd think somebody would have noticed an African missing a finger," was Wallander's comment.

"Maybe he doesn't exist," said Martinson.

"We've got the finger," said Wallander. "Whoever lost it was no spook."

Then Wallander reported on how far he had gotten. They all agreed he should go to Stockholm. There could be a link, no matter how unlikely it seemed, between the murders of Louise Åkerblom and Tengblad.

They concluded the meeting by going through the heirs to the house that had been blown up.

"They can wait," said Wallander afterwards. "There's not a lot here that looks like it will get us anywhere."

He sent Svedberg and Martinson home and stayed behind in his office a little longer. He called the prosecutor, Per Åkeson, at home, giving him a brief summary of where they stood.

"It's not good if we can't solve this murder quickly," said Åkeson.

Wallander agreed. They decided to meet first thing Monday morning to go through the investigation so far, step by step. Wallander could see Åkeson was afraid of being accused later of allowing a carelessly conducted investigation to go ahead. He ended the conversation, turned off his desk lamp, and left the station. He drove down the long-drawn-out hill and turned into the hospital parking lot.

Björk was feeling better and expected to be discharged some time Monday. Wallander gave him a report, and Björk also thought Wallander ought to go to Stockholm.

"This used to be a quiet district," said Björk as Wallander was getting ready to leave. "Nothing much used to happen here to attract attention. Now that's all changed."

"It's not just here," said Wallander. "What you are talking about belongs to a different age."

"I guess I'm getting old," sighed Björk.

"You're not the only one," said Wallander.

The words were still echoing in his ears as he left the hospital. It was nearly half past six, and he was hungry. He did not feel like cooking at home, and he decided to eat out. He went home, took a shower, and changed. Then he tried to call his daughter Linda in Stockholm. He let the phone ring for quite some time. In the end he gave up. He went down to the basement and booked himself a time in the laundry room. Then he walked in to the town center. The wind had dropped, but it was chilly.

Getting old, he thought to himself. I'm only forty-four and I'm already feeling worn out.

His train of thought suddenly made him angry. It was up to him and nobody else to decide if he was getting old before his time. He could not blame his work, nor his divorce that was already five years ago. The only question was how he would be able to change things.

He came to the square and wondered where he ought to eat. In a sudden fit of extravagance, he decided to go to the Continental. He went down Hamngatan, paused for a moment to look at the display in the lamp shop, then continued as far as the hotel. He nodded to the girl at the front desk, recalling that she had been in the same class as his daughter.

The dining room was almost empty. Just for a moment he had second thoughts. Sitting all by himself in a deserted dining room seemed like too much solitude. But he sat down anyway. He had made up his mind, and couldn't be bothered to start rethinking now.

I'll turn over a new leaf tomorrow, he thought, grimacing. He always put off the most important matters affecting his own life. When he was at work, on the other hand, he insisted on arguing for precisely the opposite approach. Always do the most important things first. He had a split personality.

He took a seat in the bar. A young waiter came over to the table and asked what he would like to drink. Wallander had a feeling he recognized the waiter, but could not quite place him.

"Whiskey," he said. "No ice. But a glass of water on the side."

He emptied the glass the moment it reached his table, and immediately ordered another. He did not often drink to get drunk. But tonight he was not going to hold back.

When he got his third whiskey, he remembered who the waiter was. A few years previously Wallander had interrogated him about a series of robberies and car thefts. He was later arrested and found guilty.

So things have turned out all right for him at least, he thought. And I'm not going to remind him about his past. Maybe you could say things have gone better for him than they have for me? If you take the circumstances into account.

He could feel the effects of the liquor almost immediately.

Shortly afterwards Wallander moved over to the dining section and ordered dinner. He drank a bottle of wine with the food, and two brandies with his coffee.

It was half past ten when he left the restaurant. He was pretty drunk by then, but had no intention of going home to lie down.

He crossed over to the taxi stand opposite the bus station and took a cab to the only dance club in town. It was surprisingly full, and he had some difficulty finding room at a table near the bar. Then he drank a whiskey and went out on the dance floor. He was not a bad dancer, and always performed with a certain degree of self-confidence. Music from the Swedish hit parade made him sentimental and maudlin. He invariably fell in love right away with every woman he danced with. He always planned to take them back to his apartment afterwards. But the illusion was shattered on this occasion when he suddenly started to feel queasy, barely managing to get outside before throwing up. He did not go back in, but staggered back to town instead. When he got back to his apartment, he stripped and stood naked in front of the hall mirror.

"Kurt Wallander," he said aloud. "This is your life."

Then he decided to call Baiba Liepa in Riga. It was two in the morning, and he knew he shouldn't do it. But he hung on until she eventually answered.

All of a sudden, he had no idea what to say. He could not find the English words he needed. He had obviously awoken her, and she had been frightened by the telephone ringing in the middle of the night.

Then he told her he loved her. She did not know what he meant at first. Once it had dawned on her, she also realized he was drunk, and Wallander himself felt the whole thing was a terrible mistake. He apologized for disturbing her and went straight into the kitchen and took a half bottle of vodka from the refrigerator. Although he still felt sick, he forced it down.

He woke at dawn on the sofa in the living room. He had a king-size hangover. What he regretted most was the call to Baiba Liepa.

He groaned at the thought of it, staggered into the bedroom, and sank into his bed. Then he forced his mind to go blank. It was late in the afternoon before he got up and made coffee. He sat in front of the television and watched one program after another. He did not bother to call his father, nor did he try to contact his daughter. At about seven he heated up some fish au gratin, which was all he had in the freezer. Then he returned to the television. He tried to avoid thinking about last night's telephone call.

At eleven o'clock he took a sleeping pill and pulled the covers over his head.

Everything will be better tomorrow, he thought. I'll call her then and explain everything. Or maybe I'll write a letter. Or something.

Monday, May 4 turned out to be very different than Wallander had imagined, however.

Everything seemed to happen all at once.

He had just arrived at his office shortly after half past seven when the telephone rang. It was Lovén in Stockholm.

"There's a rumor going around town," he said. "A rumor about a contract on an African. He can be recognized first and foremost by the bandage he has on his left hand."

It was a second before it dawned on Wallander what kind of a contract Lovén was talking about.

"Oh, shit," he said.

"I thought that's what you would say," said Lovén. "If you can tell me when you'll arrive, we can drive out and pick you up."

"I don't know yet," said Wallander. "But it won't be before this afternoon. Björk, if you remember who that is, has gallstones. I have to sort things out here first. But I'll call as soon as I get things straightened out."

"We'll be waiting," said Lovén.

Wallander had just replaced the receiver when the telephone rang again. At the same time, Martinson marched into the room waving a sheet of paper around in excitement. Wallander pointed to a chair, and answered the phone.

It was the pathologist in Malmö, Högberg, who had completed the preliminary autopsy on Louise Åkerblom's body. Wallander had dealt with him before, and knew the man was thorough. Wallander pulled a notebook towards him and gesticulated to Martinson to give him a pen.

"There is absolutely no trace of rape," said Högberg. "Unless the attacker used a condom, and it all took place in peaceful fashion. Nor does she have any injuries to suggest there was any other kind of violence. Just a few abrasions she could easily have suffered in the well. I couldn't find any sign of her having had handcuffs on either her wrists or her ankles. All that happened to her is that she was shot."

"I need the bullet as soon as possible," said Wallander.

"You'll get it this morning," said Högberg. "But it will be some time before you get the comprehensive report, of course."

"Thank you for your efforts," said Wallander.

He hung up and turned to Martinson.

"Louise Åkerblom was not raped," he said. "We can exclude any sexual motives."

"So now we know," said Martinson. "In addition, we also know the black finger is the index finger of a black man's left hand. The man is probably about thirty. It's all here in this fax we just got from Stockholm. I wonder how they do things when they're as precise as this."

"No idea," said Wallander. "But the more we know, the better. If Svedberg is around, I thing we'd better have a meeting right away. I'm going to Stockholm this afternoon. I've also promised to hold a press conference at two o'clock. You and Svedberg had better take care of that. If anything else important happens, give me a call in Stockholm."

"Svedberg will be pleased when he hears that," said Martinson. "Are you sure you can't travel a little later?"

"Absolutely certain," said Wallander, getting to his feet.

"I hear our colleagues in Malmö have brought Morell in," said Martinson when they were out in the corridor.

Wallander stared at him uncomprehendingly.

"Who?" he asked.

"Morell. That fence in Malmö. The one with the water pumps."

"Oh, him," said Wallander absentmindedly. "You mean him."

He went out into reception and asked Ebba to book him a flight at about three that afternoon. He also asked her to reserve a room at the Central Hotel on Vasagatan in Stockholm, which wasn't too expensive. Then he went back to his office and reached the receiver, intending to call his father. But he had second thoughts. He did not dare risk getting into a bad mood. He would need all his powers of concentration today. Then he had a brainstorm. He would ask Martinson to call Löderup later in the day, pass on greetings to his father, and explain that Wallander had been forced to go off to Stockholm at short notice. That might convince the old man that Wallander was up to his neck in important business.

The thought cheered him up. It could be a useful ploy for the future.

At five minutes to four Wallander landed at Arlanda, where it was drizzling slightly. He passed through the hangar-like terminal and saw Lovén waiting outside the swinging doors.

Wallander noticed he had a headache. It had been a very intense day. He had spent nearly two hours with the prosecutor. Per-Åkeson had many questions and critical observations. Wallander wondered how to explain to a prosecutor that cops were occasionally forced to rely on instinct when priorities had to be set. Åkeson criticized the reports he had received so far. Wallander defended the investigation, and by the end of the meeting the atmosphere was tense between them. Before Peters drove Wallander to Sturup Airport, he managed to stop by at home and throw a few clothes into a bag. That was when he finally managed to get hold of his daughter on the telephone. She was pleased to hear he was coming, he could hear that. They agreed he would call her that night, no matter how late it was.

Only when Wallander was in his seat and the plane had taken off did he realize how hungry he was. The SAS sandwiches were the first food to pass his lips that day.

As they drove to the police station at Kungsholmen, Wallander was filled in about the hunt for Tengblad's murderer. Lovén and his colleagues obviously had no real clues to follow up, and he could see their search was characterized by frustration. Lovén also managed to give him a summary of what had happened at the discothèque where the tear gas attack took place. It all seemed to point to either a heavy-handed prank or an act of revenge. There were no definite clues here, either. In the end Wallander asked about the contract. As far as he was concerned, this was something new and frightening. Something that had only come into the mix in the last few years, and then only in the three largest cities in the country. But he had no illusions. Before long it would be happening in his own back yard. Contracts were made between a customer and a professional killer, with the aim of murdering people. The whole affair was a business deal. It seemed to Wallander this must be the ultimate proof that the brutalization of society had reached incomprehensible proportions.

"We have people out there trying to find out what's actually going on," said Lovén as they passed the Northern Cemetery on the way into Stockholm.

"I can't figure it all out," said Wallander. "It's like it was last year, when that raft drifted ashore. Nothing added up then, either."

"We'll have to hope our technical guys can come up with something," said Lovén. "They might be able to make something of the bullets."

Wallander tapped his jacket pocket. He had with him the bullet that had killed Louise Åkerblom.

They drove into the underground garage and then took the elevator straight up to headquarters, where the hunt for Tengblad's killer was being organized.

As Wallander entered the room, he was struck by the number of cops present. Fifteen or more were staring at him, and he thought about how different it was from Ystad.

Lovén introduced him, and Wallander took the chorus of mumbles as a greeting. A short, balding man in his fifties introduced himself as Stenberg, the officer in charge of the investigation.

Wallander suddenly felt nervous and badly prepared. He was also a little worried that they might not understand his Scanian dialect. Nevertheless, he sat down at the table and filled them in on everything that had happened. He had to field a lot of questions, and it was obvious he was dealing with experienced detectives who were very quick to get to the heart of an investigation, locate the weak points, and formulate the right questions.

The meeting dragged on and on, and lasted for more than two hours. In the end, when everyone was obviously beginning to feel washed out and Wallander was forced to ask for some aspirin, Stenberg gave a summary.

"We need a rapid response regarding the results of the ammunition analysis," he said by way of conclusion. "If we can establish a link between the weapons used, then if nothing else, we've succeeded in muddying the waters a bit more."

One or two of the cops managed a smile, but most of them just sat staring into space.

It was nearly eight by the time Wallander left the Kungsholmen police station. Lovén drove him to his hotel on Vasagatan.

"Will you be OK?" asked Lovén as he dropped Wallander off.

"I have a daughter here in town," Wallander replied. "By the way, what's the name of that disco where they threw the tear gas canisters?"

"Aurora," said Lovén. "But I hardly think it's the sort of place for you."

"I'm sure it isn't," said Wallander.

Lovén nodded, and drove off. Wallander picked up his key and resisted the temptation to look for a bar close to the hotel. The memory of Saturday night in Ystad was still all too vivid. He took the elevator to his room, showered, and changed his shirt. After a catnap for an hour on top of the bed, he looked up the address of the Aurora in the telephone book. He left the hotel at a quarter to nine. He wondered whether he should call his daughter before going out. In the end, he decided to wait. His excursion to the Aurora should not take too long. Besides, Linda was a night owl. He crossed over toward Central Station, found a cab and gave an address in the Söder district. Wallander gazed thoughtfully at the city as they drove through it. Somewhere out there was his daughter Linda, and somewhere else his sister Kristina. Hidden among all those houses and people was presumably also an African missing the index finger of his left hand.

He suddenly felt uneasy. It was like he expected something to happen any minute. Something he'd better start worrying about even now.

Louise Åkerblom's smiling face flashed across his mind's eye.

What had she stumbled upon? he wondered. Had she realized she was going to die?

A staircase led down from ground level to a black-painted iron door. Above it was a filthy red neon sign. Several of the letters had gone out. Wallander began to wonder why he had decided to take a look at the place into which somebody had thrown a few tear gas canisters a couple of days previously. But he was groping so much in the dark, he couldn't afford not to follow up the very slightest chance of finding a black man with a severed finger. He went down the stairs, opened the door, and entered a dark room where he had difficulty seeing anything at all at first. He could barely hear some music coming from a loudspeaker hanging from the ceiling. The room was full of smoke, and he thought at first he was the only one there. Then he made out some shadows in a corner with the whites of their eyes gleaming, and a bar counter slightly more illuminated than the rest of the room. When he'd gotten used to the light, he went over to the bar and ordered a beer. The bartender had a shaven head.

"We can manage on our own, thank you," he said.

Wallander did not know what he was talking about.

"We can supply all the security cover we need ourselves," the guy said.

Wallander realized to his surprise that the bartender was onto him.

"How do you know I'm a cop?" he asked, wishing he hadn't even as the words crossed his lips.

"Trade secret," the bartender replied.

Wallander noticed he was starting to get angry. The guy's arrogant self-assurance irritated him.

"I have a few questions," he said. "Since you already know I'm a cop, I don't need to show you my ID."

"I very rarely answer questions," said the bartender.

"You will this time," said Wallander. "God help you if you don't."

The man stared at Wallander in astonishment.

"I might answer," he said.

"You get a lot of Africans in here," said Wallander.

"They just love this joint."

"I'm looking for a black guy about thirty, and there's something very special about him."

"Such as?"

"He's missing a finger. On his left hand."

Wallander did not expect the reaction he got. The bald guy burst out laughing.

"What's so funny about that?" Wallander wondered.

"You're number two," said the bartender.

"Number two?"

"Who's asking. There was a guy here last night who was also wondering if I'd seen an African with a maimed left hand."

Wallander thought for a moment before going on.

"What did you tell him?"

"No."

"No?"

"I ain't seen nobody missing a finger."

"Sure?"

"Sure."

"Who was asking?"

"Never seen him before," he said, starting to wipe a glass.

Wallander suspected the man was lying.

"I'll ask you one more time," he said. "But only once."

"I have nothing more to say."

"Who was doing the asking?"

"Like I said. No idea."

"Did he speak Swedish?"

"Sort of."

"What do you mean by that?"

"That he didn't sound like you and me."

Now we're getting somewhere, thought Wallander. I must make sure he doesn't wriggle off the hook.

"What did he look like?"

"Don't remember."

"There'll be hell to pay if you don't give me a straight answer."

"He looked kinda ordinary. Black jacket. Blond hair."

Wallander suddenly got the feeling the man was scared.

"Nobody can hear us," said Wallander. "I promise you I'll never repeat what you tell me."

"His name might have been Konovalenko," said the man. "The beer's on the house if you get out right now."

"Konovalenko?" said Wallander. "Are you sure?"

"How the hell can you be sure of anything in this world?" said the man.

Wallander left and managed to flag down a cab right away. He sank back into the back seat, and gave the name of his hotel.

When he got back to his room, he reached for the phone and

was about to call his daughter. Then he let it be. He would call her early next morning.

He lay in bed for a long time, wide awake.

Konovalenko, he thought. A name. Would it put him on the right track?

He thought through everything that had happened since the morning Robert Åkerblom first came to his office.

It was dawn before he finally fell asleep.

Chapter Sixteen

When Wallander got to the police station the next morning, he was told Lovén was already in a meeting with the team investigating Tengblad's killer. He got himself some coffee, went to Lovén's office, and called Ystad. After a brief pause Martinson answered.

"What's new?" asked Martinson.

"I'm concentrating on a guy who might be Russian and whose name could be Konovalenko," said Wallander.

"I hope to God you haven't found yourself another Balt," said Martinson.

"We don't even know if Konovalenko really is his name," said Wallander. "Or if he really is Russian. He could easily be Swedish."

"Alfred Hanson," said Martinson. "He told us the man who rented the house had a foreign accent."

"That's exactly what I was thinking," said Wallander. "But I have my doubts whether that was Konovalenko."

"How come?"

"Just a hunch. The whole of this investigation is full of hunches. I don't like it at all. He also said the guy who rented the room was very fat. That doesn't fit in with the guy who shot Tengblad. If it was the same man, that is."

"Where does this African with the severed finger fit in?"

Wallander gave him a quick rundown on his visit to the Aurora the previous night.

"You could be onto something," said Martinson. "You'll be staying longer in Stockholm?"

"Yeah. I have to. One more day at least. Everything quiet in Ystad?"

"Robert Åkerblom has asked via Pastor Tureson when he can bury his wife."

"There's nothing stopping him, is there?"

"Björk said I should talk to you."

"Well, now you have. What's the weather like?"

"As it should be."

"What do you mean by that?"

"It's April. Changes by the minute. But I can't pretend we're having a heat wave."

"Can you call my dad again and tell him I'm still in Stockholm?"

"The last time he invited me to go and visit. But I didn't have time."

"Can you do it?"

"Right away."

Wallander hung up, then called his daughter. He could hear she was half asleep when she answered.

"You were supposed to call last night," she said.

"I had to work until very late," said Wallander.

"I can see you this morning," she said.

"I'm afraid that's not possible. I'm going to be extremely busy these next few hours."

"Maybe you don't want to see me at all?"

"You know I do. I'll call you later."

Wallander hung up abruptly as Lovén stomped into the office. He knew he had offended his daughter. Why didn't he want Lovén to hear he was talking with Linda? He didn't know himself.

"You look like shit," said Lovén. "Did you get any sleep last night?"

"Maybe I slept too long," replied Wallander evasively. "That can be just as bad. How's it going?"

"No breakthroughs. But we're getting there."

"I have a question," said Wallander, deciding he would not mention his visit to the Aurora just yet. "They've had an anonymous tip in Ystad that a Russian whose name could be Konovalenko might be mixed up in this police murder."

Lovén frowned.

"Is that something we should take seriously?"

"Could be. The informant seemed to know what he was talking about."

Lovén thought for a moment before responding.

"It's true we do have a lot of trouble with Russian gangsters who are taking up residence in Sweden. We're also well aware that little problem is likely to get worse rather than better over the next few years. That's why we've tried to find out what's happening on that score."

He groped around among some files in a bookcase before he found the one he was looking for.

"We have a guy called Rykoff," he said. "Vladimir Rykoff. He lives out at Hallunda. If there's anybody by the name of Konovalenko in this town, that guy ought to know."

"Why?"

"He's said to be extremely well informed about what goes on in that particular circle of immigrants. We could drive out and say hello."

Lovén handed Wallander the file.

"Just read through this," he said. "It'll tell you a lot."

"I can go and see him myself," said Wallander. "We don't both need to go."

Lovén shrugged.

"I'm happy to get out of it," he said. "Let's face it, we have a lot more leads to follow up in this Tengblad business, even if there is no sign of a breakthrough yet. By the way, the technical guys think your woman in Skåne was shot by the same weapon. But of course, they can't be absolutely certain. It was probably the same weapon. There again, of course, we don't know if it was wielded by the same hand."

It was nearly one o'clock by the time Wallander found his way out to Hallunda. He stopped off at a motel on the way and had lunch while reading through the material Lovén had given him about Vladimir Rykoff. When he finally got to Hallunda and tracked down the apartment building, he paused for a while and observed the environment. It struck him that hardly any of the people who passed by were speaking Swedish.

This is where the future is, he thought. A kid growing up here and maybe becoming a cop will have experiences very different from mine.

He entered the hallway and found the name Rykoff. Then he took the elevator up.

A woman opened the door. Wallander could see right away she was on her guard, despite the fact he had not yet explained he was a cop. He showed her his ID.

"Rykoff," he said. "I have a few questions for him."

"What about?"

Wallander could hear she was foreign. She probably came from one of the eastern bloc countries.

"That's a matter for me and him."

"He's my husband."

"Is he at home?"

"I'll go get him for you."

As the woman disappeared through a door that he assumed led into the bedroom, he took a look around. The apartment was expensively furnished. Even so, he got the feeling everything was temporary. As if whoever lived there was ready to pack up at any moment and move on.

The door opened and Vladimir Rykoff entered the room. He was dressed in a robe that looked pretty expensive to Wallander. His hair was a mess. Wallander guessed he had been asleep.

He got the distinct impression Rykoff was also on his guard.

It suddenly dawned on him he was getting somewhere. Something was about to boost the investigation that had started almost two weeks ago when Robert Åkerblom came to his office and reported his wife was missing. An investigation that had tended to get deeper and deeper bogged down in a maze of confusing tracks, criss-crossing without providing any coherent context he could come to grips with.

He'd had a similar feeling in previous investigations. The sense of being on the verge of a breakthrough. It often turned out to be true.

"I apologize for disturbing you," he said, "but I have some questions I'd like to ask you."

"What about?"

Rykoff had still not asked him to sit down. His tone was brusque and dismissive. Wallander decided to take the bull by the horns. He sat down in a chair and gestured to Rykoff and his wife to follow suit.

"According to my information you came here as an Iranian refugee," Wallander began. "You were granted Swedish citizenship in the 1970s. The name Vladimir Rykoff doesn't sound especially Iranian."

"My name's my business."

Wallander's eyes were glued to Rykoff's face.

"Of course," he said. "But in some circumstances the case for granting citizenship in this country can be reexamined. If it turns out that it was based on false information."

"Are you threatening me?"

"Not at all. What's your job?"

"I run a travel agency."

"Called?"

"Rykoff's Travel Service."

"What countries do you organize trips to?"

"It varies."

"Can you give me some examples?"

"Poland."

"More!"

"Czechoslovakia."

"Keep going!"

"What the hell! What are you getting at?"

"Your travel agency is registered as an independent enterprise with the local authority. But according to the tax people you have made no declarations the last two years. As I naturally assume you're not trying to evade taxes, I have to conclude that your travel business hasn't being operating for the last few years."

Rykoff stared at him, dumbstruck.

"We're living on the profits from the good years," said his wife all of a sudden. "There's no law that says you have to keep working every year."

"Absolutely," said Wallander. "Mind you, most people do. For whatever reason."

The woman lit a cigarette. Wallander could see she was nervous. Her husband stared at her disapprovingly. Demonstratively, she got up and opened a window. It was stuck, and Wallander was about to help her when it finally opened.

"I have a lawyer who takes care of everything concerning the travel agency," said Rykoff, who was beginning to look agitated. Wallander wondered if that was due to anger, or fear.

"Let's be frank," said Wallander. "You have as many roots in Iran as I have. You come from Russia. It would probably be impossible to take your Swedish citizenship away from you. In any case, that's not why I'm here. But you are Russian, Rykoff. And you know what's going on in Russian immigrant circles. Not least among those of your countrymen who are on the wrong side of the law. A few days ago a cop was shot here in Stockholm. That's the stupidest thing a guy can do. We get angry in a very special way. If you know what I mean."

Rykoff seemed to have regained his composure. But Wallander could see his wife was still uneasy, although she was trying to hide it. She kept looking at the wall behind him.

Before sitting down he had noticed a clock hanging there.

Something's supposed to happen, he thought. And they don't want me here when it does.

"I'm looking for a man called Konovalenko," said Wallander calmly. "Do you know anyone of that name?"

"No," said Rykoff. "Not that I can think of."

At that moment, three things became clear to Wallander. First, that Konovalenko existed. Second, that Rykoff knew exactly who he was. And third, that he was not at all happy about the cops asking after him.

Rykoff denied everything. But Wallander had glanced at Rykoff's wife as he asked the question, trying to make it look coincidental. Her face, the sudden twitch in her eye, had given him the answer he was looking for.

"Are you absolutely sure? I thought Konovalenko was quite a common name."

"I don't know anybody called that."

Then Rykoff turned to his wife.

"We don't know anybody of that name, do we?"

She shook her head.

Oh yes, thought Wallander. You know Konovalenko all right. We're going to get to him through you.

"That's a pity," said Wallander.

Rykoff stared at him in surprise.

"Was that all you wanted to know?"

"For the time being," said Wallander. "But I've no doubt you'll be hearing from us again. We won't give up until we've nailed whoever shot that policeman."

"I know nothing about that," said Rykoff. "I think like everybody else, of course: it's very sad when a young cop gets killed."

"Of course," said Wallander, getting to his feet. "There was just one other thing," he went on. "You might have read in the newspapers about a woman who was murdered in the south of Sweden a few weeks ago? Or maybe you saw something about it on the TV. We think Konovalenko was involved in that, too."

This time it was Wallander who reacted by stiffening up.

He had noticed something about Rykoff that did not quite register right away.

Then he realized what it was. The man was totally expressionless.

That was the question he'd been expecting, thought Wallander as his pulse quickened. He started prowling around the room in order to conceal his reaction.

"Do you mind if I take a look around?" he asked.

"Be my guest," said Rykoff. "Tania, open all the doors for our visitor."

Wallander took a look through all the doors. But all his attention was focused on Rykoff's reaction.

Lovén did not know how right he was, thought Wallander. We have a lead in this apartment in Hallunda.

He was surprised at how calm he felt. He ought to have left the apartment right away, called Lovén, and requested a full-scale raid. Rykoff would have been subjected to interrogation, and the police would not have relaxed until he had admitted the existence of Konovalenko, and preferably also revealed where he could be found.

It was when he looked into the little room he assumed was reserved for guests that something attracted his attention, although he could not put his finger on it. There was nothing striking about the room. A bed, a desk, a Windsor-style chair, and blue drapes. A few ornaments and books occupied a bookcase on one wall. Wallander tried hard to figure out what it was he had seen, without having seen it. He memorized the details, then turned on his heel.

"Time to leave you in peace," he said.

"We've nothing to hide from the police," said Rykoff.

"Then you have nothing to fear," Wallander replied.

He drove back to town.

Now we'll pounce, he thought. I'll tell Lovén and his boys this remarkable story, and we'll get either Rykoff or his wife to spill the beans.

But now we'll get them, he thought. Now we'll get them.

Konovalenko had very nearly missed Tania's signal. When he parked his car in front of the apartment block in Hallunda, he glanced up at the façade as usual. They had agreed that Tania would leave a window open if it was dangerous for him to come up, for some reason or other. The window was closed. As he was on the way to the elevator, it dawned on him he had left the carrier bag with the two bottles of vodka in the car. He went back to fetch them, and from pure habit happened to look up at the façade again. This time the window was open. He returned to the car, and sat behind the wheel to wait.

When Wallander appeared, he realized immediately that this was the cop Tania had warned him about.

Tania confirmed his suspicions later on. The man was called Wallander, and was a detective inspector. She had also noted that his ID revealed he came from Ystad.

"What did he want?" asked Konovalenko.

"He wanted to know if I knew anybody called Konovalenko," said Rykoff.

"Good," said Konovalenko.

Both Tania and Rykoff stared blankly at him.

"Of course it's good," said Konovalenko. "Who could possibly have told him about me? If you haven't? There's only one possibility: Victor Mabasha. We can get to Mabasha through this cop."

Then he asked Tania for some glasses. They drank vodka.

Without saying a word, Konovalenko toasted the cop from Ystad. He was suddenly very pleased with himself.

Wallander went straight back to his hotel after the excursion to Hallunda. The first thing he did was to call his daughter.

"Can we meet?" he asked.

"Now?" she said. "I thought you were working."

"I've got a few hours off. If you can make it."

"Where do you want us to meet? You don't know Stockholm at all."

"I know where the Central Station is."

"Why don't we meet there, then? In the middle of the big hall? In forty-five minutes?"

"Sounds great."

They hung up. Wallander went down to reception.

"I'm incommunicado for the rest of the afternoon," he said. "Whoever comes looking for me, in person or by telephone, gets the same message. I'm on important business and can't be contacted."

"Until when?" asked the receptionist.

"Until further notice," said Wallander.

He crossed over the road and walked to Central Station. When he saw Linda enter the big hall, he hardly recognized her. She had dyed her hair and cut it. She was also heavily made up. She was wearing black overalls and a bright red raincoat. Boots with high heels. Wallander saw how several men turned to look at her, and suddenly felt both angry and embarrassed. This was his daughter. But the lady who turned up was a self-assured young woman. No sign of the shyness so characteristic of her in the old days. He gave her a hug, but felt there was something about it that wasn't quite right.

She said she was hungry. It had started raining, and they ran to a café on Vasagatan, across from the main post office.

He watched her eat. He shook his head when she asked if he wanted anything.

"Mom was here last week," she announced suddenly in between chews. "She wanted to show off her new man. Have you met him?"

"I haven't spoken with her for more than six months," said Wallander.

"I don't think I like him," she went on. "In fact, I got the impression he was more interested in me than he was in Mom."

"Really?"

"He imports machine tools from France," she said. "But he went on and on about playing golf. Did you know Mom had taken up golf?"

"No," said Wallander, taken aback. "I didn't know that."

She stared at him for a moment before continuing.

"It's not right that you don't know what she's up to," she said. "I mean, she is the most important woman in your life to date. She knows all about you. She knows about that woman in Latvia, for instance."

Wallander was surprised. He had never mentioned Baiba Liepa to his ex-wife.

"How come she knows about her?"

"Somebody must have told her."

"Who?"

"Does it matter?"

"I just wondered."

She suddenly changed the subject.

"What are you doing here in Stockholm?" she asked. "It can't be just to see me."

He told her what had happened. Traced all the events back to the day two weeks ago when his father had announced he was going to get married, and Robert Åkerblom came to his office to report that his wife was missing. She listened attentively, and for the very first time he had the impression his daughter was a grown-up. A person who undoubtedly had much more experience in certain fields than he did himself.

"I've been missing somebody to talk to," he said when he'd finished. "If only Rydberg were still alive. Do you remember him?"

"Was he the one who always seemed so miserable?"

"That's the one. He could appear strict as well."

"I remember him. I hoped you'd never be like him."

Now it was his turn to change the subject.

"What do you know about South Africa?" he asked.

"Not a lot. Just that the blacks are treated like slaves. And I'm against that, of course. We had a visit at school by a black woman from South Africa. You just couldn't believe what she had to say was true."

"You know more than I do in any case," he said. "When I was in Latvia last year, I often used to wonder how I could have gotten to be over forty without having a clue about what was going on in the world."

"You just don't keep in touch," she said. "I remember when I was twelve, thirteen, and tried to ask you things. Neither you nor

Mom had the slightest idea about what was going on beyond your own back yard. All you wanted to know about was the house and the flower beds and your work. Nothing else. Is that why you divorced?"

"You think?"

"You had made your lives a matter of tulip bulbs and new faucets in the bathroom. That's all you ever talked about, when you did talk with each other, that is."

"What's wrong with talking about flowers?"

"The flower beds grew so high, you couldn't see anything that was happening beyond them."

He decided to put an end to that discussion.

"How much time do you have?"

"An hour, at least."

"No time at all, really. How about meeting tonight, if you feel like it?"

They went out into the street when the rain had stopped.

"Don't you find those high heels difficult to walk in?" he asked.

"Of course," she replied. "But you get used to them. Like a try?"

Wallander was just pleased that she existed. Something inside him eased up. He watched as she walked to the subway, waving to him.

At that very moment it dawned on him what he had seen in the apartment in Hallunda earlier that day. What it was that had caught his attention, although he couldn't say why.

Now he knew.

There was a shelf hanging on the wall, and on it was an ashtray. He'd seen an ashtray like that somewhere before. It might have been a coincidence. But he did not think so.

He remembered his meal at the Continental Hotel in Ystad. He'd started out in the bar. On the table in front of him was a glass ashtray. Exactly the same as the one in the guest room in Tania's and Vladimir's guest room.

Konovalenko, he thought.

At some time or other, he's been at the Continental Hotel. He might even have been sitting at the same table as me. He couldn't resist the temptation to take home one of their heavy glass ashtrays. A human failing, one of the most common. He could never have imagined that a detective inspector from Ystad would ever take a look at the little room in Hallunda where he occasionally spends his nights.

Wallander went up to his hotel room and thought he might not be such an incompetent cop after all. The times had not passed him by completely, not just yet. Maybe he was still capable of solving the pointless and brutal murder of a woman who happened to take a wrong turn not far from Krageholm.

He synopsized what he thought he had established so far. Louise Åkerblom and Klas Tengblad had been shot by the same weapon. Tengblad by a white man with a foreign accent. The black African who had been around when Louise Åkerblom was killed had been chased by a man who also had a foreign accent, and was probably called Konovalenko. This Konovalenko was known to Rykoff, even though he denied it. To judge by his build, Rykoff could very well be the guy who had rented the house from Alfred Hanson. And in Rykoff's apartment was an ashtray that proved somebody had been to Ystad. It was not a lot to go on, and had it not been for the bullets, the link would have been tenuous, to say the least. But he also had his hunches, and he knew it made sense to pay attention to them. A raid on Rykoff could provide the answers they were so eager to obtain.

That evening he had dinner with Linda in a restaurant not far from the hotel.

This time he felt more secure in her presence. When he got to bed shortly before one, it occurred to him that this was the most pleasant evening he'd had for a long time.

Wallander arrived at the Kungsholmen police station just before eight the next morning. An audience of cops listened in astonishment to what he had discovered in Hallunda, and the conclusions he had drawn. As he spoke, he could feel the skepticism that surrounded him. But the desire of the cops to catch the man who had shot their colleague was overwhelming, and he could feel the mood slowly changing. In the end, nobody challenged his conclusions.

Things moved quickly throughout the morning. The apartment block in Hallunda was placed under observation while the raid was prepared. An energetic young prosecutor had no hesitation in approving plans for arrest.

The raid was set for two o'clock. Wallander kept discreetly in the background while Lovén and his colleagues went through what was going to happen in detail. At about ten, right in the middle of the most chaotic phase of the preparations, he went to Lovén's office and made a call to Björk in Ystad. He explained about the action planned for that afternoon, and how the murder of Louise Åkerblom might soon be solved.

"I have to say it all sounds pretty improbable," said Björk.

"We live in an improbable world," said Wallander.

"Whatever happens, you've done a good job," said Björk. "I'll let everybody at this end know what's going on."

"No press conference, though," said Wallander. "And nobody is to speak with Robert Åkerblom yet, either."

"Of course not," said Björk. "When do you think you'll be back?"

"As soon as possible," said Wallander. "How's the weather?"

"Terrific," said Björk. "It feels like spring is on the way. Svedberg is sneezing like a man with hay fever. That's usually a sure sign of spring, as you well know."

Wallander felt vaguely homesick as he put the phone down. But his excitement over the imminent raid was even stronger.

At eleven Lovén called together everybody who would be taking part in the raid. Reports from those watching the building suggested both Vladimir and Tania were in the apartment. It was not possible to establish whether anybody else was there.

Wallander listened carefully to Lovén's summary. He could see that a raid in Stockholm was very different from anything he was used to. Besides, operations of this size were practically unknown in Ystad. Wallander could only remember one incident the previous year, when a guy high on narcotics had barricaded himself into a summer cottage in Sandskogen.

Before the meeting Lovén had asked Wallander if he wanted to play an active role.

"Sure," he replied. "If Konovalenko is there, in a sense he's my baby. Half of him at least. Besides, I'm looking forward to seeing Rykoff's face."

Lovén brought the meeting to a close at half past eleven.

"We really don't know what we'll be up against," he said. "Probably just two people who'll go along with the inevitable. But it could turn out different."

Wallander had lunch in the police canteen with Lovén.

"Have you ever asked yourself what you've gotten involved in?" asked Lovén, all of a sudden.

"That's something I think about every day," said Wallander. "Don't most cops?"

"I don't know," said Lovén. "I only know what I think. And the thoughts that go through my head depress me. We're on the brink of losing control here in Stockholm. I don't know how it is in a smaller district like Ystad, but being a crook in this city must be a pretty pleasant existence. At least as far as the chances of getting caught are concerned."

"We're still in control, I guess," said Wallander. "But the differences between different districts are decreasing all the time. What's happening here happens in Ystad as well."

"Lots of cops in Stockholm can't wait to get transferred to the provinces," said Lovén. "They think they'd have an easier time there."

"I guess there are quite a few who'd like to transfer here as well," Wallander countered. "They think they lead too quiet a life out in the sticks, or in some little town."

"I doubt if I'd be able to change," said Lovén.

"Me neither," said Wallander. "Either I'm an Ystad cop, or I'm not a cop at all."

The conversation petered out. Afterwards Lovén had things to do.

Wallander found a quiet spot where he could stretch out on a sofa. It occurred to him that he had not had a good night's sleep since the moment Robert Åkerblom came into his office.

He dozed off for a few minutes, and awoke with a start.

Then he just lay there, thinking about Baiba Liepa.

The raid on the apartment in Hallunda took place at exactly two o'clock. Wallander, Lovén, and three other cops climbed the stairs.

After ringing twice without reply, they broke down the door with a crowbar. Specially trained men with automatic weapons were waiting in the background. All the cops on the stairs carried pistols, apart from Wallander. Lovén asked him if he wanted a gun. But he declined. On the other hand, he was glad he was wearing a bullet-proof vest like the others.

They stormed into the apartment, spread out, and it was all over before it had even begun.

The apartment was empty. All that remained was the furniture.

The cops looked at each other in bewilderment. Then Lovén took out his walkie-talkie and contacted the officer in charge down below.

"The apartment's empty," he said. "There will be no arrests. You can call the special units off. But you can send in the technical guys to go over the place."

"They must have left last night," said Wallander. "Or at the crack of dawn."

"We'll get 'em," said Lovén. "Within half an hour there'll be a country-wide APB."

He handed Wallander a pair of plastic gloves.

"Maybe you'd like to do some dusting," he said.

While Lovén was talking to headquarters in Kungsholmen on his mobile, Wallander went into the little guest room. He put on the gloves and carefully removed the ashtray from the shelf. His eyes had not deceived him. It was an exact copy of the ashtray he had been staring at a couple of nights previously, when he had a skinful of whiskey. He handed the ashtray to a technician.

"There's bound to be fingerprints on this," he said. "We probably won't have them in our files. But Interpol might have them."

He watched the technician put the ashtray into a plastic bag.

Then he went over to the window and absentmindedly contemplated the surrounding buildings and the gray sky. He remembered vaguely that this was the window Tania had opened the day before, to let out the smoke that was irritating Vladimir. Without really being able to decide whether he was depressed or annoyed at the failure of the raid, he went into the big bedroom. He examined the wardrobes. Most of the clothes were still there. On the other hand, there was no sign of any suitcases. He sat on the edge of one of the beds and casually opened a drawer in the other bedside table. It was empty save for a cotton reel and half a pack of cigarettes. He noted that Tania smoked Gitanes.

Then he bent down and looked under the bed. Nothing but a pair of dusty slippers. He walked around the bed and opened the drawer in the other bedside table. It was empty. Standing on the table were a used ashtray and a half-eaten bar of chocolate.

Wallander noticed the cigarette butts had filters. He picked one of them up and saw it was a Camel.

He suddenly became pensive.

He thought back to the previous day. Tania had lit a cigarette. Vladimir had immediately displayed his annoyance, and she had opened a window that was stuck.

It was not usual for smokers to complain about others with the same habit. Especially when the room was not smoky. Did Tania smoke several different brands? That was hardly likely. So, Vladimir smoked as well.

Thinking hard, he went back into the living room. He opened the same window Tania had opened. It was still sticking. He tried the other windows and the glazed door leading to the balcony. They all opened with no problem.

He stood in the middle of the floor, frowning. Why had she chosen to open a window that stuck? And why was that window so difficult to open?

It suddenly dawned on him. After a moment he realized there was only one possible answer.

Tania had opened the window that stuck because there was some pressing reason for that particular window to be opened. And it was sticking because it was opened so seldom.

He went back to the window. It occurred to him that if you were in a car in the parking lot, this was the window that could most clearly be seen. The other window was adjacent to the projecting balcony. The balcony door itself was completely invisible from the parking lot.

He thought through the whole sequence one more time.

He'd cracked it. Tania seemed nervous. She had been looking at the wall clock behind his head. Then she opened a window that was only used to signal to somebody in the parking lot that they should not go up to the apartment.

Konovalenko, the thought. He'd been that close.

In a gap between two phone calls, he told Lovén about his conclusions.

"You may well be right," said Lovén. "Unless it was somebody else."

"Of course," said Wallander. "Unless it was somebody else."

They drove back to Kungsholmen while the technicians continued their work. They had barely entered Lovén's office when the telephone rang. The technicians out at Hallunda had discovered a tin box containing the same kind of tear gas canisters that had been thrown into that disco the previous week.

"It's all falling into place," said Lovén. "Unless it's just getting more confusing. I don't understand what they had against that particular disco. In any case, the whole country is looking out for them. And we'll make sure there's wide coverage on the television and in the newspapers."

"That means I can go back to Ystad tomorrow," said Wallander. "When you pick up Konovalenko, maybe we can borrow him down in Skåne for a while."

"It's always annoying when a raid goes wrong," said Lovén. "I wonder where they're holed up."

The question remained unanswered. Wallander went back to his hotel and decided to pay a visit to the Aurora that evening. Now he had some more questions for the bald guy behind the bar.

He had a feeling that things were coming to a head.

Chapter Seventeen

The man outside President de Klerk's office had been waiting a long time.

It was already midnight, and he'd been there since eight o'clock. He was completely alone in the dimly lit antechamber. A security guard occasionally looked in and apologized for his being kept waiting. The latter was an elderly man in a dark suit. He was the one who had put out all the lights just after eleven, apart from the single lamp that was still burning.

Georg Scheepers had the feeling the guy could easily have been employed at a funeral parlor. His discretion and unobtrusiveness, his servility bordering on submission, reminded him of the guy who had taken charge of his own mother's funeral a few years back.

It's a symbolic comparison that could be pretty close to the truth, thought Scheepers. Maybe President de Klerk is in charge of the last, dying remnants of the white South African empire? Maybe this is more of a waiting room for a man planning a funeral, than the office of somebody leading a country into the future?

He had plenty of opportunity to think during the four hours he had been kept waiting. Now and then the security guard opened the door quietly and apologized—the president was held up by some urgent business. At ten o'clock he brought him a cup of lukewarm tea.

Georg Scheepers wondered why he had been summoned to see President de Klerk that evening, Wednesday, May 7. The previous day, at lunchtime, he had taken a call from the secretary to his superior, Henrik Wervey. Georg Scheepers was an assistant of the widely feared chief prosecutor in Johannesburg, and he was not used to meeting him except in court or at the regular Friday meetings. As he hurried through the corridors, he wondered what Wervey wanted. Unlike this evening, he had been shown straight into the prosecutor's office. Wervey indicated a chair, and continued signing various documents a secretary was waiting for. Then they were left alone.

Wervey was a man feared not only by criminals. He was nearly sixty, almost two meters tall, and sturdily built. It was a well-known fact that he occasionally demonstrated his great strength by performing various feats. Some years ago, when his offices were being refurbished, he had singlehandedly carried out a cupboard that later needed four men to lift it onto a truck. But it was not his bodily strength that made him so fearsome. During his many years as prosecutor he had always pressed for the death penalty whenever there was the slightest possibility of winning it. On those occasions, and there were many of them, when the court accepted his plea and sentenced a criminal to be hanged, Wervey was generally a witness when the sentence was carried out. That had given him the reputation of being a brutal man. Then again, no one could accuse him of racial discrimination in applying his principles. A white criminal had just as much to fear as a black one.

Georg Scheepers sat there worrying if he had done something to invoke censure. Wervey was well known for his ruthless criticism of his assistants, if he considered it justified.

But the conversation turned out to be completely unlike what he expected. Wervey had left his desk and sat down in an easy chair beside him.

"Late last night a man was murdered in his hospital bed at a private clinic in Hillbrow," he began. "His name was Pieter van Heerden, and he worked for BOSS. The homicide squad think everything points to robbery with violence. His wallet is missing. Nobody saw anybody enter the room, nobody saw the murderer leave. It looks like whoever did it was alone, and there is evidence to suggest he pretended to be a messenger from a laboratory used by Brenthurst. As none of the night nurses heard anything, the murderer must have used a gun with a silencer. It looks very much as though the police theory about robbery being the motive is correct. On the other hand, we must also bear in mind that van Heerden worked for the intelligence service."

Wervey raised his eyebrows, and Georg Scheepers knew he was waiting for a reaction.

"That sounds reasonable," said Scheepers. "There should be an investigation to see if it was in fact an opportunist robbery."

"There's another aspect which complicates matters," Wervey went on. "What I'm about to say is extremely confidential. You must be absolutely clear about that."

"I understand," said Scheepers.

"Van Heerden was responsible for keeping President de Klerk informed about secret intelligence activities outside the usual channels," said Wervey. "In other words, he was in an extremely sensitive post."

Wervey fell silent. Scheepers waited tensely for him to continue.

"President de Klerk called me a few hours ago," he said. "He wanted me to select one of my prosecutors to keep him specially informed about the police investigation. He seems convinced the motive for the murder had something to do with van Heerden's intelligence work. Although he has no proof, he rejects outright any suggestion that this was a routine robbery."

Wervey looked at Scheepers.

"We cannot know exactly what van Heerden was keeping the president informed about," he said pensively.

Georg Scheepers nodded. He understood.

"I have picked you as the man to keep President de Klerk informed," he said. "From now on you will drop all other matters and concentrate exclusively on the investigation into the circumstances surrounding van Heerden's death. Is that understood?"

Georg Scheepers nodded. He was still trying to grasp the full implications of what Wervey had just said.

"You will be summoned regularly to the president," he said. "You will keep no minutes of those meetings, only a few brief notes that you will later burn. You will speak only with the president and me. If anybody in your section wonders what you're doing, the official explanation is that I've asked you to look into the recruitment requirements regarding prosecutors over the next ten-year period. Is that clear?"

"Yes," said Georg Scheepers.

Wervey stood up, took a plastic wallet from his desk, and handed it to Scheepers.

"Here is what little investigative material the police have so far," he said. "Van Heerden has been dead for only twelve hours. The hunt for the assassin is being led by an inspector called Borstlap. I suggest you go to Brenthurst Clinic and speak with him."

That concluded the business.

"Do a good job," said Wervey. "I've chosen you because you have proved to be a good prosecutor. I don't like to be disappointed."

Georg Scheepers went back to his office and tried to come to terms with what was actually required of him. Then he thought he should buy himself a new suit. None of the clothes he possessed would be suitable for meeting the president.

Now he was in the dimly lit antechamber, wearing a dark blue suit that had been very expensive. His wife wondered why he had bought it. He said he was to take part in an inquiry chaired by the Minister of Justice. She accepted this explanation without any further questions.

It was twenty minutes to one before the discreet security guard opened the door and told him the president was now ready to receive him. Georg Scheepers jumped up from his chair, aware of how nervous he felt. He followed the guard who marched up to a high double door, knocked, and opened it for him.

Sitting at a desk, illuminated by a single lamp, was the balding man he was destined to meet. Scheepers remained standing hesitantly in the doorway until the man at the desk beckoned him to approach and gestured towards a visitor's chair.

President de Klerk looked weary. Georg Scheepers noticed he had large bags under his eyes.

The president came straight to the point. His voice had a note of impatience about it, as if he was always having to talk with people who did not understand anything.

"I am convinced the death of Pieter van Heerden had nothing to do with robbery," said de Klerk. "It's your job to insure the police investigators are properly aware of the fact that it's his intelligence work that lies behind the murder. I want all his computer files investigated, all his index files and documents, everything he's worked on over the last year. Is that understood?"

"Yes," said Georg Scheepers.

De Klerk leaned forward so that the desk lamp lit up his face and gave it an almost ghost-like appearance.

"Van Heerden told me he suspected there was a conspiracy afoot that was a serious threat to South Africa as a whole," he said. "A plot that could result in complete chaos. His death must be seen in this context. Nothing else."

Georg Scheepers nodded.

"You don't need to know any more than that," said de Klerk, leaning back in his chair again. "Chief Prosecutor Wervey selected you to keep me informed because he considers you to be completely reliable and loyal to the government authorities. But I want to stress the confidential nature of this assignment. Revealing what I have just told you would be high treason. As you are a prosecutor, I don't need to tell you what the punishment is for that particular crime."

"Of course not," said Georg Scheepers, shifting uncomfortably on his chair.

"You will report directly to me whenever you have anything to say," de Klerk went on. "Talk to one of my secretaries, and they will make an appointment. Thank you for coming."

The audience was over. De Klerk turned back to his papers.

Georg Scheepers stood up, bowed, and walked over the thick carpet back to the double doors.

The security guard accompanied him down the stairs. An armed guard escorted him as far as the parking lot, where he had left his car. His hands were sweaty as he slid behind the wheel.

A conspiracy, he thought. A plot? Which could threaten the whole country and lead to chaos? Aren't we there already? Can things get any more chaotic than they already are?

He left the question unanswered and started the engine. Then he opened the glove pocket, where he kept a pistol. He loaded a magazine, released the safety catch, and placed it on the seat beside him.

Georg Scheepers did not like driving at night. It was too unsafe, too dangerous. Armed robbery and assault took place all the time, and the level of brutality was getting worse.

Then he drove home through the South African night. Pretoria was asleep.

He had a lot to think about.

Chapter Eighteen

Days and nights had merged to form a vague whole from which he was no longer able to pick out the parts. Victor Mabasha did not know how long it was since he left the dead body of Konovalenko behind in the remote house set in muddy fields. The man who had suddenly come back to life and shot at him in the disco filled with tear gas. That was a shock for him. He was convinced he had killed Konovalenko with the bottle. But despite the smarting in his eyes, he had seen Konovalenko through the clouds of smoke. Victor Mabasha escaped from the premises via a back staircase full of screaming, kicking people in a panic, trying to flee the smoke. For a brief moment, he thought he was back in South Africa, where tear gas attacks on black townships were not uncommon. But he was in Stockholm and Konovalenko had risen from the dead and was now chasing him in order to kill him.

He had reached town at dawn and spent hours driving around the streets, not knowing what to do. He was very tired, so weary he did not really dare trust his own judgment. That made him scared. Before, he had always felt that his judgment, his ability to think himself out of difficult situations with a clear head, was his ultimate life insurance. He wondered whether to take a room in a hotel somewhere. But he had no passport, no documents at all to establish his identity. He was a nobody among all these people, an armed man without a name, that was all.

The pain in his hand kept returning at irregular intervals. Soon he would have to see a doctor. The black blood had seeped through the bandages, and he could not afford to succumb to infections and fever. That would make him completely defenseless. But the bloody stump hardly affected him. His finger might never have existed. In his thoughts he had transformed it into a dream. He was born without an index finger on his left hand.

He slept in a cemetery in a sleeping bag he bought. He was cold in spite of it. In his dreams he was pursued by the singing hounds. As he lay awake watching the stars, he thought how he might never return to his homeland. The dry, red, swirling soil would never again be touched by the soles of his feet. The thought filled him with sudden sorrow, so intense he could not remember feeling anything like it since the death of his father. It also occurred to him that in South Africa, a country founded upon an all-embracing lie, there was seldom room for simple untruths. He thought about the lie that formed the very backbone of his own life.

The nights he spent in the cemetery were filled with the *songoma's* words. It was also during these nights, surrounded by nothing but the unknown dead, white people he had never met and would never meet until he entered the underworld, the world of spirits, that he remembered his childhood. He saw his father's face, his smile, and heard his voice. It also occurred to him that the spirit world might be divided, just like South Africa. Perhaps even the underworld consisted of a black and a white world? He was filled with sorrow as he imagined the spirits of his forefathers being forced to live in smoky, slummy townships. He tried to get his *songoma* to tell him how it was. But all he got was the singing hounds, and their howls he was unable to interpret.

At dawn the second day he left the cemetery after hiding his sleeping bag in a tomb where he had managed to pry open an air vent. A few hours later he stole another car. It all happened very quickly: an opportunity arose, and he grasped it without hesitation. Once again his judgment was beginning to assist him. He had turned a corner onto a street where he saw a man leave his car with the engine running and disappear into a doorway. There was nobody around. He recognized the make, a Ford; he had driven lots of them before.

He sat behind the wheel, threw a briefcase the man had left behind onto the street, and drove off. He eventually managed to find his way out of town and had searched for a lake where he could be alone with his thoughts.

He could not find a lake, but he came upon the seashore. Or rather, he thought it had to be the seashore. He did not know which sea it was or what it was called, but when he tasted the water it was salty. Not as salty as he was used to, from the beaches at Durban and Port Elizabeth. But there could hardly be salt lakes in this country? He clambered over a few rocks, and imagined he was gazing into infinity through a narrow gap between two islands in the archipelago. There was a chill in the air and he felt cold. Even so, he remained standing on a rock as far out as he could get, thinking that this was where his life had taken him. A very long way. But what would the future look like?

Just as he used to do in his childhood, he squatted down and made a spiral-shaped labyrinth from pebbles that had broken loose from the rock. At the same time he tried to delve so deeply into himself that he could hear the voice of his *songoma*. But he couldn't get that far. The noise of the sea was too strong and his own concentration too weak. The stones he had arranged to form a labyrinth did not help. He just felt scared. If he could not talk to the spirits, he would grow so weak he might even die. He would no longer have any resistance to illnesses, his thoughts would desert him, and his body would become a mere shell that cracked the moment it was touched.

Feeling uneasy, he tore himself away from the sea and returned to his car. He tried to concentrate on the most important things. How was it possible for Konovalenko to trace him so easily to the disco recommended by some Africans from Uganda he started talking to in a burger bar?

That was the first question.

The second was how he could get out of this country and return to South Africa.

He realized he would be forced to do what he wanted to do least of all. Find Konovalenko. That would be very difficult. Konovalenko would be as hard to track down as an individual *spriengboek* in the endless African bush. But somehow or other he would have to entice Konovalenko. He was the one with a passport, he was the one who could be forced to help him get away from this country. He did not think he could see any alternative.

He still hoped he would not need to kill anybody, apart from Konovalenko.

That evening he went back to the disco. There were not many people there, and he sat in a corner, drinking beer. When he went to the bar with his empty glass for another beer, the bald man spoke to him. At first Victor Mabasha did not understand what he was saying. Then he realized that two different people had been there the day before, looking for him. He could tell from the description that one of them was Konovalenko. But what about the other one? The man behind the bar said he was a cop. A cop with an accent that showed he came from the southern part of the country.

"What did he want?" wondered Victor Mabasha.

The bald man nodded at his filthy bandage.

"He was looking for a black man missing a finger," he said.

He drank no more beer, but left the disco without more ado. Konovalenko might come back. He was still not prepared to face him, even though his gun was at the ready, tucked into his belt.

When he came out onto the street, he knew right away what he was going to do. This cop would help him find Konovalenko.

Somewhere or other there was an investigation going on into the disappearance of a woman. Maybe they had found her body already, wherever Konovalenko had hidden it. But if they had managed to find out about him, they might know about Konovalenko as well?

I left a clue, he thought. A finger. Maybe Konovalenko also left something behind?

He spent the rest of the evening hovering in the shadows outside the disco. But neither Konovalenko nor the cop showed up. The bald man had given him a description of the cop. It occurred to Victor Mabasha that a white man in his forties was not going to be a regular customer at the disco.

Late that night he went back to the tomb in the cemetery. The next day he stole another car, and that evening he hovered once more in the shadows outside the disco.

At exactly nine o'clock, a cab came to a halt at the entrance.

Victor was in the front seat of his car. He sank down so that his head was level with the steering wheel. The cop got out of the taxi and disappeared into the underworld. As soon as he had vanished, Victor drove up to the entrance and got out. He withdrew to the darkest shadows, and waited. His pistol was in his jacket pocket, within easy reach.

The man who emerged a quarter of an hour later and looked around vaguely or possibly lost in thought was not on his guard. He gave the impression of being completely harmless, a solitary, unprotected nocturnal prowler. Victor Mabasha drew his pistol, took a few swift strides, and pressed the gun against the underside of the man's chin.

"Not a move," he said in English. "Not a single move."

The man gave a start. But he understood English. He did not move.

"Go to the car," said Victor Mabasha. "Open the door and get into the passenger seat."

The man did as he was told. He was evidently very scared.

Victor quickly ducked into the car and punched him on the chin. Hard enough to knock him out, but not hard enough to break his jaw. Victor Mabasha knew his strength when he was in control of the situation. Something that did not apply that catastrophic last evening with Konovalenko.

He went through the cop's pockets. Oddly enough, no gun. Victor Mabasha was even more convinced he was in a very strange country, with unarmed cops. Then he bound the man's arms to his chest and taped over his mouth. A narrow trickle of blood was seeping from the side of his mouth. It was never possible to avoid injuring somebody altogether. The man had presumably bitten his own tongue.

During the three hours available to Victor Mabasha that afternoon, he had memorized the route he intended to take. He knew exactly where he was going and had no desire to risk a wrong turn. When he stopped at the first red light, he took out the man's wallet and saw he was called Kurt Wallander, forty years old.

The lights changed, and he moved on. He kept a close eye on the rear mirror the whole time.

After the second red light he started to think he had a car on his tail. Could the cop have had a backup? If so, there would soon be problems. When he came to a multi-lane highway, he stepped on the gas. He suddenly felt he could have been imagining things. Maybe they were on their own after all?

The man in the passenger seat started groaning and moving. Victor Mabasha could see he must have hit him precisely as hard as he had intended.

He turned into the cemetery and came to a halt in the shadow of a green building containing a shop that sold flowers and wreaths during the day. Now it was closed and in darkness. He turned off his lights and watched the cars taking the slip road. None of them seemed to be slowing down.

He waited another ten minutes. But nothing happened, apart from the policeman coming to.

"Not a sound," said Victor Mabasha, ripping off the tape over the man's mouth.

A cop understands, he thought. He knows when a guy means what he says. He then began to wonder if a man who abducted a policeman risked hanging in Sweden.

He got out of the car, listened, and looked around. All was quiet, apart from the passing traffic. He walked round the car, opened the door and motioned to the man to get out. Then he led him to one of the iron gates and they soon disappeared in the darkness consuming the gravel paths and gravestones.

Victor Mabasha led him over to the burial vault where he had managed to open the iron door without difficulty. It smelled musty in the damp vault, but he was not scared by graveyards. He had often hidden among the dead in the past.

He had bought a hurricane lamp and an extra sleeping bag. At first the cop refused to go with him into the vault, and put up a show of resistance.

"I'm not going to kill you," he said. "I'm not going to hurt you, either. But you've got to go in there."

He tucked the cop into one of the sleeping bags, lit the lamp, and went out to see if the light could be seen. But it was all dark.

Once again he stood still and listened. The many years he had spent constantly on the alert had developed his hearing. Something had moved on a gravel path. The cop's backup, he thought. Or some nocturnal animal.

In the end he decided it was not a threat. He went back into the vault and squatted opposite the cop, whose name was Kurt Wallander.

The fear Wallander had first felt had now become positive fright, perhaps even terror.

"If you do as I say no harm will come to you," said Victor Mabasha. "But you must answer my questions. And you must tell the truth. I know you're a cop. I can see you're looking at my left hand and the bandage all the time. That means you've found my finger. The one Konovalenko cut off. I want to tell you right away he was the one who killed the woman. It's up to you if you believe me or not. I only came to this country to stay for a short time, and I've decided to kill only one person. Konovalenko. But you have to help me first by telling me where he is. Once Konovalenko's dead, I'll let you go right away."

Victor Mabasha waited for a reply. Then he remembered something he had forgotten.

"I don't suppose you have a shadow?" he asked. "A car following you?"

The man shook his head.

"You're on your own?"

"Yes," said the policeman, making a face.

"I had to make sure you didn't start struggling," said Victor Mabasha. "But I don't think my punch did too much damage."

"No," said the man, grimacing.

Victor Mabasha sat there in silence. There was no rush for the moment. The cop would feel calmer if everything was quiet.

Victor Mabasha did not blame him for being afraid. He knew how abandoned a man could feel when he was terrified.

"Konovalenko," he said quietly. "Where is he?"

"I don't know," said Wallander.

Victor Mabasha eyed him up and down, and realized the cop knew who Konovalenko was, but did not actually know where he was. That was unfortunate. That would make everything more difficult, would take more time. But it wouldn't really change anything fundamentally. Together, they would be able to find Konovalenko.

Victor Mabasha slowly recounted everything that had happened when the woman was killed. But he said nothing about why he was in Sweden in the first place.

"So he was the one who blew the house up?" said Wallander when he was through.

"You know what happened now," said Victor Mabasha. "Now it's your turn to put me in the picture."

The cop had suddenly calmed down, even if he did seem put out at being in a cold, damp burial vault. Behind their backs were caskets inside sarcophagi, stacked on top of one another.

"Do you have a name?" he asked.

"Just call me Goli," said Victor Mabasha. "That'll do."

"And you come from South Africa?"

"Maybe. But that's not important."

"It's important for me."

"The only thing that's important for both of us is where Konovalenko is."

The last part of this claim was spat out. The policeman understood. The fear returned to his eyes.

That very same moment Victor Mabasha stiffened. He had not relaxed his guard while talking to the policeman. Now his sensitive ears had picked up a noise outside the vault. He gestured to the cop to keep still. Then he took out his pistol and turned down the flame in the hurricane lamp.

There was somebody outside the vault. And it was not an animal. The movements were too meticulously cautious.

He leaned rapidly over the cop and grabbed him by the throat.

"For the last time," he hissed, "was there anybody tailing you?"

"No. Nobody. I swear."

Victor Mabasha let go. Konovalenko, he thought in a fury. I don't know how you do it, but I do know now why Jan Kleyn wants you working for him in South Africa.

They could not stay in the vault. He eyed the hurricane lamp. That was their chance.

"When I open the door, throw the lamp to the left," he said to the cop, untying his hands at the same time. He turned up the flame as far as it would go, and handed it over.

"Jump to the right," he whispered. "Crouch down. Don't get in my line of fire."

He could see the cop wanted to protest. But he raised his hand and Wallander said nothing. Then he cocked the pistol and they got ready for action.

"I'll count to three," he said.

He flung open the iron door and the cop hurled the lamp to the left. Victor Mabasha fired at the same moment. The cop came stumbling behind him and he almost overbalanced. Just then he heard shots from at least two different weapons. He threw himself to one side and crawled behind a gravestone. The cop crawled off in some other direction. The hurricane lamp lit up the burial vault. Victor Mabasha detected a movement in one corner and fired. The bullet hit the iron door and disappeared whining into the vault. Another shot shattered the hurricane lamp and everything went black. Somebody scampered away along one of the gravel paths. Then all was quiet once more.

Kurt Wallander could feel his heart pounding like a piston against his ribs. He did not seem able to breathe properly, and thought he'd been hit. But there was no blood, and he couldn't feel any pain apart from his tongue, which he had bitten some time ago. With great care he crawled behind a tall gravestone. He lay there absolutely still. His heart was still pounding away. Victor Mabasha was nowhere to be seen. Once he was sure he was alone, he started running. He stumbled his way forward along the gravel paths, running towards the lights on the main road, and the noise from what cars were still out. He kept running until he was outside the boundary fence of the cemetery. He stopped at a bus stop and managed to wave down a cab on its way back to the city from Arlanda airport.

"Central Hotel," he gasped.

The driver eyed him up and down in suspicion.

"I don't know if I want you in my cab," he said. "You'll make everything filthy."

"I'm a cop, dammit," Wallander roared. "Just drive!"

The driver pulled away from the bus stop. When they got to the hotel he paid for the taxi without waiting for either a receipt or his change, and collected his key from the receptionist, who stared at his clothes in astonishment. It was midnight when he closed the door behind him and collapsed onto the bed.

When he had calmed down, he called Linda.

"Why are you calling as late as this?" she wondered.

"I've been busy until now," he said. "I didn't have a chance to call you earlier."

"Why do you sound so funny? Is something the matter?"

Wallander had a lump in his throat and was on the point of bursting into tears. But he managed to control himself.

"It's nothing," he said.

"Are you sure everything's all right?"

"Everything's fine. Why shouldn't it be?"

"You know better than I do."

"Don't you remember from when you used to live at home that I was always out working at strange hours?"

"I guess so," she said. "I'd forgotten."

He made up his mind on the spur of the moment.

"I'm coming over to your place in Bromma," he said. "Don't ask me why. I'll explain later."

He left the hotel and took a cab to where she lived in Bromma. Then they sat at the kitchen table with a beer each, and he told her what had happened.

"They say it's good for kids to get some idea of what their parents do at work," she said, shaking her head. "Weren't you scared?"

"Of course I was scared. These people have no respect at all for human life."

"Why don't you send the cops after them?"

"I'm a cop myself. And I need to think."

"Meanwhile they might kill a few more people."

He nodded.

"You're right," he said. "I'll go to the station at Kungsholmen. But I felt I needed to talk to you first."

"I'm glad you came."

She went out into the hall with him.

"Why did you ask if I was at home?" she asked suddenly, as he was about to leave. "Why didn't you say you stopped by yesterday?"

Wallander did not know what she meant.

"What are you talking about?" he asked.

"I met Mrs. Nilson when I got home, she lives next door," she said. "She told me you'd been here asking if I was in. You have a key, don't you?"

"I haven't spoken with any Mrs. Nilson," said Wallander.

"Maybe I got her wrong, then," she said.

A shiver suddenly ran down Wallander's spine.

"What did she say?"

"One more time," he said. "You came home. You met Mrs. Nilson. She said I'd been asking after you?"

"Yep."

"Repeat what she said, word for word."

"Your dad's been asking after you. That's all."

Wallander felt scared.

"I've never met Mrs. Nilson," he said. "How can she know what I look like? How can she know I'm me?"

It was a while before she caught on.

"You mean it could have been somebody else? But who? Why? Who would want to pretend they were you?"

Wallander looked at her in all seriousness. Then he switched off the light and went cautiously over to one of the living room windows.

The street down below was deserted.

He went back to the hall.

"I don't know who it was," he said. "But you're going back with me to Ystad tomorrow. I don't want you around here on your own right now."

She could tell he was deadly serious.

"OK," she said simply. "Do I need to be scared tonight?"

"You don't need to be scared at all," he said. "It's just that you shouldn't be here on your own for the next few days."

"Don't say any more," she begged. "Right now I want to know as little as possible."

She made up a bed for him on a mattress.

Then he lay there in the dark, listening to her breathing. Konovalenko, he thought.

When he was certain she was asleep, he got up and went over to the window.

The street down below was just as deserted as before.

Wallander had called a prerecorded information service and established there was a train to Malmö at three minutes past seven, and they left the apartment in Bromma soon after six.

He had slept restlessly, dozing off then waking up with a start.

He wanted to spend a few hours in a train. Flying would mean he got to Malmö too quickly. He needed to rest, and he needed to think.

They came to a standstill just outside Mjölby with an engine failure, and waited there nearly an hour. But Wallander was just grateful for the extra time. They occasionally exchanged a few words. But just as often she was buried in a book, and he was lost in thought.

Fourteen days, he thought as he watched a lonely tractor plowing what looked like a never-ending field. He tried counting the seagulls following the plow, but could not manage it.

Fourteen days since Louise Åkerblom had disappeared. The image of her was already beginning to melt away from the two small children's consciousness. He wondered if Robert Åkerblom would be able to cling to his God. What sort of answers could Pastor Tureson give him?

He looked at his daughter, who had fallen asleep with her cheek resting against the window. What did her mostly solitary fear look like? Was there a landscape where their abandoned and deserted thoughts could arrange to meet, without their knowing about it? We don't really know anybody, he thought. Least of all ourselves.

Had Robert Åkerblom known his wife?

The tractor disappeared into a dip in the field. Wallander imagined it sinking slowly into a bottomless pit of mud.

The train suddenly jerked into motion. Linda woke up and looked at him.

"Are we there?" she asked, drowsily. "How long have I been asleep?"

"A quarter of an hour, maybe," he said with a smile. "We haven't reached Nässjö yet."

"I could use a cup of coffee," she said, yawning. "How about you?"

They sat in the buffet car as far as Hässleholm. For the first time he told her the full story of his two trips to Riga the previous year. She listened in fascination.

"It doesn't sound like you at all," she said when he had finished.

"That's how I feel as well," he said.

"You could have died," she said. "Did you never think about me and Mom?"

"I thought about you," he said. "But I didn't think about your mother."

When they got to Malmö, they only had to wait half an hour for a train to Ystad. They were back in his apartment shortly before four. He made up a bed for her in the guest room, and when he went to look for some clean sheets it struck him that he had forgotten all about the time he had booked in the laundry room. At about seven they went out to one of the pizzerias on Hamngatan and had dinner. They were both tired, and were back home again before nine.

She called her grandfather, and Wallander stood by her side, listening. She promised to go and see him the next day.

He was surprised at how his father could sound so different when he talked to her.

He thought he had better call Lovén. But he put it off, since he was not yet sure how he was going to explain why he did not contact the police immediately after the incident in the cemetery. He could not understand that himself. It was a breach of duty, no doubt about it. Had he started to lose control over his own judgment? Or had he been so scared that he lost the ability to act?

Long after she fell asleep he stood in the window, looking down at the deserted street.

The images in his mind's eye were alternating between Victor Mabasha and the man known as Konovalenko.

While Wallander was standing in his window in Ystad, Vladimir Rykoff was noting that the police were still interested in his apartment. He was two floors higher up in the same building. It was Konovalenko who once suggested they should have an escape route in case the usual apartment could not or ought not to be used. It was also Konovalenko who explained how the safest haven was not always the one furthest away. The best plan is to do the unexpected. And so Rykoff rented an identical apartment in Tania's name, two floors higher up. That made it easier to move the necessary clothes and other baggage.

The previous day Konovalenko had told them to leave the apartment. He questioned Vladimir and Tania, and realized the cop from Ystad was evidently no fool. He should not be underestimated. Nor could they exclude the possibility that the cops might search the place. But most of all, Konovalenko was afraid Vladimir and Tania might be subjected to more serious interrogation. He was not convinced they were always capable of distinguishing between what they could say, and what not.

Konovalenko had also wondered whether the best solution might be to shoot them. But he decided that was unnecessary. He still needed Vladimir's legwork. Besides, the cops would only get more excited than they already were.

They moved to the other apartment that same night. Konovalenko had given Vladimir and Tania strict instructions to stay at home the next few days.

Among the first things Konovalenko learned as a young KGB officer was that there were deadly sins in the shadowy world of the intelligence service. Being a servant of secrecy meant joining a brotherhood where the most important rules were written in invisible ink. The worst sin of all, of course, was being a double agent. Betraying one's own organization, but at the same time doing it in the service of an enemy power. In the mystical hell of the intelligence service, the moles were closest to the center of the inferno.

There were other deadly sins. One was to arrive too late.

Not just to a meeting, emptying a secret letter box, a kidnapping, or even nothing more complicated than a journey. Just as bad was being too late with regard to oneself, one's own plans, one's own decisions.

Nevertheless, that is what had happened to Konovalenko early in the morning of May 7. The mistake he made was to put too much faith in his BMW. As a young KGB officer, his superiors had always taught him to plan a journey on the basis of two parallel possibilities. If one vehicle proved to be unserviceable, there should always be time to resort to a planned alternative. But that Friday morning, when his BMW suddenly stopped on St. Erik's Bridge and refused to start again, he had no alternative. Of course, he could take a cab or the subway. Besides, since he did not know if and when the cop or his daughter would leave the apartment in Bromma, it was not even certain he would be too late, anyway. Nevertheless, it seemed to him like the mistake, all the guilt, was his, not the car's. He spent nearly twenty minutes trying to restart it, and it seemed like he was trying to bring about a resurrection. But the engine was dead as far as he was concerned.

In the end he gave up, and flagged down a cab. He had planned to be outside the red-brick apartment block by seven at the latest. As it was, he did not get there until nearly a quarter to eight.

It had not been difficult to find out that Wallander had a daughter and that she was the one living in Bromma. He called the police station in Ystad and was told that Wallander was staying at the Central Hotel in Stockholm. He claimed to be a cop himself. Then he went to the hotel and pretended to be discussing a block booking for a sizable group of tourists a couple of months later. When he was not being observed, he stole a look at a message left for Wallander and quickly memorized the name Linda and a telephone number. He left the hotel, and then traced the number to an address in Bromma. He chatted to a woman on the stairs there, and soon figured out how things stood.

That morning he waited on the street outside the apartment until half past eight. Just then, an elderly woman emerged from the building. He went over to her and wished her good morning; she recognized the pleasant guy who had spoken to her previously.

"They left early this morning," she said in reply to his question.

"Both of them?"

"Both of them."

"Are they going to be away long?"

"She promised to call."

"She told you where they were going, no doubt?"

"They were going abroad on vacation. I didn't quite catch where."

Konovalenko could see she was trying hard to remember. He waited.

"France, I think it was," she said eventually. "I'm not absolutely sure, mind you."

Konovalenko thanked her for her assistance, and left. He would send Rykoff later to go over the apartment.

As he needed time to think and was in no special hurry, he walked to Brommaplan where he could no doubt find a cab. The BMW had served its purpose, and he would give Rykoff the job of finding him another car before the day was out.

Konovalenko immediately rejected the possibility that they had gone abroad. The cop from Ystad was a cold, calculating sort of guy. He had discovered that somebody had been asking the old lady questions the day before. Somebody who would doubtless come back and ask some more questions. And so he left a false trail, pointing to France.

Where can they have gone, Konovalenko wondered. In all probability he has taken his daughter back with him to Ystad. But he might have chosen some other place I couldn't possibly track down.

A temporary retreat, thought Konovalenko. I'll give him a start that I can recover later.

He drew one more conclusion. The cop from Ystad was worried. Why else would he take his daughter with him?

Konovalenko gave a little smile at the thought that they were thinking along the same lines, he and the insignificant little cop called Wallander. He recalled something a KGB colonel said to his new recruits shortly after they started their long period of training. A high level of education, a long line of ancestors, or even a high level of intelligence is no guarantee of becoming an outstanding chess player.

The main thing just now was to find Victor Mabasha, he thought. Kill him. Finish off what he had failed to do in the disco and the cemetery.

With a vague feeling of unease, he recalled the previous evening.

Shortly before midnight he called South Africa and spoke with Jan Kleyn on his special emergency number. He had rehearsed what he was going to say very carefully. There were no more excuses to explain away Victor Mabasha's continued existence. And so he lied. He said Victor Mabasha had been killed the previous day. A hand grenade in the gas tank. When the rubber band holding back the firing pin had been eaten away, the car exploded. Victor Mabasha had perished instantaneously.

All the same, Konovalenko sensed a degree of dissatisfaction in Jan Kleyn. A crisis of confidence between himself and the South African intelligence service that he could not afford. That could put his whole future at risk.

Konovalenko resolved to step on the gas. There was no longer any time to spare. Victor Mabasha had to be tracked down and killed within the next few days.

This unfathomable dusk slowly set in. But Victor Mabasha barely noticed it.

Now and again he thought about the man he was to kill. Jan Kleyn would understand. He would allow him to retain his assignment. One of these days, he would have the South African president in his sights. He would not hesitate, he would carry out the assignment he had taken on.

He wondered if the president was aware that he would soon be dead. Did white people have their own *songomas* who came to them in their dreams?

In the end he concluded they must have. How could any man survive without being in contact with the spirit world that controlled our lives, that had power over life and death?

On this occasion the spirits had been kind to him. They had told him what he had to do.

Wallander woke up soon after six in the morning. For the first time since starting to track down Louise Åkerblom's killer, he was starting to feel properly rested. He could hear his daughter snoring through the half-open door. He got up and stood in the doorway, watching her. He was suddenly overwhelmed by intense joy, and it occurred to him that the meaning of life was quite simply to take care of one's children. Nothing else. He went to the bathroom, took a long shower, and decided to make an appointment with the police doctor. It must be possible to give some kind of medical help to a cop with the serious intention of losing weight and getting fitter.

Every morning he recalled the occasion the previous year when he woke up in the middle of the night, in a cold sweat, and thought he was having a heart attack. The doctor who examined him said it was a warning. A warning that there was something completely wrong in his life. Now, a year later, he had to admit he had done nothing at all to change his life style. In addition, he had put on at least three kilos.

He drank coffee at the kitchen table. There was a thick fog over Ystad this morning. But soon spring would really have arrived, and he resolved to go and talk with Björk this coming Monday about vacation plans.

He left the apartment at a quarter past seven, after scribbling down his direct number on a scrap of paper and leaving it on the kitchen table.

When he came out onto the street, he was enveloped by fog. It was so thick, he could hardly make out his car parked a short way from the apartment block. He thought maybe he should leave it where it was, and walk to the station.

Suddenly he had the feeling something had moved on the other side of the street. A lamppost seemed to sway slightly.

Then he saw there was a man standing there, enveloped by fog just like himself.

The next moment he recognized who it was. Goli had returned to Ystad.

Chapter Nineteen

Jan Kleyn had a weakness, a well-preserved secret. Her name was Miranda, and she was as black as a raven's shadow.

She was his secret, the crucial counterpoint in his life. Everyone who knew Jan Kleyn would have considered her an impossibility. His colleagues in the intelligence service would have dismissed any rumor about her existence as preposterous fantasy. Jan Kleyn was one of those very rare suns that were considered free from spots.

But there was one, and her name was Miranda.

They were the same age, and had been aware of each other's existence since they were kids. But they did not grow up together. They lived in two different worlds. Miranda's mother, Matilda, worked as a servant for Jan Kleyn's parents in their big, white house on a hill outside Bloemfontein. She lived a few kilometers away in one of a cluster of tin shacks where the Africans had their homes. Every morning, at the first light of dawn, she would make her way laboriously up the steep hill to the white house, where her first task of the day was to serve the family breakfast. That hill was a sort of penance she had to pay for the crime of being born black. Jan Kleyn, like his brothers and sisters, had special servants whose only assignment was to take care of the children. Even so, he used to turn to Matilda all the time. One day when he was eleven, he suddenly started to wonder where she came from every morning, and where she went back to when her day's work was done. As part of a forbidden adventure—he was not allowed to leave the walled-in yard on his own—he followed her in secret. It was the first time he had seen at close range the clutter of tin shacks where African families lived. Of course, he had been aware that the blacks lived in quite different conditions from his own. He was always hearing from his parents how it was part of the natural order of things that whites and blacks lived differently. Whites, like Jan Kleyn, were human beings. The blacks hadn't yet got that far. Some time in the distant future they might possibly be able to reach the same level as the whites. The color of their skins would grow lighter, their powers of understanding would grow greater, and it would all be as a result of the patient upbringing the whites gave them. Even so, he had never imagined their houses would be as awful as those he could see before him.

But there was also something else that attracted his attention. Matilda was met by a girl of his own age, lanky and slim. That must be Matilda's daughter. It had never occurred to him that Matilda might have children of her own. Now he realized for the first time that Matilda had a family, a life apart from the work she did in his home. It was a discovery that affected him badly. He could feel himself getting angry. It was as if Matilda had deceived him. He always imagined she was there for him alone.

Two years later Matilda died. Miranda had never explained to him how it happened, just that something had eaten away her insides until all life left her. Matilda's home and family had broken up. Miranda's father took two sons and a daughter with him to where he came from, the barren countryside far away on the Lesotho border. The idea was that Miranda would grow up with one of Matilda's sisters. But Jan Kleyn's mother, in a fit of unexpected generosity, decided to take Miranda under her wing. She was to live with the master gardener, who had a little cottage in some remote corner of their large grounds. Miranda would be trained to take over her mother's job. In that way, the spirit of Matilda would live on inside the white house. Jan Klein's mother was not a Boer for nothing. As far as she was concerned, maintaining traditions was a guarantee for the continuation of the family and Afrikaner society. Keeping the same family of domestic servants, generation after generation, helped to provide a sense of permanence and stability.

Jan Kleyn and Miranda continued to grow up near each other. But the distance between them was unchanged. Even though he could see she was very beautiful, there was in fact no such thing as black beauty. It belonged to what he had been taught was a forbidden area. He heard young men his own age telling secret stories about white Afrikaners traveling to neighboring Mozambique on weekends, in order to bed black women. But that just seemed to confirm the truth he had learned never to question. And so he went on seeing Miranda without actually wanting to discover her, when she served his breakfast on the terrace. But she had started appearing in his dreams. The dreams were violent and sent his pulse racing when he recalled them the following day. Reality was transformed in his dreams. In them, not only did he recognize Miranda's beauty, he accepted it. In his dreams he was allowed to love her, and the girls from Afrikaner families he associated with normally faded away in comparison with Matilda's daughter.

Their first real meeting took place when they were both nineteen. It was a Sunday in January, when everyone but Jan Kleyn had gone to a family dinner in Kimberley. He was not able to join them because he was still feeling weak and depressed after a lengthy bout of malaria. He was sitting out on the terrace, Miranda was the only servant in the house, and suddenly he stood up and went to her in the kitchen. Long afterwards he would often think he had never really left her after that. He had stayed in the kitchen. From that moment on, she had him in her power. He would never be able to shake her off.

Two years later she got pregnant.

He was then studying at Rand University in Johannesburg. His love for Miranda was his passion and at the same time his horror. He realized he was betraying his people and their traditions. He often tried to break off contact with her, to force himself out of this forbidden relationship. But he could not. They would meet in secret, their moments together dominated by fear of being discovered. When she told him she was pregnant, he beat her. The next moment it dawned on him that he would never be able to live without her, even if he would never be able to live with her openly either. She gave up her position at the white house. He arranged a job for her in Johannesburg. With the help of some English friends at the university, who had a different attitude toward affairs with black women, Jan Kleyn bought a little house in Bezuidenhout Park in eastern Johannesburg. He arranged for her to live there under the pretense of being a servant for an Englishman who spent most of his time on his farm in Southern Rhodesia. They could meet there, and there, in Bezuidenhout Park, their daughter was born and, without any discussion being necessary, christened Matilda. They continued to see each other, had no more children, and Jan Kleyn never married a white woman, to the sorrow and sometimes even bitterness of his parents. A Boer who did not form a family and have lots of children was odd, a person who failed to live up to Afrikaner traditions. Jan Kleyn became more and more of a mystery to his parents, and it was clear to him he would never be able to explain that he loved their servant Matilda's daughter, Miranda.

Jan Kleyn lay in bed thinking about all this, that Saturday morning of May 9. In the evening he would be visiting the house in Bezuidenhout Park. It was a habit he regarded as sacrosanct. The only thing that could get in the way was something connected with his work for BOSS. That particular Saturday he knew his visit to Bezuidenhout would be very much delayed. He needed to have an important meeting with Franz Malan. That could not be postponed.

As usual, he woke up early that Saturday morning. Jan Kleyn went to bed late and woke up early. He had disciplined himself to get by with only a few hours sleep. But that morning he allowed himself the luxury of sleeping late. He could hear faint noises from the kitchen where his servant, Moses, was making breakfast.

He thought about the telephone call he had received just after midnight. Konovalenko had finally given him the news he was waiting for. Victor Mabasha was dead. That did not only mean a problem had ceased to exist. It also meant the doubt he had been entertaining the last few days about Konovalenko's abilities had been put to rest.

He was due to meet Franz Malan in Hammanskraal at ten. It was time to decide when and where the assassination would take place. Victor Mabasha's successor had also been chosen. Jan Kleyn had no doubt he had once again made the right choice. Sikosi Tsiki would do what was required of him. The selection of Victor Mabasha had not been an error of judgment. Jan Kleyn knew there were invisible depths in everybody, even the most uncompromising of people. That was why he had decided to let Konovalenko test the man he had chosen. Victor Mabasha had been weighed in Konovalenko's scales and found wanting. Sikosi Tsiki would undergo the same test. Jan Kleyn could not believe that two people in succession would turn out to be too weak.

Shortly after half past eight he left his house and drove towards Hammanskraal. Smoke hung low over the African shanty town alongside the freeway. He tried to imagine Miranda and Matilda being forced to live there, among the tin shacks and homeless dogs, the charcoal fires constantly making their eyes water. Miranda had been lucky and escaped from the inferno of the slums. Her daughter Matilda had inherited her good fortune. Thanks to Jan Kleyn and his concession to forbidden love, they had no need to share the hopeless lives of their African brothers and sisters.

It seemed to Jan Kleyn that his daughter had inherited her mother's beauty. But there was a difference, hinting at the future. Matilda's skin was lighter than her mother's. When she eventually had a child with a white man, the process would continue. Sometime in the future, long after he had ceased to exist, his descendants would give birth to children whose appearance would never betray the fact that there was black blood somewhere in the past.

Jan Kleyn liked driving and thinking about the future. He had never been able to understand those who claimed it was impossible to predict what it would be like. As far as he was concerned, it was being shaped at that very minute.

Franz Malan was waiting on the veranda at Hammanskraal when Jan Kleyn turned into the forecourt. They shook hands and went straight in to where the table with the green felt cloth was waiting for them.

"Victor Mabasha is dead," said Jan Kleyn when they had sat down.

A broad smile lit up Franz Malan's face.

"I was just wondering," he said.

"Konovalenko killed him yesterday," said Jan Kleyn. "The Swedes have always been very good at making hand grenades."

"We have some of them here in South Africa," said Franz Malan. "It's always hard to get hold of them. But our agents can generally get around the problems."

"I suppose that's about the only thing we have to thank the Rhodesians for," said Jan Kleyn.

He recalled briefly what he had heard about events in Southern Rhodesia nearly thirty years ago. As part of his training for his work in the intelligence service, he heard an old officer describing how the whites in Southern Rhodesia had managed to evade the world-wide sanctions imposed upon them. It had taught him that all politicians have dirty hands. Those vying for power set up and break rules according to the state of the game. Despite the sanctions imposed by every country in the world apart from Portugal, Taiwan, Israel, and South Africa, Southern Rhodesia had never run short of the goods they needed to import. Nor had their exports suffered any serious downturn. This was due not least to American and Soviet politicians who flew discreetly to Salisbury and offered their services. The American politicians were mainly senators from the South, who considered it important to support the white minority in the country. Through their contacts, Greek and Italian businessmen, hastily established airlines and an ingenious network of intermediaries, they had taken it upon themselves to lift the sanctions by back-door methods. In their turn Russian politicians had used similar means to guarantee access to the Rhodesian metals they needed for their own industries. Soon there was nothing left but a mirage of isolation. Nevertheless, politicians throughout the world continued to preach condemnation of the white racist regime and praise the success of sanctions.

Jan Kleyn realized later that white South Africa also had many friends throughout the world. The support they received was less noticeable than what the blacks were getting. But Jan Kleyn had no doubt that what was happening in silence was at least as valuable as the support being proclaimed in the streets and public squares. This was a fight to the death, and in such circumstances everything goes.

"Who'll replace him?" wondered Franz Malan.

"Sikosi Tsiki," said Jan Kleyn. "He was number two on the list I made earlier. He's twenty-eight, born near East London. He's managed to get himself banned by both the ANC and Inkatha. In both cases for disloyalty and theft. He's now full of such hatred for both organizations, I'd call it fanatical."

"Fanatics," said Franz Malan. "There's generally something about fanatics that can't be completely controlled. They have absolutely no fear of death. But they don't always stick to the plans that have been laid."

Jan Kleyn was irritated by Franz Malan's magisterial tone. But he managed to conceal that when he responded.

"I'm the one calling him fanatical," he said. "That doesn't necessarily mean he'll live up to the description in practice. He's a man whose cold-bloodedness is scarcely any less intense than yours or mine."

Franz Malan was happy with the response. As usual, he had no reason to doubt what Jan Kleyn said.

"I've talked to the rest of our friends on the committee," Jan Kleyn went on. "I called a vote, since we were talking about picking a replacement after all. Nobody disagreed."

Franz Malan could picture the committee members in his mind's eye. Sitting round the oval-shaped walnut table, slowly raising their hands one after another. There were never any secret votes. Open decisions were necessary in order to make sure members' loyalty never wavered. Apart from a determination to use drastic methods to secure the rights of Afrikaners and by extension all whites in South Africa, the committee members had little or nothing to do with each other. The fascist leader Terrace Blanche was regarded with ill-concealed contempt by many of the other committee members. But his presence was a necessity. The representative of the diamond family de Beers, an elderly man whom no one had ever seen laugh, was treated with the double-edged respect often aroused by extreme wealth. Judge Pelser, the Broederbond representative, was a man whose contempt for humankind was notorious. But he had great influence and was seldom contradicted. And finally there was General Stroesser, one of the air force high command, a man who disliked the company of civil servants or mine owners.

But they had voted to give Sikosi Tsiki the assignment. That meant he and Jan Kleyn could go through with their plans.

"Sikosi Tsiki will be leaving in three days," said Jan Kleyn. "Konovalenko is ready to receive him. He'll fly to Copenhagen via Amsterdam on a Zambian passport. Then he'll be ferried over to Sweden by boat."

Franz Malan nodded. Now it was his turn. He took some black-and-white enlarged photographs from his brief case. He had taken the pictures himself and developed them in the laboratory he had installed at home. He had copied the map at work when no one was looking.

"Friday, June 12," he began. "The local police think there'll be at least forty thousand in the crowd. There are lots of reasons why this could be a suitable occasion for us to pounce. To start with, there's a hill, Signal Hill, just to the south of the stadium. The distance from there to where the podium will be is about 700 meters. There are no buildings on the summit. But there is a serviceable access road from the south side. Sikosi Tsiki shouldn't have any problems getting there, or making his retreat. If necessary, he can even lie low up there before making his way down the hillside later and mixing with the blacks who'll be milling around in the chaos that's bound to follow."

Jan Kleyn studied the photos carefully. He waited for Franz Malan to continue.

"My other argument," said Franz Malan, "is that the assassination should take place in the heart of what we can call the English part of our country. Africans tend to react primitively. Their first reaction will be that somebody from Cape Town is responsible for the killing. Their rage will be directed at the locals who live in the town. All those liberal-minded Englishmen who wish the blacks so well will be forced to face up to what is in store for them if ever the blacks come to power in our country. That will make it much easier for us to stir up a backlash."

Jan Kleyn nodded. He had been thinking along the same lines. He reflected briefly on what Franz Malan had said. In his experience every plan had some kind of weakness.

"What is there against it?" he asked.

"I have difficulty in finding anything at all," replied Franz Malan.

"There's always a weak point," said Jan Kleyn. "We can't make a final decision until we've put our finger on what it is."

"I can only think of one thing that could go wrong," said Franz Malan after a few moments' silence. "Sikosi Tsiki could miss."

Jan Kleyn looked surprised.

"He won't miss," he said. "I only pick people who hit their targets."

"All the same, 700 meters is a long way," said Franz Malan. "A sudden puff of wind. A flash of reflected sun nobody could have foreseen. The bullet misses by a couple of centimeters. Hits somebody else."

"That just cannot happen," said Jan Kleyn.

It occurred to Franz Malan that while they might not be able to find the weak point in the plan they were developing, he had found a weakness in Jan Kleyn. When rational arguments ran out, he reverted to fate. Something simply could not happen.

But he said nothing.

A servant brought them tea. They ran through the plan once more. Spelled out details, noted questions that needed answering. Not until nearly four in the afternoon did they think they had gotten as far as they could.

"Tomorrow it's exactly a month to June 12," said Jan Kleyn. "That means we don't have much time to make up our minds. We'll have to decide by next Friday if it's going to be Cape Town or not. By then we must have weighed everything, and answered all the outstanding questions. Let's meet here again on May 15, in the morning. Then I'll get the whole committee together at twelve o'clock. During the coming week we'll both have to go through the plans, independently, looking for cracks or weaknesses. We already know the strengths, the positive arguments. Now we'll have to find the bad ones."

Franz Malan nodded. He had no objections.

They shook hands and left the house at Hammanskraal ten minutes apart.

Jan Kleyn drove straight to the house in Bezuidenhout Park.

Miranda Nkoyi contemplated her daughter. She was sitting on the floor, staring into space. Miranda could see her eyes were not vacant, but alert. Whenever she looked at her daughter, she sometimes felt, as if in a brief fit of giddiness, that she was seeing her mother. Her mother was as young as that, barely seventeen years old, when she gave birth to Miranda. Now her own daughter was that same age.

What is she looking at, Miranda wondered. She sometimes felt a cold shudder running down her spine when she recognized features characteristic of Matilda's father. Especially that look of intense concentration, even though she was staring into empty space. That inner vision that no one else could understand.

"Matilda," she said tenderly, as if hoping to bring her back down to earth by treating her gently.

The girl came out of her reverie with a start, and looked her straight in the eye.

"I know my father will soon be here," she said. "As you won't let me hate him while he's here, I do it while I'm waiting. You can dictate when. But you can never take the hatred away from me."

Miranda wanted to cry out that she understood her feelings. She often thought that way herself. But she could not. She was like her mother, Matilda senior, who was saddened by the continual humiliation of not being permitted to lead a satisfactory life in her own country. Miranda knew she had grown soft just like her mother, and remained silently in a state of impotence she could only make up for by constantly betraying the man who was the father of her daughter.

Soon, she thought. Soon I must tell my daughter that her mother has retained a little bit of her life force, despite everything. I shall have to tell her, in order to win her back, to show how the gap between us is not an abyss after all.

In secret, Matilda was a member of the ANC youth organization. She was active, and had already undertaken several undercover assignments. She had been arrested by the police on more than one occasion. Miranda was always frightened she would be injured or killed. Every time the coffins of dead blacks were being carried in swaying, chanting processions to their graves, she would pray to all the gods she believed in that her daughter might be spared. She turned to the Christian god, to the spirits of her ancestors, to her dead mother, to the *songoma* her father always used to talk about. But she was never completely convinced they had really heard her. The prayers merely made her feel better by dint of tiring her out.

Miranda could understand the confused feeling of impotence in her daughter because her father was a Boer, knowing herself to be sired by the enemy. It was like being inflicted with a mortal wound at the very moment of birth.

Nevertheless, she knew a mother could never regret the existence of her own daughter. That time seventeen years ago she had loved Jan Kleyn just as little as she loved him today. Matilda was conceived in fear and subservience: It was like the bed they were lying in was floating in a remote, airless universe. Afterwards, she just did not have the strength to cast aside her subservience. The child would be born, it had a father, and he had organized a life for her, a house in Bezuidenhout, money to live on. Right from the start she was resolved never to have another child by him. If necessary Matilda would be her only offspring, even if her African heart was horrified by the thought. Jan Kleyn had never openly stated he wanted another child by her; his demands on her as far as lovemaking were concerned were always equally hollow. She let him spend nights with her, and could stick it out because she had learned how to take revenge by betraying him.

She observed her daughter, who had once again lost herself in a world to which her mother was not allowed access. She could see Matilda had inherited her own beauty. The only difference was that her skin was lighter. She sometimes wondered what Jan Kleyn would say if he knew that what his daughter wanted most of all was a darker skin.

My daughter betrays him as well, Miranda thought. But our betrayal is not malice. It's the lifeline we cling to as South Africa burns. Any malice is all on his side. One of these days it will destroy him. The freedom we achieve will not be primarily the voting slips we find in our hands, but the release from those inner chains that have been holding us prisoner.

The car came to a stop on the drive outside the garage.

Matilda got up and looked at her mother.

"Why have you never killed him?" she asked.

What Miranda heard was his voice in hers. But she had convinced herself that Matilda's heart was not that of an Afrikaner. Her appearance, her light-colored skin, those were things she could do nothing about. But she had preserved her heart, hot and inexhaustible as it was. That was a line of defense, albeit the last one, which Jan Kleyn could never overcome.

The shameful thing was that he never seemed to notice anything. Every time he came to Bezuidenhout his car was laden with food so that she could make him a *braai*, just as he remembered it from the white house where he grew up. He never realized he was transforming Miranda into her own mother, the enslaved servant. He could never see that he was forcing her to play different roles: cook, lover, valet. He did not notice the resolute hatred emanating from his daughter. He saw only a world that was unchanging, petrified, something he considered it his main task in life to preserve. He did not see the falseness, the dishonesty, the bottomless artificiality on which the whole country was based.

"Is everything OK?" he asked as he placed all the bags of food in the hall.

"Yes," said Miranda. "Everything's fine."

Then she made *braai* while he tried to talk to his daughter, who was hiding behind the role of the shy and timid girl. He tried stroking her hair, and Miranda could see through the kitchen door how her daughter stiffened. They ate their meal of Afrikaner sausages, big chunks of meat and cabbage salad. Miranda knew Matilda would go out to the bathroom and force herself to throw up the whole lot, once the meal was over. Then he wanted to talk about unimportant matters, the house, the wallpaper, the yard. Matilda withdrew to her room, leaving Miranda alone with him, and she gave him the answers he was expecting. Then they went to bed. His body was as hot as only a freezing object can be. The next day would be Sunday. As they could not be seen together, they took their Sunday stroll inside the four walls of the house, walking around and around each other, eating, and sitting in silence. Matilda always went out just as soon as she could and didn't come back until he had left. Only when Monday came would everything begin to return to normal.

When he had fallen asleep and his breathing was calm and steady, she got carefully out of bed. She had learned how to move around the bedroom in absolute silence. She went out to the kitchen, leaving the door open so she could check the whole time that he did not wake up. If he did, and wondered why she was up, her excuse was a glass of water she had poured earlier.

As usual, she had draped his clothes over a chair in the kitchen. It was positioned so he could not see it from the bedroom. He did once ask why she always hung his clothes in the kitchen rather than in the bedroom, and she explained she wanted to brush them down for him every morning before he got dressed.

She carefully went through his pockets. She knew his wallet would be in the left inside pocket of his jacket, and his keys in his right pants pocket. The pistol he always carried was on the bedside table.

That was generally all she found in his pockets. That particular evening, however, there was a scrap of paper with something written on it in what she recognized as his handwriting. With one eye on the bedroom, she quickly memorized what it said.

Cape Town, she read.

12 June.
Distance to location? Wind direction? Roads?

She put the scrap of paper back where she had found it, once she was certain it was folded exactly as it had been.

She could not understand what the words on the piece of paper meant. But even so she would do what she was told to do whenever she found something in his pockets. She would tell the man she always met the day after Jan Kleyn had been to visit her. Together with their friends, they would try and work out what the words meant.

She drank the water and went back to bed.

He sometimes talked in his sleep. When that happened it was nearly always within an hour of his falling asleep. She would also memorize the words he sometimes mumbled, sometimes yelled out, and tell the man she met the following day. He would write down everything she could remember, just as he did with everything else that had happened during Jan Kleyn's visit. Sometimes he would say where he had come from, and sometimes where he was going as well. But most often he said nothing at all. He had never consciously or accidentally revealed anything about his work for the intelligence service.

A long time ago he had said he was working as a chief executive officer in the Ministry of Justice in Pretoria.

Later, when she was contacted by the man who was looking for information and heard from him that Jan Kleyn worked for BOSS, she was told she must never breathe a word about knowing what he did for a living.

Jan Kleyn left her house on the Sunday evening. Miranda waved goodbye as he drove away.

The last thing he said was that he would come back late in the afternoon the following Friday.

As he drove along, he decided he was looking forward to the coming week. The plan had begun to take shape. He had everything that was going to happen under control.

What he did not know, however, was that Victor Mabasha was still alive.

* * *

In the evening of May 12, exactly a month before he was due to carry out the assassination of Nelson Mandela, Sikosi Tsiki left Johannesburg on the regular KLM flight to Amsterdam. Like Victor Mabasha, Sikosi Tsiki had spent a long time wondering who his victim was going to be. Unlike Victor, though, he had not concluded it must be President de Klerk. He left the question open.

That it might involve Nelson Mandela had never even occurred to him.

On Wednesday, May 13, shortly after six in the evening, a fishing boat pulled into the harbor at Limhamn.

Sikosi Tsiki jumped ashore. The fishing boat pulled out right away, headed back to Denmark.

An unusually fat man was standing on the dark to welcome him.

That particular afternoon there was a southwesterly gale blowing over Skåne. The wind did not die down until the evening.

Then came the heat.

Chapter Twenty

Shortly after three o'clock on Sunday afternoon, Peters and Norén were driving through central Ystad in their patrol car. They were waiting for their shift to come to an end. It had been a quiet day with only one real incident. Just before noon they received a call to say a naked man had started demolishing a house out in Sandskogen. His wife made the call. She explained how the man was in a rage because he had to spend all his leisure time repairing her parents' summer cottage. In order to secure some peace and quiet in his life, he decided to pull it down. She explained how he would prefer to sit by a lake, fishing.

"You'd better go straight there and calm the guy down," said the operator at the emergency center.

"What's it called?" asked Norén, who was looking after the radio while Peters did the driving. "Disorderly conduct?"

"There's no such thing anymore," said the operator. "But if the house belongs to his in-laws, you could say it's taking the law into his own hands. Who cares what it's called? Just calm the guy down. That's the main thing."

They drove out toward Sandskogen without speeding up.

"I guess I understand the guy," said Peters. "Having a house of your own can be a pain in the ass. There's always something that needs to be done. But you never have time, or it's too expensive. Having to work on somebody else's house in the same way can't make things any better."

"Maybe we'd better help him pull the house down instead," said Norén.

They managed to find the right address. Quite a crowd had gathered on the road outside the fence. Norén and Peters got out of the car and watched the naked guy crawling around on the roof, prying off tiles with a crowbar. Just then his wife came running up. Norén could see she had been crying. They listened to her incoherent account of what had happened. The main thing was, he obviously did not have permission to do what he was doing.

They went over to the house and yelled up at the guy sitting astride the roof ridge. He was concentrating so hard on the roof tiles, he hadn't noticed the patrol car. When he saw Norén and Peters he was so surprised, he dropped the crowbar. It came sliding down the roof, and Norén had to leap to one side to avoid being hit.

"Careful with that!" yelled Peters. "I guess you'd better come down. You have no right to be demolishing this house."

To their astonishment the guy obeyed them right away. He let down the ladder he had pulled up behind him, and climbed down. His wife came running up with a robe, which he put on.

"You gonna arrest me?" asked the guy.

"No," said Peters. "But you'd better quit pulling that house down. To tell you the truth, I don't really think they'll be asking you to do any more repairs."

"All I want to do is to go fishing," said the man.

They drove back through Sandskogen. Norén reported back to headquarters.

Just as they were about to turn into the Österleden highway, it happened.

"Here comes Wallander," he said.

Norén looked up from his notebook.

As the car drove past, it looked like Wallander had not seen them. That would have been very strange if true, as they were in a marked patrol car painted blue and white. What attracted the attention of the two cops most of all, however, was not Wallander's vacant stare.

It was the guy in the passenger seat. He was black.

Peters and Norén looked at each other.

"Wasn't that an African in the car?" wondered Norén.

"Yeah," said Peters. "He sure was black."

They were both thinking about the severed finger they had found a few weeks earlier, and the black man they'd been searching for all over the country.

"Wallander must have caught him," said Norén hesitantly.

"Why is he traveling in that direction, then?" objected Peters. "And why didn't he stop when he saw us?"

"It was like he didn't want to see us," said Norén. "Like kids do. If they close their eyes, they think nobody can see them."

Peters nodded.

"Do you think he's in trouble?"

"No," said Norén. "But where did he manage to find the black guy?"

Then they were interrupted by an emergency call about a suspected stolen motorcycle found abandoned in Bjäresjö. When they finished their shift they went back to the station. To their surprise, when they asked about Wallander in the coffee room they discovered he had not shown up. Peters was just going to tell everybody how they had seen him when he saw Norén quickly put his finger over his lips.

"Why shouldn't I say anything?" he asked when they were together in the locker room, getting ready to go home.

"If Wallander hasn't shown up, there must be some reason why," said Norén. "Just what, is nothing to do with you or me. Besides, it could be some other African. Martinson once said Wallander's daughter had something going with a black man. It could have been him, for all we know."

"I still think it's weird," Peters insisted.

That was a feeling that stayed with him even after he got back home to his row house on the road to Kristianstad. When he had finished his dinner and played with his kids for a while, he went out with the dog. Martinson lived in the same neighborhood, so he decided to stop by and tell him what he and Norén had seen. The dog was a Labrador bitch and Martinson had inquired recently if he could join the waiting list for puppies.

Martinson himself answered the door. He invited Peters to come in.

"I must get back home in a minute," said Peters. "But there is one thing I'd like to mention. Do you have time?"

Martinson had some position or other in the Liberal Party and was hoping for a seat on the local council before long; he had been reading some boring political reports the party had sent him. He lost no time putting on a jacket, and came out to join Peters. The latter told him what had happened earlier that afternoon.

"Are you sure about this?" asked Martinson when Peters had finished.

"We can't both have been seeing things," said Peters.

"Strange," said Martinson thoughtfully. "I'd have heard right away if it was the African who's missing a finger."

"Maybe it was his daughter's boyfriend," hazarded Peters.

"Wallander said that was all over and done with," said Martinson.

They walked in silence for a while, watching the dog straining at its leash.

"It was like he didn't want to see us," said Peters tentatively. "And that can only mean one thing. He didn't want us to know what he was up to."

"Or at least about the African in the passenger seat," said Martinson, lost in thought.

"I guess there'll be some natural explanation," said Peters. "I mean, I don't want to suggest Wallander is up to something he shouldn't be."

"Of course not," said Martinson. "But it was good you told me about it."

"I mean, I don't want to go spreading gossip," Peters insisted.

"This isn't gossip," said Martinson.

"Norén will be mad," said peters.

"He doesn't need to know," said Martinson.

They separated outside Martinson's house. Peters promised Martinson he could buy a puppy when the time came.

Martinson wondered if he ought to call Wallander. Then he decided to wait and talk to him the next day. With a sigh, he returned to his endless political documents.

When Wallander showed up at the police station the next morning shortly before eight, he had an answer ready for the question he knew would come. The previous day when, after much hesitation, he had decided to take Victor Mabasha out with him in the car, he thought the risk of bumping into a police colleague or anybody he knew was small. He had taken roads he knew patrol cars seldom used. But needless to say, he ran into Peters and Norén. He noticed them so late there was no time to tell Victor Mabasha to crouch down and make himself invisible. Nor had he managed to turn off in some other direction. He could see in the corner of his eye that Peters and Norén had noticed the man in the seat beside him. They would ask for an explanation the next day, that was clear to him right away. At the same time he cursed his luck, and wished he had never set out.

Was there no end to it, he asked himself.

Then, when he had calmed down, he turned to his daughter for help once more.

"Herman Mboya will have to be resurrected as your boyfriend," he said. "If anybody should ask. Which is pretty unlikely."

She stared at him, then burst out laughing in resignation.

"Don't you remember what you told me when I was a kid?" she asked. "That one lie leads to another? And eventually you get into such a mess, nobody knows what's true any more."

"I dislike this just as much as you do," said Wallander. "But it'll soon be over. He'll soon be out of the country. Then we can forget he was ever here."

"Sure I'll say Herman Mboya has come back," she said. "To tell you the truth, I sometimes wish he had."

When Wallander got to the police station on Monday morning, then, he had an explanation ready for why there was an African sitting beside him in the car on Sunday afternoon. In a situation where most things were complicated and threatening to slide out of control, that seemed to him the least of his problems. When he noticed Victor Mabasha on the street that morning, shrouded in fog and looking like nothing more than a mirage, his first instinct was to rush back to the apartment and summon his colleagues for assistance. But something held him back, something at odds with all his usual police logic. Even when they were together in the cemetery that night in Stockholm, he had the distinct impression the black man was telling the truth. He was not the killer of Louise Åkerblom. He might have been there, but he was innocent. It was another guy, a guy called Konovalenko, and later he'd tried to kill Victor Mabasha as well. There was a possibility the black man missing a finger had tried to prevent what happened at the deserted house. Wallander had been thinking non-stop about what was behind it all.

That was the spirit in which he took him back to the apartment, well aware that he might be making a mistake. On several occasions Wallander had used unconventional methods, to say the least, when dealing with suspects or convicted criminals. More than once Björk had felt obliged to remind Wallander of the regulations regarding correct police procedures. Even so, he required the black man to surrender any weapon he was carrying while they were still on the street. He accepted the pistol, and then frisked him. The black man had seemed strangely unaffected, as if he expected nothing less of Wallander than an invitation to join him in his home. Just to prove he was not completely naive, Wallander asked how he had managed to track down his address.

"On the way to the cemetery," said the man, "I looked through your wallet. I memorized your address."

"You attacked me," he said. "And now you've traced me to my home, many miles away from Stockholm. You'd better have some good answers to the questions I'm going to ask you."

They sat down in the kitchen, and Wallander closed the kitchen door so they wouldn't wake Linda. Afterwards, he would remember those hours they sat opposite each other at the table as the most remarkable conversation he had ever taken part in. It was not just that Wallander received his first real insight into the strange world from which Victor Mabasha originated and to which he would soon return. He was also forced to ask himself how it was possible for a human being to be made up of so many incompatible parts. How could a man be a cold-blooded killer who approached his contracts as if they were part of an accountable day's work, and at the same time be a rational, sensitive human being with well-thought-out political views? He did not realize the conversation was part of a confidence trick that had him fooled. Victor Mabasha had seen how the wind was blowing. His ability to give the impression of reliability could give him the freedom to return to South Africa. The spirits had whispered in his ear that he should seek out the cop who was hunting Konovalenko and obtain his help to flee the country.

What Wallander remembered most vividly in retrospect was what Victor Mabasha said about a plant that grew exclusively in the Namibian desert. It could live as long as two thousand years. It grew long leaves like protective shadows to shield its flowers and its complicated root system. Victor Mabasha regarded this unusual plant as a symbol of the opposing forces in his homeland, and also struggling for supremacy in his own being.

"People don't surrender their privileges voluntarily," he said. "These privileges have become a habit with roots so deep, they've become a sort of extra limb. It's a mistake to believe it's all down to a racial defect. Where I come from it's the whites who reap the benefits of this habit. But if things had been different it could just as easily have been me and my brothers. You can never fight racism with racism. What has to happen in my country, so battered and bruised for so many hundreds of years, is that the habits of submission have to be broken. The whites must be made to understand that if they're to survive the immediate future, they must step down. They have to hand over land to the deprived blacks who have been robbed of their land for centuries. They have to transfer most of their riches to those who have nothing, they have to learn how to treat the blacks as human beings. Barbarism has always had a human face. That's precisely what makes barbarism so inhuman. The blacks, who are so used to being submissive, to regarding themselves as nobodies in a community of nobodies, have to change their habits. Could it be that submissiveness is the most difficult of all human failings to shake off? It's a habit so deeply ingrained, it deforms one's whole being and leaves no part of the body untouched. Progressing from being a nobody to being a somebody is the longest journey a human being can undertake. Once you've learned to put up with your inferiority, it becomes a habit which dominates your whole life. And I believe a peaceful solution is an illusion. The apartheid system in my country has gone so far, it's already begun to flounder because it's become impossible. New generations of blacks have grown up and refused to submit. They're impatient, they can see the imminent collapse. But everything is progressing so slowly. Besides, there are too many whites who think the same way. They refuse to accept privileges requiring them to live as if all the blacks in their country were invisible, as if they only existed as servants or some strange sort of animals confined to remote shanty towns. In my country we have large nature reserves where wild animals can rove unhindered. At the same time, we have large human reserves where people are constantly hindered. Where I come from, wild animals are better off than humans."

Victor Mabasha fell silent, and looked at Wallander as if expecting him to ask questions or make objections. It seemed to Wallander that all whites were the same to Victor Mabasha, whether they lived in South Africa or anywhere else.

"A lot of my black brothers and sisters think this feeling of inferiority can be overcome by its opposite, superiority," Victor Mabasha went on. "But that's wrong, of course. That just leads to antipathy, and tensions between various groups where there should be cooperation. For instance, it can split a family in two. And you should know, Inspector Wallander, that where I come from if you don't have a family, you are nothing. For an African, the family is the be-all and end-all."

"I thought your spirits fulfilled that role," said Wallander.

"Spirits are part of our families," said Victor Mabasha. "The spirits are our ancestors, keeping watch over us. They are invisible members of our family. We never forget their existence. That's why the whites have committed such an incomprehensible crime in driving us out of the land where we have lived for so many generations. Spirits don't like being forced to quit the land that was once theirs. The spirits hate the shanty towns the whites have forced us to live in even more than we do."

He stopped abruptly, as if the words he had just spoken had given him such terrible insight he had trouble in believing what he just said.

"I grew up in a family that was split from the very start," he said after a long pause. "The whites knew they could break down our resistance by splitting up our families. I could see how my brothers and sisters started reacting more and more like blind rabbits. They just ran around in circles, around and around, and no longer knew where they came from or where they were headed. I saw all that, and chose a different route. I learned how to hate. I drank of the dark waters that arouse the desire for revenge. But I also realized that despite their superiority, their arrogant assumption that their supremacy was God-given, they also had their weak points. They were scared. They talked about making South Africa a perfect work of art, a white palace in Paradise.

"But they could never see how impossible that dream of theirs really was. And those who did refused to admit as much. So the very foundation on which everything was built became a lie, and fear came to them in the night. They filled their houses with weapons.

But fear found its way inside even so. Violence became a part of the everyday program of fear. I could see all that, and I resolved to keep my friends close by me, but my enemies even closer. I would play the role of the black man who knew what white men wanted. I would feed my contempt by running errands for them. I would work in their kitchens, and spit into the soup before carrying it in to their tables. I would continue to be a nobody who, in secret, had become a somebody."

He fell silent. Wallander thought he had said all he wanted to say. But how much had Wallander really understood? How could all this help him to understand what brought Victor Mabasha to Sweden? What did it all mean? He had always had a vague understanding that South Africa was a country in the process of being destroyed by an awful political system based on racial discrimination, and he now had a clearer understanding of what it was all about. But the assassination? Who was it aimed at? Who was behind it all? An organization?

"I have to know more," he said. "You still haven't said who's behind all this. Who paid for your ticket to Sweden?"

"Those ruthless people are mere shadows," said Victor Mabasha. "Their ancestors abandoned them long ago. They meet in secrecy to plan the downfall of our country."

"And you run their errands?"

"Yes."

"Why?"

"Why not?"

"You kill people."

"Sooner or later others will kill me."

"What do you mean by that?"

"I know it will happen."

"But you didn't kill Louise Åkerblom?"

"No."

"A man called Konovalenko did that?"

"Yes."

"Why?"

"Only he can tell you that."

"A guy comes here from South Africa, another from Russia. They meet up at a remote house in Skåne. They have a powerful radio transmitter there, and they have weapons. Why?"

"That's how it was arranged."

"By whom?"

"By the ones who asked us to make the journey."

We're going around in circles, Wallander thought. I'm not getting any answers.

But he tried again, forced himself to make one more effort.

"I've gathered this was some kind of preparation," he said. "A preparation for some crime or other that was going to take place back home where you come from. A crime you were to be responsible for. A murder? But who was going to be killed? Why?"

"I've tried to explain what my country's like."

"I'm asking you straightforward questions, and I want straightforward answers."

"Maybe the answers have to be what they are."

"I don't understand you," said Wallander after a long silence. "You're a man who doesn't hesitate to kill, and you do it to order if I understand you rightly. At the same time you seem to me a sensitive person who's suffering as a result of circumstances in your country. I can't make it all add up."

"Nothing adds up for a black man living in South Africa."

Then Victor Mabasha went on to explain how things were in his battered and bruised homeland. Wallander had difficulty believing his ears. When Victor Mabasha finally finished, it seemed to Wallander that he had been on a long journey. His guide had shown him places he never knew existed.

I live in a country where we've been taught to believe that all truths are simple, he thought. And also that the truth is clear and unassailable. Our whole legal system is based on that principle. Now I'm starting to realize that the opposite is true. The truth is complicated, multi-faceted, contradictory. On the other hand, lies are black and white. If one's view of humans, of human life, is disrespectful and contemptuous, then truth takes on another aspect than if life is regarded as inviolable.

He contemplated Victor Mabasha, who was looking him straight in the eye.

"Did you kill Louise Åkerblom?" asked Wallander, getting the impression that this was the last time he would ask.

"No," replied Victor Mabasha. "Afterward, I lost one of my fingers for the sake of her soul."

"You still don't want to tell me what you're supposed to do when you get back?"

Before Victor Mabasha replied Wallander felt that something had changed. Something in the black man's face was different. Thinking about it later, he thought maybe it was that the expressionless mask suddenly started to melt away.

"I still can't say what," said Victor Mabasha. "But it won't happen."

"I don't think I understand," said Wallander slowly.

"Death will not come from my hands," said Victor Mabasha. "But I can't stop it coming from somebody else's."

"An assassination?"

"That it was my job to carry out. But now I'm washing my hands of it. I'm going to drop it and walk away."

"You're talking in riddles," said Wallander. "What are you going to drop? I want to know who was going to be assassinated."

But Victor Mabasha did not answer. He shook his head, and Wallander accepted, albeit reluctantly, that he would not get any further. Afterward he would also realize he still had a long way to go before he could recognize the truth in circumstances outside his normal range of experience. To put it briefly, it was only later that it dawned on him that the last admission, when Victor Mabasha allowed his mask to drop, was false through and through. He did not have the slightest intention of walking away from his assignment. But he realized the lie was necessary if he were to receive the help he needed to get out of the country. To be believed, he was forced to lie—and to do so skillfully enough to deceive the Swedish cop.

Wallander had no more questions for the moment.

He felt tired. But at the same time, he seemed to have achieved what he wanted to achieve. The assassination was foiled, at least as far as Victor Mabasha was concerned. Assuming he was telling the truth. That would give his unknown colleagues in South Africa more time to sort things out. And he was bound to think that whatever it was Victor Mabasha was not going to do must mean something positive as far as the blacks in South Africa were concerned.

That will do, thought Wallander. I'll contact the South African police via Interpol and tell them all I know. That's about all I can do. All that's left now is our friend Konovalenko. If I try to get Per

Åkeson to have Victor Mabasha arrested, there's a big risk that everything could become even more confused. Besides, the chances of Konovalenko fleeing the country would only increase. I don't need to know any more. Now I can carry out my last illegal action as far as Victor Mabasha is concerned.

Help him to get out of here.

His daughter had been present for the latter part of the conversation. She had woken up, and come out into the kitchen in surprise. Wallander explained briefly who the man was.

"The guy who hit you?" she asked.

"The very same."

"And now he's here drinking coffee with you?"

"Yes."

"Even you must think that's a little strange."

"A cop's life is a little strange."

She asked no more questions. When she was dressed, she returned and sat quietly on a chair, listening. Afterward Wallander sent her to the pharmacy to buy a bandage for the man's hand. He also found some penicillin in the bathroom and gave some to Victor Mabasha, well aware that he really ought to have called a doctor. Then he reluctantly cleaned up the wound around the severed finger, and applied a clean bandage.

Next he called Lovén and got him almost right away. He asked about the latest news on Konovalenko and the others who had disappeared from the apartment block in Hallunda. He said nothing to Lovén about the fact that Victor Mabasha was with him in his kitchen.

"We know where they went from their apartment when we made the raid," said Lovén. "They just moved up two floors in the same building. Cunning, and convenient, too. They had a second apartment there, in her name. But they're gone now."

"Then we know something else as well," said Wallander. "They're still in this country. Presumably in Stockholm, where it's easiest to lose yourself."

"If need be I'll personally kick down the front door of every apartment in this town," said Lovén. "We have to get them now. And quick."

"Concentrate on Konovalenko," said Wallander. "I think the African is less important."

"If only I could understand the connection between them," said Lovén.

"They were in the same place when Louise Åkerblom was murdered," said Wallander. "Then Konovalenko did a bank job and shot a cop. The African wasn't there then."

"But what does that mean?" asked Lovén. "I can't see any real connection, just a vague link that doesn't make sense."

"We know quite a bit even so," said Wallander. "Konovalenko seems to be obsessed with wanting to kill that African. The most likely explanation is they started out friends but had a falling out."

"But where does your real estate agent fit into all this?"

"She doesn't. I guess we can say she was killed by accident. Like you just said, Konovalenko is ruthless."

"All that boils down to one single question," said Lovén. "Why?"

"The only person who can answer that is Konovalenko," said Wallander.

"Or the African," said Lovén. "You're forgetting him, Kurt."

After the telephone call to Lovén, Wallander finally made up his mind to get Victor Mabasha out of the country. But before he could do anything he must be quite certain the African wasn't the one who had shot Louise Åkerblom after all.

How am I going to establish that, he wondered. I've never come across anybody with a face so expressionless. With him I can't decide where truth stops and lies start.

"The best thing you can do is to stay here in the apartment," he told Victor Mabasha. "I still have a lot of questions I want answered. You might just as well get used to that."

Apart from the car trip on Sunday, they spent the whole weekend in the apartment. Victor Mabasha was exhausted, and slept most of the time. Wallander was worried that his hand would turn septic. At the same time he regretted ever having let him into his apartment. Like so often before, he had followed his intuition rather than his reason. Now he could see no obvious way out of his dilemma.

On Sunday evening he drove Linda out to see his father. He dropped her on the main road so he would not have to put up with his father's complaints about not even having time for a cup of coffee.

Monday finally came, and he returned to the police station. Björk welcomed him back. Then they got together with Martinson and Svedberg in the conference room. Wallander reported selectively on what had happened in Stockholm. There were lots of questions. But the bottom line was that nobody had much to say. The key to the whole business was in Konovalenko's hands.

"In other words, we just have to wait until we pick him up," was Björk's conclusion. "That'll give us some time to sort out the stacks of other matters waiting for our attention."

They sorted out what needed needed dealing with most urgently. Wallander was assigned to find out what happened to three trotting horses that had been rustled from stables near Skårby. To the astonishment of his colleagues, he burst out laughing.

"It's a bit absurd," he said, apologetically. "A missing woman. And now missing horses."

He hardly got back to his office before he received the visit he was expecting. He was not sure which of them would actually turn up to ask the question. It could be any one of his colleagues. But it was in fact Martinson who knocked and entered.

"Have you got a minute?" he asked.

Wallander nodded.

"There's something I need to ask you," Martinson went on.

Wallander could see he was embarrassed.

"I'm listening," said Wallander.

"You were seen with an African yesterday," said Martinson. "In your car. I just thought . . ."

"You thought what?"

"I don't really know."

"Linda is back together with her Kenyan again."

"I thought that would be it."

"You said a moment ago you didn't really know what you thought."

Martinson threw out his arms and made a face. Then he retreated in a hurry.

Wallander ignored the case of the missing horses, shut the door

Martinson had left open, and sat down to think. Just what were the questions he wanted to ask Victor Mabasha? And how would he be able to check his answers?

In recent years Wallander had often encountered foreign citizens in connection with various investigations, and had spoken to them both as victims and possible perpetrators. It often occurred to him that what he used to regard as absolute truth when it came to right and wrong, guilt and innocence, might not necessarily apply any more. Nor had he realized that what was regarded as a crime, serious or petty, might vary according to the culture one grew up in. He often felt helpless in such situations. He felt he simply did not have the grounds for asking questions that could lead to a crime being solved or a suspect released. The very year his former colleague and mentor, Rydberg, died, they had spent a lot of time discussing the enormous changes that were taking place in their country, and indeed the world at large. The police would be faced with quite different demands. Rydberg sipped his whiskey and prophesied that within the next ten years Swedish cops would be forced to cope with bigger changes than they had ever experienced before. This time, though, it would not be just fundamental organizational reforms, but it would affect police work on the ground.

"This is something I'm not going to have to face," Rydberg had said one evening as they sat on his cramped little balcony. "Death comes to us all. I sometimes feel sad that I won't be around to see what comes next. It's bound to be difficult. But stimulating. You'll be there, though. And you'll have to start thinking along completely different lines."

"I wonder if I'll manage to cope," was Wallander's reply. "I keep wondering more and more often whether there's life beyond the police station."

"If you're thinking of sailing to the West Indies, make sure you never come back," said Rydberg ironically. "People who go off somewhere and then come back again are seldom any better off for their adventure. They're fooling themselves. They haven't come to terms with the ancient truth that you can never run away from yourself."

"That's something I'll never do," said Wallander. "I don't have room for such big plans in my makeup. The most I can do is wonder whether there might be some other job I'd enjoy."

"You'll be a cop as long as you live," said Rydberg. "You're like me. Just acknowledge that."

Wallander banished all thought of Rydberg from his mind, took out a blank note pad, and reached for a pen.

Then he just sat there. Questions and answers, he thought. That's probably where I'm making the first mistake. Lots of people, not least those who come from continents a long way away from ours, have to be allowed to tell the story their own way in order to be able to formulate an answer. That's something I ought to have learned by now, considering the number of Africans, Arabs, and Latin Americans I've met in various contexts. They are often scared by the hurry we're always in, and they think it's really a sign of our contempt. Not having time for a person, not being able to sit in silence together with somebody, that's the same as rejecting them, as being scornful about them.

Tell their own story, he wrote at the top of the note pad.

He thought that might put him on the right path.

Tell their own story, that's all.

He slid the note pad on one side and put his feet up on his desk. Then he called home and was told that everything was quiet. He promised to be back in a couple of hours.

He absentmindedly read through the memo on the stolen horses. It told him nothing more than that three valuable animals had disappeared on the night of May 5. They had been put into their stalls for the night. The next morning, when one of the stable girls opened the doors at about half past five, the stalls were empty.

He glanced at his watch and decided to drive out to the stables. After speaking to three grooms and the owner's personal secretary, Wallander was inclined to believe the whole thing could very well be a sophisticated form of insurance fraud. He made a few notes and said he'd be coming back.

On the way home to Ystad he stopped by a café for a cup of coffee.

He wondered if they had race horses in South Africa.

Chapter Twenty-one

Sikosi Tsiki came to Sweden on the evening of Wednesday, May 13.

That very same evening he was told by Konovalenko he would be staying in the southern part of the country. This was where his preparatory training would take place, and he would also leave the country from there. When Konovalenko heard from Jan Kleyn that the replacement was on his way, he had considered the possibility of setting up camp in the Stockholm area. There were lots of possibilities, especially around Arlanda, where the noise of airplanes landing and taking off would drown most other sounds. The necessary shooting practice could take place there. Furthermore there was the problem of Victor Mabasha and the Swedish policeman he hated. If they were still in Stockholm, he would have to stay there until they had been liquidated. Nor could he ignore the probability that the general level of vigilance throughout the country would be higher, now that he had killed the cop. To be on the safe side he decided to proceed on two fronts at the same time. He kept Tania with him in Stockholm, but sent Rykoff to the southern part of the country again with orders to find a suitable house in a remote area. Rykoff had then pointed out on a map an area to the north of Skåne called Småland, claiming it was much easier to find remotely situated houses there. But Konovalenko wanted to be near Ystad. If they did not catch Victor Mabasha and the policeman in Stockholm, they would turn up sooner or later in Wallander's home town. He was as sure of that as he was that some kind of unexpected relationship had formed between the black man and Wallander. He had some difficulty in understanding what was going on. But nevertheless he was increasingly sure they would be not far away from each other. If he could find one of them, he would also find the other.

Through a travel agency in Ystad, Rykoff rented a house north east of Ystad, on the way to Tomelilla. The location could have been better, but adjacent to the site was an abandoned quarry that could be used for target practice. As Konovalenko had decreed that Tania could go with them if they did in fact decide to go ahead with this alternative, Rykoff did not need to fill the freezer with food. Instead and on Konovalenko's orders, he spent his time finding out where Wallander lived, and then keeping his apartment under observation. But Wallander did not show up. The day before Sikosi Tsiki was due to arrive, Tuesday, May 12, Konovalenko decided to stay in Stockholm. Although none of those he sent out looking for Victor Mabasha had seen him, Konovalenko had the distinct feeling he was lying low somewhere in town. He also found it difficult to believe that a cop as careful and well organized as Wallander would return too quickly to his home, which he must expect to be watched.

Nevertheless that is where Rykoff finally found him, shortly after five o'clock on Tuesday afternoon. The door opened and Wallander stepped out onto the street. He was on his own, and Rykoff, who was sitting in his car, could see right away he was on guard. He left the building on foot, and Rykoff realized he would be spotted at once if he tried to follow him in his car. He was still there ten minutes later when the front door opened once again. Rykoff stiffened. This time two people left the building. The young girl had to be Wallander's daughter, whom he had never seen before. Behind her was Victor Mabasha. They crossed the street, got into a car, and drove off. Rykoff did not bother following them this time either. Instead he stayed where he was and dialed the number of the apartment in Järfälla where Konovalenko was staying with Tania. She answered. Rykoff greeted her briefly and asked to speak to Konovalenko. After hearing what Rykoff had to say, Konovalenko made up his mind right away. He and Tania would go to Skåne early the next day. They would stay there until they had collected Sikosi Tsiki and killed Wallander and Victor Mabasha; the daughter as well, if necessary. Then they could make up their minds what to do next. But the flat in Järfälla would be a possibility.

Konovalenko drove down to Skåne with Tania overnight. Rykoff met them at a parking lot on the western edge of Ystad. They drove straight to the house he had rented. Later that afternoon Konovalenko also paid a visit to Mariagatan. He spent some time observing the block where Wallander lived. On the way back he also paused for a while on the hill outside the police station.

The situation seemed very simple to him. He could not afford to fail again. That would mean the end of his dreams about a future life in South Africa. He was already living dangerously, and knew it. He had not told Jan Kleyn the truth, not admitted that Victor Mabasha was still alive. There was a risk, albeit a small one, that Jan Kleyn had someone passing on information without Konovalenko knowing. He had occasionally sent out scouts to see if they could find anyone shadowing him. But nobody had come across any kind of surveillance that might have been organized by Jan Kleyn.

Konovalenko and Rykoff spent the day deciding how to proceed. Konovalenko made up his mind from the very first to act resolutely and ruthlessly. It would be a brutal, direct attack.

"What kind of weapons do we have?" he asked.

"Practically anything you like short of a rocket launcher," Rykoff had told him. "We have explosives, long-distance detonators, grenades, automatic rifles, shotguns, pistols, radio equipment."

Konovalenko drank a glass of vodka. He would really like most of all to capture Wallander alive. There were some questions he wanted answering before he killed him. But he banished the thought. He could not afford to take any risks.

Then he made up his mind what to do.

"Tomorrow morning when Wallander is out, Tania can enter the building and see what the staircase and apartment doors look like," he said. "You can pretend to be distributing advertising brochures. We can pick up some leaflets from a supermarket. Then the building has to be kept under constant observation. If we're certain they're at home tomorrow evening, we'll make our move then. We'll blow up the door and rush in with guns blazing. If nothing unexpected happens we'll kill the pair of them and make our escape."

"There are three of them," observed Rykoff.

"Two or three," said Konovalenko. "We can't let anybody survive."

"This new African I'm going to pick up this evening, will he be in on it?" wondered Rykoff.

"No," said Konovalenko. "He waits here with Tania."

His expression was serious as he eyed Rykoff and Tania.

"The fact is, Victor Mabasha has been dead for several days," he said. "At least, that's what Sikosi Tsiki has to believe. Is that clear?"

They both nodded.

Konovalenko poured himself and Tania another glass of vodka. Rykoff refused, since he was going to prepare the explosives and did not want to be affected by the alcohol. Besides, he was going to drive to Limhamn later to collect Sikosi Tsiki.

"Let's put on a welcoming dinner for the man from South Africa," said Konovalenko. "None of us enjoys sitting at dinner with an African. But sometimes you have to do it for the sake of the job in hand."

"Victor Mabasha didn't like Russian food," said Tania.

Konovalenko thought for a moment.

"Chicken," he said eventually. "All Africans like chicken."

At six o'clock Rykoff met Sikosi Tsiki at Limhamn. A few hours later they were all sitting around the table. Konovalenko raised his glass.

"You have a day off tomorrow," he said. "We get started on Friday."

Sikosi Tsiki nodded. The replacement was just as silent as his predecessor.

Quiet guys, thought Konovalenko. Ruthless when the chips are down. Just as ruthless as I am.

Wallander devoted most of the first few days after his return to Ystad to planning various forms of criminal activities. He paved the way for Victor Mabasha's escape from Sweden with dogged persistence. After much soul-searching he had decided it was the only way to get the situation under control. He had severe pangs of guilt, and could not avoid being constantly reminded that what he was doing was downright reprehensible. Even if Victor Mabasha had not killed Louise Åkerblom himself, he was present when the murder was committed. Moreover, he had stolen cars and robbed a store. As if that were not enough, he was an illegal immigrant in Sweden, and had been planning to commit a serious crime back home in South Africa. Wallander convinced himself that in spite of everything, this was a way of preventing the crime. In addition, Konovalenko could be prevented from killing Victor Mabasha. He would be punished for the murder of Louise Åkerblom once he was caught. What he intended to do now was to send a message to his colleagues in South Africa via Interpol. But first he wanted to get Victor Mabasha out of the country. So as not to attract unnecessary attention, he contacted a travel agency in Malmö to find out how Victor Mabasha could get a flight to Lusaka in Zambia. Mabasha had told him he could not get into South Africa without a visa. But with a fake Swedish passport, he did not need a visa to enter Zambia. He still had enough money for both an airline ticket and the next stage of the journey from Zambia, via Zimbabwe and Botswana. Once he got to South Africa he would slip over the border at an unguarded point. The travel agent in Malmö explained the various choices. They decided in the end that Victor Mabasha would go to London and then take a Zambia Airways flight from there to Lusaka. It meant Wallander would have to get him a false passport. That caused him not only the severest practical problems, but also the worst pangs of conscience. Arranging a false passport at his own police station seemed to him a betrayal of his profession. It did not make things any better to know he had made Victor Mabasha promise to destroy the passport as soon as he had gone through the checks in Zambia.

"The very same day," Wallander had insisted. "And it must be burned."

Wallander bought a cheap camera and took passport photographs. The big problem that could not be resolved until the last minute was how Victor Mabasha would get through Swedish passport control. Even if he had a Swedish passport that was technically genuine and did not appear on the blacklist held by the border police, there was a big risk that something could go wrong. After a lot of thought Wallander decided to get Victor Mabasha out via the hovercraft terminal in Malmö. He would buy him a first-class ticket. He assumed the embarkation card might help to ensure that passport officials were not especially interested in him. Linda would play the role of his girlfriend. They would kiss goodbye right under the.

noses of the immigration officials, and Wallander would teach him a few phrases of perfect Swedish.

The connections and the confirmed tickets meant he would be leaving Sweden on the morning of May 15. Wallander would have to produce a false passport for him by then.

On Tuesday afternoon he completed a passport application form for his father, and took with him two photographs. The whole procedures for issuing passports had recently been revised. The document was now produced while the applicant waited. Wallander hung around until the woman dealing with passports had finished with the last of her customers and was about to close.

"Excuse me for being a little late," said Wallander. "But my dad is going on a senior citizens trip to France. He managed to burn his passport when he was sorting some old papers."

"These things happen," said the woman, whose name was Irma. "Does he have to have it today?"

"If possible," said Wallander. "Sorry I'm late."

"You can't solve the murder of that woman either," she said, taking the photos and the application form.

Wallander watched closely as she created the passport. Afterwards, when he had the document in his hand, he was confident he could repeat exactly what she had done.

"Impressively simple," he said.

"But boring," said Irma. "Why is it that all jobs get more boring when they're made easier?"

"Become a cop," said Wallander. "What we do is never boring."

"I am a cop," she said. "Besides, I don't think I'd want to change places with you. It must be awful, pulling a body out of a well. What does it feel like, in fact?"

"I don't really know," said Wallander. "I suppose it feels so awful you get numb and so you don't feel anything at all. But you can bet your boots there'll be some committee in the Ministry of Justice looking into what policemen feel when they pull dead women out of wells."

He stayed chatting while she locked up. All the things you needed to make a passport were locked away in a cupboard. But he knew where the keys were kept.

They had decided Victor Mabasha would leave the country as the Swedish citizen Jan Berg. Wallander had tried out endless combinations of names to find out which ones Victor Mabasha found easiest to pronounce. They went for Jan Berg. Victor Mabasha asked what the name meant. He was satisfied with the translation he was given. Wallander had realized during their conversations these last few days that the man from South Africa lived in close contact with a spirit world that was completely alien to him. Nothing was coincidental, not even a chance change of name. Linda had been able to help him with some explanations of why Victor Mabasha thought as he did. Even so, he thought he was looking at a world he had absolutely no basis for understanding. Victor Mabasha talked about his ancestors as if they were alive. Wallander was sometimes unsure whether incidents had taken place a hundred years ago, or yesterday. He could not help but be fascinated by Victor Mabasha. It became more and more difficult to comprehend that this man was a criminal preparing to commit a serious crime in his home country.

Wallander stayed in his office until late that Tuesday evening. To help the time pass he began a letter to Baiba Liepa in Riga. But when he read through what he had written, he tore it up. One of these days he would write a letter and send it to her. But it would take some time, he realized that.

By about ten o'clock only those on night duty were still at the station. As he did not dare to switch the light on in the room where the passports were assembled, he had acquired a flashlight that produced a blue light. He walked along the corridor, wishing he was on his way to someplace quite different. He thought of Victor Mabasha's spirit world, and wondered briefly if Swedish cops had a special patron saint who would watch over them when they were about to do something forbidden.

The key was hanging on its hook in the filing cabinet. He paused for a moment, staring at the machine that transformed the photographs and the application forms with all their completed answers and crosses into a passport.

Then he put on his rubber gloves and started work. At one point he thought he heard footsteps approaching. He ducked down behind the machine and turned off his flashlight. When the footsteps died away, he started once again. He could feel sweat streaming down under his shirt. In the end, though, he had a passport in his hand. He switched off the machine, returned the key to its rightful place in the cabinet, and locked the door. Sooner or later some check would show that a passport template had disappeared. Bearing the registration numbers in mind, it could even happen the very next day, he thought. That would cause Björk some sleepless nights. But nothing could be traced to Wallander.

Not until he was back in his office and slumped down behind his desk did it occur to him that he had forgotten to stamp the passport. He cursed himself, and flung the document down on the desk in front of him.

Just then the door burst open and Martinson marched in. He gave a start when he saw Wallander in his chair.

"Oh, excuse me," he said. "I didn't think you were here. I was just going to see if I could find my cap."

"Cap?" asked Wallander. "In the middle of May?"

"I can feel a cold coming on," said Martinson. "I had it with me when we were sitting here yesterday."

Wallander could not remember Martinson having a cap with him the previous day when he and Svedberg had been in Wallander's office to go through the latest developments in the investigation and the hitherto fruitless search for Konovalenko.

"Look on the floor under the chair," said Wallander.

When Martinson bent down Wallander hastily stuffed the passport into his pocket.

"Nothing," said Martinson. "I'm always losing my caps."

"Ask the cleaner," Wallander suggested.

Martinson was about to leave when something struck him.

"Do you remember Peter Hanson?" he asked.

"How could I ever forget him?" wondered Wallander.

"Svedberg called him a few days ago and asked about a few details in the interrogation report. Then he told Peter Hanson about the break-in at your apartment. Thieves generally know what each other is up to. Svedberg thought it might be worth a try. Peter Hanson called in today and said maybe he knew who did it."

"Well, I'll be damned!" said Wallander. "If he can arrange for me to get back my records and tapes, I'll forget about the hi-fi."

"Have a word with Svedberg tomorrow," said Martinson. "And don't stay here all night."

"I was just about to leave," said Wallander, getting to his feet.

Martinson paused in the doorway.

"Do you think we'll get him?" he asked.

"Sure," said Wallander. "Of course we'll get him. Konovalenko isn't going to get away."

"I wonder if he's still in the country," said Martinson.

"We have to assume that," said Wallander.

"What about the African who's missing a finger?"

"No doubt Konovalenko can explain that."

Martinson nodded doubtfully.

"One other thing," he added. "It's Louise Åkerblom's funeral tomorrow."

Wallander looked at him. But he said nothing.

The funeral was at two o'clock on Wednesday afternoon. Wallander wondered whether or not he should go right to the last minute. He had no personal connections with the Åkerblom family. The woman they were burying had been dead when he first came into contact with her. On the other hand, might it be misunderstood if somebody from the police was there? Not least in view of the fact that the killer had not yet been nailed. Wallander had trouble figuring out why he was thinking of going. Was it curiosity? Or a guilty conscience? All the same, at one o'clock he changed into a dark suit and spent some time looking for his white necktie. Victor Mabasha sat watching him tying the knot in front of the hall mirror.

"I'm going to a funeral," said Wallander. "The woman Konovalenko killed."

Victor Mabasha stared at him in astonishment.

"Only now?" he asked in surprise. "Back home we bury our dead as soon as possible. So they don't walk."

"We don't believe in ghosts," said Wallander.

"Spirits aren't ghosts," said Victor Mabasha. "I sometimes wonder how it's possible for white folk to understand so little."

"Maybe you're right," said Wallander. "Or maybe you're wrong. It could be the other way around."

Then he went out. He noticed that Victor Mabasha's question had annoyed him.

Does that black bastard think he can come here and tell me what to think? he thought irreverently. Where would he be without me and the help I've given him?

He parked his car some way from the chapel at the crematorium and waited while the bells were ringing and the black-clad congregation entered. Only when a janitor started closing the doors did he go in himself and sit in the back. A man a couple of rows in front of him turned round and greeted him. He was a journalist from the *Ystad Chronicle*.

Then he listened to the organ music and felt a lump in his throat. Funerals were a great strain as far as he was concerned. He dreaded the day he would have to follow his father to the grave. His mother's funeral eleven years ago could still conjure up unpleasant memories. He was supposed to make a short speech over the bier, but had broken down and rushed out of the church.

He tried to control his emotions by contemplating the rest of the congregation. Robert Åkerblom was on the front row with his two daughters, both wearing white dresses. Next to them was Pastor Tureson, who would be in charge of the burial.

He suddenly started thinking about the handcuffs he found in a desk drawer at the Åkerbloms' house. It was over a week since he last thought about them.

He thought how policemen have a sort of curiosity that goes beyond the immediate investigative work. Maybe it's a kind of occupational hazard brought on by having to spend so many years delving into the most private parts of peoples' lives. I know those handcuffs can be excluded from the murder investigation. They have no significance. All the same I'm ready to spend time and effort trying to figure out why they were in that drawer. Trying to figure out what they meant to Louise Åkerblom, and maybe also her husband.

He shuddered at the unpleasant implications of his train of thought, and concentrated on the funeral service. At one point during Pastor Tureson's homily he caught the eye of Robert Åkerblom. Despite the distance he could sense the depths of sorrow and forlornness. The lump came back into his throat, and tears started to flow. In order to regain control of his emotions he started thinking about Konovalenko. Like most of the other cops in Sweden, no doubt, Wallander was secretly pro death penalty. Quite apart from the scandal that it had been enforced against traitors during the war, it was not that he saw it as a knee-jerk reaction to a certain kind of crime. It was rather that certain murders, certain assaults, certain drug offenses were so appallingly immoral, so crass in their disregard of human dignity, that he could not help feeling the perpetrators had forfeited all right to life themselves. He could see that his thinking was riddled with contradictions, and that laws to introduce it would be impossible and unjust. It was just his raw experience speaking, unrefined yet painful. What he was forced to come up against because he was a cop. Things that caused reactions, irrational and excruciating.

After the interment he shook hands solemnly with Robert Åkerblom and the other principal mourners. He avoided looking at the two daughters, afraid of bursting into tears.

Pastor Tureson took him to one side outside the chapel.

"Your presence was very much appreciated," he told Wallander. "Nobody had expected the police to send a representative to the funeral."

"I'm representing nobody but myself," said Wallander.

"So much the better that you came," said Pastor Tureson. "Are you still looking for the man behind the tragedy?"

Wallander nodded.

"But you will catch him?"

Wallander nodded again.

"Yes," he said. "Sooner or later. How's Robert Åkerblom taking it? And the daughters?"

"The support they're getting from the church is all-important to them just now," said Pastor Tureson. "And then, he has his God."

"You mean he still believes?" wondered Wallander quietly.

Pastor Tureson frowned.

"Why should he abandon his God for something human beings have done to him and his family?"

"No," said Wallander quietly. "Why should he do that?"

"There'll be a meeting at the church in an hour," said Pastor Tureson. "You're welcome to come."

"Thanks," said Wallander. "But I've got to get back to work."

They shook hands and Wallander returned to his car. It suddenly dawned on him that spring had really arrived.

Just wait till Victor Mabasha has left, he thought. Just wait till we've caught Konovalenko. Then I can devote myself to spring.

On Thursday morning Wallander drove his daughter out to his father's house in Löderup. When they got there, she suddenly decided to stay overnight. She took one look at the overgrown yard and announced her intention to tidy it up before returning to Ystad. That would take her at least two days.

"If you change your mind, just give me a call," said Wallander.

"You should thank me for cleaning up your apartment," she said. "It looked awful."

"I know," he said. "Thanks."

"How much longer do I have to stay?" she asked. "I've got lots to do in Stockholm, you know."

"Not much longer," said Wallander, aware that he did not sound very convincing. But to his surprise, she seemed satisfied with his reply.

Afterwards he had a long talk with the prosecutor, Åkeson. When he got back, Wallander gathered together all the investigation material with the help of Martinson and Svedberg.

At about four in the afternoon he went shopping and bought some food before driving home. Outside the apartment door was an unusually big stack of leaflets from some store or other. Without looking to see what they were, he shoved them into the garbage sack. Then he made dinner and went through all the practical details of the journey with Victor Mabasha one more time. The lines he had memorized sounded better every time he pronounced them.

After dinner they went through the finer points. Victor Mabasha would have an overcoat over his left arm to hide the bandage he still had on his injured hand. He practiced taking his passport from his inside pocket while keeping the coat over his left arm. Wallander was satisfied. Nobody would be able to see the injury.

"You'll be flying to London with a British airline," he said. "SAS would be too risky. Swedish air hostesses will probably read the newspapers and see the TV news. They'd notice your hand and sound the alarm."

Later that evening, when there were no more practical details to discuss, silence fell and neither seemed inclined to break it for a long time. In the end Victor Mabasha got up and stood in front of Wallander.

"Why have you been helping me?" he asked.

"I don't know," answered Wallander. "I often think I ought to slip the handcuffs on you. I can see I'm taking a big risk in letting you go. Maybe it was you who killed Louise Åkerblom after all? You say yourself how good a liar everybody becomes back home in your country. Maybe I'm letting a murderer go?"

"But you're doing it even so?"

"I'm doing it even so."

Victor Mabasha took off his necklace and handed it to Wallander. He could see that it featured the tooth of a wild animal.

"The leopard is the solitary hunter," said Victor Mabasha. "Unlike the lion, the leopard goes its own way and only crosses its own tracks. During the day when the heat is at its height, it rests in the trees alongside the eagles. At night it hunts alone. The leopard is a skillful hunter. But the leopard is also the biggest challenge for other hunters. This is a canine tooth from a leopard. I want you to have it."

"I'm not sure I understood what you mean," said Wallander, "but I'll be glad to have the tooth."

"Not everything is understandable," said Victor Mabasha. "A story is a journey without an end."

"That's probably the difference between you and me," said Wallander. "I'm used to stories having an end, and expect one. You say a good story doesn't have one."

"That may be so," said Victor Mabasha. "It can be a good thing to know you'll never meet a certain person again. That means that something will live on."

"Perhaps," said Wallander. "But I doubt it. I wonder if that's the way things really are."

Victor Mabasha did not answer.

An hour later he was asleep under a blanket on the sofa, while Wallander sat looking at the tooth he had been given.

Suddenly he felt uneasy. He went out into the dark kitchen and looked down at the street. All was quiet. Then he went out into the hall and checked that the door was securely locked. He sat down on a stool by the telephone, and thought maybe he was just tired. Another twelve hours and Victor Mabasha would be gone.

He examined the tooth once more.

Nobody would believe me, he thought. If for no other reason, I'd better keep quiet about the days and nights I spent with a black man who once had a finger cut off in a remote house in Skåne.

That's a secret I'd better take to the grave.

When Jan Kleyn and Franz Malan met at Hammanskraal in the morning of Friday, May 15, it did not take them long to establish that neither of them had found any significant weaknesses in the plan.

The assassination would take place in Cape Town on June 12. Nelson Mandela would be speaking in the stadium, and from the summit of Signal Hill Sikosi Tsiki would have an ideal position for his long-range rifle. Then he could disappear unnoticed.

But there were two things Jan Kleyn had not mentioned to Franz Malan, nor to the other committee members. In fact, they were matters he had no intention of mentioning to anybody at all. In order to ensure the continued dominance of white rule in South Africa, he was prepared to take certain selected secrets with him to the grave. Certain events and connections would never be revealed in the history of the country.

The first thing was that he was not prepared to take the risk of allowing Sikosi Tsiki to live with the knowledge of whom he had killed. He did not doubt for a moment that Sikosi Tsiki could keep his mouth shut. But just as the pharaohs of ancient times killed off those who had built the secret chambers in the pyramids, to ensure that any knowledge of their existence would be lost, he would sacrifice Sikosi Tsiki. He would kill him himself, and make sure the body would never be found.

The other secret Jan Kleyn would keep to himself was the fact that Victor Mabasha had been alive as recently as the previous afternoon. Now he was dead, no doubt about that. But it was a personal defeat for Jan Kleyn that Victor Mabasha had managed to survive as long as he had. He felt personally responsible for Konovalenko's errors and repeated inability to bring the Victor Mabasha chapter to a close. The KGB man had displayed unexpected weaknesses. His attempt to cover up his shortcomings by lying was the biggest weakness of all. Jan Kleyn always regarded it as a personal slight when anybody doubted his ability to keep abreast of the information he needed. Once the assassination of Mandela was accomplished, he would decide whether or not he was ready to receive Konovalenko into South Africa. He did not doubt the man's ability to take care of the necessary preliminary training of Sikosi Tsiki. On the other hand, he thought it could well be that the downfall of the Soviet empire had been ultimately due to the same kind of unreliable skills that Konovalenko had. He did not exclude the possibility that even Konovalenko might have to go up in smoke, together with his henchmen Vladimir and Tania. The whole operation needed a thorough spring cleaning. He had no intention of delegating that job to anyone else.

They were sitting at the table with the green felt cloth, going over the plan one more time. The previous week Franz Malan had been to Cape Town to examine the stadium where Nelson Mandela was due to speak. He also spent an afternoon at the spot where Sikosi Tsiki was to fire his rifle. He made a videotape, which they watched three times on the television set in the room. The only thing still missing was a report on Cape Town's usual wind conditions. Pretending to represent a yacht club, Franz Malan had been in touch with the national weather center, which had promised to send him the information he had asked for. The name and address he gave would never be traced.

Jan Kleyn had not done any legwork. His contribution was of a different kind. His specialty was a theoretical dissection of the plan. He had considered unexpected developments, tried out a one-man role-play, and kept at it until he was convinced no undesirable problems could crop up.

After two hours their work was completed.

"There's just one more thing," said Jan Kleyn. "We have to establish before June 12 exactly how the Cape Town police will be deployed."

"I can take care of that," said Franz Malan. "We can send out a flyer to all the police districts in the country requesting copies of their security plans, to give us time to prepare all the political measures that need to be taken when big crowds are expected."

They went out onto the veranda, waiting for the rest of the committee to arrive. They contemplated the view in silence. On the far horizon was a heavy blanket of smoke over a black shanty town.

"There'll be a bloodbath," said Franz Malan. "I still have trouble envisioning what will happen."

"Regard it as a purification process," said Jan Kleyn. "Those words sound rather better than bloodbath. Besides, that's what we are hoping to achieve."

"Nevertheless," said Franz Malan. "I sometimes feel uneasy. Will we be able to control what happens?"

"The answer to that is simple," said Jan Kleyn. "We have to."

That fatalism again, thought Franz Malan. He glanced surreptitiously at the man standing a few meters away from him. Was Jan Kleyn crazy? A psychopath hiding the violent truth about himself behind a public mask that was always under control?

He did not like the thought. All he could do was suppress it.

The whole committee gathered at two o'clock. Franz Malan and Jan Kleyn showed the videotape and presented their summary. There were not many questions, and objections were easily fended off. The whole thing lasted less than an hour. They took a vote shortly before three. The decision was made.

Twenty-eight days later Nelson Mandela would be killed while speaking at a stadium near Cape Town.

The members of the committee left Hammanskraal at intervals of a few minutes. Jan Kleyn was the last to leave.

The countdown had started.

Chapter Twenty-two

T he attack came just after midnight.
Victor Mabasha was asleep on the sofa, wrapped in a blanket. Wallander was standing by the kitchen window, trying to decide whether he was hungry or should just have a cup of tea. At the same time he was wondering whether his father and daughter were still up. He assumed so. They always had a surprising number of things to talk about.

As he was waiting for the water to boil it occurred to him it was three weeks since they had started looking for Louise Åkerblom. Now, three weeks later, they knew she had been killed by a guy called Konovalenko. The same guy who had most probably killed the cop Tengblad as well.

In a few more hours, when Victor Mabasha was out of the country, he would be able to tell people what had happened. But he would do so anonymously, even though he realized hardly anybody would believe the unsigned letter he intended to send to the police. In the end everything depended on what they could make Konovalenko confess to. And it was doubtful whether even he would be believed either.

Wallander poured the boiling water into the pot and left it to brew. Then he pulled out one of the kitchen chairs and sat down.

As he did so the apartment door and hall blew up. Wallander was thrown backwards by the blast, and hit his head against the refrigerator. The kitchen started to fill up rapidly with smoke, and he groped his way to the bedroom door. Just as he got to his bed and was fumbling for his pistol on the bedside table he heard four shots in rapid succession behind him. He flung himself flat on the floor. The shots came from the living room.

Konovalenko, he thought frantically. Now he's coming for me.

He wriggled under the bed as fast as he could. He was so scared, he wasn't sure his heart could cope with the strain. Looking back later on, he would recall being struck by how degrading it would be, having to die under one's own bed.

He heard some thuds and breathless groans from the living room. Somebody came into the bedroom, stood motionless for a moment, then went out again. Wallander heard Victor Mabasha shouting something. So he was still alive. Then came footsteps fading away into the stairway. At the same time somebody started yelling, though he could not tell if it came from the street or from one of the neighboring apartments.

He crept out from under the bed and hoisted himself up carefully so he could see the street through the window. The smoke was choking, and he had difficulty in making anything out. But then he saw two men dragging Victor Mabasha between them. One of them was Rykoff. Without thinking Wallander flung open the bedroom window and fired straight up into the air. Rykoff let go of Victor Mabasha and turned around. Wallander just managed to hit the floor before a salvo from an automatic weapon shattered the window pane. Splinters showered down over his face. He heard people shrieking and a car starting. He just had time to see it was a black Audi before it disappeared down the street. Wallander rushed downstairs and onto the sidewalk, where half-dressed people were starting to gather. When they saw Wallander with a pistol in his hand, they jumped aside screaming. Wallander opened the door of his car with fumbling fingers, cursed as he stabbed at the ignition lock with his key before getting it right, then set off after the Audi. He could hear the sound of sirens approaching from a distance. He decided to head for the Österleden highway and got lucky. The Audi came skidding around the corner from Regementsgatan and took off bearing east. Wallander thought they might not realize it was him in the car. The only reason the man in the bedroom had not looked under the bed must have been the fact that it was still made, indicating Wallander was not at home.

Wallander did not normally bother to make his bed in the morning, but that day his daughter, upset by all the mess, had cleaned up the apartment and changed his bed linen.

They left the town at high speed. Wallander kept his distance, and felt like he was in the middle of a nightmare. No doubt he was breaking all the rules for how to arrest dangerous criminals. He started to brake, intending to stop and turn back. Then he changed his mind and kept going. They had already passed Sandskogen, with the golf course on the left, and Wallander began to wonder if the Audi would take a left towards Sandhammaren or keep going straight on towards Simrishamn and Kristianstad.

He suddenly noticed the back lights on the car in front shuddering, and getting closer. The Audi must have a flat. He watched the car slide into a ditch and come to rest on its side. Wallander hit the brakes outside the driveway to a house by the roadside, and turned in. When he got out of the car he saw a man standing in the doorway with a light on.

Wallander had his pistol in his hand. When he started talking he made an effort to sound friendly and firm at the same time.

"My name's Wallander and I'm a cop," he said, noticing how breathless he was. "Call the police and tell them I'm chasing a guy called Konovalenko. Explain where you live and tell them to start searching the military training ground. Is that clear?"

The man nodded. He seemed to be in his thirties.

"I recognize you," he said. "I've seen you in the papers."

"Call right away," said Wallander. "You do have a telephone?"

"Sure I have a phone," said the man. "Don't you need a better weapon than that pistol?"

"Of course I do," said Wallander. "But I don't have time to change right now."

Then he ran out onto the road.

He could see the Audi some way ahead. He tried to stick to the shadows as he approached cautiously. He was still wondering how long his heart would cope with the strain. All the same, he was glad he hadn't died under his bed. Now it seemed as if his fear was driving him on. He paused behind a road sign and listened. There was nobody left in the car. Then he noticed that a section of the fence around the military training ground had been destroyed. Fog was drifting in rapidly from the sea and settling densely over the artillery range. He could see a group of sheep lying motionless on the ground. Then he suddenly heard a bleat from a sheep he could not see through the fog, and another answering restlessly.

There, he thought. The sheep can guide me. He crouched down

and ran toward the hole in the fence, then lay down staring into the fog. He could see and hear nothing. A car approached from the direction of Ystad and slowed to a halt. A man got out. Wallander saw it was the man who had promised to call the police. He had a shotgun in his hand. Wallander crept back through the fence.

"Stay here," he said. "Back the car up about a hundred meters. Stay there and wait till the police arrive. Show them this hole in the fence. Say there are at least two guys with weapons out there. One of them has some kind of automatic. Can you remember all that?"

The man nodded.

"I brought this shotgun," he said.

Wallander hesitated a moment.

"Show me how it works," he said. "I know next to nothing about shotguns."

The guy looked at him in surprise. Then he showed him the safety catch and how to load. Wallander could see it was a pump-action model. He grabbed it and stuffed a handful of spare cartridges in his pocket.

The guy went back to his car and Wallander crawled through the fence again. A sheep bleated once more. The sound came from the right, somewhere between a clump of trees and the slope down to the sea. Wallander tucked his pistol into his belt and started to edge his way toward where the sheep were bleating restlessly.

The fog was very thick by now.

Martinson was woken up by the telephone call from emergency headquarters. They told him about the shooting and fire on Mariagatan, and also the message Wallander had given the guy on the outskirts of Ystad. He was wide awake immediately, and started getting dressed as he dialed Björk's number. It seemed to Martinson it took forever for the message to penetrate Björk's sleepy brain, but half an hour later the largest squad the Ystad police could possibly muster at such short notice was assembled outside the police station. Reinforcements were also on their way from surrounding districts. In addition, Björk had found time to call and wake up the police commissioner, who had asked to be informed as soon as the arrest of Konovalenko was imminent.

Martinson and Svedberg regarded the crowd of cops with some

displeasure. They both felt that a smaller squad could be just as effective in a much shorter time. But Björk was going by the book. He did not dare risk exposing himself to criticism afterward.

"This'll be a disaster," said Svedberg. "We've got to take care of this ourselves, you and me. Björk will just mess things up. If Wallander is out there on his own and Konovalenko is as dangerous as we think he is, he needs us right now."

Martinson nodded and went over to Björk.

"While you are assembling the squad, Svedberg and I will go on ahead," he said.

"Out of the question," said Björk. "We have to follow the rules."

"You do that while Svedberg and I use our common sense," said Martinson angrily, and walked away. Björk yelled after him, but Svedberg and Martinson leapt into a squad car and drove off. They also signaled Norén and Peters that they should follow.

They drove out of Ystad at very high speed. They allowed the patrol car to overtake and then lead the way with flashing blue lights and siren. Martinson drove, with Svedberg by his side fumbling with his pistol.

"What have we got?" asked Martinson. "The training ground just before the turnoff to Kåseberga. Two armed men. One of them Konovalenko."

"We've got nothing," said Svedberg. "I can't say I'm looking forward to this."

"Explosion and shooting on Mariagatan," Martinson went on. "How does it all hang together?"

"Let's hope Björk can figure that out with the help of his rule book," said Svedberg.

Outside the police station in Ystad things were rapidly deteriorating into chaos. Telephone calls were pouring in from terrified people living on Mariagatan. The fire brigade was busy putting out the fire. Now it was up to the police to find out what lay behind the shooting. The fire chief, Peter Edler, announced that the street in front of the house was covered with blood.

Björk was under pressure from all sides, but finally made up his mind to let Mariagatan wait. His first priority was to catch Konovalenko and the other man, and to give Wallander some assistance.

"Is there anybody here who knows how big the training ground is?" asked Björk.

Nobody knew how long it was, but Björk was sure it stretched from the road right down to the beach. He could see they knew too little to think of doing anything but try and surround the whole area.

More cars kept arriving from surrounding districts. Because they were after someone who had killed a cop, even off-duty men were turning up.

After consulting an officer from Malmö, Björk decided they would make final plans for surrounding the place once they got there. A car had also been sent to the army barracks to pick up some reliable maps.

The long caravan of cars left Ystad shortly before one in the morning. A few private cars that happened to be passing by joined in out of curiosity. The fog was now drifting down over central Ystad.

At the training ground they met the man who had spoken first with Wallander, and then with Martinson and Svedberg.

"Has anything happened?" asked Björk.

"Nothing at all," said the man.

Just then a single shot rang out somewhere in the middle of the training ground. It was followed shortly afterwards by a long salvo. Then all was silent again.

"Where are Martinson and Svedberg?" asked Björk in a voice betraying his fear.

"They ran into the training ground," answered the man.

"And Wallander?"

"I haven't seen him since he went off into the fog."

The searchlights on the squad car roofs were lighting up the fog and the sheep.

"We must let them know we're here," said Björk. "We'll surround the place as best as we can."

A few minutes later his voice rang out over the whole training ground. The loudspeaker echoed spookily. Then they spread themselves around the perimeter, and started the wait.

Once Wallander had crawled into the training ground, he had been completely swallowed up by the fog. Things happened very fast. He walked toward the bleating sheep. He was moving quickly, crouching down, as he had the distinct impression he was in danger of arriving too late. Several times he tripped over sheep lying on the ground, and they ran off bleating. He realized the sheep he was using to guide him were also betraying the fact that he was on his way.

Then he came upon them.

They were at the far side of the artillery range, where it started sloping down to the sea. It was like a still photograph from a film. Victor Mabasha had been forced down on his knees. Konovalenko was standing in front of him, pistol in hand, and Rykoff a few paces to the side, looking fatter than ever. Wallander could hear Konovalenko repeating the same question over and over again.

"Where's the cop?"

"I don't know."

Wallander could hear Victor Mabasha's voice was defiant. That made him see red. He hated the man who had killed Louise Åkerblom, and no doubt Tengblad as well. At the same time his mind was racing in an attempt to figure out what he should do. If he tried to crawl any closer, they would notice him. He doubted whether he could hit them with his pistol, given the distance. They were out of shotgun range. If he tried to storm them, he would simply be signing his own death warrant. The automatic pistol in Rykoff's hand would wipe him out.

The only thing he could do was wait and hope his colleagues would turn up soon. But he could hear Konovalenko getting more and more annoyed. He wondered if they could get there in time.

He had his pistol ready. He tried lying so that he could aim with steady hands. He was aiming straight at Konovalenko.

But the end came too soon. And it came so fast, Wallander had no time to react before it was too late. Looking back, he could see more clearly than ever before how quickly you can waste a life.

Konovalenko repeated his question one last time. Victor Mabasha gave his negative, defiant response. Then Konovalenko raised his pistol and shot Victor Mabasha right through the head. Just as he had killed Louise Åkerblom three weeks previously.

Wallander yelled out and fired. But it was all over. Victor Mabasha had fallen backwards and was lying at an unnatural angle, motionless. Wallander's bullet had missed Konovalenko. He could see now that the biggest threat was Rykoff's automatic pistol. He aimed at the fat man and fired shot after shot. To his amazement, he saw Rykoff suddenly twitch, then fall in a heap. When Wallander turned his gun on Konovalenko, he saw that the Russian had lifted up Victor Mabasha and was using him as a shield as he shuffled backwards toward the beach. Although Wallander knew Victor Mabasha was dead, he could not bring himself to shoot. He stood up and yelled at Konovalenko to drop his gun and give himself up. His answer came in the form of a bullet. Wallander flung himself to one side. Victor Mabasha's body had saved him from being hit. Not even Konovalenko could aim with a steady hand while holding a heavy corpse upright in front of him. In the distance he could hear a single siren approaching. The fog got thicker as Konovalenko got closer to the beach. Wallander followed him, holding both his weapons in position. Suddenly Konovalenko dropped the dead body and disappeared down the slope. Just then Wallander heard a sheep bleat behind him. He spun around and raised both the pistol and the shotgun.

Then he saw Martinson and Svedberg emerging from out of the fog. Their faces were pictures of astonished horror.

"Drop your guns!" yelled Martinson. "It's us, can't you see!"

Wallander knew Konovalenko was about to escape yet again. There was no time for explanations.

"Stay where you are," he yelled. "Don't follow me!"

Then he started backing away, still pointing his guns. Martinson and Svedberg did not move a muscle. Then he disappeared into the fog.

Martinson and Svedberg looked at each other in horror.

"Was that really Kurt?" wondered Svedberg.

"Yeah," said Martinson. "But he seemed out of his mind."

"He's alive," said Svedberg. "He's still alive despite everything."

They cautiously approached the slope down to the beach where Wallander had disappeared. They could not detect any movements in the fog, but could hear the gentle lapping of the sea on the sand.

Martinson contacted Björk while Svedberg started to examine the two men lying on the ground. Martinson gave Björk precise directions, and called for ambulances.

"What about Wallander?" asked Björk.

"He's still alive," replied Martinson. "But I can't tell you where he is just now."

Then he switched off his walkie-talkie, before Björk could ask any more questions.

He went over to Svedberg and looked at the man Wallander had killed. Two bullets had gone in just above Rykoff's navel.

"We'll have to tell Björk," said Martinson. "Wallander seemed completely out of his mind."

Svedberg nodded. He could see they had no choice.

They went over to the other body.

"The man without a finger," said Martinson. "Now he's also dead." He bent down and pointed to the bullet hole in his forehead.

Both of them were thinking the same thing. Louise Åkerblom.

Then the police cars arrived, followed by two ambulances. As the examination of the two bodies got under way, Svedberg and Martinson took Björk aside and led him over to one of the squad cars. They told him what they had seen. Björk looked at them doubtfully.

"This all sounds very strange," he said. "Even if Kurt can be strange at times, I find it hard to imagine him going crazy."

"You should have seen what he looked like," said Svedberg. "He seemed to be on the verge of a breakdown. He pointed guns at us. He had one in each hand."

Björk shook his head.

"And then he disappeared along the beach?"

"He was following Konovalenko," said Martinson.

"Along the beach?"

"That's where he disappeared."

Björk said nothing, trying to let what he had heard sink in.

"We'd better send in dog patrols," he said after a few moments. "Set up roadblocks, and call in helicopters as soon as it gets light and the fog lifts."

As they got out of the car, a single shot rang out in the fog. It came from the beach, somewhere to the east of where they were standing. Everything got very quiet. Police, ambulance men and dogs all waited to see what would happen next.

Finally a sheep bleated. The desolate sound made Martinson shudder.

"We've got to help Kurt," he said eventually. "He's on his own out there in the fog. He's up against a guy who won't hesitate to shoot. We've got to help Kurt. Now, Otto."

Svedberg had never heard Martinson call Björk by his first name before. Even Björk was startled, as if he did not realize at first who Martinson meant.

"Dog handlers with bulletproof vests," he said.

Within a short space of time the hunt was on. The dogs picked up the scent immediately, and started straining at their leashes. Martinson and Svedberg followed close on the heels of the dog handlers.

About two hundred meters from the murder scene the dogs discovered a patch of blood in the sand. They searched around in circles without finding anything else. Suddenly one of the dogs set off in a northerly direction. They were on the perimeter of the training ground, following the fence. The trail the dogs found led over the road and then toward Sandhammaren.

After a couple of kilometers the trail fizzled out. Disappeared into thin air.

The dogs whimpered and started backtracking the way they had just come.

"What's going on?" Martinson asked one of the dog handlers. He shook his head.

"The trail's gone cold," he said.

Martinson looked uncomprehending.

"Wallander can't just have gone up in smoke?"

"It looks like it," said the dog handler.

They kept on searching as dawn came. Roadblocks were erected. The whole southern Swedish police force was involved one way or another in the hunt for Konovalenko and Wallander. When the fog lifted, helicopters joined the search.

But they found nothing. The two men had disappeared.

By nine o'clock in the morning Svedberg and Martinson were sitting with Björk in the conference room. Everybody was tired and soaked through from the fog. Martinson was also displaying the first symptoms of a cold coming on.

"What am I going to tell the Commissioner of Police?" asked Björk.

"Sometimes it's best to tell it like it is," said Martinson softly.

Björk shook his head.

"Can't you just see the headlines?" he asked. "'Crazy cop is Swedish police secret weapon in hunt for police killer.'"

"A headline has to be short," Svedberg objected.

Björk stood up.

"Go home and get something to eat," he said. "Get changed. Then we have to get going again."

Martinson raised his hand, as if in a classroom.

"I think I'll drive out to his father's place at Löderup," he said. "His daughter's there. She might be able to tell us something useful."

"Do that," said Björk. "But get moving."

Then he went into his office and called the commissioner.

When he eventually managed to end the conversation, his face was red with anger.

He had received the negative criticism he was expecting.

Martinson was sitting in the kitchen of the house in Österlen. Wallander's daughter was making coffee as they talked. When he arrived, he went straight out to the studio to say hello to Wallander's father. He said nothing to him about what had happened during the night, however. He wanted to talk to the daughter first.

He could see she was shocked. There were tears in her eyes.

"I should really have been sleeping at the apartment on Mariagatan last night, too," she said.

She served him coffee. He noticed her hands were shaking.

"I don't understand it all," she said. "That he's dead. Victor Mabasha. I just don't understand it."

Martinson mumbled something vague in reply.

He suspected she could tell him quite a lot about what had been going on between her father and the dead African. He realized it was not her Kenyan boyfriend in Wallander's car a few days earlier. But why had he lied?

"You've got to find Dad before something happens," she said, interrupting his train of thought.

"We'll do what we can," said Martinson.

"That's not good enough," she said. "Do more."

Martinson nodded.

"Yeah," he said. "We'll do more than we can."

Martinson left the house half an hour later. She had promised to tell her grandfather what had happened. He in turn had promised to keep her informed as things developed. Then he drove back to Ystad.

After lunch Björk sat down with Svedberg and Martinson in the conference room at the police station in Ystad. Björk did something most unusual. He locked the door.

"We need to be undisturbed," he said. "It's essential that we put a stop to this catastrophic mess before we lose control."

Martinson and Svedberg stared down at the table. Neither of them knew what he was going to say next.

"Has either of you noticed any signs that Kurt was losing his mind?" asked Björk. "You must have seen something. I've always thought he could be strange at times. But you're the ones who work with him every day."

"I don't think he's out of his mind," said Martinson after a long pause. "Maybe he's overworked?"

"If that were anything to go by every cop in the country would go crazy now and then," said Björk dismissively. "And they don't normally do that. Of course he's out of his mind. Or mentally unbalanced, if that sounds better. Does it run in the family? Didn't somebody find his dad wandering around in a field a year or two back?"

"He was drunk," said Martinson. "Or temporarily senile. Kurt isn't suffering from senility."

"Do you think he might have Alzheimer's?" wondered Björk.

"I don't know what you're talking about," said Svedberg suddenly. "For God's sake, let's stick to the facts. Whether or not Kurt has had some kind of mental breakdown is something only a doctor can decide. Our job is to find him. We know he was involved in a violent shoot-out in which two people died. We saw him out there in the training ground. He pointed his gun at us. But he wasn't dangerous. It was more like desperation. Or confusion. I'm not sure which. Then he disappeared."

Martinson nodded slowly.

"Kurt wasn't at the scene by chance," he said thoughtfully. "His apartment had been attacked. We must assume the black man was there with him. What happened next we can only guess. But Kurt must be onto something, something he never had a chance to tell us about. Or maybe something he chose not to tell us about for the moment. We know he does that sometimes, and we get annoyed. But right now only one thing counts. Finding him."

Nobody said a word.

"I never thought I'd have to do anything like this," said Björk eventually.

Martinson and Svedberg understood what he meant.

"But you've got to do it," said Svedberg. "You have to get the whole force looking for him. Put out an APB on him."

"Awful," muttered Björk. "But I have no choice."

There was nothing else to say.

With a heavy heart, Björk went back to his office to put out an APB on his colleague and friend, Chief Inspector Kurt Wallander.

It was May 15, 1992. Spring had arrived in Skåne. It was a very hot day. Toward evening a thunderstorm moved in over Ystad.

The
White
Lioness

Chapter Twenty-three

The lioness seemed completely white in the moonlight.

Georg Scheepers held his breath as he stood in the back of the safari vehicle, watching her. She was lying motionless down by the river, about thirty meters away. He glanced at his wife Judith, who was standing beside him. She looked back at him. He could see she was scared. He shook his head carefully.

"It's not dangerous," he said. "She won't hurt us."

He believed what he said. But even so, deep down, he was not convinced. Animals in the Kruger National Park, where they were, were used to people watching them from the back of open safari vehicles, even at midnight as in this case. But he could not forget that the lioness was a beast of prey, unpredictable, governed by instinct and nothing else. She was young. Her strength and speed would never be greater than they were now. It would take her three seconds at most to shake herself out of her sprawling langor and bound powerfully over to their car. The black driver did not seem to be particularly alert. None of them carried a gun. If she wanted to, she could kill them all within the space of a few seconds. Three bites from those powerful jaws, on their necks or spines, was all that was needed.

Suddenly it seemed as if the lioness had read his thoughts. She lifted her head and gazed at the car. He felt Judith grab hold of his arm. It was as if the lioness was looking straight at them. The moonlight was reflected in her eyes, making them luminous. Georg Scheepers' heart started beating faster. He wished the driver would start the engine, but the black man was sitting motionless behind the wheel. It suddenly occurred to Georg Scheepers in horror that the guy might have fallen asleep.

At that moment the lioness got up from the sand. She never took her eyes off the people in the car for a moment. Georg Scheepers knew there was such a thing as freezing. You were able to think about being afraid and running away, but had no strength to move.

She stood absolutely still, watching them. Her powerful shoulders rippled prominently under her skin. He thought how beautiful she was. Her strength is her beauty, her unpredictability her character.

He also thought how she was first and foremost a lion. Being white was only a secondary thing. That thought stuck fast in his mind. It was a sort of reminder to himself of something he had forgotten about. But what? He couldn't remember.

"Why doesn't he drive away?" whispered Judith by his side.

"It's not dangerous," he said. "She won't come over here."

The lioness stood motionless, watching the people in the car parked right out by the water's edge. The moonlight was very strong. The night was clear, and it was warm. Somewhere in the dark river they could hear the lazy sounds of hippos moving.

It seemed to Georg Scheepers the whole situation was a reminder. The feeling of imminent danger, which could turn into uncontrollable violence at any moment, was the normal daily state of affairs in his country. Everybody went around waiting for something to happen. The beast of prey was watching them. The beast of prey inside them. The blacks who were impatient because developments were taking place so slowly. The whites with their fears of losing their privileges, their fear of the future. It was like being there on the river bank with a lion watching them.

She was white because she was an albino. He thought of all the myths attached to people and animals that had been born albino. Their strength was mighty, and they could never die.

Suddenly the lioness began to move, coming straight towards them. Her concentration was unbroken, her movements stealthy. The driver hastily started the engine and switched on the headlights. The light blinded her. She stopped in mid-movement, one paw in the air. Georg Scheepers could feel his wife's fingernails piercing his khaki shirt.

Drive, he thought. Drive away now, before she attacks.

The driver shifted into reverse. The engine coughed. Georg Scheepers thought his heart would stand still when the engine almost stopped. But the driver increased pressure on the gas pedal and the car started rolling backwards. The lioness turned her head away to avoid being blinded.

It was all over. Judith's fingernails were no longer digging into his arm. They clung tightly onto the rail as the safari vehicle bumped and jerked its way back to the bungalow where they were staying. The nocturnal outing would soon be over. But the memory of the lioness, and the thoughts her presence on the riverbank aroused, would stay with him.

It was Georg Scheepers who suggested to his wife they should go up to the Kruger for a few days. He had spent a week or more trying to sort out and understand the papers van Heerden left behind after his death. He needed time to think. They would be away on Friday and Saturday, but on Sunday, May 17, he would spend his time trying to master van Heerden's computer files. He wanted to do that when he was alone at work, when there was nobody in the corridors at the prosecutor's office. The police investigators had made sure all his material, all his diskettes, had been placed in a cardboard box and sent to the public prosecutor's office. His boss Wervey had given the order for the intelligence service to hand over all the material. Officially Wervey himself, in his capacity as chief public prosecutor of Johannesburg, should be going through the material, which BOSS had immediately classified as top secret. When van Heerden's superiors refused to release the material until their own people had gone through it, Wervey threw a fit and immediately contacted the Minister of Justice. A few hours later BOSS relented. The material would be delivered to the prosecutor's office. It would be Wervey's responsibility. But it was in fact Georg Scheepers who would go through it all, in circumstances of extreme secrecy. That was why he intended to work on Sunday, when the building would be deserted.

They left Johannesburg early in the morning of Friday, May 15. The N4 freeway to Nelspruit took them quickly to their destination. They turned off onto a minor road and entered the Kruger National Park at the Nambi Gate. Judith had called to book a bungalow in one of the most remote camps, Nwanetsi, not far from the Mozambique border. They had been there several times before, and liked going back. The camp, with its bungalows, restaurant, and safari office, appealed primarily to guests looking for peace and quiet, people who went to bed early and got up at dawn in order to see the animals coming to the river to drink. On the way to Nelspruit Judith had asked him about the investigation he was undertaking for the minister of justice. He said he did not know much about it yet. But he needed time to figure out the best way of approaching the matter. She asked no more questions as she knew her husband was a man of few words.

During their two days at Nwanetsi they were out on game drives all the time. They looked at animals and scenery, leaving Johannesburg and its troubles far behind them. After meals Judith would bury her head in one of her books while Georg Scheepers thought over what he now knew about van Heerden and his secret work.

He had started methodically by going through van Heerden's filing cabinet, and very soon realized he would have to step up his ability to read between the lines. In among formally correct memoranda and reports he found loose scraps of paper with hurriedly scribbled notes. Reading them was slow work and needed a lot of effort; the difficult handwriting reminded him of a pedantic schoolteacher. It seemed to him they were sketches for poems. Lyrical insights, outlines for metaphors and images. It was then, when he tried to penetrate the informal part of van Heerden's work, that he had a premonition something was going to happen. The reports, memos and loose notes—*divine poems*, as he began to regard them—went back a long way. At first they were often precise observations and reflections expressed in a cool, neutral style. But about six months before van Heerden died, they began to change character. It seemed like a different, darker tone had crept into his thoughts. Something had happened, Scheepers thought. Something had changed dramatically either in his work or his private life. Van Heerden was starting to think different thoughts. What had previously been certain suddenly became unsure, the clear voice became hesitant, tenuous. He thought he could see another difference as well. Before, the loose papers had been haphazard. From now on van Heerden noted down the date and sometimes even the time. Scheepers could see van Heerden had often worked late into the night. Most of the notes were timed after midnight. It all started to look like a poetically expressed diary. He tried to find a basic and consistent theme as a starting point. Because van Heerden never mentioned his private life, Scheepers assumed he was only writing about what happened at work. There was no concrete information to assist him. Van Heerden's diary was formulated in synonyms and parallels. It was obvious that *Homeland* stood for South Africa. But who was *The Chameleon*? Who were *The Mother and Child*? Van Heerden was not married. He had no close relations, according to what Chief Inspector Borstlap of the Johannesburg police had written in a personal memo responding to Scheepers's request. Scheepers entered the names into his computer and tried to figure out the connections, without success. Van Heerden's language was evasive, as if he would prefer not to be associated with what he was writing. Over and over again Scheepers had the feeling there was a note of threatening danger. A trace of confession. Van Heerden was onto something significant. His whole world suddenly seemed under threat. He wrote about a kingdom of death, seeming to imply we all had it inside ourselves. He had visions of something falling apart. At the same time Scheepers seemed to detect feelings of guilt and sorrow in van Heerden, which grew dramatically stronger during his last weeks before he died.

Scheepers noted that what he wrote about all the time was the blacks, the whites, the Boers, God and forgiveness. But nowhere did he use the words conspiracy or plot. The thing I'm supposed to be looking for, the thing van Heerden informed President de Klerk about. *Why is there nothing about it?*

On the Thursday evening, the day before he and Judith were due to drive to Nwanetsi, he stayed in his office until very late. He had switched off all the lights apart from his desk lamp. Now and then he could hear the night guards talking outside his window, which he had left ajar.

Pieter van Heerden had been the ideal loyal servant, he thought. In the course of his work for the intelligence service that was growing more divided, acting more autonomously, he had come across something significant. A conspiracy against the state. A conspiracy whose aim was somehow or other to spark off a coup d'état. Van Heerden was sparing no effort in attempting to track down the center of the conspiracy. There were a lot of questions. And van Heerden wrote poems about his worries and the kingdom of death he had discovered inside himself.

Scheepers looked at his filing cabinet. That was where he had locked away the diskettes Wervey had demanded from van Heerden's superiors. That is where the solution must be, he thought. Van Heerden's increasingly confused and introspective musings, as expressed on the loose scraps of paper, could only be part of the whole picture. The truth must be in his diskettes.

Early in the morning of Sunday, May 17, they left the Kruger Park and returned to Johannesburg. He took Judith home, and after breakfast he drove in to the ominous-looking building in the city center in which the public prosecutor's offices were housed. The city was deserted, as if it had suddenly been evacuated and people would never return. The armed guards let him in, and he walked along the echoing corridor to his office.

The moment he walked through the door, he knew someone had been there. There were tiny, barely noticeable changes betraying a visit by an outsider. Presumably the cleaners, he thought. But he could not be sure.

I'm starting to let my assignment get to me, he said to himself. Van Heerden's unrest, his constant fear of being watched, threatened, is now starting to affect me.

He shook off his uneasy feeling, took off his jacket and opened his filing cabinet. Then he slid the first diskette into his computer.

Two hours later he had sorted out the material. Van Heerden's computer files revealed nothing of significance. Most striking was how immaculately everything was organized.

There was just one diskette left.

Georg Scheepers could not manage to open it. He had the instinctive feeling this was where van Heerden's secret testimony was to be found. The blinking message on his screen demanded a password before the diskette would open the doors to its many secret chambers. This is impossible, thought Scheepers. The password is just one single word, but it could be any word at all. I suppose I could run the diskette with a program containing a whole dictionary. But is the password in English or Afrikaans? Even so, he did not believe the answer would be found by working systematically through a dictionary. Van Heerden would not lock his most important diskette with a meaningless password. He would choose something significant as his secret key.

Scheepers rolled up his shirtsleeves, filled his coffee cup from the thermos he had brought with him from home, and started looking through the loose papers one more time. He began to worry that van Heerden might have programed the diskette so it erased everything of its own accord after a certain number of failed efforts to find the unknown password. He compared it with trying to storm an ancient fortress. The drawbridge is up, the moat full of water. There's only one way left. Climb up the walls. Somewhere there must be steps carved into the walls. That's what I'm looking for. The first step.

By two in the afternoon he had still not succeeded. Despondency was not far away, and he could sense a vague feeling of anger boiling up inside, aimed at van Heerden and the lock he was unable to prize open.

A couple of hours later he was on the point of giving up. He had run out of ideas about how to open the diskette. He also had the feeling he was nowhere near finding the correct word. Van Heerden's choice of password had a context and significance he had not yet managed to pin down. Without expecting any particular help he turned to the memos and investigation documents he had received from Chief Inspector Borstlap. Maybe there would be something there which could point him in the right direction? He read the autopsy report with distaste, and shut his eyes when he came to photographs of the dead man. He wondered whether it was just robbery with violence after all. The long-winded report of police proceedings gave him no clues. He turned to the personal memoranda.

Right at the back of Borstlap's file was an inventory of what the police had found in his office at BOSS headquarters. Chief Inspector Borstlap had made the ironic comment that of course, there was no way of knowing if van Heerden's superiors had removed any papers or objects they considered unsuitable for the police to get their hands on. He glanced casually down the list of ashtrays, framed photographs of his parents, some lithographs, a pen rack, diaries, blotting pad. He was just going to put it on one side when he suddenly paused. Among the items listed by Borstlap was a little ivory sculpture of an antelope. *Very valuable, antique*, Borstlap had written.

He put down the memo and typed *antelope* on the keyboard. The computer responded by asking for the correct password. He thought for a moment. Then he typed *kudu*. The computer's response was negative. He picked up the telephone and called home to Judith.

"I need your help," he said. "Can you look up antelopes in our wildlife encyclopedia?"

"What on earth are you doing?" she asked in surprise.

"My assignment includes formulating a stance on the development of our antelope species," he lied. "I just want to make sure I don't forget any."

She got the book and recited the various species of antelope for him.

"When will you be home?" she asked when she had finished.

"Either very soon, or very late," he answered. "I'll call you."

When he hung up he saw right away which word it must be, assuming the little sculpture in the list was in fact the right link.

Springbok, he thought to himself. Our national symbol. Can it really be as easy as that?

He keyed the word in slowly, pausing for a moment before the last letter. The computer responded right away. Negative.

One more possibility, he thought. Same word. But in Afrikaans. He keyed in *spriengboek*.

Immediately the screen started flashing. Then a list of contents appeared.

He had cracked it. He had found his way into van Heerden's world.

He noticed he was sweating. The elation of a criminal when he's just opened a bank vault, he thought.

Then he sat down to read the screen. Afterwards, at nearly one in the morning when he came to the end of the texts, he knew two things. In the first place he was now certain van Heerden had been murdered because of the work he was doing. Second, the premonition of imminent danger he had felt previously was justified.

He leaned back in his chair and stretched.

Then he shuddered.

Van Heerden had compiled the notes recorded on his diskette with cool precision. He could see now that van Heerden was a deeply split personality. The discoveries he made in connection with the conspiracy had reinforced the feeling he had earlier, that his life as an Afrikaner was based on a lie. The deeper he penetrated into the reality of the conspirators, the deeper he penetrated his own. The world as depicted in the loose sheets of paper, and the cool precision of the diskette, existed in the very same person.

It occurred to him that in a sense, van Heerden had been close to his own destruction.

He stood up and walked over to the window. Somewhere in the distance he could hear police sirens.

Just what have we believed? he asked himself. That our dreams of an unchanging world were in fact true? That the small concessions we made to the blacks would be sufficient, although they did not really change anything?

He was overcome by a feeling of shame. For even if he was one of the new Afrikaners, one of those who did not regard de Klerk as a traitor, the many years of passivity on the part of Judith and himself had enabled the racist policies to continue. He too had inside himself the kingdom of death van Heerden had written about.

It was ultimately this silent acceptance that formed the basis of the conspirators' intentions. They were counting on his continued passivity. His silent acceptance.

He sat down at the screen once more.

Van Heerden had done good work. The conclusions Scheepers was now able to draw, and which he would pass on to President de Klerk the very next day, were impossible to miss.

Nelson Mandela, the self-evident leader of the blacks, was going to be murdered. During his last days van Heerden had worked feverishly to try and find the answers to the crucial questions of where, and when. He had not found the answer when he switched off his computer for the last time. But the indications were that it would be very soon, in connection with a speech given by Mandela to a large public gathering. Van Heerden had drawn up a list of possible locations and dates over the coming three months. Among them were Durban, Johannesburg, Soweto, Bloemfontein, Cape Town and East London, with dates attached. Somewhere abroad a professional killer was making preparations. Van Heerden had managed to discover that a former KGB officer was hovering indistinctly in the murderer's background. But there were a lot of other things to be clarified.

Ultimately there was the most important question. Georg Scheepers read one more time the section where van Heerden analyzed his way to the very center of the conspiracy. He spoke of a *Committee*. A loose collection of people, representatives of dominant groups among the Afrikaners. But van Heerden did not have all their names. The only ones he knew about were Jan Kleyn and Franz Malan.

Georg Scheepers was now convinced the chameleon was Jan Kleyn. On the other hand, he had not identified Franz Malan's code name.

He realized van Heerden regarded this pair as the chief actors. By concentrating on them, he hoped to be able to figure out who the other members of the committee were, and just what they were intending to achieve.

Coup d'état, van Heerden had written at the end of the last text, dated two days before he was killed. *Civil war? Chaos?* He did not answer the questions. He merely asked them.

But there was one more note, made the same day, the Sunday before he went into the hospital.

Next week, wrote van Heerden. *Take it further. Bezuidenhout. 559.*

That's his message to me from the grave, thought Georg Scheepers. That's what he would have done. Now I have to do it instead. But what? Bezuidenhout is a suburb of Johannesburg, and the number must surely be part of the address of a house.

He suddenly noticed he was very tired and very worried. The responsibility he had been given was greater than he could ever have imagined.

He switched off the computer and locked the diskettes in his filing cabinet. It was nine o'clock already, and dark outside. Police sirens were wailing non-stop, like hyenas, keeping watch in the darkness of the night.

He left the deserted prosecutor's offices and walked to his car. Without really having decided to do so, he drove toward the eastern edge of the city, to Bezuidenhout. It did not take him long to find what he was looking for. Number 559 was a house bordering the park that gave Bezuidenhout its name. He parked by the curb, switched off the engine and put out the headlights. The house was white, in glazed brick. A light was on behind drawn drapes. He could see a car in the drive.

He was still too tired and worried to think about how he should proceed next. First of all, the whole of this long day would have to sink into his consciousness. He thought of the lioness lying motionless by the riverbank. How she stood and came towards them. The wild beast is clawing at us, he thought.

It suddenly dawned on him what was the most important thing.

The murder of Nelson Mandela would be the worst thing that could happen to the country just now. The consequences would be horrific. Everything they were trying to achieve, this brittle attempt to reach a settlement between blacks and whites would be demolished in a fraction of a second. The dikes would be breached and the flood would rage over the whole country.

There were people who wanted this apocalyptic flood to take place. They had formed a committee to open the floodgates.

That was as far as he got in his thoughts. Then he saw a man leave the house and get into the car. At the same time one of the drapes was pulled back in a window. He could see a black woman, and another one behind her, younger. The older woman waved, but the one behind her did not move a muscle.

He could not see the man in the car. It was too dark. Even so, he knew it was Jan Kleyn. He crouched down in his seat as the other car passed. When he sat up again, the drapes were back in place.

He frowned. Two black women? Jan Kleyn had come out of their house. *The chameleon, mother and child?* He could not see the connection. But he had no reason to doubt van Heerden. If he had written that it was important, then so it was.

Van Heerden had stumbled upon a secret, he thought. I must go down the same track.

The next day he called President de Klerk's office and asked for an urgent appointment. He was told the president could see him at ten that night. He spent the day writing a report on the conclusions he had drawn. He was superficially nervous as he sat waiting in the president's antechamber, having been welcomed by the same somber security guard as before. This evening, however, he was not forced to wait. At exactly ten o' clock the security guard announced the President was ready to see him. When Scheepers entered the room, he had the same impression as last time. President de Klerk seemed to be very tired. His eyes were dim and his face pale. The heavy bags under his eyes seemed to weigh him down to the ground.

As briefly as possible he reported what he had discovered the previous day. For the moment, however, he said nothing about the house in Bezuidenhout Park.

President de Klerk listened, his eyes half-closed. When Scheepers was finished, de Klerk sat there without moving. For a brief moment he thought the president had fallen asleep while he was talking. Then de Klerk opened his eyes and looked straight at him.

"I often wonder how it is that I'm still alive," he said slowly. "Thousands of *boere* regard me as a traitor. Even so, Nelson Mandela is the one picked out in the report as the intended victim of an assassination attempt."

President de Klerk fell silent. Scheepers could see he was thinking hard.

"There is something in the report that disturbs me," he said. "Let us assume there are red herrings laid out in appropriate places. Let us imagine two different sets of circumstances. One is that it's me, the president, who is the intended victim. I'd like you to read the report with that in mind, Scheepers. I'd also like you to consider the possibility that these people intend to attack both my friend Mandela and myself. That doesn't mean I'm excluding the possibility that it really is Mandela these lunatics are after. I just want you to think critically about what you are doing. Pieter van Heerden was murdered. That means there are eyes and ears everywhere. Experience has taught me that red herrings are an important part of intelligence work. Do you follow me?"

"Yes," said Scheepers.

"I'll be expecting your conclusions within the next two days. I'm afraid I can't give you any more time than that."

"I still believe Pieter van Heerden's conclusions indicate it's Nelson Mandela they intend to kill," said Scheepers.

"Believe?" said de Klerk. "I believe in God. But I don't know if he exists. Nor do I know if there is more than one."

Scheepers was dumbfounded by the response. But he understood what de Klerk meant.

The president raised his hands, then let them drop on his desk.

"A committee," he said thoughtfully. "That wants to frustrate all we've achieved. Dismantling in a just way policies that have gone wrong. They are trying to open the floodgates over our country. They will not be allowed to do that."

"Of course not," said Scheepers.

De Klerk was lost in thought once more. Scheepers waited without saying anything.

"Every day I expect some crazy fanatic to get to me," he said circumspectly. "I think about what happened to my predecessor Verwoerd. Stabbed to death in parliament. I am aware the same could happen to me. It does not scare me. What does frighten me, though, is that there isn't really anybody who can take over after me."

De Klerk looked at him, smiling slightly.

"You are still young," he said. "But right now the future of this country is in the hands of two old men, Nelson Mandela and me. That's why it would be desirable for both of us to live a little bit longer."

"Shouldn't Nelson Mandela get a greatly increased bodyguard?" asked Scheepers.

"Nelson Mandela is a very special man," replied de Klerk. "He's not particularly fond of bodyguards. Outstanding men rarely are. Just look at de Gaulle. That's why everything will have to be handled very discreetly. But of course I have arranged for his guard to be strengthened. He doesn't need to hear about it, though."

The audience was at an end.

"Two days," said de Klerk. "No more."

Scheepers got to his feet and bowed.

"One more thing," said de Klerk. "You mustn't forget what happened to van Heerden. Be careful."

It was not until he had left the government building that what President de Klerk said really sunk in. Unseen eyes were watching over him as well. He broke into a cold sweat as he got into his car and drove home.

One again his mind wandered to the lioness that had seemed almost white in the cold, clear moonlight.

Chapter Twenty-four

Kurt Wallander had always imagined death as black.

Now, as he stood on the beach shrouded in fog, he realized that death did not respect colors. Here it was white. The fog enclosed him completely; he thought he could hear the gentle lapping of waves on the shore, but it was the fog that dominated and strengthened his feeling of not knowing which way to turn.

When he had been higher up on the training ground, surrounded by invisible sheep, and it was all over, he did not have a single clear thought in his head. He knew Victor Mabasha was dead, that he himself had killed a human being, and that Konovalenko had escaped yet again, swallowed up by all the whiteness surrounding them. Svedberg and Martinson had emerged from the fog like two pale ghosts of themselves. He could see in their faces his own horror at being surrounded by dead bodies. He had felt simultaneously a desire to run away and never come back, but also to continue the hunt for Konovalenko. Afterwards he recalled what happened in those few moments as something peripheral to him, seen from a distance. It was a different Wallander standing there, waving his guns around. Not him, but somebody who had temporarily possessed him. Only when he yelled at Martinson and Svedberg to keep their distance, then skidded and scrambled up the slope finding himself being alone in the fog, did he slowly begin to understand what had happened. Victor Mabasha was dead, shot through the head, just like Louise Åkerblom. The fat man had started back and flung his hands in the air. He was also dead, and Wallander had shot him.

He yelled out, like a solitary human foghorn in the mist. There's no turning back, he told himself desperately. I'll disappear into this fog. When it lifts, I won't exist any more.

He tried to gather the last vestiges of reason he thought he still had left. Go back, he told himself. Go back to the dead men. Your colleagues are there. You can continue the search for Konovalenko together.

Then he walked away. He could not go back. If he had one duty left, it was to find Konovalenko, kill him if that could not be avoided, but preferably catch him and hand him over to Björk. Once that was done he could sleep. When he woke up again, the nightmare would be over. But that was not true. The nightmare would still be there. In shooting Rykoff, he had done something he would never be able to shake off. And so he might just as well go hunting for Konovalenko. He had a vague feeling he was already trying to find some way to atone for the killing of Rykoff.

Konovalenko was somewhere out there in the fog. Maybe close by. Helplessly, Wallander fired a shot straight into the whiteness, as if trying to split the fog. He brushed aside the sweaty hair that was sticking to his forehead. Then he saw he was bleeding. He must have cut himself when Rykoff shattered the window panes on Mariagatan. He looked down at his clothes, and saw they were soaked in blood. It was dripping down onto the sand. He stood still, waiting for his breathing to calm down. Then he continued. He could follow Konovalenko's tracks in the sand. He tucked the pistol in his belt. He held the shotgun cocked and ready, at hip level. It seemed to him from Konovalenko's footprints that he had been moving quickly, running perhaps. He speeded up, following the scent like a dog. The thick fog suddenly gave him the impression he was standing still while the sand was moving. Just then, he noted that Konovalenko had stopped and turned around before running off in a different direction. The tracks led back up to the cliff. Wallander realized they would disappear as soon as they came to the grass. He scrambled up the slope and saw he was at the eastern edge of the training ground. He stopped to listen. Far behind him he could hear the sound of a siren fading away into the distance. Then a sheep bleated, very close by. Silence once again. He followed the fence northwards. It was the only bearing he had. He half-expected Konovalenko to loom up out of the fog at any moment. Wallander tried to imagine what it must be like to be shot through the head.

But he could not feel anything. The whole purpose of his life just now was to follow that fence along the perimeter of the training ground, nothing else. Konovalenko was somewhere out there with his gun and Wallander was going to find him.

When Wallander hit the road to Sandhammaren, there was nothing to see but fog. He thought he could make out the dim shape of a horse on the other side, standing motionless, ears cocked.

Then he stood in the middle of the road and urinated. In the distance he could hear a car going by on the road to Kristianstad.

He started walking towards Kåseberga. Konovalenko had disappeared. He had escaped yet again. Wallander was walking aimlessly. Walking was easier than standing still. He wished Baiba Leipa would emerge from the whiteness and come towards him. But there was nothing. Just him and the damp asphalt.

A bicycle leaned against the remains of an old milk pallet. It was unlocked, and it seemed to Wallander someone had left it there for him. He used the baggage rack for the shotgun and cycled off. As soon as possible he turned off the road onto the dirt roads crisscrossing the plain. Eventually he came to his father's house. It was dark, apart from a single lamp outside the front door. He stood still and listened. Then he hid the bicycle behind the shed. He tiptoed carefully over the gravel. He knew his father had a spare key hidden underneath a broken flowerpot on the outside stairs leading down to the cellar. He unlocked the door to his father's studio. There was an inside room where he kept his paints and old canvases. He closed the door behind him and switched on the light. The brightness from the bulb took him by surprise. It was as if he expected the fog to be here as well. He ducked under the cold water tap and tried to rinse the blood off his face. He could see his reflection in a broken mirror on the wall. He did not recognize his own eyes. They were staring, bloodshot, shifting anxiously. He heated up some coffee on the filthy electric hot plate. It was four in the morning. He knew his father generally got up at half past five. He would have to be gone by then. What he needed just now was a hideaway. Various alternatives, all of them impossible, flashed through his mind. But in the end he decided what to do. He drank his coffee, left the studio, crossed over the courtyard, and carefully unlocked the door to the main house. He stood in the hall, and could smell the acrid, old-mannish aroma in his nostrils. He listened. Not a sound. He went cautiously into the kitchen where the telephone was, closing the door behind him. To his surprise he remembered the number. With his hand on the receiver, he thought about what he was going to say. Then he dialed.

Sten Widén answered almost right away. Wallander could hear he was already wide awake. Horsey people get up early, he thought.

"Sten? It's Kurt Wallander."

Once upon a time they had been very close friends. Wallander knew he hardly ever displayed a trace of surprise.

"I can hear that," he said. "You're calling at four in the morning?"

"I need your help."

Sten Widén said nothing. He was waiting to hear more.

"On the road to Sandhammaren," said Wallander. "You'll have to come and get me. I need to hide in your house for a while. A few hours at least."

"Where?" asked Sten Widén.

Then he started coughing.

He's still smoking those cheroots, thought Wallander.

"I'll wait for you at the Kåseberga exit," he said. "What kind of car do you have?"

"An old Duett."

"How long will it take you?"

"It's thick fog. Say forty-five minutes. Maybe a little less."

"I'll be there. Thanks for your help."

He hung up and left the kitchen. Then he could not resist the temptation. He walked through the living room where the old television set was, and carefully pulled aside the curtain to the guest room where his daughter was sleeping. In the weak light from the lamp outside the kitchen door, he could see her hair and forehead, some of her nose. She was fast asleep.

Then he left the house and cleaned up after himself in the inside room of the studio. He cycled down to the main road and turned right. When he came to the Kåseberga exit he put the bicycle behind a hut belonging to the telephone company, concealed himself in the shadows, and settled down to wait. The fog was just as thick as before. Suddenly a police car flashed past on the way to Sandhammaren. Wallander thought he recognized Peters behind the wheel.

His thoughts turned to Sten Widén. They had not met for over a year. In connection with a criminal investigation Wallander had gotten the idea of calling on him at his stables near the ruined castle at Stjärnsund. That was where he trained a number of trotting horses. He lived alone, probably drank too much and too often, and had unclear relationships with his female employees. Once upon a time they had shared a common dream. Sten Widén had a fine baritone voice. He was going to become an opera singer, and Wallander would be his impresario. But the dream faded away, their friendship dissolved, and finally ceased to be.

Even so, he's perhaps the only real friend I've ever had, thought Wallander as he waited in the fog. If I don't count Rydberg. But that was something different. We'd never have gotten close to each other if we hadn't both been cops.

Forty minutes later the wine-red Duett came gliding through the fog. Wallander emerged from behind the hut and got into the car. Sten Widén looked at his face, dirty, smeared with blood. But as usual he displayed no surprise.

"I'll explain later," said Wallander.

"When it suits you," said Sten Widén. He had an unlit cigarette in his mouth, and smelled of strong liquor.

They passed the training ground. Wallander crouched down and made himself invisible. There were several police cars by the side of the road. Sten Widén slowed down but did not stop. The road was clear, no roadblocks. He looked across at Wallander, who was still trying to hide. But he said nothing. They drove past Ystad, Skurup, then took a right towards Stjärnsund. The fog was still as thick as ever when they turned into the stable yard. A girl of about seventeen stood yawning and smoking in front of the stalls.

"My face has been in the newspapers and on TV," said Wallander. "I'd prefer to be anonymous."

"Ulrika doesn't read the papers," said Sten Widén. "If she ever watches TV, it's just videos. I have another girl, Kristina. She won't say anything either."

They went into the untidy, chaotic house. Wallander had the feeling it looked exactly the same as the last time he was there. Sten Widén asked if he was hungry. Wallander nodded and they sat down in the kitchen. He had some sandwiches and a cup of coffee. Sten Widén occasionally went out into the next room. Whenever he came back he smelled even more strongly of spirits.

"Thanks for coming for me," said Wallander.

Sten Widén shrugged.

"No problem," he said.

"I need a few hours' sleep," Wallander went on. "Then I'll tell you what's going on."

"The horses have to be looked after," said Sten Widén. "You can sleep in here."

He got up and Wallander followed him. His exhaustion caught up with him. Sten Widén showed him into a little room with a sofa.

"I doubt if I have any clean sheets. But you can have a pillow and a blanket."

"That's more than enough," said Wallander.

"You know where the bathroom is?"

Wallander nodded. He could remember.

Wallander took off his shoes. You could hear the sand crunching underfoot. He slung his jacket over a chair. Sten Widén stood watching him in the doorway.

"How are things?" Wallander inquired.

"I've started singing again," said Sten Widén.

"You must tell me all about it," said Wallander.

Sten Widén left the room. Wallander could hear a horse whinnying out in the yard. The last thing he thought before falling asleep was that Sten Widén was just the same as ever. The same tousled hair, the same dry eczema on his neck.

Nevertheless there was something different.

When he woke up, he was not sure where he was at first. He had a headache, and pain all over his body. He put his hand on his forehead and could feel he had a temperature. He lay still under the blanket, which smelled of horses. When he went to check his watch, he found he must have dropped it at some point during the night. He got up and went out into the kitchen. A clock on the wall showed half past eleven. He had slept for over four hours. The fog had lifted somewhat, but was still there. He poured himself a cup of coffee and sat down at the kitchen table. Then he stood up and opened various cabinets until he found some painkillers. Shortly afterwards the telephone rang. Wallander heard Sten Widén come in and answer it. The call had to do with hay. They were discussing the price of a delivery. When he finished talking, he came into the kitchen.

"Awake?" he asked.

"I needed some sleep," said Wallander.

Then he told him what had happened. Sten Widén listened in silence, expressionless. Wallander started with the disappearance of Louise Åkerblom. He talked about the man he had killed.

"I just had to get away," he concluded. "I know of course my colleagues will be looking for me now. But I'll have to tell them a white lie. Say I passed out and lay behind a bush. But I'd be grateful if you could do one thing for me. Call my daughter and tell her I'm OK. And tell her she should stay where she is."

"Should I tell her where you are?"

"No. Not yet. But you've got to convince her."

Sten Widén nodded. Wallander gave him the number. But there was no answer.

"You'll have to keep on trying until you reach her," he said.

One of the stable girls came into the kitchen. Wallander nodded, and she introduced herself as Kristina.

"You can go get a pizza," said Sten Widén. "Buy a few newspapers, too. There isn't a bite to eat in the house."

Sten Widén gave the girl some money. She drove off in the Duett.

"You said you started singing again," said Wallander.

Sten Widén smiled for the first time. Wallander could remember that smile, but it was many years since he had last seen it.

"I've joined the church choir at Svedala," ha said. "I sometimes sing solos at funerals. I realized I was missing it. But the horses don't like it if I sing in the stables."

"Do you need an impresario?" wondered Wallander. "It's hard to see how I can keep going as a cop after all this."

"You killed in self-defense," said Sten Widén. "I'd have done the same thing. Just thank your lucky stars you had a gun."

"I don't think anybody can understand what it feels like."

"It'll pass."

"Never."

"Everything passes."

Sten Widén tried calling again. Still no answer. Wallander went out to the bathroom and took a shower. He borrowed a shirt from Sten Widén. That also smelled like horses.

"How's it going?" he asked.

"How's what going?"

"The horse business."

"I've got one that's good. Three more that might become good. But Fog's got talent. She'll bring in the money. She might even be a possibility for the Derby this year."

"Is she really called Fog?"

"Yes. Why?"

"I was thinking about last night. If I'd had a horse I might have been able to catch up with Konovalenko."

"Not on Fog you wouldn't. She throws riders she doesn't know. Talented horses are often a handful. Like people. Full of themselves, and whimsical. I sometimes wonder if she should have a mirror in the horse box. But she runs fast."

The girl called Kristina came back with the pizza and some newspapers. Then she went out again.

"Isn't she going to eat?" asked Wallander.

"They eat in the stables," said Sten Widén. "We have a little kitchen there." He took the top newspaper and leafed through. One of the pages attracted his attention.

"It's about you," he said.

"I'd rather not know. Not yet."

"As you like."

Sten Widén got a reply the third time he called. It was Linda who answered, not Wallander's father. Wallander could hear she was insisting on asking lots of questions. But Sten Widén only said what he was supposed to.

"She was very relieved," he said when the call was over. "She promised to stay put."

The ate their pizzas. A cat jumped up onto the table. Wallander gave it a piece. He noticed the cat smelled like horses, too.

"The fog's lifting," said Sten Widén. "Did I ever tell you I'd been in South Africa? Apropos of what you were just saying."

"No," said Wallander, surprised. "I didn't know that."

"When nothing came of the opera-singing business, I went away," he said. "I wanted to get away from everything, you'll remember that. I thought I might become a big game hunter. Or go looking for diamonds in Kimberley. Must have been something I'd read. And I actually went. Got as far as Cape Town. I stayed for three weeks, and then I'd had enough. Ran away. Came back here. And so it was horses instead, when Dad died."

"Ran away?"

"The way those blacks were treated. I was ashamed. It was their country, but they were forced to go around cap in hand, apologizing for their existence. I've never seen anything like it. I'll never forget it."

He wiped his mouth and went out. Wallander thought about what he had said. Then he realized he would soon have to go back to the police station in Ystad.

He went into the room where the telephone was, and found what he was looking for. A half-empty whiskey bottle. He unscrewed the cap, took a large mouthful, and then another. He watched Sten Widén ride past the window on a brown horse.

First I get burgled. Then they blow my apartment up. What next?

He lay down on the sofa again, and pulled the blanket up to his chin. His fever had been imagined, and his headache was gone. He would have to get up again soon.

Victor Mabasha was dead. Konovalenko had shot him. The investigation into Louise Åkerblom's disappearance and death was littered with dead bodies. He could see no way out. How were they ever going to catch up with Konovalenko?

After a while he fell asleep. He did not wake up again for another four hours.

Sten Widén was in the kitchen, reading an evening paper.

"You're wanted," he said.

Wallander looked at him uncomprehendingly.

"Who is?"

"You," repeated Sten Widén. "You're wanted. They've sent out an APB. You can also read between the lines that they think you've gone temporarily insane."

Wallander grabbed hold of the newspaper. There was a picture of him, and of Björk.

Sten Widén was telling the truth. He was a wanted man. He and Konovalenko. They also suspected he might not be fit to look after himself.

Wallander stared in horror at Sten Widén.

"Call my daughter," he said.

"I already did," he said. "And I told her you were still *compos mentis.*"

"Did she believe you?"

"Yes. She believed me."

Wallander sat there motionless. Then he made up his mind. He would play the role they had given him. A chief detective inspector from Ystad, temporarily out of his mind, missing and wanted. That would give him the thing he needed above all else.

Time.

When Konovalenko caught sight of Wallander in the fog down by the sea, in the field with the sheep, he realized to his astonishment that he was up against a worthy opponent. It was at the very moment Victor Mabasha was thrown backwards and was dead before he hit the ground. Konovalenko heard a roar coming out of the fog, and turned around while crouching down. And there he was, the chubby provincial cop who had defied him time and time again. Konovalenko could now see he had underestimated him. He watched as Rykoff was hit by two bullets that ripped open his rib cage. Using the dead African as a shield, Konovalenko backed up as far as the beach, knowing that Wallander would come after him. He would not give up, and it was clear now that he was dangerous.

Konovalenko ran along the beach in the fog. At the same time he called Tania on the mobile phone he had with him. She was waiting at the square in Ystad with a car. He got as far as the perimeter fence, scrambled up onto the road, and saw a sign pointing to Kåseberga. He directed her out of Ystad by telephone, talking to her all the time, and urged her to drive carefully. He said nothing about Vladimir being dead. That would come later. All the time he kept an eye out behind him. Wallander was not far away and he was dangerous, the first ruthless Swede he had come up against at close quarters. He could not believe what had happened. Wallander was just a provincial cop, after all. There was something about his behavior that simply did not add up.

Tania arrived, Konovalenko took over the wheel, and they drove back to the house near Tomelilla.

"Where's Vladimir?" she asked.

"He'll be coming later," replied Konovalenko. "We were forced to split up. I'll get him later."

"What about the African?"

"Dead."

"The cop?"

No answer. Tania realized something had gone wrong. Konovalenko was driving too fast. There was something bugging him.

It was while they were still in the car that Tania realized Vladimir was dead. But she said nothing, and managed to keep up the façade until they got back to the house where Sikosi Tsiki was sitting on a chair watching them, his face devoid of expression. Then she started screaming. Konovalenko slapped her, on the cheek with the flat of his hand at first, then harder and harder. But she kept on screaming until he managed to force some sedatives down her throat, so many they practically knocked her out. Sikosi Tsiki sat watching them the whole time from the sofa, without moving. Konovalenko had the impression he was performing on a stage, with Sikosi Tsiki the only member of the audience, albeit an attentive one. Once Tania had sunk into the no-man's-land between deep sleep and unconsciousness, Konovalenko got changed and poured himself a glass of vodka. The fact that Victor Mabasha was dead at last did not give him the satisfaction he had expected. It solved the immediate practical problems, not least his sensitive relationship with Jan Kleyn. But he knew Wallander would come after him.

He would not give in. He would pick up the trail once more.

Konovalenko drank another glass of vodka.

The African on the sofa is a dumb animal, he thought. He watches me all the time, not in a friendly way, not unfriendly either, just watching. He says nothing, asks nothing. He could sit like that for days on end if anyone asked him to.

Konovalenko still had nothing to say to him. With every minute that passed, Wallander would be getting closer. What was needed now was an offensive on his part. Preparing for the actual assignment, the assassination in South Africa, would have to wait for a while.

He knew Wallander's weak spot. That was what Konovalenko wanted to get at. But where was his daughter? Somewhere not far away, presumably in Ystad. But not in the apartment.

It took him an hour to figure out a solution to the problem. It was a very risky plan. But he had realized there was no such thing as a risk-free strategy as far as this remarkable cop Wallander was concerned.

Since Tania was the key to his plan and she was going to be asleep for many hours, all he needed to do was to wait. But he did not forget for one moment that Wallander was out there in the fog and darkness, and that he was getting closer all the time.

"I gather the big man won't be coming back," Sikosi Tsiki said suddenly. His voice was very husky, his English singsong.

"He made a mistake," said Konovalenko. "He was too slow. Perhaps he thought there was a way back. But there isn't."

That was all Sikosi Tsiki said that night. He got up from the sofa and went back to his room. It occurred to Konovalenko that, despite everything, he preferred the replacement Jan Kleyn had sent. He would remember to point that out when he called South Africa the following night.

He was the only one still awake. The drapes were carefully drawn, and he refilled his glass with vodka.

He went to bed shortly before five in the morning.

Tania arrived at the police station in Ystad just before one in the afternoon on Saturday, May 16. She was still groggy, as a result of the shock over Vladimir's death and the strong sedatives Konovalenko had given her. But she was also determined. Wallander was the guy who had killed her husband. The cop who visited them in Hallunda. Konovalenko had described Vladimir's death in a way that bore little resemblance to what actually happened in the fog. As far as Tania was concerned, Wallander was a monster of uncontrolled, sadistic brutality. For Vladimir's sake she would play the part Konovalenko had given her. Eventually there would be an opportunity to kill him.

She entered the reception area at the police station. A woman in a glass cage smiled at her.

"How can I help you?" she asked.

"My car was broken into," said Tania.

"Oh, dear," said the receptionist. "I'll see if there's anybody who can deal with you. The whole place is upside down today."

"I can imagine," said Tania. "Wasn't it awful, what happened."

"I never thought we'd live to see anything like this happening in Ystad," said the receptionist. "But obviously, you never know."

She tried several numbers. Eventually someone answered.

"Is that Martinson? Do you have time to deal with a theft from a car?"

Tania could hear an excited voice at the other end of the line, harassed, negative. But the woman would not give up.

"We have to try and function normally, in spite of everything," she said. "I can't find anybody but you. And it won't take long."

The man on the phone conceded.

"You can talk to Detective Inspector Martinson," she said, pointing. "Third door on the left."

Tania knocked and entered the office, which was in a terrible mess. The man behind the desk looked weary and harassed. His desk was stacked up with paper. He looked at her with ill-concealed irritation, but he invited her to sit down and started rummaging through a drawer for a form.

"Car break-in," he said.

"Yes," said Tania. "The thief got away with my radio."

"They usually do," said Martinson.

"Please excuse me," said Tania, "but I wonder if could have a glass of water? I have such a nagging cough."

Martinson looked at her in surprise.

"Yes, of course," he said. "Of course you can have a glass of water."

He got up and left the room.

Tania had already noticed the address book on his desk. As soon as Martinson went out, she picked it up and found the letter W. Wallander's home number at the Mariagatan apartment was listed, and his father's number as well. Tania wrote it down quickly on a piece of paper she had in her coat pocket. Then she replaced the address book and looked around the office.

Martinson came back with a glass of water, and a cup of coffee for himself. The telephone started ringing, but he picked up the receiver and laid it on the desk. Then he asked his questions and she described the imaginary break-in. She gave the registration number of a car she had seen parked in the center of town. They had taken a radio, and a bag containing liquor. Martinson wrote it all down, and when he had finished he asked her to read it through and sign. She called herself Irma Alexanderson, and gave an address on the Malmö Road. She handed the sheet of paper back to Martinson.

"You must be very worried about your colleague," she said in a friendly tone. "What was his name, now? Wallander?"

"Yes," said Martinson. "It's not easy."

"I'm sorry for his daughter," she said. "I used to be her music teacher once upon a time. But then she moved to Stockholm."

Martinson looked at her with somewhat renewed interest.

"She's back here again now," he said.

"Really?" said Tania. "She must have been very lucky, then, when the apartment burned down."

"She's with her grandfather," said Martinson, replacing the telephone receiver.

Tania got up.

"I won't disturb you any longer," she said. "Many thanks for your help."

"No problem," said Martinson, shaking her by the hand.

Tania knew he would forget her the moment she left the room. The dark wig she was wearing over her own blond hair meant he would never be able to recognize her.

She nodded to the woman in reception, passed by a crowd of journalists who were waiting for a press conference due to begin any time now, and left the police station.

Konovalenko was waiting in his car at the gas station on the hill leading to the town center. She got into the car.

"Wallander's daughter is staying with his father," she said. "I've got his telephone number."

Konovalenko looked at her. Then he broke into a smile.

"We've got her," he said quietly. "We've got her. And when we've got her, we've got him as well."

Chapter Twenty-five

Wallander dreamed he was walking on water.

The world he found himself in was a strange blue color. The sky and its jagged clouds were blue, the edge of a forest in the far distance was also blue, and the cliff face was cluttered with blue birds roosting. And there was the sea he was walking on as well. Konovalenko was also somewhere in the dream. Wallander had been following his tracks in the sand. But then, instead of turning up toward the slope leading away from the beach, they went straight out into the sea. In his dream it was obvious that he should follow them. And so he walked on water. It was like walking over a thin layer of fine glass splinters. The surface of the water was uneven, but it bore his weight. Somewhere, beyond the last of those blue islets, close to the horizon, was Konovalenko.

He remembered his dream when he woke up early on Sunday morning, May 17. He was on the sofa in Sten Widén's house. He padded out into the kitchen and noted it was half past five. A quick look into Sten Widén's bedroom revealed that he was up already, and had gone out to the horses. Wallander poured himself a cup of coffee and sat down at the kitchen table.

The previous evening he had tried to start thinking again.

In one sense his situation was easy to assess. He was a wanted man, and they were looking for him. But he could be wounded, he could be dead. Moreover, he had pointed guns at his colleagues and thus demonstrated that he was out of his mind. In order to catch Konovalenko they would also have to track down Chief Inspector Wallander from Ystad. So far, his situation was quite clear. The previous day, when Sten Widén told him what was in the evening papers, he had decided to play the part assigned to him. That would give him time. And he needed that time in order to catch up with Konovalenko and, if necessary, kill him.

Wallander realized he was setting up a sacrificial lamb. Himself. He doubted whether the police could arrest Konovalenko without more cops being injured, perhaps killed. And therefore he would sacrifice himself. The very thought terrified him. But he felt he could not run away. He had to achieve what he had set out to do, regardless of the consequences.

Wallander tried to imagine what Konovalenko was thinking. He concluded that Konovalenko could not be completely indifferent to his existence. Even if Konovalenko did not regard him as a worthy adversary, he must have gathered that Wallander was a cop who went his own way and did not hesitate to use a gun if necessary. If nothing else that should have earned him a certain amount of respect, even if Konovalenko knew deep down that the basic assumption was false. Wallander was a cop who never took unnecessary risks. He was both cowardly and cautious. When he reacted in primitive fashion, it was always because he was in desperate circumstances. But by all means let Konovalenko go on thinking I'm not the man I really am, thought Wallander.

He had also tried to figure out what Konovalenko had in mind. He had returned to Skåne, and succeeded in killing Victor Mabasha. Wallander had difficulty in believing he was acting on his own. He had brought Rykoff with him, but how had he managed to get away without outside help? Rykoff's wife, Tania, must be around, and maybe other henchmen Wallander didn't know about. They had rented a house under a false name before. Maybe they've hidden themselves away again in some remote house out in the sticks.

Having got that far, Wallander realized there was another important question still waiting to be resolved.

What happens after Victor Mabasha, he wondered. What about the assassination that was the center of everything that's happened? What about the invisible organization that's pulling all the strings, even Konovalenko's? Will the whole thing be called off? Or will these faceless men keep on trekking towards their goal?

He drank his coffee, and concluded there was only one thing open to him. He had to make sure Konovalenko could find him. When they attacked the apartment, they were looking for him as well. Victor Mabasha's last words were that he didn't know where Wallander was. Konovalenko wanted to know.

He could hear footsteps in the hall. Sten Widén came in. He was dressed in dirty overalls and muddy boots.

"We're racing at Jägersro today," he said. "How about coming along?"

Wallander was tempted, just for a moment. He welcomed anything that could divert his thoughts.

"Is Fog running?" he asked.

"She's running, and she's going to win," said Sten Widén. "But I doubt whether the gamblers will have enough faith in her. That means you could earn a few kronor."

"How can you be so sure she's the best?" wondered Wallander.

"She's a temperamental beast," said Sten Widén, "but today she's raring to go. She's restless in her box. She can sense the chips are down. And the opposition is not all that brilliant. There are a few horses from Norway I don't know much about. But I guess she can beat them as well."

"Who's the owner of this horse?" asked Wallander.

"Some businessman by the name of Morell."

Wallander recognized the name. He had heard it not long ago, but could not remember the context.

"Stockholmer?"

"No. From Skåne."

Something clicked for Wallander. Peter Hanson and his pumps. A fence by the name of Morell.

"What line of business is this Morell in?" asked Wallander.

"To tell you the truth, I think he's a little shady," said Sten Widén. "Or so rumor has it. But he pays his training bills on time. No business of mine where the money comes from."

Wallander had no more questions.

"I don't think I'll come, thanks all the same," he said.

"Ulrika bought in some food," said Sten Widén. "We'll be taking the horses off in an hour or two. You'll have to look after yourself."

"What about the Duett? asked Wallander. "Will you leave it here?"

"You can borrow it if you like," said Sten Widén. "But remember to fill the tank. I keep forgetting."

Wallander watched the horses being led into the big horse boxes, and driven off. Not long afterwards he was also on his way. When he got to Ystad he took the risk of driving down Mariagatan. It looked pretty desolate. A yawning hole in the wall, surrounded by filthy bricks, showed where the window used to be. He stopped only briefly, before driving right through town. As he passed the military training ground he noted a squad car parked a long way from the perimeter. Now the fog had disappeared, the distance seemed shorter than he remembered it. He drove on and turned off down to the harbor at Kåseberga. He knew there was a risk he might be recognized, but the photo of him in the newspapers was not a particularly good likeness. The problem was he might bump into somebody he knew. He went into a phone booth and called his father. Just as he had hoped, his daughter answered.

"Where are you?" she asked. "What are you up to?"

"Just listen," he said. "Can anybody overhear you?"

"How could anybody? Grandad's painting."

"Nobody else?"

"There's nobody here, I told you!"

"Haven't the police stationed a guard yet? Isn't there a car parked on the road?"

"There's Nilson's tractor in one of the fields."

"Nothing else?"

"Dad, there's nobody here. Stop worrying about it."

"I'll be with you in a few minutes," he said. "Don't say anything to your grandad."

"Have you seen what they put in the papers?"

"We can talk about that later."

He replaced the receiver, thinking how pleased he was nobody had yet confirmed that he killed Rykoff. Even if the police knew, they wouldn't release the information until Wallander returned. He was quite sure of that, after all his years in the force.

He drove straight to his father's house from Kåseberga. He left the car on the main road and walked the last bit, taking a path where he knew he could not be seen.

She was standing at the door, waiting for him. When they got into the hallway, she hugged him. They stood there in silence. He did not know what she was thinking. As far as he was concerned, though, it was proof that they were on the way to establishing a relationship so close that words were sometimes unnecessary.

They sat in the kitchen, opposite each other at the table.

"Grandad won't show up for quite some time yet," she said. "I could learn a lot from his working discipline."

"Or stubbornness," he said.

They both burst out laughing at the same time.

Then he grew serious again. He told her slowly what had happened, and why he had decided to accept the role of a wanted man, a half-crazy cop on the loose.

"Just what do you think you'll achieve? All by yourself?"

He could not make up his mind whether fear or skepticism lay behind her question.

"I'll lure him out. I'm well aware I'm no one-man army. But if this thing is going to be solved, I have to take the first step myself."

Quickly, as if in protest at what he had just said, she changed the subject.

"Did he suffer a lot?" she asked. "Victor Mabasha?"

"No," Wallander replied. "It was over in a flash. I don't think he had any idea he was going to die."

"What'll happen to him now?"

"I don't know," said Wallander. "I guess there'll be an autopsy. Then it's a matter of whether his family want him buried here, or in South Africa. Assuming that's where he comes from."

"Who is he, in fact?"

"I don't know. I sometimes felt I'd established some kind of contact with him. But then he slipped away again. I can't say I know what he was thinking deep down. He was a remarkable man, very complicated. If that's how you get when you live in South Africa, it must be a country you wouldn't even want to send your worst enemy to."

"I want to help you," she said.

"You can," said Wallander. "I want you to call the police station and ask to speak with Martinson."

"That's not what I mean," she said. "I'd like to do something nobody else can do."

"That's not the kind of thing you can plan in advance," said Wallander. "That just happens. When it happens."

She called the police station and asked to speak with Martinson.

But the switchboard could not track him down. She put her hand over the mouthpiece and asked what she should do. Wallander hesitated. But then he realized he could not afford to wait, nor pick and choose. He asked her to get Svedberg instead.

"He's in a meeting," she said. "Not to be disturbed."

"Tell her who you are," said Wallander. "Say it's important. He has to leave the meeting."

It was a few minutes before Svedberg came to the phone. She handed the receiver to Wallander.

"It's me," he said. "Kurt. Don't say anything. Where are you?"

"In my office."

"Is the door closed?"

"Just a moment."

Wallander could hear him slamming the door.

"Kurt," he said. "Where are you?"

"I'm somewhere where you'll never be able to find me."

"Damn, Kurt."

"Just listen. Don't interrupt. I need to meet you. But only on condition you don't say a word to anybody. Not to Björk, not to Martinson, nobody. If you can't promise that I'll hang up right away."

"Right now we're in the conference room discussing how to scale up the search for you and Konovalenko," said Svedberg. "It'll be absurd if I can't go back to that meeting and not say I've just been talking with you."

"That can't be helped," said Wallander. "I think I have good reason for doing what I'm doing. I'm intending to cash in on the fact that I'm wanted."

"How?"

"I'll tell you when we meet. Make up your mind now!"

There was a long pause. Wallander waited. He could not predict what Svedberg would decide.

"I'll come," said Svedberg eventually.

"Sure?"

"Yeah."

Wallander described the way to Stjärnsund.

"Two hours from now," said Wallander. "Can you make that?"

"I'll have to make sure I can," said Svedberg.

Wallander hung up.

"I want to be certain somebody knows what I'm doing," he said.

"In case something happens?"

Her question came so suddenly Wallander had no time to think of an evasive answer.

"Yes," he said. "In case something happens."

He stayed for another cup of coffee. As he was getting ready to leave, he suddenly hesitated.

"I don't want to make you any more worried than you already are," he said, "but I don't want you to leave these four walls for the next few days. Nothing's going to happen to you. It's probably just to make me sleep easier at night."

She patted his cheek.

"I'll stay here," she said. "Don't you worry."

"Just a few more days," he said. "It can hardly be more than that. This nightmare will be over by then. Then I'll have to get used to the fact that I killed somebody."

He turned and left before she had chance to say anything. He could see in the rearview mirror that she had followed him to the road and was watching him drive away.

Svedberg was on time.

It was ten to three when he turned into the courtyard.

Wallander put on his jacket and went out to meet him.

Svedberg looked at him and shook his head.

"What are you doing?" he asked.

"I think I can handle it," said Wallander. "But thanks for coming."

They went out onto the bridge over the old moat around the ruined castle. Svedberg stopped, leaned over the rail and contemplated the green sludge below.

"It's hard to grasp that this sort of thing can happen," he said.

"I've come to the conclusion that we nearly always act against our better judgment," said Wallander. "We think we can stop something happening just by refusing to acknowledge it."

"But why Sweden?" Svedberg wondered. "Why choose this country as their starting point?"

"Victor Mabasha had a possible explanation," said Wallander.

"Who?"

Wallander realized Svedberg did not know what the dead African was called. He repeated the name. Then he went on.

"It was partly because this is where Konovalenko was established, of course," he said. "But it was just as important to lay a smoke screen. The crucial thing for the guys behind this business is that nothing can be tracked down. Sweden is a country where it's easy to get lost. It's simple to cross the border without being noticed, and it's easy to disappear. He had a simile for it. He said South Africa is a cuckoo who often lays her eggs in other people's nests."

They continued towards the castle that had collapsed long ago. Svedberg looked around.

"I've never been here before," he said. "I wonder what it was like, being a cop when this castle was in its prime."

They wandered in silence around the crumbled remains of what had once been high walls.

"You have to understand, Martinson and I were really shaken," said Svedberg. "You were covered in blood, your hair was standing on end, and you were waving guns around in both hands."

"Yes, I realize that," said Wallander.

"But it was wrong of us to tell Björk you seemed to be out of your mind."

"I sometimes wonder if I am, in fact."

"What are you thinking of doing?" asked Svedberg.

"I'm thinking of enticing Konovalenko to come after me," said Wallander. "Now I think that's the only way to make him come out of hiding."

Svedberg looked at him, a serious expression on his face.

"What you're doing is dangerous," he said.

"It's less risky when you can anticipate the danger," said Wallander, wondering as he did so what his words really meant.

"You've got to have backup," Svedberg insisted.

"He wouldn't come out then," said Wallander. "It's not enough for him just to think I'm on my own. He'll check. He won't pounce until he's absolutely certain."

"Pounce?"

Wallander shrugged.

"He'll try to kill me," he said. "But I'll make sure he doesn't succeed."

"How?"

"I don't know yet."

Svedberg stared at him in amazement. But he said nothing.

They started back, and stopped once again on the bridge.

"There's something I want to ask you," said Wallander. "I'm worried about my daughter. Konovalenko's unpredictable. That's why I want you to give her a bodyguard."

"Björk will want an explanation," said Svedberg.

"I know," said Wallander. "That's why I'm asking you. You can talk with Martinson. Björk doesn't really need to know."

"I'll try," said Svedberg. "I can see why you're worried."

They started walking again, left the bridge and puffed their way up the hill.

"By the way, somebody who knows your daughter came to see Martinson," said Svedberg, trying to change the subject to something less solemn.

Wallander stared at him in amazement.

"At home?"

"In his office. She was reporting a theft from her car. She'd been your daughter's teacher or something. I don't remember exactly."

Wallander stopped dead.

"One more time," he said. "Just what are you saying?"

Svedberg said it again.

"What was her name?" asked Wallander.

"I've no idea."

"What did she look like?"

"You'd better ask Martinson that."

"Try and remember exactly what he said!"

Svedberg pondered.

"We were having coffee," he said. "Martinson was complaining about being interrupted all the time. He says he'll get an ulcer from all the work piling up. 'At least they could stop breaking into cars just now. A woman came in, by the way. Somebody had broken into her car. She asked about Wallander's daughter. If she was still living in Stockholm.' Something along those lines."

"What did Martinson tell her? Did he tell that woman my daughter is here?"

"I don't know."

"We must call Martinson," said Wallander. He started rushing towards the house. He broke into a run, with Svedberg after him.

"Get Martinson on the phone," said Wallander when they were inside. "Ask him if he said where my daughter is right now. Find out what that woman was called. If he asks why, just tell him you'll explain later."

Svedberg nodded.

"You don't believe there was a car theft?"

"I don't know. But I can't take any risks."

Svedberg got hold of Martinson almost right away. He wrote down a few notes on a scrap of paper. Wallander could hear Martinson was very perplexed by Svedberg's questions.

When the call was over, Svedberg had started to share Wallander's worry.

"He said he'd told her."

"Told her what?"

"That she was staying with your father out at Österlen."

"Why did he do that?"

"She asked him."

Wallander looked at the kitchen clock.

"You'd better make the call," he said. "My father might answer. He's probably eating just now. Ask to talk to my daughter. Then I'll take over."

Wallander gave him the number. It rang for a long time before anybody answered. It was Wallander's father. Svedberg asked to speak to his granddaughter. When he heard the reply, he cut the conversation short.

"She went down to the beach on her bike," he said.

Wallander felt a stabbing pain in his stomach.

"I told her to stay indoors."

"She left half an hour ago," said Svedberg.

They took Svedberg's car, and drove fast. Wallander did not say a word. Svedberg occasionally glanced at him. But he said nothing.

They came to the Kåseberga exit.

"Keep going," said Wallander. "Next exit."

They parked as close to the beach as they could get. There were no other cars. Wallander raced onto the sands with Svedberg behind him. The beach was deserted. Wallander could feel panic rising.

Once again he had the invisible Konovalenko breathing down his neck.

"She could be behind one of the sand dunes," he said.

"Are you sure this is where she'll be?" wondered Svedberg.

"This is her beach," said Wallander. "If she goes to the beach, this is where she comes. You go that way, I'll go this way."

Svedberg walked back towards Kåseberga while Wallander continued in an easterly direction. He tried to convince himself that he had no need to worry. Nothing had happened to her. But he couldn't understand why she hadn't stayed inside the house as promised. Was it really possible that she did not understand how serious it was? In spite of all that had happened?

Occasionally he would turn around and look toward Svedberg. Nothing as yet.

Wallander suddenly thought of Robert Åkerblom. He would have said a prayer in this situation, he told himself. But I have no god to pray to. I don't even have any spirits, like Victor Mabasha. I have my own joy and sorrow, that's all.

There was a guy with a dog on top of the cliff, gazing out to sea. Wallander asked him if he had seen a solitary girl walking along the beach. But the guy shook his head. He had been on the beach with his dog for twenty minutes, and had been alone the whole time.

"Have you seen a man?" asked Wallander, and described Konovalenko.

The guy shook his head again.

Wallander walked on. He felt cold even though there was a trace of spring warmth in the wind. He started walking faster. The beach seemed endless. Then he looked around again. Svedberg was a long way away, but Wallander could see somebody standing by his side. Suddenly, Svedberg started waving.

Wallander ran all the way back. When he got to Svedberg and his daughter he was shattered. He looked at her without saying anything while he waited to get his breath back.

"You were supposed not to leave the house," he said. "Why did you?"

"I didn't think a walk along the beach would matter," she said. "Not when it's light. It's nighttime when things happen, isn't it?"

Svedberg drove and the other two sat in the back seat.

"What shall I tell Grandad?" she asked.

"Nothing," answered Wallander. "I'll talk to him tonight. I'll play cards with him tomorrow. That will cheer him up."

They separated on the road not far from the house.

Svedberg and Wallander drove back to Stjärnsund.

"I want that guard starting tonight," said Wallander.

"I'll go and tell Martinson right away," said Svedberg. "We'll arrange it somehow."

"A police car parked on the road," said Wallander. "I want it to be obvious the house is being watched."

Svedberg got ready to leave.

"I need a few days," said Wallander. "Until then you can keep on looking for me. But I'd like you to call me here occasionally."

"What shall I tell Martinson?" wondered Svedberg.

"Tell him you got the idea of guarding my father's house yourself," said Wallander. "You can figure out how best to convince him."

"You still don't want me to fill Martinson in?"

"It's enough for you to know where I am," said Wallander.

Svedberg left. Wallander went to the kitchen and fried a couple of eggs. Two hours later the horse trailer returned.

"Did she win?" asked Wallander as Sten Widén came into the kitchen.

"She won," he replied. "But barely."

Peters and Norén were in their patrol car, drinking coffee.

They were both in a bad mood. They had been ordered by Svedberg to guard the house where Wallander's father lived. The longest shifts were when your car was standing still. They would be sitting here until somebody came to relieve them. That was many hours away yet. It was a quarter past eleven at night. Darkness had fallen.

"What do you think's happened to Wallander?"

"No idea," said Norén. "How many times do I have to say the same thing? I don't know."

"It's hard not to think about it," Peters went on. "I'm sitting here wondering whether he might be an alcoholic."

"Why should he be?"

"Do you remember that time we caught him drunk?"

"That's not the same as being alcoholic."

"No. But still."

The conversation petered out. Norén got out of the car and stood legs apart to urinate.

That was when he saw the fire. At first he thought it was the reflection from a car's headlights. Then he noticed smoke spiraling up from where the fire was burning.

"Fire!" he shouted to Peters.

Peters got out of the car.

"Can it be a forest fire?" wondered Norén.

The blaze was in a clump of trees on the far side of the nearest group of fields. It was hard to see where the center was because the countryside was undulating.

"We'd better drive over and take a look," said Peters.

"Svedberg said we weren't to leave our posts," said Norén. "No matter what happened."

"It'll only take ten minutes," said Peters. "We have a duty to intervene if we find a fire."

"Call Svedberg first and get permission," said Norén.

"It'll only take ten minutes," said Peters. "What are you scared of?"

"I'm not scared," said Norén. "But orders are orders."

They did as Peters wanted even so. They found their way to the fire via a muddy tractor track. When they got there, they found an old oil drum. Somebody had filled it with paper and plastic to make a good blaze. By the time Peters and Norén arrived, the fire was almost out.

"Funny time to burn garbage," said Peters, looking round.

But there was no sign of anybody. The place was deserted.

"Let's get back," said Norén.

Barely twenty minutes later they were back at the house they were supposed to be guarding. All seemed to be quiet. The lights were out. Wallander's father and daughter were asleep.

Many hours later they were relieved by Svedberg himself.

"All quiet," said Peters.

He did not mention the excursion to the burning oil drum.

Svedberg sat dozing in his car. Dawn broke, and developed into morning.

By eight o'clock he started wondering why there was nobody up. He knew Wallander's father got up early.

By half past eight, he had the distinct impression something was wrong. He got out of his car, crossed the courtyard to the front door and tried the handle.

The door was not locked. He rang the bell and waited. Nobody opened. He entered the dark vestibule and listened. Not a sound. Then he thought he could hear a scratching sound somewhere or other. It sounded like a mouse trying to get through a wall. He followed the noise until he found himself in front of a closed door. He knocked. By way of answer he could hear a muffled bellowing. He flung open the door. Wallander's father was lying in bed. He was tied up, with a length of black tape over his mouth.

Svedberg stood quite still. He carefully removed the tape and untied the ropes. Then he searched through the whole house. The room in which he assumed Wallander's daughter slept was empty. There was nobody in the house but Wallander's father.

"When did it happen?" he asked.

"Last night," said Wallander's father. "Just after eleven."

"How many of them were there?"

"One."

"One?"

"Just one. But he had a gun."

Svedberg stood up. His head was a complete blank.

Then he went out to the telephone to call Wallander.

Chapter Twenty-six

The acrid smell of winter apples.

That was the first thing she noticed when she came to. But then, when she opened her eyes in the darkness, there was nothing but solitude and terror. She was lying on a stone floor and it smelled of damp earth. There was not a sound to be heard, even though fear sharpened all her senses. Carefully, she felt the rough surface of the floor with one hand. It was made of individual slabs fitted together. She realized she was in a cellar. In the house at Österlen where her grandfather lived and where she had been brutally woken and abducted by an unknown man, there was a similar floor in the potato cellar.

When there was nothing more for her senses to register, she felt dizzy and her headache got steadily worse. She could not say how long she had been there in darkness and silence; her wristwatch was still on the bedside table. Nevertheless she had the distinct impression it was many hours since she had been woken up and dragged away.

Her arms were free. But she had a chain around her ankles. When she felt it with her fingers she discovered there was a padlock. The feeling of being confined by an iron lock turned her cold. It occurred to her that people are usually tied up with ropes. They were softer, more flexible. Chains belonged to the past, to slavery and ancient witch trials.

But worst of all during this waking up period were the clothes she had on. She could feel right away they were not hers. They were unfamiliar—their shape, the colors she could not see but seemed to think she could feel with her fingertips, and the smell of a strong washing powder. They were not her clothes, and somebody must have dressed her in them. Somebody had taken off her nightie and dressed her in everything from underclothes to stockings and shoes, an outrage that made her feel sick. The dizziness immediately got stronger. She put her head in her hands and rocked backwards and forwards. It's not true, she thought in desperation. But it was true, and she could even remember what had happened.

She had been dreaming something but could no longer remember the context. She was woken by a man pressing a handkerchief over her nose and mouth. A pungent smell, then she was overcome by a feeling of numbness and fading senses. The light from the lamp outside the kitchen door produced a faint glow in her room. She could see a man in front of her. His face was very close when he bent over her. Now when she thought about him she recalled a strong smell of shaving lotion even though he was unshaven. He said nothing, but although it was almost dark in the room she could see his eyes and had time to think she would never forget them. Then she remembered nothing else until she woke up on the damp stone floor.

Of course she understood why it had happened. The guy who bent over her and anaesthetized her must have been the one who was hunting and being hunted by her father. His eyes were Konovalenko's eyes, just as she had imagined them. The man who killed Victor Mabasha, who killed a policeman and wanted to kill another, her own father. He was the one who had sneaked into her room, dressed her and put chains around her ankles.

When the hatch in the cellar ceiling opened, she was completely unprepared. It occured to her afterward that the man had doubtless been standing up there, listening. The light shining through the hole was very strong, perhaps specially planned to dazzle her. She caught a glimpse of a ladder being dropped down and a pair of brown shoes, a pair of trouser legs approaching her. Then, last of all, the face, the same face and the same eyes that had stared at her as she was being knocked out. She looked away in order not to be dazzled and because her fear had returned and was paralyzing her. But she noticed the cellar was larger than she had thought. In the darkness the walls and ceiling seemed close to her. Maybe she was in a cellar extending under the whole ground floor of a house.

The man stood in such a way that he shielded her from the light streaming down. He had a flashlight in one hand. In the other he had a metal object she could not make out at first.

Then she realized it was a pair of scissors.

She screamed. Shrill, long. She thought he had climbed down the ladder in order to kill her, and that he would do it with the scissors. She grabbed the chains around her legs and started pulling at them, as if she could break free despite everything. All the time he was staring at her, and his face was no more than a silhouette against the strong background light.

Suddenly he turned the flashlight onto his own face. He held it under his chin so that his face looked like a lifeless skull. She fell silent. Her screaming had only increased her fear. And yet she felt strangely exhausted. It was already too late. There was no point in offering resistance.

The skull suddenly started talking.

"You're wasting your time screaming," said Konovalenko. "Nobody will hear you. Besides, there's a risk I'll get annoyed. Then I might hurt you. Better keep quiet."

His last words were like a whisper.

Daddy, she thought. You've got to help me.

Then everything happened very quickly. With the same hand in which he held the flashlight, he grabbed her hair, pulled it and started cutting it off. She started back, in pain and surprise. But he was holding her so tightly, she could not move. She could hear the dry sound of the sharp scissors clipping away around the back of her neck, just under her earlobes. It happened very quickly. Then he let her go. The feeling of wanting to vomit came back. Her cropped hair was another outrage, just like him dressing her without her being aware of it.

Konovalenko rolled up the hair into a ball and put it in his pocket.

He's sick, she thought. He's crazy, a sadist, a madman who kills and feels nothing.

Her thoughts were interrupted by him talking again. The flashlight was shining on her neck, where she was wearing a necklace. It was in the form of a lyre, and she had gotten it from her parents for her fifteenth birthday.

"The necklace," said Konovalenko. "Take it off."

She did as she was told and was careful to avoid touching his hands when she held it out. He left her without a word, climbed up the ladder, and returned her to the darkness.

She crawled away, to one side, until she came up against a wall. She groped along till she came to a corner. Then she tried to hide there.

The previous night, after successfully abducting the cop's daughter, Konovalenko had ordered Tania and Sikosi Tsiki out of the kitchen. He had a great need to be alone, and the kitchen suited him best just now. The house, the last one Rykoff had rented in his life, was planned so that the kitchen was the biggest room. It was arranged in old-fashioned style, with exposed beams, a deep baking oven, and open china cupboards. Copper pots were hanging along one wall. Konovalenko was reminded of his own childhood in Kiev, the big kitchen in the *kolkhoz* where his father had been a political superintendent.

He realized to his surprise that he missed Rykoff. It was not just a feeling of now having to shoulder an increased practical workload. There was also a feeling that could hardly be called melancholy or sorrow, but which nevertheless made him occasionally feel depressed. During his many years as a KGB officer, the value of life, for everybody but himself and his two children, had gradually been reduced to calculable resources or, at the opposite pole, to expendable persons. He was always surrounded by sudden death, and all emotional reactions gradually disappeared more or less completely. But Rykoff's death had affected him, and it made him hate even more this cop who was always getting in his way. Now he had his daughter under his feet, and he knew she would be the bait that would entice him out into the open. But the thought of revenge could not liberate him entirely from his depression. He sat in the kitchen drinking vodka, being careful not to get too drunk, and occasionally looking at his face in a mirror hanging on the wall. It suddenly occurred to him that his face was ugly. Was he starting to get old? Had the collapse of the Soviet empire resulted in some of his own hardness and ruthlessness softening?

At two in the morning, when Tania was asleep or at least pretending to be, and Sikosi Tsiki had shut himself away in his room, he went out into the kitchen where the telephone was, and called

Jan Kleyn. He had thought carefully about what he was going to say. He decided there was no reason to conceal the fact that one of his assistants was dead. It would do no harm for Jan Kleyn to be aware that Konovalenko's work was not without its risks. Then he decided to lie to him one more time. He would say that damned nuisance of a cop had been liquidated. He was so sure he would get him, now that he had his daughter locked up in the cellar, that he dared to declare Wallander dead in advance.

Jan Kleyn listened and made no special comment. Konovalenko knew Jan Kleyn's silence was the best approval he could get for his efforts. Then Jan Kleyn had mentioned that Sikosi Tsiki ought to return to South Africa soon. He asked Konovalenko if there was any doubt about his suitability, if he had displayed any signs of weakness, as Victor Mabasha had done. Konovalenko replied in the negative. That was also a claim made in advance. He had been able to devote very little time to Sikosi Tsiki so far. The main impression he had was of a man completely devoid of emotion. He hardly ever laughed at all, and was just as controlled as he was impeccably dressed. He thought that once Wallander and his daughter were out of the way he would spend a few intensive days teaching the African all he needed to know. But he said Sikosi Tsiki would not let them down. Jan Kleyn seemed satisfied. He concluded their conversation by asking Konovalenko to call again in three days. Then he would receive precise instructions for Sikosi Tsiki's return to South Africa.

The conversation with Jan Kleyn restored some of the energy he thought he had lost thanks to his depression after Rykoff's death. He sat at the kitchen table and concluded that the abduction of Wallander's daughter had been almost embarrassingly easy. It had only taken him a few hours to locate her grandfather's house, once Tania had been to the Ystad police station. He made the call himself and a housekeeper answered the phone. He introduced himself as a representative of the telephone company and inquired whether there was likely to be any change of address before the next edition of the telephone directory went to press. Tania bought a large-scale map of Skåne from the local bookstore, and then they drove out to the house and kept it under observation from a distance. The housekeeper went home late in the afternoon, and a few hours later a single police car parked on the road. When he was certain there were no further guards posted, he rapidly planned a diversion. He drove back to the house in Tomelilla, prepared an oil drum he found lying around in a shed, and told Tania what she had to do. They rented a car from a nearby gas station, then drove back to the house in two cars, found the copse, decided on a time and set to work. Tania made the fire blaze up as intended and then, as planned, left the scene before the cops showed up to investigate the fire. Konovalenko realized he did not have much time, but that was just an extra challenge for him. He flung open the outside door, tied up and silenced the old man in his bed, then chloroformed the daughter and carried her out to the waiting car. The whole operation took less than ten minutes, and he made his escape before the police car got back. Tania had bought some clothes for the girl during the day, and dressed her while she was still unconscious. Then he dragged her down into the cellar and secured her legs with a padlock and chain. It was all so easy, and he wondered whether things would continue to be equally uncomplicated. He had noticed her necklace and thought her father would be able to identify her by it. But he also wanted to give Wallander a different picture of the circumstances, something threatening that would leave no doubt about what he was fully prepared to do. That was when he resolved to cut off her hair and send it to him along with the necklace. Cropped female hair smells of death and ruin, he thought. He's a cop, he'll get the picture.

Konovalenko poured himself another glass of vodka and gazed out the window. Dawn was already rising. There was warmth in the air, and he thought about how he would soon be living in constant sunshine, far away from this climate where you never knew from one day to the next what the weather would be like.

He went to bed for a few hours. When he woke up he looked at his wristwatch. A quarter past nine, Monday, May 18. By this stage Wallander must know that his daughter has been abducted. Now he would be waiting for Konovalenko to contact him.

He can wait a little bit longer, Konovalenko thought. The silence will grow increasingly unbearable with every hour that passes, and his worry greater than his ability to control it.

The hatch leading down to the cellar where Wallander's daughter was imprisoned was just behind his chair. Occasionally he listened for any noises, but everything was silent.

Konovalenko sat there a bit longer, gazing thoughtfully out of the window. Then he got up, got an envelope and put the cropped hair and necklace into it.

Soon he would be in touch with Wallander.

The news of Linda's abduction hit Wallander like an attack of vertigo.

It made him desperate and furious. Sten Widén happened to be in the kitchen when the telephone rang, answered it, and looked on in astonishment as Wallander tore the instrument from the wall and hurled it through the open door into Sten Widén's office. But then he saw how scared Wallander was. His fear was completely bare, naked. Widén realized something awful must have happened. Sympathy often aroused ambivalent reactions in him, but not this time. Wallander's agony over what had happened to his daughter and the fact that nothing could be done about it had hit him hard. He squatted down beside him and patted him on the shoulder.

Meanwhile Svedberg had worked up a frenzy of energy. Once he had made sure Wallander's father was uninjured and did not seem to be especially shocked, he called Peters at home. His wife answered, and said her husband was in bed asleep after his night shift. Svedberg's bellowing left no doubt in her mind that he should be woken immediately. When Peters came to the phone, Svedberg gave him half an hour to get hold of Norén and then come to the house they were supposed to have been guarding. Peters knew Svedberg well and realized he would not have woken him up unless something serious had happened. He asked no questions but promised to hurry. He called Norén, and when they arrived at the grandfather's house, Svedberg confronted them with the brutal truth about what had happened.

"All we can do is tell you the truth," said Norén, who had been vaguely worried the previous evening that there was something odd about the burning oil drum.

Svedberg listened to what Norén had to say. The night before it was Peters who insisted they should go and investigate the fire, but he said nothing. Norén did not pin the blame on him, however. In his report he stated the decision was a joint one.

"I hope nothing happens to Wallander's daughter, for your sake," said Svedberg afterwards.

"Abducted?" asked Norén. "By whom? And why?"

Svedberg gave them a long, serious look before answering.

"I'm going to make you promise me something," he said. "If you keep that promise, I'll try and forget that you acted in complete disregard of clearly expressed orders last night. If the girl comes out of this unharmed, nobody will get to know a thing. Is that clear?"

They both nodded.

"You heard nothing, and you saw nothing last night," he said. "And most important of all, Wallander's daughter has not been abducted. In other words, nothing has happened."

Peters and Norén stared at him, nonplused.

"I mean what I say," said Svedberg again. "Nothing has happened. That's what you have to remember. You'll just have to believe me when I say it's important."

"Is there anything we can do?" asked Peters.

"Yes," said Svedberg. "Go home and get some sleep."

Then Svedberg searched in vain for clues in the courtyard and inside the house. He searched the copse where the oil drum had been. There were tire tracks leading there, but nothing else. He went back to the house and spoke again with Wallander's father. He was in the kitchen drinking coffee, and was scared stiff.

"What's happened?" he asked, worried. "There's no sign of Linda."

"I don't know," said Svedberg, honestly. "But it'll all work itself out, that's for sure."

"You think?" said Wallander's father. His voice was full of doubt. "I could hear how upset Kurt was on the telephone. Where is he, come to that? What's going on?"

"I guess it'll be best if he explains that himself," said Svedberg, getting to his feet. "I'm going to see him."

"Say hello from me," said the old man. "Tell him I'm doing just fine."

"I'll do that," said Svedberg, and left.

Wallander was barefoot on the gravel outside Sten Widén's house when Svedberg drove up. It was nearly eleven in the morning. Svedberg explained in detail what must have happened while they were still out in the courtyard. He did not refrain from mentioning how easily Peters and Norén had been lured away for the short time needed to abduct his daughter. Finally he passed on the greeting from his father.

Wallander listened attentively all the time. Even so, Svedberg had the impression there was something distant about him. Normally he could always look Wallander in the eye when he spoke to him, but now his eyes were wandering about aimlessly. Svedberg could see that mentally, he was with his daughter, wherever she might be.

"No clues?" asked Wallander.

"Nothing at all."

Wallander nodded. They went into the house.

"I've been trying to think," said Wallander when they sat down. Svedberg could see his hands were shaking.

"This is Konovalenko's work, of course," he continued. "Just as I'd feared. It's all my fault. I ought to have been there. Everything should have been different. Now he's using my daughter to get hold of me. He evidently has no assistants. He's working on his own."

"He must have at least one," objected Svedberg cautiously. "If I understood Peters and Norén right, he couldn't possibly have had time to light the fire himself, then tie up your dad and run off with your daughter."

Wallander thought for a moment.

"The oil drum was lit by Tania," he said. "Rykoff's wife. So there are two of them. We don't know where they are. Presumably in a house somewhere in the countryside. Not far from Ystad. A remotely situated house. A house we could have found if circumstances had been different. We can't now."

Sten Widén tiptoed to the table and served coffee. Wallander looked at him.

"I need something stronger," he said.

Sten Widén returned with a half-empty bottle of whiskey. Without hesitation Wallander took a gulp straight from the bottle.

"I've been trying to figure out what'll happen next," said Wallander. "He'll get in touch with me. And he'll use my dad's house. That's where I'll wait until I hear from him. I don't know what he'll propose. At best my life for hers. At worst, God only knows."

He turned to Svedberg.

"That's how I see it," he said. "Do you think I'm wrong?"

"You're probably right," replied Svedberg. "The question is just what we're going to do about it."

"Nobody should do anything," said Wallander. "No cops around the house, nothing. Konovalenko will smell the slightest whiff of danger. I'll have to be alone in the house with my father. Your job will be to make sure nobody goes there."

"You can't handle this on your own," said Svedberg. "You've got to let us help you."

"I don't want my daughter to die," said Wallander quite simply. "I have to sort this out myself."

Svedberg realized the conversation was over. Wallander had made up his mind.

"I'll take you to Löderup," said Svedberg.

"That won't be necessary. You can take the Duett," said Sten Widén.

Wallander nodded.

He almost fell as he stood up. He grabbed the edge of the table.

"No problem," he said.

Svedberg and Sten Widén stood in the courtyard, watching him drive off in the Duett.

"How will it all end?" asked Svedberg.

Sten Widén did not answer.

When Wallander reached Löderup he found his father painting in his studio.

Wallander saw that for the first time ever he had abandoned his eternal theme, a landscape in the evening sun, with or without a wood grouse in the front corner. This time he was painting a different landscape, darker, more chaotic. The picture did not hang together. The woods were growing directly out of the lake, and the mountains in the background overwhelmed the viewer.

He put down his brushes after Wallander had been standing behind his back for a while. When he turned around Wallander could see he was scared.

"Let's go in," said his father. "I sent the aide home."

His father placed his hand on Wallander's shoulder. He could not remember the last time the old man had made a gesture like that.

When they were inside Wallander told him everything that had happened. He could see his father was incapable of separating out the various incidents as they crisscrossed one another. Even so he wanted to give him an idea of what had been going on these last three weeks. He did not want to hide the fact that he had killed another human being, nor that his daughter was in great danger. The man holding her prisoner, who had tied him up in his own bed, was absolutely ruthless.

Afterwards his father sat looking down at his hands.

"I can deal with it," said Wallander. "I'm a good cop. I'll stay here until this man contacts me. It could be any time now. Or he could wait until tomorrow."

The afternoon was close to being evening, and still no word from Konovalenko. Svedberg called twice, but Wallander had nothing new to tell him. He sent his father out into the studio to go on painting. He couldn't stand him sitting in the kitchen, staring at his hands. His father would normally have been furious at the thought of having to do what his son told him, but on this occasion he just stood up and went. Wallander paced up and down, sat down on a chair for a moment, then got up again right away. Occasionally he would go out into the courtyard and gaze out over the fields. Then he would come back in and start pacing again. He tried eating twice, but could not tolerate anything. His anguish, his worry and his helplessness made it impossible for him to think straight. On several occasions Robert Åkerblom came into his mind. But he sent him packing, scared that the very thought could be a bad omen for what might happen to his daughter.

Evening came and Konovalenko still had not made contact. Svedberg called to say he could be reached at home from now on. Wallander called Sten Widén but did not really have anything to say. At ten o'clock he sent his father to bed. It was spring, and still light outside. He sat on the steps outside the kitchen door for a while. When he was sure his father was asleep, he called Baiba Liepa in Riga. No reply at first. But she was home when he tried again half an hour later. He was icily calm as he told her his daughter had been abducted by a very dangerous man. He said he had no one to talk to, and just then he felt he was telling the absolute truth. Then he apologized once again for the night when he had been drunk and woken her up with his call. He tried to explain his feelings for her, but without success. The words he needed were outside his grasp of English. Before hanging up he promised to get back to her. She listened to what he had to say, but hardly said anything herself from start to finish. Afterwards he wondered whether he really had been talking to her, or whether it was all in his imagination.

He spent a sleepless night. Occasionally he slumped down into one of his father's worn old armchairs and closed his eyes. But just as he was about to doze off, he would wake up again with a start. He started pacing up and down once more, and it was like reliving the whole of his life. Toward dawn he stood staring at a solitary hare sitting motionless in the courtyard.

It was now Tuesday, May 19.

Shortly after five o'clock it started raining.

The message came just before eight.

A taxi from Simrishamn turned into the courtyard. Wallander heard the car approaching from some way off, and went out onto the steps when it came to a halt. The driver got out and handed over a fat envelope.

The letter was addressed to his father.

"It's for my father," he said. "Where is it from?"

"A lady handed it in at the taxi station in Simrishamn," said the driver, who was in a hurry and did not want to get wet. "She paid for it to be delivered. It's all fixed. I don't need a receipt."

Wallander nodded. Tania, he thought. She has taken over her husband's role as errand boy.

The cab disappeared. Wallander was alone in the house. His father was already out painting in his studio.

It was a padded envelope. He examined it carefully before starting to open it along one of the short sides. At first he could not see what was inside. Then he saw Linda's hair, and the necklace he had once given her.

He sat still as a statue, staring at the cropped hair lying on the table in front of him. Then he started crying. His pain had passed another limit, and he could not fight it any more. What had Konovalenko done to her? It was all his fault, getting her involved in this.

Then he forced himself to read the enclosed letter.

Konovalenko would be in touch again in exactly twelve hours.

They needed to meet in order to sort out their problems, he wrote. Wallander would just have to wait until then. Any contact with the police would put his daughter's life in danger.

The letter was unsigned.

He looked again at his daughter's hair. The world was helpless in the face of such evil. How could he stop Konovalenko?

He imagined these were exactly the thoughts Konovalenko wanted him to be having. He had also given him twelve hours with no hope of doing anything other than what Konovalenko had dictated.

Wallander sat frozen like a statue on his chair.

He had no idea what to do.

Chapter Twenty-seven

A long time ago, Karl Evert Svedberg had decided to become a cop for a very particular reason, and one reason only—a reason he tried to keep secret.

He was terrified of the dark.

Ever since he was a child he had slept with the bedside lamp lit. Unlike most other people, he did not notice his fear of the dark receding as he grew older. On the contrary, it had become worse when he was a teenager. And so had his feeling of shame at suffering from a defect that could hardly be classified as anything other than cowardice. His father was a baker who rose at half past two every morning; he therefore suggested his son should follow him into the business. As he would sleep in the afternoons, the problem would solve itself. His mother was a milliner, considered by her dwindling circle of customers to be very skillful at creating individual and expressive ladies' hats, and she regarded the problem as altogether more serious. She took her son to a child psychologist, who was convinced the problem would disappear in time. But the opposite occurred. He became even more scared. He could never figure out what was the cause of it all, though. In the end he decided to become a cop. He thought his fear of the dark might be countered by boosting his personal courage. But now, this spring day, Tuesday, May 19, he woke up with his bedside lamp on. Moreover, it was his custom to lock the bedroom door. He lived alone in an apartment in central Ystad. He was born in the town, and disliked leaving it—even for short periods.

He put the light out, stretched, and got up. He had slept badly. The developments concerning Kurt Wallander had made him upset and scared. He could see that he had to assist Wallander. During the night he had worried about what he could do without breaking the vow of silence Wallander had imposed upon him. In the end, shortly before dawn, he made up his mind. He would try to track down the house where Konovalenko was hiding. He guessed it was highly likely that Wallander's daughter was being held prisoner there.

He got to the police station just before eight. The only starting point he had was what had happened at the military training ground a few hours previously. It was Martinson who had gone though the few belongings he found in the dead men's clothes. There was nothing remarkable. Nevertheless, as dawn broke, Svedberg decided to go through the material one more time. He went to the room where the various pieces of evidence and other finds from several crime scenes were kept, and identified the relevant plastic bags. Martinson had found nothing at all in the African's pockets, which seemed significant in itself. Svedberg replaced the bag containing nothing more than a few grains of dust. Then he carefully tipped out onto the table the contents of the other bag. Martinson had found cigarettes, a lighter, grains of tobacco, unclassifiable bits of dust, and other odds and ends one would expect to find in the fat man's pocket. Svedberg contemplated the objects on the table in front of him. His interest was immediately focused on the cigarette lighter. It had an advertising slogan that was almost completely worn away. Svedberg held it up to the light and tried to figure out what it said. He replaced the bag, and took the lighter to his office. At ten-thirty they were due at a meeting to establish how things were going in the attempt to capture Konovalenko and Wallander. He wanted the time before that meeting to himself. He took a magnifying glass from a drawer, adjusted the desk lamp, and started to study the lighter. After a minute or so, his heart started beating faster. He had managed to figure out the text, and it presented a clue. If the clue would lead to a solution was too early to say, of course. But the lighter sported an advertising slogan for ICA in Tomelilla. That was not conclusive evidence in itself. Rykoff could have picked it up more or less anywhere. But if Rykoff had in fact been at the ICA store in Tomelilla, it was not impossible that a checkout assistant might be able to remember a man who spoke broken Swedish, and most obviously of all, was incredibly fat. He put the lighter in his pocket and left the police station without saying where he was going.

He drove to Tomelilla, went into the ICA store, showed his ID, and asked to see the manager. This turned out to be a young man by the name of Sven Persson. Svedberg showed him the lighter and explained what he wanted to know. The manager thought for a while, then shook his head. He could not remember a fat guy being in the store recently.

"Talk to Britta," he said. "The girl at the check-out. But I'm afraid she has a pretty bad memory. Well, she's scatterbrained at least."

"Is she the only check-out person?" wondered Svedberg.

"We have an extra one on Saturdays," said the manager. "She's not in today."

"Call her," said Svedberg. "Ask her to come here at once."

"Is it that important?"

"Yes. Immediately."

The manager disappeared to make the call. Svedberg had left no doubt about what he wanted. He waited until Britta, a woman in her fifties, was through with the customer she was dealing with and who had produced a wad of various coupons for discounts and special offers. Svedberg identified himself.

"I want to know if you've had a big, fat guy shopping here recently," he said.

"We get lots of fat guys shopping here," said Britta unsympathetically.

Svedberg rephrased the question.

"Not just fat," he said. "Positively obese. Absolutely enormous. And a guy who speaks bad Swedish as well. Has anyone of that description been here?"

She tried to remember. At the same time Svedberg could see her growing curiosity was affecting her concentration.

"He hasn't done anything in the least exciting," said Svedberg. "I just want to know if he's been in here."

"No," she said. "If he was that fat, I'd have remembered the guy. I'm dieting myself, you see. So I look at people."

"Have you been away at all lately?"

"No."

"Not even for an hour?"

"Well, I sometimes have to go out an errand."

"Who does the check-out then?"

"Sven."

Svedberg could feel any hope he had ebbing away. He thanked her for her assistance and wandered around the shop while waiting for the part-timer. As he did so, his mind was working overtime, trying to figure what to do if the lead given by the inscription on the cigarette lighter went nowhere. Where could he find another starting point?

The girl who worked Saturdays was young, barely more than seventeen. She was strikingly corpulent, and Svedberg dreaded having to talk with her about fat people. The manager introduced her as Annika Hagström. Svedberg was unsure how to start. The manager had withdrawn discreetly. They were standing by some shelves stacked high with food for dogs and cats.

"I gather you work here on Saturdays," Svedberg began hesitantly.

"I'm out of work," said Annika Hagström. "There aren't any jobs. Sitting here on Saturdays is all I do."

"It can be pretty bad just now," said Svedberg, trying to sound understanding.

"Actually, I've wondered about becoming a cop," said the girl.

Svedberg stared at her in astonishment.

"But I'm not sure I'm the type to wear a uniform," she went on. "Why aren't you wearing a uniform?"

"We don't always have to," said Svedberg.

"Maybe I'll think again, then," said the girl. "Anyway, what have I done?"

"Nothing," said Svedberg. "I just wanted to ask if you'd seen a male personage in this shop who looked a little unusual."

He groaned inwardly at his clumsy way of putting it.

"What do you mean, unusual?"

"A guy who is very fat, and speaks bad Swedish."

"Oh, him," she said immediately.

Svedberg stared at her.

"He was here last Saturday," she continued.

Svedberg took a notebook out of his pocket.

"When?" he asked.

"Shortly after nine."

"Was he alone?"

"Yes."

"Do you remember what he bought?"

"Quite a lot. Several packets of tea, among other things. He filled four bags."

That's him, thought Svedberg. Russians drink tea like we drink coffee.

"How did he pay?"

"He was carrying money loose in his pocket."

"How did he seem? Was he nervous? Or what?"

Her answers were all immediate and specific.

"He was in a hurry. He practically stuffed the food into the bags."

"Did he say anything?"

"No."

"How do you know he had a foreign accent, then?"

"He said hello and thank you. You could tell right away."

Svedberg nodded. He had just one more question.

"You don't happen to know where he lives, I suppose?" he wondered.

She furrowed her brow and thought hard.

Surely she can't have an answer for that one as well, Svedberg thought quickly.

"He lives somewhere in the direction of the quarry," she said.

"Quarry?"

"Do you know where the college is?"

Svedberg nodded. He knew.

"Drive past there then take a left," she said. "Then left again."

"How do you know he lives there?"

"Then next in line was an old guy called Holgerson," she said. "He always gossips when he pays. He said he'd never seen a guy as fat as that before. Then he said he'd seen him outside a house down by the quarry. There are quite a few empty houses there. Holgerson knows about everything that happens in Tomelilla."

Svedberg put his notebook away. He was in a hurry now.

"I'll tell you something." he said. "I guess you really should become a cop."

"What did he do?" she asked.

"Nothing," said Svedberg. "If he comes back it's very important you don't say somebody's been asking about him. Least of all a cop."

"I won't say a word," she said. "Would it be possible to come and see you at the police station some time?"

"Just call and ask for me," said Svedberg. "Ask for Svedberg. That's me. I'll show you around."

Her face lit up.

"I'll do that," she said.

"Not just now, though," said Svedberg. "Wait a few weeks. We're pretty busy right now."

He left the store and followed the directions she had given him. When he came to an exit leading to the quarry, he stopped the car and got out. He had a pair of binoculars in the glove compartment. He walked to the quarry and climbed up onto an abandoned stone crusher.

There were two houses on the other side of the quarry, a fair distance apart. One of them was rather decrepit, but the other seemed to be in better condition. He could see no cars parked in the courtyard, and the house looked deserted. Even so, he had the feeling that this was the place. It was remote. There was no road nearby. Nobody would take that dead-end track unless they had business at the house.

He waited, binoculars ready. It started drizzling.

After nearly half an hour, the door suddenly opened. A woman stepped out. Tania, he thought. She stood quite still, smoking. Svedberg could not see her face because she was half-hidden by a tree.

He dropped his binoculars. It must be the place, he thought. The girl in the store had her eyes and ears about her, and a good memory as well. He climbed down from the stone crusher and went back to his car. It was already after ten. He decided to call the police station and report sick. He had no time to sit around in meetings.

Now he must talk to Wallander.

Tania threw down her cigarette and stubbed it out with her heel. She was standing out in the courtyard, in the drizzle. The weather was in tune with her mood. Konovalenko had withdrawn with the new African, and she had no interest in whatever they were talking about. Vladimir had kept her informed while he was alive. She knew some important politician in South Africa was going to be killed.

But she had no idea who or why. No doubt Vladimir had told her, but she had forgotten.

She went out into the yard in order to have a few minutes to herself. She still had barely had time to work out the implications of Vladimir's death. She was also surprised by the sorrow and pain she felt. Their marriage had never been more than a practical arrangement that suited them both. When they fled the collapsing Soviet Union, they were able to give each other some support. Afterwards, when they came to Sweden, she gave her life some purpose by helping Vladimir with his various undertakings. All that changed when Konovalenko suddenly turned up. At first Tania was quite attracted to him. His decisive manner, his self-confidence stood in sharp contrast to Vladimir's personality, and she did not hesitate when Konovalenko started to take a serious interest in her. It did not take her long to see he was just using her, however. His lack of emotion, his intense contempt for other people horrified her. Konovalenko came to dominate their lives totally. Occasionally, late at night, she and Vladimir had talked about getting out, starting all over again, far away from Konovalenko's influence. But nothing had ever come of it, and now Vladimir was dead. She was standing in the courtyard, thinking about how much she missed him. She had no idea what would happen next. Konovalenko was obsessed with wiping out this policeman who had killed Vladimir and caused him so much trouble. She guessed thoughts about the future could wait until it was all over, the cop dead and the African back in South Africa to carry out his assignment. She realized she was dependent on Konovalenko, whether she liked it or not. She was in exile, and there was no going back. She had vague and increasingly rare thoughts about Kiev, the city both she and Vladimir came from. What hurt was not all the memories, but her conviction that she would never again see the place and the people who used to be the foundation of her life. The door had slammed inexorably behind her. It was locked, and the key had been tossed away. The final remnants had gone with Vladimir.

She thought about the girl being held prisoner in the cellar. That was the only thing she had asked Konovalenko about these last few days. What would happen to her? He said they would let her go once he had captured her father. But she wondered from the first if he really meant that. She shuddered at the thought of him killing her as well.

Tania had trouble sorting out her own feelings on this matter. She could feel unreserved hatred for the girl's father, who had killed her husband, and barbarically to boot, although Konovalenko had not explained in any detail what he meant by that. But sacrificing the policeman's daughter as well was going too far, she thought. At the same time she knew she could do nothing to prevent it happening eventually. The slightest sign of resistance on her part would only result in Konovalenko turning his deadly attention to her as well.

She was shivering in the rain, which had grown heavier, and went back into the house. The mumbling sound of Konovalenko's voice could be heard from behind the closed door. She went out into the kitchen and looked at the hatch in the floor. The clock on the wall indicated it was time to give the girl something to eat and drink. She had already prepared a plastic carrier bag with a flask and some sandwiches. So far the girl in the cellar had never touched the food she had been given. Each time Tania came back up with what she had taken down last time. She switched on the light Konovalenko had rigged up. She carried a flashlight in one hand.

Linda had crept into a corner. She lay there rolled up, as if suffering severe stomach cramps. Tania shone the flashlight on the pot they had left on the stone floor. It was unused. She was full of pity for the girl. At first she was so preoccupied with the pain she felt after Vladimir's death, there had been no room for anything else. But now, when she saw the girl rolled up, paralyzed with fear, she had the feeling there was no limit to Konovalenko's cruelty. There was absolutely no reason why she should be in a dark cellar. And with chains around her legs. She could have been kept locked in one of the rooms upstairs, tied so she could not leave the house.

The girl did not move, but she followed Tania's movements with her eyes. Her cropped hair made Tania feel sick. She crouched down beside the motionless girl.

"It'll be over soon," she said.

The girl did not answer. Her eyes stared straight into Tania's.

"You must try and eat something," she said. "It'll be over soon."

Her fear has already started to consume her, Tania thought. It's gnawing away at her from the inside.

Suddenly she knew she would have to help Linda. It could cost her her life. But she had no choice. Konovalenko's evil was to great to bear, even for her.

"It'll be over soon," she whispered, placing the bag by the girl's face and going back up the stairs. She closed the hatch and turned around.

Konovalenko was standing there. She gave a start and squealed softly. He had a way of creeping up on people without a sound. She sometimes had the feeling his hearing was unnaturally well developed. Like a nocturnal animal, she thought. He hears what other people can't.

"She's asleep," said Tania.

Konovalenko looked at her sternly. Then he suddenly smiled and left the kitchen without saying a word.

Tania flopped into a chair and lit a cigarette. She noticed her hands were shaking. But she knew now the resolve that had formed within her was irreversible.

Shortly after one o'clock Svedberg called Wallander.

He picked up the receiver after the first ring. Svedberg had been sitting in his apartment for some time, trying to figure out how to convince Wallander he should not challenge Konovalenko on his own again. But he realized Wallander was no longer acting rationally. He had reached a point where emotional impulses were just as strong as reason in guiding his actions. The only thing he could do was to urge Wallander not to confront Konovalenko on his own. In a way he is not responsible for his actions, Svedberg thought. He is being driven by fear of what might happen to his daughter. There's no telling what he might do.

He came straight to the point.

"I've found Konovalenko's house," he said.

He had the feeling Wallander winced at the other end of the line.

"I found a clue in the stuff Rykoff had in his pockets," he went on. "I don't need to go into details, but it led me to an ICA store in Tomelilla. A check-out girl with a phenomenal memory pointed me in the right direction. The house is just to the east of Tomelilla. By a quarry that doesn't seem to be in commission any more. It used to be a farm."

"I hope nobody saw you," said Wallander.

Svedberg could hear how tense and weary he was.

"Not a soul," he said. "No need to worry."

"How could I not worry?" asked Wallander.

Svedberg did not answer.

"I think I know where that quarry is," Wallander went on. "If what you say is right, that gives me an advantage over Konovalenko."

"Have you heard from him again?" asked Svedberg.

"Twelve hours means eight o'clock tonight," said Wallander. "He'll be on time. I'm not going to do anything until he contacts me again."

"It'll be catastrophic if you try to take him on your own," said Svedberg. "I can't bear to think what would happen."

"You know there's no other possibility," said Wallander. "I'm not going to tell you where I shall meet him. I know you mean well. But I can't take any risks. Thank you for finding the house for me. I won't forget that."

Then he hung up.

Svedberg was left sitting there with the receiver in his hand.

What should he do now? It had not occurred to him that Wallander might simply withhold vital information.

He replaced the receiver, convinced that while Wallander might not think he needed any help, Svedberg certainly did. The only question was who he could get to go with him.

He went over to a window and looked out at the church tower half-hidden by the rooftops. When Wallander was on the run after that night at the military training ground, he had chosen to contact Sten Widén, he thought. Svedberg had never met the guy before. He had never even heard Wallander mention him. Nevertheless, they were obviously close friends who had known each other for a long time. He was the one Wallander turned to for help. Now Svedberg decided to do the same thing. He left the apartment and drove out of town. The rain had grown heavier, and a wind was getting up. He followed the coast road, thinking how all the things that had happened lately must come to an end soon. It was all too much for a little police district like Ystad.

He found Sten Widén out in the stable. He was standing in front of a stall fitted with bars in which a horse was pacing up and down restlessly and occasionally delivering a vicious kick at the woodwork.

Svedberg said hello and stood by his side. The restless horse was very tall and thin. Svedberg had never sat on a horse's back in his whole life. He had a great fear of horses and could not understand how anyone would voluntarily spend his life training them and looking after them.

"She's sick," said Sten Widén suddenly. "But I don't know what's matter with her."

"She seems a bit restless," said Svedberg cautiously.

"That's the pain," said Sten Widén.

Then he drew the bolt and entered the stall. He grabbed the halter and the horse calmed down almost immediately. Then he bent down and examined her left foreleg. Svedberg leaned carefully over the edge of the stall to look.

"It's swollen," said Sten Widén. "Can you see?"

Svedberg could not see anything of the sort. But he muttered something in agreement. Sten Widén patted the horse for a while, then emerged from the stall.

"I need to talk to you," said Svedberg.

"Let's go in," said Sten Widén.

When they entered the house Svedberg saw an elderly lady sitting on a sofa in the untidy living room. She did not seem to fit in with Sten Widén's surroundings. She was strikingly elegantly dressed, heavily made up, and wearing expensive jewelry. Sten Widén noticed he had seen her.

"She's waiting for her chauffeur to fetch her," he said. "She owns two horses I have in training."

"So that's it," said Svedberg.

"A master builder's widow from Trelleborg," said Sten Widén. "She'll be on her way home soon. She comes occasionally and just sits there. I think she's very lonely."

Sten Widén said the last words with a degree of understanding that surprised Svedberg.

They sat in the kitchen.

"I don't really know why I'm here," said Svedberg. "Or rather, I do know, of course. But what exactly is involved if I ask you to help, I have no idea."

He explained about the house he had discovered near the quarry outside Tomelilla. Sten Widén stood up and groped around in a drawer crammed full of papers and racing programs. Eventually he produced a dirty, torn map. He unfolded it on the table and Svedberg used a blunt pencil to point out where the house was situated.

"I've no idea what Wallander intends to do," said Svedberg. "All I know is that he intends to confront Konovalenko on his own. He can't take any risks for the sake of his daughter. One can understand that, of course. The problem is simply that Wallander hasn't a chance in hell of getting Konovalenko into safe custody on his own."

"So you're intending to help him?" said Sten Widén.

Svedberg nodded.

"But I can't do that on my own either," he said. "I couldn't think of anybody to talk to apart from you. It's just not possible to take another cop. That's why I came here. You know him, you're his friend."

"Maybe," said Sten Widén.

"Maybe?" said Svedberg, puzzled.

"It's true we've known each other for a long time," said Sten Widén. "But we haven't been in close touch for over ten years."

"I didn't know that," said Svedberg. "I thought things were different."

A car turned into the courtyard. Sten Widén got up and went out with the builder's widow. It seemed to Svedberg he had made a mistake. Sten Widén was not as close a friend of Wallander's as he thought.

"What exactly are you thinking of?" asked Sten Widén when he returned to the kitchen.

Svedberg told him. Some time after eight o'clock he would call Wallander. He would not be able to find out exactly what Konovalenko had said. Nevertheless, Svedberg hoped he might be able to persuade Wallander to tell him when the meeting was to take place, if nothing else. Once he knew the time of the meeting, he and preferably somebody else as well would go to the house during the night so they would be there on hand, invisible, in case Wallander needed help.

Sten Widén listened, expressionless. When Svedberg had finished, he got up and left the room. Svedberg wondered if he had gone to the bathroom, perhaps. But when Sten Widén reappeared, he had a rifle in his hand.

"We'd better try and help him," he said abruptly.

He sat down to examine the rifle. Svedberg put his pistol on the table to show that he was armed as well. Sten Widén made a face.

"Not much to go hunting a desperate madman with," he said.

"Can you leave the horses?" asked Svedberg.

"Ulrika sleeps here," he said. "One of the girls who assist me."

Svedberg felt hesitant in Sten Widén's presence. His taciturnity and odd personality made it hard for Svedberg to relax. But he was glad he would not be on his own.

Svedberg went home at three in the afternoon. They agreed he would be in touch as soon as he had spoken to Wallander. On the way to Ystad he bought the evening papers that had just arrived. He sat in the car leafing through them. Konovalenko and Wallander were still big news, but they had already been relegated to the inside pages.

Svedberg's attention was suddenly caught by some headlines. The headlines he had been dreading more than anything else.

And alongside them a photo of Wallander's daughter.

He called Wallander at twenty past eight.

Konovalenko had made contact.

"I know you won't want to tell me what's going to happen," said Svedberg. "But at least tell me when."

Wallander hesitated before replying.

"Seven o'clock tomorrow morning," he said.

"Not at the house, though," said Svedberg.

"No," said Wallander. "Somewhere else. But no more questions now."

"What's going to happen?"

"He's promised to release my daughter. That's all I know."

You know all right, thought Svedberg. You know he'll try to kill you.

"Be careful, Kurt," he said.

"Sure," said Wallander, and hung up.

Svedberg was certain now the meeting would take place at the house by the quarry. Wallander's reply had come a little bit too readily. He sat quite still.

Then he called Sten Widén. They agreed to meet at Svedberg's place at midnight, then drive out to Tomelilla.

They drank a cup of coffee in Svedberg's kitchen.

It was still raining outside.

They set out at a quarter to two in the morning.

Chapter Twenty-eight

The man outside her house in Bezuidenhout Park had come back again. It was the third morning in succession Miranda had seen him standing on the other side of the street, motionless, waiting. She could see him through the thin drapes in the living room window. He was white, dressed in a suit and tie, and looked like a lost soul in this world of hers. She had noticed him early in the morning, not long after Matilda left for school. She reacted immediately, for people very rarely used her street. Every morning the men living in the detached houses drove off in their cars to the center of Johannesburg. Later on the womenfolk would set out in their own cars to do the shopping, go to the beauty parlor, or simply to get away. Bezuidenhout was the haunt of frustrated and restless members of the white middle class. The ones who could not quite make it into the very top white echelons. Miranda knew many of these people were thinking about emigrating. It had occurred to her that yet another fundamental truth was inevitably about to be revealed. For these people South Africa was not the natural fatherland where soil and blood had run in the same veins and furrows. Even if they had been born here, they did not hesitate to start thinking about running away as soon as de Klerk made his speech to the nation that February. Nelson Mandela had been released from prison, and a new age was dawning. A new age that might perhaps see other blacks as well as Miranda living in Bezuidenhout.

But the man in the street was a stranger. He did not belong there, and Miranda wondered what he was after. Anyone standing still on a street at dawn must be looking for something, something lost or dreamed about. She had stood behind the thin curtains for a long time, watching him; in the end she concluded it was her house he was keeping under observation. At first that scared her. Was he from some unknown authority, one of those incomprehensible supervisory organizations that were still governing the lives of blacks in South Africa? She had expected him to announce his presence, to ring the doorbell. But the longer he stood there, motionless, the more she began to doubt that. Besides, he was not carrying a briefcase. Miranda was used to white South Africa always addressing blacks through the medium of dogs, police, swinging batons and armored cars, or papers. But he had no briefcase, and his hands were empty.

The first morning Miranda kept returning to the window to check if he was still there. She thought of him as a sort of statue no one was sure where to place, or that nobody wanted. By shortly before nine, the street was empty. But the next day he was back again, in the same place, staring straight at her window. She had a nasty suspicion he might be there because of Matilda. He could be from the secret police; in the background, invisible to her eyes, there could be cars waiting, full of uniformed men. But something about his behavior made her hesitate. That was when she first had the idea he might be standing there precisely for her to see him, and realize he was not dangerous. He was not a threat, but was giving her time to get used to him.

Now it was the third morning, Wednesday, May 20, and he was there again. Suddenly he looked around, then crossed the street, opened her gate and walked along the path to her front door. She was still behind the drapes when the bell rang. That particular morning Matilda had not gone to school. She had a headache and a temperature when she woke up, possibly malaria, and now she was asleep in her room. Miranda carefully closed her bedroom door before going to answer the front door. He had only rung once. He knew somebody was at home, and it seemed he was also sure somebody would answer.

He's young, thought Miranda when she confronted him in the doorway.

The man's voice was clear when he spoke.

"Miranda Nkoyi? I wonder if I might come in for a moment? I promise not to disturb you for long."

Alarm bells were ringing somewhere inside her. But she let him in even so, showed him into the living room and invited him to take a seat.

As usual, Georg Scheepers felt insecure when he was alone with a black woman. It did not happen often in his life. Mostly it would be one of the black secretaries that had appeared in the prosecutor's office when the race laws were relaxed recently. This was in fact the first time he had ever sat with a black woman in her own home.

He had the recurrent feeling that black people despised him. He was always looking for traces of enmity. The vague feeling of guilt was never so clear as when he was alone with a black. He could sense his feeling of helplessness growing, now that he was sitting opposite a black woman. It might have been different with a man. As a white man he normally had the upper hand. But now he had lost that advantage, and his chair sank beneath him until he felt like he was sitting on the floor.

He had spent the last few days and previous weekend trying to delve as far as possible into Jan Kleyn's secret. He knew now that Jan Kleyn was always visiting this house in Bezuidenhout. It was something that had been going on for many years, ever since Jan Kleyn moved to Johannesburg after graduating from the university. With the assistance of Wervey and some of his own contacts, he had also managed to get around the bank confidentiality regulations, and knew Jan Kleyn transferred a large sum of money to Miranda Nkoyi every month.

The secret had opened up before his very eyes. Jan Kleyn, one of the most respected members of BOSS, an Afrikaner who carried his high esteem with pride, lived in secret with a black woman. For her sake he was prepared to take the greatest of risks. If President de Klerk was considered a traitor, Jan Kleyn was another.

But Scheepers had the impression he was only just scraping the surface of the secret, and decided to visit the woman. He would not explain who he was, and it was possible she might never tell Jan Kleyn he had been there, the next time her lover came to visit. If she did, he would soon have identified the visitor as Georg Scheepers. But he would not be sure why; he would be afraid that his secret had been exposed and that Scheepers would have a hold over Jan Kleyn in the future. Of course, there was a risk that Jan Kleyn would decide to kill him. But Scheepers believed that he had insured himself against that possibility as well. He would not leave the house until Miranda understood quite clearly that several other people were aware of Jan Kleyn's secret life outside the closed world of the intelligence service.

She looked at him, looked through him. She was very beautiful. Her beauty had survived; it survived everything, subjugation, compulsion, pain, as long as the spirit of resistance was there. Ugliness, stunted growth, degeneration, all those things followed in the wake of resignation.

He forced himself to tell her how things stood. That the man who paid her visits, paid for her house, and was presumably her lover, was a man under grave suspicion of conspiracy against the state and the lives of individuals. As he spoke he got the impression she knew some of what he was telling her, but that some parts were new to her. At the same time he had a strange feeling that she was somehow relieved, as if she had been expecting, or even fearing, something different. He immediately started wondering what that could be. He suspected it had something to do with the secret, the elusive impression that there was yet another secret door waiting to be opened.

"I need to know," he said. "I really don't have any questions. You shouldn't think either that I'm asking you to give testify against your own husband. But what is as stake is very big. A threat to the whole country. So big I can't even tell you who I am."

"But you are his enemy," she said. "When the herd senses danger, some animals run off on their own. And they are doomed. Is that how it is?"

"Maybe," said Scheepers. "It may be."

He was sitting with his back to the window. Just when Miranda was talking about the animals and the herd, he detected the slightest of movements at the door directly behind her. It was like someone had started to turn the handle but then had a change of heart. It dawned on him he had not seen the young woman leave the house that morning. The young woman who must be Miranda's daughter.

It was one of the strange circumstances he had discovered while doing his research these last few days. Miranda Nkoyi was registered as the single housekeeper for a man named Sidney Houston, who spent most of his time on his cattle ranch miles away in the vast plains east of Harare. Scheepers had no difficulty in seeing through this business of the absentee rancher, especially when he found out that Jan Kleyn and Houston had studied together at university. But the other woman, Miranda's daughter? She did not exist. And now here she was, standing behind a door, listening to their conversation.

He was overwhelmed by the thought. Afterwards, he would see his prejudices had misled him, the invisible racial barriers that organized his life. He suddenly realized who the listening girl was. Jan Kleyn's big and well-preserved secret had been exposed. It was like a fortress finally giving way under siege. It had been possible to conceal the truth for so long because it was quite simply unthinkable. Jan Kleyn, the star of the intelligence service, the ruthless Afrikaner fighting for his rights, had a daughter with a black woman. A daughter he presumably loved above all else. Perhaps he imagined that Nelson Mandela would have to die so that his daughter could continue to live and be refined by her proximity to the whites of this country. As far as Scheepers was concerned, this hypocrisy deserved nothing more than scorn. He felt that all his own resistance had now been broken down. At the same time he thought he could understand the enormity of the task President de Klerk and Nelson Mandela had taken upon themselves. How could they possibly create a feeling of kinship among peoples if everybody regarded everybody else as traitors?

Miranda did not take her eyes off him. He could not imagine what she was thinking, but he could see she was upset.

He let his gaze wander, first to her face and then to a photograph of the girl, standing on the mantelpiece.

"Your daughter," he said. "Jan Kleyn's daughter."

"Matilda."

Scheepers recalled what he had read about Miranda's past.

"Like your mother."

"Like my mother."

"Do you love your husband?"

"He's not my husband. He's her father."

"What about her?"

"She hates him."

"At this very moment she's standing behind her door, listening to our conversation."

"She's sick. She has a fever."

"But she's listening even so."

"Why shouldn't she listen?"

Scheepers nodded. He understood.

"I need to know," he said. "Think carefully. The slightest little thing might help us to find the men who are plotting to throw our country into chaos. Before it's too late."

It seemed to Miranda the moment she had been awaiting for so long had finally arrived. Before now she had always imagined nobody else would be present when she confessed to how she went through Jan Kleyn's pockets at night, and noted down the words he uttered in his sleep. There would just be the two of them, herself and her daughter. But now she realized things would be different. She wondered why, without even knowing his name, she trusted him so implicitly. Was it his own vulnerability? His lack of confidence in her presence? Was weakness the only thing she dared to trust?

The joy of liberation, she thought. That's what I feel right now. Like emerging from the sea and knowing I'm clean.

"I thought for ages he was just an ordinary civil servant," she began. "I knew nothing about his crimes. But then I heard."

"Who from?"

"I might tell you. But not yet. You should only say things when the time is ripe."

He regretted having interrupted her.

"But he doesn't know I know," she went on. "That has been the advantage I had. Maybe it was my salvation, maybe it'll be my death. But every time he came to visit us, I got up during the night and emptied his pockets. I copied even the smallest scrap of paper. I listened to the random words he muttered in his sleep. And I passed them on."

"Who to?"

"To the people who look after us."

"I look after you."

"I don't even know your name."

"That doesn't matter."

"I spoke with black men who lead lives just as secret as Jan Kleyn's."

He had heard rumors. But nothing had ever been proved. He knew the intelligence service, both the civilian and military branches, were always running after their own shadows. There was a persistent rumor that the blacks had their own intelligence service. Maybe linked directly to the ANC, maybe an independent organization. They investigated what the investigators were doing. Their strategies and their identities. He realized this woman, Miranda, was confirming the existence of these people.

Jan Kleyn is a dead man, he thought. Without his knowing it, his pockets have been picked by the people he regards as the enemy.

"These last few months," he said. "I don't care about the time before then. But what have you found recently?"

"I've already passed it on, and forgotten," she said. "Why should I strain myself to remember?"

He could see she was telling the truth. He tried appealing to her one more time. He had to talk with one of the men whose job it was to interpret whatever she found in Jan Kleyn's pockets. Or what he heard him muttering in his sleep.

"Why should I trust you?" she asked.

"You don't have to," he said. "There are no guarantees in this life. There are only risks."

She sat in silence, and seemed to be thinking.

"Has he killed a lot of people?" she asked. She was speaking very loudly, and he gathered this was so that her daughter could hear.

"Yes," he said. "He's killed a lot of people."

"Blacks?"

"Blacks."

"Who were criminals?"

"Some were. Some weren't."

"Why did he kill them?"

"They were people who preferred not to talk. People who had rebelled. Causers of instability."

"Like my daughter."

"I don't know your daughter."

"But I do."

She stood up suddenly.

"Come back tomorrow," she said. "There might be somebody here who wants to meet you. Go now."

He left the house. When he got to his car parked on a side street, he was sweating. He drove off, thinking about his own weakness. And her strength. Was there a future in which they could come together and be reconciled?

*　*　*

Matilda did not leave her room when he left. Miranda left her in peace. But that evening she sat on the edge of her bed for a long time.

The fever came and went in waves.

"Are you upset?" Miranda asked.

"No," replied Matilda. "I hate him even more now."

Afterwards Scheepers would remember his visit to Kliptown as a descent into a hell he had thus far managed to avoid in his life. By sticking to the white path mapped out for Afrikaners from the cradle to the grave, he had trodden the path of the one-eyed man. Now he was forced to take the other path, the black path, and what he saw he thought he would never forget. It moved him, it had to move him, because the lives of twenty million people were affected. People who were not allowed to live normal lives, who died early, after lives that were artificially restricted and never given the opportunity to develop.

He returned to the house in Bezuidenhout at ten the next morning. Miranda answered the door, but it was Matilda who would take him to the man who had expressed a willingness to talk to him. He had the feeling of having been granted a great privilege. Matilda was just as beautiful as her mother. Her skin was lighter, but her eyes were the same. He had difficulty in making out any features of her father in her face. Perhaps she kept him at such a distance, she simply prevented herself from growing to look like him. She greeted him very shyly, merely nodding when he offered his hand. Once again he felt insecure, in the presence of the daughter as well, even though she was only a teenager. He started to feel uneasy about what he had let himself in for. Perhaps Jan Kleyn's influence over this house was altogether different from what he had been led to believe? But it was too late to back out now. A rusty old car, its exhaust pipe trailing along the ground and the fenders broken off, was parked in front of the house. Without a word Matilda opened the door, and turned to him.

"I thought he'd be coming here," said Scheepers doubtfully.

"We're going to visit another world," said Matilda.

He got into the back seat and was hit by a smell he only later recognized as reminiscent of his childhood's henhouse. The man behind the wheel had a baseball cap pulled down over his eyes. He turned and looked at him without saying a word. Then they drove away, and the driver and Matilda started a conversation in a language Scheepers did not understand but recognized as Xhosa. They took a southwesterly direction, and Scheepers thought the man was driving much too fast. They soon left central Johannesburg behind them and came onto the complicated network of highways with exits leading off in all directions. Soweto, thought Scheepers. Is that where they're taking me?

But they were not headed for Soweto. They passed Meadowland, where the choking smoke lay thick over the dusty countryside. Not far beyond the conglomeration of crumbling houses, dogs, children, hens, wrecked and burned-out cars, the driver slowed down and came to a halt. Matilda got out then came to sit beside him in the back seat. She had a black hood in her hand.

"You're not allowed to see from now on," she said.

He protested and pushed her hand away.

"What is there to be afraid of?" she asked. "Make up your mind."

He took hold of the hood.

"Why?" he asked.

"There are a thousand eyes," she said. "You are not to see anything. And nobody's going to see you, either."

"That's not an answer," he said. "It's a riddle."

"Not for me it isn't," she replied. "Make up your mind now!"

He pulled the hood over his head. They set off again. The road was getting worse all the time. But the driver did not slow down. Scheepers rode with the bumps as best he could. Even so he banged his head on the car roof several times. He lost all count of time. The hood was irritating his face, and his skin started to itch.

The car slowed down and came to a halt. Somewhere a dog was barking furiously. Music from a radio was coming and going in waves. Despite the hood he could smell the smoke from fires. Matilda helped him out of the car. Then she removed the hood. The sun shone straight into his unprotected eyes, blinding him. When his eyes got used to the light he could see they were in the middle of a mass of shacks cobbled together from corrugated iron, cardboard cartons, old sacks, sheets of plastic, venetian blinds. There were huts where a car wreck formed one of the rooms. There was a stink of garbage, and a skinny, mangy dog was sniffing at one of his legs. He observed the people who lived out their lives in this destitution. None of them seemed to notice he was there. There was no threat, no curiosity, merely indifference. He did not exist as far as they were concerned.

"Welcome to Kliptown." said Matilda. "Maybe it's Kliptown, maybe it's some other shantytown. You'd never find your way back here anyway. They all look the same. The destitution is just as bad in all of them, the smells are the same, the inhabitants are the same."

She led him into the cluster of shacks. It was like entering a labyrinth that soon swallowed him up, robbed him of his entire past. After a few paces he had totally lost all sense of direction. He thought how absurd it was that he had Jan Kleyn's daughter by his side. But absurdity was their inheritance, something that was about to be disturbed for the first time, and then destroyed.

"What can you see?" she asked.

"The same as you," he replied.

"No!" she said sternly. "Are you shocked?"

"Of course."

"I'm not. Shock is a staircase. There are many steps. We are not standing on the same one."

"Maybe you're at the very top?"

"Nearly."

"Is the view different?"

"You can see further. Zebra grazing in herds, on alert. Antelopes leaping and leaving gravity behind. A cobra that has hidden itself away in an empty termite stack. Woman carrying water."

She stopped and turned to face him.

"I see my own hatred in their eyes," she said. "But your eyes can't see that."

"What do you want me to say?" he wondered. "I think it's sheer hell, living like this. The question is, is it my fault?"

"It might be," she said. "That depends."

They continued deeper into the labyrinth. He would never be able to find his way out alone. I need her, he thought. Like we have always needed the blacks. And she knows it.

Matilda halted outside a shack that was slightly bigger than the others, even if it was made from the same materials. She squatted by the door, which was shoddily made from a sheet of hardboard.

"Go on in," she said. "I'll wait here."

Scheepers went in. At first he had difficulty in distinguishing anything at all in the darkness. Then he made out a simple wooden table, a few wooden chairs, and a smoking kerosene lamp. A man detached himself from the shadows. He gazed at him with a hint of a smile. Scheepers thought he must be about the same age as himself. But the man facing him was more powerfully built, had a beard, and radiated the same kind of dignity as he had found in both Miranda and Matilda.

"Georg Scheepers," said the man, bursting into laughter. Then he pointed to one of the chairs.

"What's so funny?" asked Scheepers. He had trouble in concealing his growing unease.

"Nothing," said the man. "You can call me Steve."

"You know why I want to meet you," said Scheepers.

"You don't want to meet me," said the man who called himself Steve. "You want to meet somebody who can tell you things about Jan Kleyn you don't know already. That person happens to be me. But it could just as easily have been somebody else."

"Can we get to the point?" said Scheepers, who was beginning to get impatient.

"White men are always short of time," said Steve. "I've never been able to understand why."

"Jan Kleyn," said Scheepers.

"A dangerous man," said Steve. "Everybody's enemy, not just ours. The ravens cry in the night. And we analyze and interpret and think we know something is going to happen, something that could cause chaos. And we wouldn't want that. Neither the ANC nor de Klerk. That's why you must first tell me what you know. Then perhaps we can combine to illuminate some of the darkest corners."

Scheepers did not tell him everything. But he did divulge the most important points, and even that was a risk. He did not know who he was talking with. Nevertheless, he had no choice. Steve listened, stroking his chin slowly the while.

"So it's gone that far," he said when Scheepers had finished. "We've been expecting this. But we really thought some crazy Boer would first try to slit the throat of that traitor de Klerk."

"A professional killer," said Scheepers. "No face, no name. But he might have cropped up before. Not least in the vicinity of Jan Kleyn. Those ravens you were talking about could perhaps do some listening. The man could be white, he could be black. I've found an indication that he could be due for a lot of money. A million rand, perhaps more."

"It ought to be possible to identify him," said Steve. "Jan Kleyn only picks the best. If he's a South African, black or white, we'll find him."

"Find him and stop him," said Scheepers. "Kill him. We have to work together."

"No," said Steve. "We're meeting now. But this is the only time. We're going from two different directions, both on this occasion and in the future. Nothing else is possible."

"Why not?"

"We don't share each other's secrets. Everything is still too unsure, too uncertain. We avoid all pacts and agreements unless they are absolutely essential. Don't forget we're enemies. And the war in our country has been going on for a very long time. Although you don't want to recognize that fact."

"We see things differently," said Scheepers.

"Yes," said Steve. "We do."

The conversation had lasted only a few minutes. Even so, Steve got to his feet and Scheepers gathered it was all over.

"Miranda exists," said Steve. "You can contact my world through her."

"Yes," said Scheepers. "She exists. We have to stop this assassination."

"Right," said Steve. "But I guess you are the ones who are going to have to do it. You are still the ones with the resources. I have nothing. Apart from a tin hut. And Miranda. And Matilda. Just imagine what would happen if the assassination came off."

"I'd rather not think about it."

Steve stared at him for a moment in silence. Then he disappeared through the door without saying goodbye. Scheepers followed him into the bright sunlight. Matilda led him back to the car without speaking. Once again he sat in the back seat with a hood over his head. In the darkness he was already preparing what to say to President de Klerk.

*　　*　　*

De Klerk had a recurrent dream about termites.

He was in a house where every floor, every wall, every piece of furniture had been attacked by the hungry insects. Why he had come to the house, he had no idea. Grass was growing up between the floorboards, the windowpanes were shattered, and the furious chewing of the termites was like an itch in his own body. In his dream he had a very short time in which to write an important speech. His usual shorthand typist had disappeared, and he had to do the work himself. But when he started writing, termites came pouring out of his pen.

At that point he usually woke up. He would lie in the dark, thinking how the dream might anticipate coming reality. Maybe everything was too late already? What he wanted to achieve, to rescue South Africa from disintegration while still preserving the influence and special status of the whites as far as possible, could well be already too far out of step with black impatience. Only Nelson Mandela could convince him there was no other course to take. De Klerk knew they both shared the same fear. Uncontrolled violence, a chaotic collapse that no one could control, a breeding ground for a brutal military coup intent on revenge, or various ethnic groupings that would fight each other until nothing was left.

It was ten at night on Thursday, May 21. De Klerk knew the young lawyer Scheepers was already waiting in his anteroom. But de Klerk did not feel ready to receive him just yet. He was tired, his head bursting with all the problems he was constantly being forced to try and solve. He got up from his desk and went over to one of the high windows. He sometimes felt petrified by all the responsibility resting on his shoulders. He thought it was too much for one man to bear. He sometimes felt an instinctive urge to run away, to make himself invisible, to go straight out into the bush and simply disappear, to fade away into a mirage. But he knew he would not do that. The God he found increasingly difficult to talk to and believe in was maybe still shielding him after all. He wondered how much time he still had. His mood was constantly changing. From being convinced he was already living on borrowed time, he could start believing he had another five years after all. And time was what he needed. His grand design—to delay the transition to a new kind of society for as long as possible, and meanwhile to entice a large number of black voters into his own party—needed time. But he could also see that Nelson Mandela would refuse to allow him time that was not used to pave the way for the transition.

It seemed to him there was an element of artificiality in everything he did. I too am really an upholder of the impossible dream, that my country will never change. The difference between me and a fanatic madman who wants to defend the impossible dream with open violence is very small.

Time is running out for South Africa, it seemed to him. What is happening now ought to have happened many years ago. But history does not follow invisible guidelines.

He returned to his desk and rang the bell. Shortly afterwards Scheepers came in. De Klerk had come to appreciate his energy and thoroughness. He overlooked the streak of naive innocence he also detected in the young lawyer. Even this young Afrikaner had to learn there were sharp rocks under the soft sand.

He listened to Scheepers's report with half-closed eyes. The words that got through to him piled up in his consciousness. When Scheepers had finished, de Klerk looked searchingly at him.

"I take it for granted everything I've just heard is true," said de Klerk.

"Yes," replied Scheepers. "No doubt about it."

"None at all?"

"No."

De Klerk thought for a moment before proceeding.

"So they're going to kill Nelson Mandela," he said. "Some miserable contract killer selected and paid by the executive branch of this secret committee. The murder will take place in the near future when Mandela is making one of his many public appearances. The consequence will be chaos, a bloodbath, total collapse. A group of influential *boere* are waiting in the wings to take over the government of this country. The constitution and the social order will be overturned. A corporate regime will be imposed, consisting of equal parts from the military, the police and civilian groups. The future will be one long, drawn-out state of emergency. Is that right?"

"Yes," said Scheepers. "If I may be allowed to venture a guess, I would say the assassination attempt will be on June 12."

"Why?"

"Nelson Mandela is due to speak in Cape Town. I have received information to the effect that the army information office has being displaying an unusual amount of interest in the plans made for dealing with the occasion by the local police. There are also other indications which suggest this is the case. I am well aware it is only a guess. But I'm convinced it's an informed guess."

"Three weeks," said de Klerk. "Three weeks in which to stop these lunatics."

"If that is in fact right," said Scheepers. "We can't ignore the possibility that June 12 and Cape Town are a red herring. The people involved in this are very cunning. The assassination attempt could easily take place tomorrow."

"In other words, at any time," said de Klerk. "Any place. And there's nothing we can do about it."

He fell silent. Scheepers waited.

"I must speak with Nelson Mandela," said de Klerk. "He has to know what's afoot."

Then he turned to Scheepers.

"These people must be stopped without delay," he said.

"We don't know who they are," Scheepers pointed out. "How can we stop something we don't know about?"

"What about the man they've hired?"

"We don't know who he is either."

De Klerk looked thoughtfully at him.

"You have a plan," he said. "I can see it in your face."

Scheepers could feel himself blushing.

"Mr. President," he said. "I think the key to all this is Jan Kleyn. The man in the intelligence service. He has to be arrested immediately. Of course, the risk is he won't talk. Or he might prefer to commit suicide. But I can see no alternative to interrogating him."

De Klerk nodded.

"Let's do that," he said. "In fact we have quite a few skillful interrogators who can usually force the truth out of people."

Out of blacks, thought Scheepers. Who then die in mysterious circumstances.

"I think it would be best if I could conduct the interrogation," he said. "I know most about it, after all."

"Do you think you can handle him?"

"Yes."

The president rose. The audience was over.

"Jan Kleyn will be arrested tomorrow," said de Klerk. "And I want running reports from now on. Once every day."

The shook hands.

Scheepers left, nodding to the old security guard waiting in the antechamber. Then he drove home through the night, with his pistol on the seat beside him.

De Klerk stood at his window for a long time, deep in thought. Then he worked at his desk for a few more hours.

Outside in the antechamber, the old guard ambled round straightening out folds in the carpets and smoothing cushions on chairs. All the time he was thinking over what he had overheard with his ear to the door of the president's private office. He realized the situation was extremely serious. He went into the room that served as his own modest office. He removed the telephone from the plug routed through the switchboard. Behind a loose wooden panel was another socket only he knew about. He lifted the receiver and got a direct line out. Then he dialed a number.

The answer came almost immediately. Jan Kleyn was not yet asleep.

After his conversation with the guard at the president's private office, he could see this was going to be a sleepless night.

Countdown
to a Vacuum

Chapter Twenty-nine

L ate in the evening Sikosi Tsiki killed a mouse with a well-aimed throw of a knife. By then Tania had already gone to bed. Konovalenko was waiting until it was late enough for him to call Jan Kleyn in South Africa and get the final instructions for Sikosi Tsiki's return journey. Konovalenko also intended to raise the question of his own future as an immigrant to South Africa. There was not a sound to be heard from the cellar. Tania had been down to look at the girl and said she was asleep. For the first time in ages he felt totally content. He had made contact with Wallander. Konovalenko had demanded an unsigned letter of safe conduct from him, in return for getting his daughter back unharmed. Wallander would give him a week's start, and personally insure the police search was wrongly directed. As Konovalenko intended to return to Stockholm immediately, Wallander would make sure the search for him was concentrated in southern Sweden.

But none of this was true, of course. Konovalenko intended to shoot both him and the girl. He wondered whether Wallander really believed what he had said. If so he would return to being the kind of cop Konovalenko had started by thinking he was, the naive provincial drudge. But he had no intention of making the mistake of underestimating Wallander yet again.

During the day he had devoted many hours to Sikosi Tsiki. Just as in preparing Victor Mabasha, Konovalenko had run through various possible turns of events in connection with the assassination attempt. He had the impression Sikosi Tsiki was quicker-witted than Victor Mabasha. Moreover, he seemed completely unaffected by the passing but unambiguous racist remarks Konovalenko could not resist making. He intended to provoke him even more over the next few days, to see if he could pin down the limit of his self-control.

There was one characteristic Sikosi Tsiki shared with Victor Mabasha. Konovalenko started to wonder whether it was something typical of the African temperament. He was thinking of their introversion, the impossible task of trying to figure out what they really thought. It irritated him. He was used to being able to see straight through people, read their thoughts, and hence give himself an opportunity to anticipate their reactions.

He gazed at the man who had just speared a mouse in a corner of the room with his strangely curved knife. He'll do a good job, thought Konovalenko. A few more days of planning and weapons training, and he'll be ready to go home. He'll be my entrance visa to South Africa.

Sikosi Tsiki stood up and retrieved his knife with the mouse speared on the end of it. Then he went out into the kitchen and removed the victim. He dropped it into a garbage pail and rinsed the blade. Konovalenko observed him, occasionally taking a sip of vodka from his glass.

"A knife with a curved blade," he said. "I've never seen one like that before."

"My ancestors used to make them over a thousand years ago," said Sikosi Tsiki.

"But the curved blade?" wondered Konovalenko. "Why?"

"Nobody knows," answered Sikosi Tsiki. "It's still a secret. The day the secret is revealed, the knife will lose its power."

Soon after he disappeared into his room. Konovalenko was annoyed by the mysterious reply he had received. He heard Sikosi Tsiki locking the door behind him.

Konovalenko was on his own now. He went around the room turning off the lights, apart from the lamp next to the table where the telephone was. He checked the time. Half past midnight. Soon he would call Jan Kleyn. He listened at the cellar hatch. Not a sound. He poured himself another glass of vodka. He would save it until after he had finished speaking with Jan Kleyn.

The call to South Africa was brief.

Jan Kleyn listened to Konovalenko's assurances that Sikosi Tsiki would cause no problems. There was no doubt about his mental stability. Then Jan Kleyn announced his verdict. He wanted Sikosi

Tsiki to return to South Africa within a week at the most. Konovalenko's job was to make arrangements immediately to get him out of Sweden, and make sure the return journey to Johannesburg was booked and confirmed. Konovalenko had the impression Jan Kleyn was in a hurry, that he was under pressure. Of course, he had no way of confirming his hunch. But it was enough to put him off his stride when it came to discussing his own journey to South Africa. The call ended without his having said a single word about the future. He felt annoyed with himself afterwards. He drained his vodka glass and wondered if Jan Kleyn intended to double-cross him. But he dismissed the thought. Besides, he was convinced they really needed his talents and experience in South Africa. He drank another glass of vodka, then went out onto the porch to urinate. It was raining. He gazed out into the mist, and decided he should be pleased with himself. Just a few more hours and all his problems would be over, for this particular job. His assignment was almost at an end. Then he would have time to devote to his future. Not the least significant decision he would have to make was whether to take Tania with him to South Africa, or if he should do what he did with his wife and leave her behind.

He locked the door, retired to his own room and lay down. He did not get undressed, but just pulled a blanket over him. Tania could sleep alone tonight. He needed some rest.

She was lying awake in her room, and heard Konovalenko shut the door and lie down on top of the bed. She lay still, listening. She was scared. Deep down she had the feeling it would be impossible to get the girl out of the cellar and then leave the house without Konovalenko hearing. Nor was it possible to lock the door to his room quietly. She had tried that earlier in the day, when Konovalenko and the African were out shooting rifles in the quarry. Besides, it was possible for him to jump out of the bedroom window even if the door was barricaded. She wished she had some sleeping pills. She could have dissolved them in one of his vodka bottles. But all she had was herself, and she knew she had to try. Earlier in the day she had prepared a little suitcase with some money and clothes. She hid it in the barn. She also left her rain clothes there, and a pair of boots.

She checked the time. A quarter past one. She knew the meeting with the cop was scheduled for dawn. She and the daughter would have to be a long way away by then. As soon as she heard Konovalenko start to snore, she would get up. She knew Konovalenko was a very light sleeper and kept waking up, but rarely during the first half hour after falling asleep.

She still was not sure why she was doing this. She knew she was risking her own life. But she did not feel the need to justify her actions to herself. Some things were just dictated by life itself.

Konovalenko turned over and coughed. Twenty-five past one. Some nights Konovalenko chose not to sleep, but just lay on the bed resting. If this was one of those nights, there was nothing she could do to help the girl. She noticed how that made her feel even more scared. It was a threat that seemed to her greater than any danger she might run herself.

At twenty to two she finally heard Konovalenko start to snore. She listened for about half a minute. Then she carefully got out of bed. She was fully dressed. All the time she had been clutching the key to the lock on the chains around the girl's ankles. She cautiously opened the door of her room and avoided the floorboards she knew would creak. She sneaked into the kitchen, switched on her flashlight and started easing up the hatch very carefully. It was a critical moment: the girl might start screaming. That had not happened so far. But it could, she realized that. Konovalenko was snoring. She listened. Then she climbed cautiously down the ladder. The girl was curled into a ball. Her eyes were open. Tania squatted beside her and whispered while stroking her cropped hair. She said they were going to run away, but she would have to be very, very quiet. The girl did not react. Her eyes were completely expressionless. Tania was suddenly afraid she would not be able to move. Perhaps she was rendered immobile by fear? She had to turn her over on her side in order to get to the padlock. The girl suddenly started kicking and punching. Tania just managed to place her hand over the girl's mouth before she started screaming. Tania was strong, and pressed as hard as she could. Just one half-stifled yell would be enough to wake Konovalenko. She shuddered at the thought. Konovalenko was quite capable of nailing down the hatch and leaving them both down there in the darkness. Tania tried to whisper to her at the same time as she pressed. The girl's eyes had come alive, and Tania hoped she would understand now. She slowly took away her hand, unlocked the padlock, and carefully removed the chains.

At the same moment she noticed Konovalenko had stopped snoring. She held her breath. He started again. She hurriedly got to her feet, reached for the hatch, and closed it. The girl had understood. She sat up, and was quiet. But her eyes had come alive again.

Tania suddenly thought her heart would stand still. She heard footsteps in the kitchen above them. Someone was walking around there. The footsteps stopped. Now he'll open the hatch, she thought, shutting her eyes. He's heard me after all.

Then came relief in the form of the clinking of a bottle. Konovalenko had got up for another glass of vodka. The footsteps died away again. Tania shone the flashlight on her face and tried to smile. Then she took the girl's hand and held it while they waited. After ten minutes she opened the hatch cautiously. Konovalenko had started snoring again. She explained to the girl what was going to happen. They would approach the front door as quietly as they could. Tania had oiled the lock during the day. She thought it would be possible to open it without a click. If all went well they would then hurry away from the house together. But if something did happen, if Konovalenko woke up, Tania would simply fling the door open and they would race off in different directions. Was that clear? Run, run for all they were worth. There was a fine drizzle outside that should make it harder for them to be seen. But she should just keep on running, without looking back. When she came to a house or saw a car on the road, she should give herself up. But the main thing was to run for her life.

Did she understand? Tania thought so. The girl's eyes were animated, she could move her legs, even if she was weak and unsteady. Tania listened again. Then she nodded to the girl. It was time to move. Tania climbed up first, listened one more time, then reached down to help the girl. Now speed was of the essence. Tania made herself hold back so as to avoid the stairs creaking. The girl emerged cautiously into the kitchen. She screwed up her eyes, even though the light was very weak. She's practically blind, thought Tania. She held her firmly by one arm. Konovalenko was snoring. Then they started walking toward the hall and the front door, one step at a time, painfully slow. There was a curtain in the hall doorway. Tania took great care in pulling it to one side, with the girl hanging onto her arm. Then they were at the door. Tania could feel she was covered in sweat. Her hands were trembling as she took hold of the key. At this point she almost dared to believe it would be OK. She turned the key. There was a point, a certain resistance, where it would click if she turned it too quickly. She could feel the resistance and kept on turning as carefully as she could. She was past the critical point. There had not been a single sound. She nodded to the girl. Then she opened the door.

As she did so, something crashed behind her. She gave a start and turned around. The girl had bumped into a stand for coats and umbrellas. It had fallen over. Tania had no need to listen in order to know what was already happening. She flung open the door, shoved the girl out into the rain and mist, and yelled at her to run. At first the girl seemed petrified. But Tania pushed her, and she started running. Within a couple of seconds she had disappeared into the grayness.

Tania knew it was already too late as far as she was concerned. But she would try even so. Most of all she did not want to turn around. She ran in the opposite direction, in an attempt to divert Konovalenko, make him unsure about where the girl was for a few more precious seconds.

Tania got to the middle of the courtyard before Konovalenko caught up with her. "What are you doing?" he yelled. "Are you sick?"

Then she realized Konovalenko did not know the hatch was open. He would not understand what had happened until they were back inside the house. The girl's start would be sufficient. Konovalenko would never be able to find her again.

Tania suddenly felt very tired.

But she knew that what she has done was right.

"I don't feel very well," she said, pretending to be dizzy.

"Let's go inside," said Konovalenko.

"Just a minute," she said. "I need some fresh air."

I'll do the best I can for her, she thought. Every breath gives her a bigger start. The game is up for me.

She ran through the night. It was raining. She had no idea where she was, she just ran. She kept falling, but simply scrambled back onto her feet and kept on running. She came out into a field. All around her frightened hares were bounding off in different directions. She felt like one of them, a hunted animal. The mud was clinging to her shoes. In the end she took them off and kept on running in her stocking feet. The field seemed to go on forever. Everything was engulfed by the fog. Only she and the hares existed. Eventually she came to a road, and lacked the strength to run any farther. She walked along the gravel road. The sharp edges of the stones were hurting her feet. Then the gravel came to an end and she found herself on an asphalt road. She could see the white line down the middle. She had no idea which direction to take. But she kept on walking even so. She still did not dare to think about what had happened. She could still feel some vague sense of evil somewhere behind her. It was neither human nor animal, rather a sort of cold breeze; but it was there all the time, forcing her to keep going.

Then she saw a pair of headlights approaching. It was a man who had been visiting his girlfriend. During the night they had started quarreling about something. He decided to go home. Now he was sitting behind the wheel of his car, thinking that if only he had the money, he would go away. Anywhere would do, anywhere far away. The windshield wipers were squeaking, and visibility was poor. He suddenly saw something in front of the car. At first he thought it was an animal, and slammed on the brakes. Then he stopped altogether. It was a human being, he could see that. He could hardly believe his eyes. A young girl, with no shoes, covered in mud, her hair a short-cropped mess. It occurred to him there might have been a car crash. Then he saw her sit down in the middle of the road. He got slowly out of the car, and went up to her.

"What happened?" he asked.

She did not answer.

He could not see any blood. Nor was there any sign of a car in the ditch. Then he lifted her up and led her to his car. She could barely stand.

"What happened?" he asked one more time.

But he received no reply.

Sten Widén and Svedberg left the apartment in Ystad at a quarter to two. It was raining as they got into Svedberg's car. Three kilometers outside town Svedberg thought he had a flat in one of the back tires. He pulled into the side, worrying that the spare might be no good as well. But it was OK when they fitted it. The flat had thrown out their schedule. Svedberg had assumed Wallander would approach the house before it got too light. That meant they would have to set off early to avoid bumping into him. Now, it was nearly three by the time they parked the car behind a clump of bushes more than a mile away from the quarry and the house. They were in a hurry, and moved quickly through the fog. They passed a field on the north side of the quarry. Svedberg had suggested they should take up position as near the house as they dared. But as they did not know what direction Wallander would come from, and they would have to be able to see to both sides if they were to avoid being discovered. They had tried to guess which direction Wallander would choose. They agreed he would probably take the western approach. It was slightly hilly on that side. There were high, dense clumps of bushes growing right up to the edge of the property. On that basis they decided to approach from the east. Svedberg had noticed a haystack on a narrow strip of ground between two fields. If necessary they could burrow into the stack itself. They were in position by half past three. Both of them had their guns ready and loaded.

The house shimmered before them in the fog. Everything was still. Without really knowing why, Svedberg had the impression that everything was not quite right. He took out his binoculars, wiped the lenses, and then examined the house wall bit by bit. There was a light in one window, probably the kitchen. He could not see anything unusual. He found it hard to imagine Konovalenko was asleep. He would be there, waiting in silence. He might even be outside the house.

They waited on tenterhooks, each of them lost in a world of his own.

It was Sten Widén who first saw Wallander. The time was five o'clock. As they had thought, he appeared on the western side of the house. Widén had good eyesight, and thought at first it was a hare or a deer moving among the bushes. But then he began to wonder, nudged Svedberg's arm gently, and pointed. Svedberg took out his binoculars again. He could just make out Wallander's face among the bushes.

Neither of them knew what would happen. Was Wallander acting according to the instructions he had received from Konovalenko? Or had he decided to try and take him by surprise? And where was Konovalenko? And Wallander's daughter?

They waited. All was quiet around the house. Sten Widén and Svedberg took turns observing Wallander's expressionless face. Again Svedberg got the feeling something was wrong. He looked at his watch. Wallander would soon have been lying in the bushes for an hour. There was still no sign of movement in the house.

Suddenly Sten Widén handed the binoculars to Svedberg. Wallander had started moving. He wriggled his way rapidly to the house, then stood there pressed against the wall. He had his pistol in one hand. So, he's decided to take Konovalenko on, thought Svedberg, and he could feel a lump in his stomach. There was nothing they could do but keep watching. Sten Widén had taken aim with his rifle, pointing it at the front door. Wallander ducked down as he passed the windows and ran as far as the front door. Svedberg could see he was listening. Then he cautiously tried the handle. The door was unlocked. Without hesitation he flung it open and rushed in. At the same time Sten Widén and Svedberg crawled out of the haystack.

They had not agreed what to do next; they just knew they had to follow Wallander. They ran up to the corner of the house and took cover. It was still deathly silent in the house. Svedberg suddenly realized why he had been uneasy.

The house was deserted. There was nobody there.

"They've moved out," he said to Sten Widén. "There's nobody there."

Sten Widén stared at him in disbelief.

"How do you know?"

"I just know," answered Svedberg, stepping out of the shadow of the wall.

He shouted Wallander's name.

Wallander came out onto the steps. He did not seem surprised to see them.

"She's gone," he said.

They could see he was very tired. It was possible he had already passed the limit of being so exhausted, he might collapse at any moment.

They entered the house and tried to interpret the clues. Sten

Widén kept in the background while Svedberg and Wallander searched the house. Wallander did not refer to their having followed him to the house. Svedberg suspected he knew deep down they would not abandon him. Perhaps he was even grateful, in fact?

It was Svedberg who found Tania. He opened the door to one of the bedrooms, and looked at the unmade bed. Without knowing why, he bent down and peered under it. There she was. For one brief, horrible moment he thought it was Wallander's daughter. Then he saw it was the other woman. Before telling the others what he had found, he quickly checked under the other beds. He looked in the refrigerator and all the closets. Only when he was certain Wallander's daughter was not lying hidden somewhere did he attract their attention. They moved the bed to one side. Wallander was standing in the background. When he saw her head he turned on his heel, rushed out of the house and threw up.

She had no face left. Just a bloody mass where it was impossible to pick out any features. Svedberg got a towel and laid it over her face. Then he examined the body. There were five bullet wounds. They formed a pattern, and that made him feel even worse than he did already. She had been shot in both feet, then in her hands, and finally through the heart.

They left her, and continued going through the house in silence. Neither of them said a word. They opened the cellar, and went down. Svedberg managed to hide the chain which he assumed had been used to tie up Wallander's daughter. But Wallander knew she had been kept down there in the darkness. Svedberg could see him biting his lips. He wondered how much longer Wallander could keep going. They went back to the kitchen. Svedberg discovered a big cauldron full of blood-colored water. When he stuck his finger in, he could feel traces of lingering heat. It was slowly dawning on him what had happened. He went through the house one more time, slowly, trying to follow up the various clues, make them reveal what had happened.

In the end, he proposed they should all sit down. Wallander was almost apathetic by this stage. Svedberg thought long and deep. Did he dare? The responsibility was enormous. But in the end he resolved to go ahead.

"I don't know where your daughter is," he said. "But she's still alive. I'm sure of that."

Wallander looked at him without saying anything.

"I think this is what happened," Svedberg went on. "I can't be sure, of course. But I'm trying to interpret the clues, piece them together, and see what kind of a story they tell. I think the dead woman tried to help your daughter to escape. I don't know whether or not she managed it. Maybe she got away, maybe Konovalenko stopped her? There are signs suggesting both possibilities. He killed Tania in such a sadistic fury, we might think your daughter must have escaped. But it could also be a reaction to the fact that she even tried to help Linda. Tania let him down, and that was enough to trigger off his evil tendencies, which seem to be limitless. He scalded her face with boiling water. Then he shot her in the feet, that was for the escape, and then in the hands and finally through the heart. I would prefer not to try and imagine what her last hour in this life was like. Afterward, he left. That is another indication that your daughter has escaped. If she managed to get away, Konovalenko could no longer regard the house as safe. But it could also be that Konovalenko was afraid somebody might have heard the shooting. That's what I think happened. But of course, it could all have been quite different."

It was seven o'clock by now. Nobody said a word.

Svedberg stood up and went to the telephone. He called Martinson, and had to wait as he was in the bathroom.

"Do me a favor," he said. "Drive to the railroad station in Tomelilla and meet me there in an hour. And don't tell anybody where you're going."

"Are you going crazy as well?" asked Martinson.

"On the contrary," said Svedberg. "This is important."

He hung up and looked at Wallander.

"Right now there's nothing you can do apart from getting some sleep. Go home with Sten. Or else we could take you to your father's."

"How could I possibly sleep?" asked Wallander as if in a dream.

"By lying down," said Svedberg. "You'd better do as I say now. If you're going to be in a position to help your daughter, you must get some sleep. In the state you're in now you'd only be a nuisance."

Wallander nodded.

"I think I'd better go to my dad's place," he said.

"Where did you leave the car?" asked Sten Widén.

"Let me go and get it," said Wallander. "I need some air."

He went out. Svedberg and Sten Widén stared at each other, too weary and upset to talk.

"I sure am glad I'm not a cop," said Sten Widén as the Duett trundled into the courtyard. He nodded towards the room where Tania was.

"Thanks for your help," said Svedberg.

He watched them drive away.

He wondered when the nightmare would end.

Sten Widén stopped the car to drop off Wallander. They had not exchanged a single word during the journey.

"I'll be in touch before the day's over," said Sten Widén.

He watched Wallander making his way slowly towards the house.

Poor devil, he thought. How much longer can he keep going?

His father was sitting at the kitchen table. He was unshaven, and Wallander could smell that he needed a bath. He sat down opposite him.

Neither of them said anything for a long time.

"She's asleep," his father said eventually.

Wallander hardly heard what he said.

"She's sleeping calmly," repeated his father.

The words slowly penetrated Wallander's befuddled head.

"Who is?" he asked wearily.

"I'm talking about my granddaughter," said his father.

Wallander stared at him. For ages. Then he slowly got to his feet and went to the bedroom. Slowly, he opened the door.

Linda was in bed, asleep. Her hair was cropped on one side of her head. But it was her all right. Wallander stood motionless in the doorway. Then he walked over to the bed and squatted down. He did nothing, just looked. He did not want to know what had happened, he did not know what had taken place or how she had got home. He just wanted to look at her. Somewhere in the back of his mind, he knew that Konovalenko was still out there. But just for the moment, he didn't care about Konovalenko. Right now she was the only person who existed.

He lay down on the floor beside her bed. He curled up and went to sleep. His father put a blanket over him and closed the door. Then he went out to his studio and carried on painting. But now he had returned to his usual motif. He was putting the finishing touches on a wood grouse.

Martinson arrived at the railroad station in Tomelilla soon after eight. He got out of his car and greeted Svedberg.

"What's so important, then?" he asked, not bothering to conceal the fact that he was annoyed.

"You'll see," said Svedberg. "But I must warn you it's not a pretty sight."

Martinson frowned.

"What's happened?"

"Konovalenko," said Svedberg. "He's struck again. We have another body to deal with. A woman."

"Good Lord!"

"Follow me," said Svedberg. "We have a lot to talk about."

"Is Wallander mixed up in all this?" asked Martinson.

Svedberg did not hear. He was already on the way to his car.

Martinson did not discover what had happened until afterwards.

Chapter Thirty

L ate on Wednesday afternoon she cut her hair.

That was how she hoped to erase her unpleasant memories.

Then she started talking about what had happened. Wallander had tried in vain to persuade her to see a doctor. But she refused.

"My hair will grow again in its own good time," she said. "No doctor can make it grow any faster than it wants to."

Wallander was afraid of what was coming next. What scared him was that his daughter might blame him for what had happened to her. He would find it hard to defend himself. It was his fault. He was responsible for dragging her into all this. It was not even an accident. But she had made up her mind not to see a doctor for the moment, and he did not try to convince her.

Only once during the course of the day did she start crying. It happened unexpectedly, just as they were going to sit down to eat. She looked at him and asked what had happened to Tania. He told her the truth, that she was dead. But he avoided saying she had been tortured by Konovalenko. Wallander hoped the newspapers would leave out the details. He also told her Konovalenko was still at large.

"But he's on the run," he said. "He's a hunted man; he can't attack whenever he likes any more."

Wallander suspected what he said was not completely true. Konovalenko was probably just as dangerous now as before. He also knew that he himself, once again, would be setting out to find him. But not yet, not this Wednesday, when his daughter had come back to him from the darkness, silence and fear.

At one point on Wednesday evening he spoke with Svedberg on the telephone. Wallander asked for the night in order to catch up on sleep and do some thinking. He would come out into the open on Thursday. Svedberg told him about the search going on at full scale. There was no trace of Konovalenko.

"But he's not alone," said Svedberg. "There was somebody else in that house. Rykoff is dead. Tania too. The man called Victor Mabasha died some days ago. Konovalenko ought to be on his own. But he isn't. There was somebody else in that house. The question is: who?"

"I don't know," said Wallander. "A new, unknown henchman?"

Shortly after Svedberg had hung up, there was a call from Sten Widén. Wallander assumed he and Svedberg were in touch with each other. Sten Widén asked about Wallander's daughter, and Wallander replied she would no doubt be OK.

"I'm thinking about that woman," said Sten Widén. "I'm trying to understand how anybody could do something like that to a fellow human being."

"There are such people," said Wallander. "Unfortunately there are more of them than we care to think."

When Linda had fallen asleep, Wallander went out to the studio where his father was painting. Although he suspected it was just a temporary change of mind, he felt they had both found it easier to talk with each other during the goings-on of the last couple of days. He also wondered how much of what had happened his father had really understood.

"Are you still determined to get married?" asked Wallander, sitting on a stool out in the studio.

"You shouldn't joke about serious matters," replied his father. "We're getting married in June."

"My daughter has been invited," said Wallander. "But I haven't."

"You will be," said his father.

"Where are you going to get married?"

"Here."

"Here? In the studio?"

"Why not? I'm going to paint a big backcloth."

"What do you think Gertrud will have to say about that?"

"It's her idea."

His father turned around and smiled at him. Wallander burst out laughing. He couldn't remember the last time he had a good laugh.

"Gertrud is an unusual woman," said his father.

"She must be," said Wallander.

On Thursday morning Wallander woke up feeling refreshed. His joy at the fact his daughter had emerged unscathed filled him with renewed energy. At the back of his mind, Konovalenko was a constant presence. He began to feel once again that he was ready to go after him.

Wallander called Björk just before eight. He had prepared his excuses meticulously.

"Kurt," said Björk. "For God's sake! Where are you? What's happened?"

"I guess I had a bit of a breakdown," said Wallander, trying to sound convincing by speaking softly and slowly. "But I'm better now. I just need a few more days of peace and quiet."

"You must take sick leave, of course," said Björk firmly. "I don't know if you realized we've had an official search on for you. All very unpleasant. But it was necessary. I'll call off the search for you right away. I'll issue a press statement. The missing detective chief inspector has returned after a short illness. Where are you, by the way?"

"In Copenhagen," Wallander lied.

"What the hell are you doing there?"

"I'm staying at a little hotel and getting some rest."

"And no doubt you're not going to tell me what that hotel is called? Or where it is?"

"I'd rather not."

"We need you as quickly as possible. But in good health. Some horrible things are happening here. Martinson and Svedberg and the rest of us feel helpless without you. We'll be asking for assistance from Stockholm."

"I'll be back on Friday. And sick leave won't be necessary."

"You'll never know how relieved I am. We've been extremely worried. What actually happened out there in the fog?"

"I'll be writing a report. I'll be with you on Friday."

He hung up, and started thinking about what Svedberg had said. Who was this unknown person? Who was hanging on Konovalenko's coattails now? He lay on his back in bed, staring up at the ceiling. Slowly, he went over all that had happened since the day

Robert Åkerblom came to his office. He recalled all the summaries he had tried to write, and attempted to find some kind of path through all the confusing tracks. The feeling of being caught up in an investigation that could never quite be pinned down came to him once more. He still had not gotten *behind* it all, it seemed to him. He hadn't found the starting point of all the things that had happened. He still did not know the real cause of it all.

He called Svedberg late in the afternoon.

"We haven't found anything to suggest where they've gone," answered Svedberg to Wallander's question. "It's all very mysterious. On the other hand, I think my theory about what happened during the night is correct. There's no other plausible explanation."

"I need your help," said Wallander. "I have to drive out to that house again tonight."

"You don't mean you're thinking of going after Konovalenko on your own again?" asked Svedberg, horrified.

"Not at all," replied Wallander. "My daughter dropped a piece of jewelry while she was being held there. I don't suppose you've found it?"

"Not as far as I know."

"Who's on guard out there tonight?"

"I expect there'll just be a patrol car checking up now and then."

"Can you keep that patrol car out of the way between nine and eleven tonight? I'm officially in Copenhagen, as you might have heard from Björk."

"Yes," said Svedberg.

"How can I get into the house?"

"We found a spare key in the gutter on the right-hand corner of the house, seen from the front that is. It's still there."

Afterwards Wallander wondered whether Svedberg had really believed what he said. Searching for a piece of jewelry was a pretty feeble excuse. If it was there, then of course the police would have found it. Then again, he had no idea what he thought he might find. During the last year Svedberg had developed into a skillful crime scene investigator. Wallander thought he might one day get up to Rydberg's level. If there had been anything significant there, Svedberg would have found it. What Wallander might possibly be able to do was to see new connections.

In any case, that is where he had to start. It was most likely, of course, that Konovalenko and his companion had returned to Stockholm. But nothing was certain.

He left for Tomelilla at half past eight. It was warm, and he drove with the window open. It occurred to him that he still hadn't discussed his vacation with Björk.

He parked in the courtyard and found the key. When he got into the house he started by switching on all the lights. He looked round, and suddenly felt unsure about where to start looking. He wandered around the house, trying to pin down what he was actually looking for. A track leading to Konovalenko. A destination. An indication of who the unknown companion might be. Something that would reveal at last what was behind it all. He sat down in one of the chairs and thought back to when he checked the room first time around. At the same time he let his gaze wander. He saw nothing that seemed to him odd, or in any way remarkable. There's nothing here, he thought. Even if Konovalenko left in a hurry, he'll have covered up his tracks. The ashtray in Stockholm was an exception. A fluke.

He got up from the chair and went around the house again, more slowly this time, and more carefully. He paused occasionally, lifted up a tablecloth, leafed through magazines, felt underneath the seats of chairs. Still nothing. He went through the various bedrooms, leaving the room where they had found Tania until last. Nothing. In the garbage pail, which Svedberg had naturally been through already, he found a dead mouse. Wallander poked at it with a fork and saw it had not been killed by a mousetrap. Somebody had stabbed it to death. A knife, he thought. He remembered that Victor Mabasha had had a knife. But he was dead, in the morgue. Wallander left the kitchen and went into the bathroom. Konovalenko had left nothing behind. He returned to the living room and sat down again. He picked a different chair this time, so he could see the room from another angle. There's always something, he thought. It's just a case of finding it. He set off to search through the house once more. Nothing. By the time he sat down again, it was already a quarter past ten. He would soon have to leave. Time was running out.

Whoever used to live in this house had been very well organized. There was a logical plan for every object, every piece of furniture, every light fixture. He looked to see if he could find anything out of place. After a while his eye settled on a bookcase against one of the walls. All the books were standing in straight lines. Except on the bottom shelf. The back of one book was sticking out there. He got up and picked out the book. It was a road atlas of Sweden. He noticed a piece of the cover had been torn off and was inserted between a couple of pages. He opened the atlas and found himself looking at a map of eastern Sweden, including sections of Småland, Kalmar County, and the island of Öland. He studied the map. Then he sat down at a table and adjusted the lamp. He could see some traces of pencil marks here and there. As if somebody had been following a route with a pencil, occasionally letting it touch the paper. One of the faint pencil marks was at the point where the Öland bridge starts out from Kalmar. Right down at the bottom of the page, more or less level with Blekinge, he found another mark. He thought for a while. Then he turned to the map of Skåne. There were no pencil marks there. He went back to the previous page. The faint pencil marks followed the coastal road towards Kalmar. He put the atlas down again. Then he went into the kitchen and called Svedberg at home.

"I'm still out there," he said. "If I say Öland, what does that mean to you?"

Svedberg pondered.

"Nothing," he said.

"You didn't find a notebook when you searched the house? No telephone book?"

"Tania had a little pocket diary in her purse," said Svedberg. "But there was nothing in it."

"No loose scraps of paper?"

"If you look in the woodstove, you'll see somebody has been burning paper," said Svedberg. "We went through the ashes. There was nothing there. Why do you mention Öland?"

"I found a map," said Wallander. "But I don't suppose it means anything."

"Konovalenko has probably gone back to Stockholm," said Svedberg. "I think he's had enough of Skåne."

"You're probably right," said Wallander. "Sorry to disturb you. I'll be leaving soon."

"No problems with the key?"

"It was where you said it would be."

Wallander returned the atlas to the bookcase. Svedberg was no doubt right. Konovalenko had gone back to Stockholm.

He went to the kitchen and poured himself a glass of water. He happened to notice the telephone was standing on a directory. He picked it up and opened it.

Somebody had written an address on the inside cover: 14 Hemmansvägen. It was written in pencil. He thought for a moment. Then he called directory assistance. When they answered he asked for the number of a subscriber by the name of Wallander who lived at 14 Hemmansvägen in Kalmar.

"There is nobody called Wallander at the address you gave," said the operator.

"It could be the phone is in his boss's name," said Wallander. "But I can't remember what he's called."

"Could it be Edelman?" wondered the operator.

"That's it," said Wallander.

He was given the number, thanked the girl and hung up. Then he stood totally motionless. Was it possible? Did Konovalenko have another hideaway, this time on Öland?

He put out the lights behind him, locked up and replaced the key in the gutter. There was a breeze blowing. The evening was warm and suggested early summer. His mind had been made up for him. He drove away from the house and headed for Öland.

He stopped in Brösarp and called home. His father answered.

"She's asleep," he said. "We've been playing cards."

"I won't be coming home tonight," said Wallander. "But don't worry. I just have to catch up with a stack of routine work. She knows I like working nights. I'll be in touch tomorrow morning."

"You come when you're ready," said his father.

Wallander replaced the receiver. Their relationship might be improving after all. There was a different tone between them. Let's hope it lasts, he thought. Maybe something good will come of this nightmare after all.

He reached the Öland bridge at four in the morning. He had stopped twice on the way, once to fill up with gas, and once to take a nap. Now that he had arrived, he no longer felt tired. He contemplated the mighty bridge looming up before him, and the water glittering in the morning sunlight. In the parking lot where he stopped was a phone booth with a ragged directory. Hemmansvägen was evidently on the other side of the bridge. He took his pistol out of the glove pocket and checked to make sure it was loaded. He suddenly remembered the time many years ago when he had visited Öland with his sister Kristina and their parents. There was no bridge then. He had a vague memory of the little ferry that took them over the sound. They spent a week camping that summer. He remembered that week as a happy experience rather than a series of separate incidents. A vague feeling of something lost forever possessed him just for a moment. Then he redirected his thoughts to Konovalenko. He tried to convince himself that he was probably mistaken. The pencil marks in the atlas and the address in the directory need not have been made by Konovalenko. He would soon be on his way back to Skåne.

He stopped when he came to the Öland side of the bridge. There was a large road map of the island there, and he got out to study it. Hemmansvägen was a side road just before the zoo entrance. He got back into the car and turned right. There was still not much traffic around. After a few minutes he found the right road. He left the car in a small parking lot. Hemmansvägen was made up of a mixture of old and new houses, all of them with large yards. He started walking. The first house had a number three on the fence. A dog eyed him suspiciously. He kept going, and figured out which house must be number fourteen. He noted that it was one of the older houses, with bay windows and elaborate ornamentation. Then he walked back the same way as he had come. He wanted to try approaching the house from the rear. He could not afford to take any risks. Konovalenko and his unknown companion could be there after all.

There was a sports field behind the houses. He clambered over the fence, ripping his trousers high up on one leg. He approached the house from behind a wooden spectator stand. It was painted yellow, with two stories and a tower in one corner. There was a boarded-up hot-dog stand next to the fence. Crouching down, he left the shelter of the spectator stand and ran over to the hut. Once there, he took his pistol out of his pocket. He stood motionless for five minutes, watching the house. Everything was very calm. There was a toolshed in one corner of the yard. He decided that was where he would hide. He looked again at the house. Then he went down carefully onto his knees and crawled over to the fence behind the shed. It was rickety and difficult to climb over. He almost fell over backward, but managed to regain his balance and jump down into the narrow gap behind the shed. He noticed he was breathing heavily. That's due to all the evil, he thought. He carefully stuck his head out and contemplated the house from his new position. All was still quiet. The yard was overgrown and in bad shape. Next to him was a wheelbarrow full of last year's leaves. He began to wonder if the house was deserted. After a while he was more or less convinced it was. He left the protection of the shed and ran to the house wall. Then he followed the wall to the right in order to get around to the other side of the house, where the front door was presumably located. He gave a start when he stumbled against a hedgehog. It hissed and raised its spikes. Wallander had put his pistol back in his pocket. Now, without being quite sure why, he took it out again. The sound of a foghorn drifted in from the sound. He crept around the corner of the house and found himself at the far gable end. What am I doing here, he wondered. If there is anybody in the house, it's bound to be some old couple who are just waking up after a good night's sleep. What on earth will they say if they find a runaway detective inspector sneaking around in their yard? He kept going to the next corner. Then he peered around it.

Konovalenko was standing on the gravel path by the flagpole, urinating. He was barefoot, dressed in trousers and an open shirt. Wallander did not move. Even so, something alarmed Konovalenko, possibly his instinct for danger that never waned. He turned around. Wallander had his pistol drawn. For a split second they both assessed the situation. Wallander realized Konovalenko had made the mistake of leaving the house without his gun. Konovalenko could see Wallander would either kill him or intercept him before he could reach the front door. Konovalenko found himself in a situation that gave him no choice. He flung himself to one side with such force that just for a moment, Wallander lost sight of him. Then he ran as fast as he could, dodging from side to side, and jumped over the fence. He was already in the road before Wallander had grasped what was happening and began chasing him. It had all happened in a flash. That is why he did not see Sikosi Tsiki standing in a window, watching what was going on.

Sikosi Tsiki knew something alarming had happened. He did not know what. But he realized the instructions Konovalenko gave him the day before must now be followed. "If anything happens," Konovalenko told him, handing over an envelope, "follow the instructions inside here. That way you'll make it back to South Africa. Get in touch with the man you already met, the one who gave you your money and your last set of instructions."

He waited by the window for a short while.

Then he sat down at a table and opened the envelope.

An hour later he left the house and was on his way.

Konovalenko had about a fifty-meter head start. Wallander wondered how he could run so incredibly fast. They were running in the direction of where Wallander had parked his car. Konovalenko had a car parked in the same lot! Wallander cursed and ran even faster. But the distance between them got no shorter. He was right. Konovalenko headed for a Mercedes, ripped open the door, which was unlocked, and started the engine. It all went so fast Wallander realized the ignition key must have been in the lock. Konovalenko was prepared, even if he had made the mistake of leaving the house without a gun. Just then Wallander saw a flash. Instinctively he threw himself to one side. The bullet whined past and hit the asphalt. Wallander huddled behind a bicycle stand and hoped he was invisible. Then he heard the car make a racing start.

He rushed towards his own car, fumbling with the keys and thinking he had doubtless lost Konovalenko already. But he was sure he would get off Öland as quickly as possible. If he stayed on the island he was bound to be cornered sooner or later. Wallander slammed down the gas pedal. He caught sight of Konovalenko at the rotary just before the bridge. Wallander overtook a slow-moving truck at vast speed and nearly lost control of the car as he clipped the flower bed in the center of the rotary. Then he raced onto the bridge. The Mercedes was in front of him. He must think of something. If it came down to a car chase, he wouldn't stand a chance against Konovalenko.

It all came to a head at the highest part of the bridge.

Konovalenko was going at very high speed, but Wallander had managed to keep on his tail. When he was sure of not hitting a car coming in the opposite direction, he stuck his pistol out of the window and shot. His aim was just to hit the car. The first shot missed. But the second was on target, and by an incredible stroke of luck he managed to burst one of the rear tires. The Mercedes immediately went into a skid, and Konovalenko could not stop it. Wallander slammed on the brakes and watched as Konovalenko careered into the concrete barrier at the outer edge of the bridge. There was an enormous crash. Wallander could not see what had happened to Konovalenko behind the wheel. But without a second thought he shifted into first gear and drove straight into the back of the wrecked car. He felt a searing pain as the safety belt bit into his chest. Wallander wrestled with the lever to find reverse. With tires screeching, he backed off and prepared for another ram. Then he repeated the maneuver one more time. The car in front was hurled a few more meters forward. Wallander backed off again, flung open the door, and took cover. Cars were already lining up behind him. When Wallander waved his pistol and yelled at the drivers to keep out of the way, several tumbled out of their cars and ran for it. Wallander could see a similar line of cars on the other side of the bridge. Still no sign of Konovalenko. Even so, he fired a shot at the crumpled car.

After the second bullet, the gas tank exploded. Wallander never knew for sure afterwards if it was his bullet that caused the fire, or whether the leaking gas had ignited for some other reason. The car was instantly engulfed by roaring flames and thick smoke. Wallander approached the car cautiously.

Konovalenko was on fire.

He was trapped on his back with half his upper body sticking out through the windshield. Afterwards, Wallander would remember his staring eyes, indicating he could not believe what was happening to him. Then his hair started burning, and a few seconds later it was obvious to Wallander he was dead. Sirens were approaching in the distance. He walked slowly back to his own car and leaned against the door.

He gazed out over Kalmar Sound. The water glistened. There was a smell of the sea. His mind was a complete blank; he could not think at all. Something had come to an end, and he felt stupefied. Then he heard a voice from a megaphone ordering somebody to lay down their arms. It was a while before he realized the voice was talking to him. He turned round and saw fire engines and patrol cars on the Kalmar side. Konavalenko's car was still ablaze. Wallander looked at his pistol. Then he threw it over the side of the bridge. Armed police were coming towards him. Wallander waved his ID.

"Chief Inspector Wallander," he yelled. "I'm a cop!"

He was soon surrounded by suspicious local colleagues.

"I'm a cop and my name's Wallander," he repeated. "You might have read about me in the papers. There's been an APB on me since last week."

"I recognize you," said one of the cops in a broad local accent.

"The guy on fire in the car is Konovalenko," said Wallander. "He's the one who shot our colleague in Stockholm. And a few more besides."

Wallander looked around.

Something that might have been joy, or maybe relief, was beginning to well up inside him.

"Shall we go?" he asked. "I could use a cup of coffee. It's all over here."

Chapter Thirty-one

Jan Kleyn was arrested in his office at BOSS headquarters around midday, Friday, May 22. Soon after eight in the morning Chief Prosecutor Wervey had listened to Scheepers's account of the circumstances and President de Klerk's decision late the previous night. Then, without comment, he signed a warrant for Jan Kleyn's arrest and another to search his house. Scheepers requested that Inspector Borstlap, who had made a good impression in connection with the murder of van Heerden, should take care of the arrest of Jan Kleyn. When Borstlap had deposited Jan Kleyn in an interrogation room, he went to an adjacent room where Scheepers was waiting. He was able to report that the arrest had taken place without any problems. But he had observed something that seemed to him important, and possibly worrisome. His information about why somebody in the intelligence service should be brought in for interrogation was scanty. Scheepers had stressed the secrecy surrounding everything to do with state security. Nevertheless, Borstlap had been told in confidence that President de Klerk was aware of what was happening. Borstlap had therefore felt instinctively that he ought to report what he had seen.

Jan Kleyn had not been surprised by his arrest. Borstlap had seen through his indignation as a poorly performed charade. Somebody must have warned Jan Kleyn about what was going to happen. Since it was clear to Borstlap that the decision to arrest Jan Kleyn had been made in great haste, he realized Kleyn must either have friends in circles close to the president or there must be a mole operating in the public prosecutor's office. Scheepers listened to what Borstlap had to say. It was less than twelve hours since de Klerk made his decision. Apart from the president only Wervey and Borstlap knew what was going to happen. It was clear to Scheepers he must inform de Klerk immediately that his office must be bugged. He asked Borstlap to wait outside while he made an important telephone call. But he did not get hold of de Klerk. His secretary said he was in a meeting and could not be reached until later in the afternoon.

Scheepers left the room and went out to Borstlap. He had made up his mind to keep Kleyn waiting. He had no illusions about the latter being worried because he was not told why he had been arrested. It was more for his own sake. Scheepers felt a degree of uncertainty about the imminent confrontation.

They drove to Jan Kleyn's house outside Pretoria. Borstlap was driving, and Scheepers was slumped in the back seat. He suddenly started to think about the white lioness he and Judith had seen. It was a symbol of Africa, he thought. The animal at rest, the calm before it gets to its feet and musters all its strength. The beast of prey one cannot afford to wound, but which must be killed if it starts to attack.

Scheepers gazed out of the car window and wondered what was happening in his life. He wondered whether the grand design worked out by de Klerk and Nelson Mandela, involving the ultimate retreat of the whites, would actually succeed. Or would it lead to chaos, uncontrolled violence, a crazy civil war with positions and alliances constantly changing and the outcome impossible to predict? The apocalypse, he thought. The doomsday we have always tried to contain like an evil genie in a bottle. Will the genie take its revenge when the bottle is broken?

They stopped outside the gate of Jan Kleyn's big house. Borstlap had already informed him on his arrest that his house would be searched, and requested the keys. Jan Kleyn played up his outraged dignity and refused. Then Borstlap threatened to break down the front door. He got the keys in the end. There was a guard posted outside the house, and a gardener. Scheepers introduced himself. He looked around the walled yard. It was designed on the basis of straight lines. In addition, it was so well tended it had lost all signs of life. That's what Jan Kleyn must be like as well, he thought to himself. His life is an extension of straight ideological lines. There is no room in his life for divergence, not in his thoughts, his emotions, nor his garden. The exception is his secret: Miranda and Matilda.

They entered the house. A black servant stared at them in astonishment. Scheepers asked him to wait outside while they searched the building. They asked him to tell the gardener and the guard not to go away until they received permission.

The house was sparsely but expensively furnished. They could see Jan Kleyn preferred marble, steel, and substantial wood in his furniture. Lithographs hung here and there on the walls. The motifs were taken from South African history. There were also some fencing swords, old pistols and game bags. A hunting trophy was mounted over the mantelpiece, a stuffed kudu with powerful, curved horns. While Borstlap went through the whole house, Scheepers shut himself into Jan Kleyn's study. The desk was empty. There was a filing cabinet against one wall. Scheepers looked for a safe but found nothing. He went downstairs to the living room where Borstlap was searching through a bookcase.

"There must be a safe," said Scheepers.

Borstlap picked up Jan Kleyn's keys and showed them to him.

"No key, though," he said.

"You can be sure he's chosen a place for the safe he thinks is the last place we'd think of looking," said Scheepers. "So that's where we'll start. Where's the last place we'd think of looking?"

"Right in front of our very eyes," said Borstlap. "The best hiding place is often the most obvious one. That's what we find hardest to see."

"Concentrate on finding the safe," said Scheepers. "There's nothing on the bookshelves."

Borstlap nodded and replaced the book he was holding in his hand. Scheepers went back to the study. He sat at the desk and started opening the drawers in turn.

Two hours later he had found nothing at all of significance for the investigation. Jan Kleyn's papers were mostly concerned with his private life and contained nothing remarkable. Or else they were to do with his coin collection. To his astonishment Scheepers discovered that Jan Kleyn was chairman of the South African Numismatic Society, and did sterling work on behalf of the country's coin collectors. Another peculiarity, he thought. But that is hardly of significance for my investigation.

Borstlap had made two thorough searches of the house without finding a safe.

"There must be one," said Scheepers.

Borstlap called in the servant and asked him where the safe was. The man stared at him uncomprehendingly.

"A secret cupboard," said Borstlap. "Hidden, always locked?"

"There isn't one," said the man.

Borstlap sent him out again in annoyance. Then they started searching anew. Scheepers tried to see if there were any irregularities in the house's architecture. It was not unusual for South Africans to have secret chambers built into their houses. He found nothing. While Borstlap was up in the cramped loft searching around with a flashlight, Scheepers went out into the yard. He observed the house from the back. The solution struck him more or less immediately. The house had no chimney. He went back inside and squatted in front of the open hearth. They had pocket flashlights with them, and he shone his up into the chimney. The safe was cut into the wall. When he tried the handle he found to his surprise that it was unlocked. Just then Borstlap came downstairs.

"A well-chosen hiding place," said Scheepers.

Borstlap nodded. He was annoyed that he had failed to find it himself.

Scheepers sat down at the marble table in front of the big leather sofa. Borstlap had gone outside for a cigarette. Scheepers sorted through the papers from the safe. There were insurance policies, some envelopes containing old coins, the house deeds, about twenty stock certificates, and some government debentures. He pushed it all to one side and concentrated on a small, black notebook. He leafed through the pages. They were full of cryptic notes, a mixture of names, places and combinations of numbers. Scheepers decided to take the book with him. He replaced the papers in the safe and went out to Borstlap.

A thought suddenly struck him. He beckoned to the three men who squatted watching them.

"Were there any visitors late last night?" he asked.

The gardener replied.

"Only Mofolo, the night watchman, can tell you that," he said.

"And he's not here, of course."

"He comes at seven o'clock."

Scheepers nodded. He would come back.

They drove back to Johannesburg. On the way they stopped for a late lunch. They separated at a quarter past four outside the police station. Scheepers could not put it off any longer. He would have to start the interrogation of Jan Kleyn now. But first he would make another attempt to get hold of President de Klerk.

When the security guard outside President de Klerk's office called near midnight, Jan Kleyn had been surprised. He knew of course that a young prosecutor by the name of Scheepers had been given the assignment of trying to sort out the suspicions of a conspiracy. All the time he was confident of being a sufficient number of steps ahead of the man trying to track him down. But now he realized Scheepers was closer to him than he had imagined. He got up, dressed, and prepared to be up all night. He guessed he had until at least ten the following morning. Scheepers would need an hour or two next day in order to arrange all the papers needed for his arrest. By then he must have made sure he had issued all the necessary instructions and ensured the operation would not run into trouble. He went down to the kitchen and made tea. Then he sat down to write a summary. There was a lot to keep in mind. But he would manage.

Getting arrested was an unexpected complication. But he had considered the possibility. The situation was annoying, but not impossible to resolve. As he could not be sure how long Scheepers was thinking of holding him, he must make plans on the assumption he would be detained until the assassination of Mandela had been carried out.

That was his first task that night. To turn what would happen the following day to his own advantage. As long as he was detained, they would not be able to accuse him of being involved in the various activities. He thought through what was going to happen. It was one in the morning by the time he called Franz Malan.

"Get dressed and come over here," he said.

Franz Malan was half-awake and confused. Jan Kleyn did not mention his name.

"Get dressed and come over here," he repeated.

Franz Malan asked no questions.

Just over an hour later, shortly after two, he entered Jan Kleyn's living room. The drapes were closed. The night watchman who opened the gate for him was threatened with instant dismissal if he ever revealed the visitors who came to the house late in the evening or during the night. Jan Kleyn paid him a very high wage in order to guarantee the guy's silence.

Franz Malan was nervous. He knew Jan Kleyn would never have summoned him unless something important had come up.

Jan Kleyn hardly let him sit down before explaining what had happened, what would happen the next morning, and what must be fixed that night. What Franz Malan heard increased his nervousness. He could see his own responsibility would increase beyond what he was really happy with.

"We don't know how much Scheepers has managed to figure out," he said. "But we must take certain precautions. The most important one is to dissolve the Committee, and divert attention from Cape Town and June 12."

Franz Malan gaped at him in astonishment. Could he be serious? Would all the executive responsibility fall on his shoulders?

Jan Kleyn could see he was worried.

"I'll be out again soon," he said. "Then I'll take over the responsibility."

"I hope so," said Franz Malan. "But dissolving the Committee?"

"We have to. Scheepers might have penetrated deeper and further than we can imagine."

"But how has he done that?"

Jan Kleyn shrugged in annoyance.

"What do we do?" he asked. "We use all our skills, all our contacts. We bribe, threaten, and lie our way to the information we need. There are no limits to what we can do. And so there are no limits for those who keep watch over our activities. The Committee must not meet again. It will cease to exist. That means it has never existed. We shall contact all the members tonight. But before that there are other things we have to do."

"If Scheepers knows we're planning something for June 12th, we'll have to postpone it," said Franz Malan. "The risk is too great."

"It's too late," said Jan Kleyn. "Besides, Scheepers can't be certain. A well-laid trail in another direction will convince him that Cape Town and June 12 are an attempt to mislead him. We turn the tables on him."

"How?"

"During the interrogation I'll be subjected to tomorrow, I'll have the chance to trick him into starting to believe something else."

"But that's hardly enough."

"Of course not."

Jan Kleyn took out a little black notebook. When he opened it, Franz Malan could see all the pages were blank.

"I'll fill this with nonsense," Jan Kleyn went on. "But here and there I'll note down a place and a date. All except one will be crossed out. The one that is left will not be Cape Town, June 12. I'll leave the book in my safe. I'll leave it unlocked, as if I'd been in a great hurry and tried to burn important papers."

Franz Malan nodded. He was beginning to think Jan Kleyn was right. It would be possible to set false trails.

"Sikosi Tsiki is on his way home," said Jan Kleyn, handing over an envelope to Franz Malan. "It will be your job to receive him, take him to Hammanskraal, and give him his final instructions the day before June 12. Everything is written down inside this envelope. Read through it now and see if anything is unclear. Then we'll have to start making our calls."

While Franz Malan was reading the instructions, Jan Kleyn started filling the notebook with meaningless combinations of words and numbers. He used several different pens to give the impression the notes had been made over a long period. He thought for a while before deciding on Durban, July 3. He knew the ANC would be holding an important meeting there on that day. That would be his red herring, and he hoped Scheepers would be fooled by it.

Franz Malan put down the papers.

"It doesn't say anything about what gun he should use," he said.

"Konovalenko has been training him to use a long-range rifle," said Jan Kleyn. "There is an exact copy in the underground store at Hammanskraal."

Franz Malan nodded.

"No more questions?" wondered Jan Kleyn.

"No," said Franz Malan.

Then they started making their telephone calls. Jan Kleyn had three separate lines. They made calls all over the country. Half-asleep men fumbled for receivers, only to become wide awake instantaneously. Some were worried about what they heard, others merely noted how things would be from now on. Some of the men who had been woken up had trouble in getting back to sleep, while others simply turned over and resumed snoring.

The Committee was dissolved. It had never existed because it had disappeared without trace. All that remained was a rumor about its existence. But it could be re-created at very short notice. Just now it was no longer needed, and indeed, could be a danger. But the state of readiness to achieve what the Committee members considered to be the only solution for the future of South Africa was as high as ever. They were all ruthless men who never rested. Their ruthlessness was real, but their ideas were based on a mixture of illusions, lies, and fanatical despair. For some of the members it was a matter of pure hatred.

Franz Malan drove home through the night.

Jan Kleyn tidied up his house and left the safe door unlocked. At half past four in the morning he went to bed and prepared to get a few hours sleep. He wondered who had provided Scheepers with all the information. He could not get away from the uncomfortable feeling that there was something he did not understand.

Somebody had betrayed him.

But he could not figure out who it was.

Scheepers opened the door of the interview room.

Jan Kleyn was sitting on a chair against one of the walls, smiling at him. Scheepers had decided to treat him in a friendly and correct manner. He had spent an hour going through the notebook. He was still doubtful whether the assassination attempt on Nelson Mandela really had been switched to Durban. He had weighed the reasons for and against without reaching any definite conclusion. He saw absolutely no prospect of Jan Kleyn actually telling him the truth. He might just be able to lure him into providing snippets of information which could indicate indirectly how things stood.

Scheepers sat opposite Jan Kleyn, and it struck him this was Matilda's father he was looking at. He knew the secret, but he realized he would not be able to make use of it. It would result in far too big a threat for the two women. Jan Kleyn could not be detained indefinitely. He already looked like he was ready to leave the interview room at any moment.

A secretary came in and sat down at a little table to one side.

"Jan Kleyn," he said. "You have been arrested because there are strong grounds for believing you are involved in and possibly even responsible for subversive activities, and plotting to commit murder. What do you have to say?"

Jan Kleyn continued smiling as he replied.

"My response is that I will not say anything until I have a lawyer at my side."

Scheepers was momentarily put off his stride. The normal procedure was that when a person is arrested, the first step is to give him the opportunity of contacting a lawyer.

"Everything has been conducted by the book," said Jan Kleyn, as if he could see right through Scheepers' hesitation. "But my lawyer hasn't arrived yet."

"We can start with personal details, then," said Scheepers. "You don't need to have a lawyer present for that."

"Of course not."

Scheepers left the room as soon as he had recorded all the details. He left instructions to send for him the moment the lawyer showed up. When he got to the prosecutor's waiting room, he was covered in sweat. Jan Kleyn's nonchalant superiority unnerved him. How could he be so indifferent when faced with charges which, if proven, could result in his being sentenced to death?

Scheepers suddenly began to wonder if he would be able to handle him as required. Maybe he should contact Wervey and suggest that a more experienced interrogator should be called in? On the other hand he knew Wervey was expecting him to carry off the assignment he had been given. Wervey never gave anybody the same challenge twice. His whole career would be under threat if he failed to live up to expectations. He took off his jacket and rinsed his face under the cold water tap. Then he ran through the questions he planned to put one more time.

He also managed to get through to President de Klerk. As soon as he could he passed on his suspicion that the president's office was bugged. De Klerk heard him through without interrupting.

"I'll have that looked into," he said when Scheepers was through. That was the end of the conversation.

It was six o'clock before he was informed that the lawyer had shown up. He returned to the interview room immediately. The lawyer by Jan Kleyn's side was about forty and called Kritzinger. They shook hands and greeted each other coolly. Scheepers could see right away that Kritzinger and Jan Kleyn were old acquaintances. It was possible Kritzinger had deliberately delayed his arrival in order to give Jan Kleyn breathing space and at the same time un-nerve the chief interrogator. The effect on Scheepers was the opposite, and he remained quite calm. All the doubts he had experienced over the last few hours had disappeared.

"I have examined the detention order," said Kritzinger. "These are serious charges."

"It's a serious crime to undermine national security," Scheepers responded.

"My client absolutely rejects all the charges," said Kritzinger. "I demand that he be released immediately. Is it sensible to detain people whose daily task it is to uphold precisely that national security you refer to?"

"For the moment I am the one asking the questions," said Scheepers. "Your client is the one required to supply the answers, not me."

Scheepers glanced down at his papers.

"Do you know Franz Malan?" he asked.

"Yes," said Jan Kleyn without hesitation. "He works in the military sector which deals with top secret security measures."

"When did you last see him?"

"In connection with the terrorist attack on the restaurant near Durban. We were both called in to assist with the investigation."

"Are you aware of a secret group of *boere* who call themselves simply the Committee?"

"No."

"Are you sure?"

"My client has already answered once," protested Kritzinger.

"There's nothing to prevent my asking the same question twice," snapped Scheepers.

"I am not aware of any such Committee," said Jan Kleyn.

"We have reason to believe the assassination of one of the black nationalist leaders is being plotted by that same Committee," said Scheepers. "Various places and dates have been mentioned. Do you know anything about that?"

"No."

Scheepers produced the notebook.

"When your house was searched, the police found this book. Do you recognize it?"

"Of course I recognize it. It's mine."

"There are various notes in it about dates and places. Can you tell me what they mean?"

"What is all this?" said Jan Kleyn, turning to his lawyer. "These are private notes about birthdays and meetings with friends."

"What do you have planned for Cape Town on June 12?"

Jan Kleyn's expression did not waver when he replied.

"I have nothing planned at all," he said. "I had thought of going there for a meeting with some of my fellow numismatists. But it was canceled."

Scheepers thought Jan Kleyn still seemed totally unconcerned.

"What do you have to say about Durban on July 3?"

"Nothing."

"You have nothing to say?"

Jan Kleyn turned to his lawyer and whispered something.

"My client declines to answer that question for personal reasons," said Kritzinger.

"Personal reasons or not, I want an answer," said Scheepers.

"This is lunacy," said Jan Kleyn, with a gesture of resignation.

Scheepers suddenly noticed Jan Kleyn was sweating. Moreover one of his hands, resting on the table, had started trembling.

"All your questions so far have been completely lacking in substance," said Kritzinger. "I shall very soon be demanding an end to all this and insisting on the immediate release of my client."

"When it comes to investigations concerning threats to national security, the police and prosecutors have wide powers," said Scheepers. "Now, will you please answer my question."

"I am having an affair with a woman in Durban," said Jan Kleyn. "As she is married, I have to meet her in extremely discreet circumstances."

"Do you meet her regularly?"

"Yes."

"What's her name?"

Jan Kleyn and Kritzinger protested with one voice.

"OK, we'll leave her name out of it for the time being," said Scheepers. "I'll come back to that. But if it's true you meet her regularly and, moreover, note down various meetings in this book, is it not a little odd that there's only one reference to Durban?"

"I get through at least ten notebooks a year," said Jan Kleyn. "I throw full ones away regularly. Or burn them."

"Where do you burn them?"

Jan Kleyn seemed to have recovered his composure.

"In the kitchen sink, or in the toilet," said Jan Kleyn. "As you know already, my fireplace has no chimney. It was bricked off by the former owners. I never got around to opening it again."

The interrogation continued. Scheepers reverted to asking questions about the secret Committee, but the answers were always the same. Kritzinger protested at regular intervals. After three hours of questioning, Scheepers decided to call it a day. He rose to his feet and said curtly that Jan Kleyn would remain in custody. Kritzinger was absolutely furious. But Scheepers overruled him. The law allowed him to detain Jan Kleyn for at least another twenty-four hours.

It was already evening by the time he went to report to Wervey, who had promised to remain in his office until he arrived. The corridors were deserted as he hurried to the chief prosecutor's office. The door was ajar. Wervey was asleep in his chair. He knocked and went in. Wervey opened his eyes and looked at him. Scheepers sat down.

"Jan Kleyn has not admitted to any knowledge whatsoever of a conspiracy or an assassination," he said. "I don't think he will, either. Moreover, we have no evidence to connect him with either offence. When we searched his house, we found only one item of interest. There was a notebook in his safe, with references to various dates and locations. All of them were crossed out except one. Durban, July 3. We know that Nelson Mandela will be giving a public address on that day. The date we first suspected, Cape Town June 12, is crossed out in the book."

Wervey quickly adjusted his chair to the upright position and asked to see the notebook. Scheepers had it in his case. Wervey leafed through it slowly in the light of his desk lamp.

"What explanation did he give?" asked Wervey when he got to the end.

"Various meetings. As far as Durban is concerned, he claims he is having an affair with a married woman there."

"Start with that tomorrow," said Wervey.

"He refuses to say who she is."

"Tell him he won't be released unless he tells us."

Scheepers looked at Wervey in surprise.

"Can we do that?"

"Young man," said Wervey. "You can do anything when you are chief prosecutor and as old as I am. Don't forget that a man like Jan Kleyn knows how to eradicate every trace of where he's been. He must be beaten in battle. Even if one has to resort to doubtful methods."

"Even so, I sometimes got the feeling he was insecure," said Scheepers hesitantly.

"He knows we're snapping at his heels in any case," said Wervey. "Really put him under pressure tomorrow. The same questions, over and over again. From different angles. But the same thrust, the same thrust every time."

Scheepers nodded.

"There was one more thing," he said. "Inspector Borstlap actually made the arrest, and he had the distinct impression Jan Kleyn had been warned. Even though only a very few people knew only a short time in advance what was going to happen."

Wervey looked at him for a long time before responding.

"This country of ours is at war," he said. "There are ears everywhere, human and electronic. Penetrating secrets is often the best weapon of all. Don't forget that."

The conversation was over.

Scheepers left the building and paused on the steps, enjoying the fresh air. He felt very tired. Then he went to his car to drive home. Just as he was about to open his car door, one of the parking attendants emerged from the shadows.

"A man left this for you," said the attendant, handing him an envelope.

"Who?" asked Scheepers.

"A black guy," said the attendant. "He didn't say his name. Just that it was important."

Scheepers handled the letter carefully. It was thin, and could not possibly contain a bomb. He nodded to the attendant, unlocked the car and got in. Then he opened the envelope and read what the note said by the light of the inside lamp.

Assassin probably a black man by the name of Victor Mabasha.

The note was signed Steve.

Scheepers felt his heart beating faster.

At last, he thought.

Then he drove straight home. Judith was waiting for him with a meal. But before sitting down, he called Inspector Borstlap at home.

"Victor Mabasha," he said. "Does that name mean anything to you?"

Borstlap considered before replying.

"No," he said.

"Tomorrow morning go through all the files and everything you have in the computer. Victor Mabasha is a black, and probably the assassin we are looking for."

"Have you managed to break Jan Kleyn?" asked Borstlap in surprise.

"No," said Scheepers. "How I got that information is neither here nor there for the moment."

End of conversation.

Victor Mabasha, he thought as he sat down at the dining table. If you're the one, we'll put a stop to you before it's too late.

Chapter Thirty-two

That day in Kalmar, Kurt Wallander began to realize how bad he actually felt. Later, when the murder of Louise Åkerblom and the sheer nightmare that followed in its wake had become a series of unreal events, a desolate charade in a distant landscape, he would insist stubbornly that it was not until Konovalenko was lying on the Öland bridge with staring eyes and blazing hair that it really struck him how rotten he felt deep down inside. That was the moment of insight, and he would not budge from that view, even though the memories and all the painful experiences came and went like changing patterns in a kaleidoscope. It was in Kalmar that he lost his grip on himself! He told his daughter it was like a countdown had started, a countdown leading to nothing but a vacuum. The doctor in Ystad, who started treating him in mid-June and tried to sort out his increasing gloom, wrote in his journal that *according to the patient the depression started over a cup of coffee at the police station in Kalmar while a man was being burned up in a car on a bridge.*

There he sat in the police station in Kalmar, drinking coffee, feeling very tired and low. Everybody who saw him hunched over his cup that half hour had the impression he was preoccupied and completely aloof. Or was he just thoughtful? In any case, nobody went to keep him company or to ask him how he was doing. The strange cop from Ystad was surrounded by a mixture of respect and hesitation. He was simply left in peace while they all dealt with the chaos on the bridge and the endless flow of telephone calls from newspapers, radio, and television. After half an hour he suddenly jumped to his feet and demanded to be taken to the yellow house on Hemmánsvägen. When they passed the place on the bridge where

Konovalenko's car had become a smoking, burned-out shell, he stared straight ahead. When he got to the house he immediately took over command, forgetting completely that the investigation was actually being led by a Kalmar detective called Blomstrand. But they deferred to him, and he worked up an enormous level of energy over the next few hours. He seemed to have put Konovalenko right out of his mind already. There were two things that interested him above all others. He wanted to know who owned the house. He also kept going on about Konovalenko not being alone. He ordered an immediate door-to-door survey of the other houses in the street, and he wanted cab drivers and bus conductors to be contacted. Konovalenko was not alone, he kept repeating, over and over again. Who was the man or woman he had with him, who had now disappeared without trace? None of his questions could be answered immediately. The local property register and the neighbors who were questioned gave completely contradictory answers about who actually owned the yellow house. About ten years previously, the owner, a widower called Hjalmarson who worked at the provincial records office, had died. His son lived in Brazil. According to some neighbors he was a representative for some Swedish firm and an arms dealer according to others. He returned home for the funeral. It had all amounted to a worrying time for Hemmansvägen, according to a retired department head at the local council offices in Kronoberg, who emerged as a spokesman for the neighbors. And so there was an invisible sigh of relief when the "For Sale" sign was taken down and a moving van drove up filled with all the belongings of a retired reserve officer. He used to be something as antiquated as a major in the Scanian hussars, an amazing relic from a former age. He was named Gustav Jernberg, and he announced his presence to the surrounding world by means of friendly bellowing. The worries returned, however, when it became apparent that Jernberg spent most of his time in Spain, on account of his rheumatism. When he was away, the house was occupied by his grandson, who was in his mid-thirties, arrogant, rude, and paid no attention to normal conventions. His name was Hans Jernberg, and all anybody knew was that he was some kind of businessman who occasionally paid fleeting visits, often accompanied by strange companions nobody recognized.

The police immediately started looking for Hans Jernberg. He was traced at about two in the afternoon to an office in Göteborg. Wallander spoke with him over the telephone. At first he claimed to have no idea what they were talking about. But Wallander was in no mood to wheedle and coax people into telling the truth that day, and threatened to hand him over to the Göteborg police besides hinting it would be impossible to keep the press out of it. Halfway through the call one of the Kalmar cops stuck a note under Wallander's nose. They had run a search on Hans Jernberg through various files and found he had strong connections with neo-nazi movements in Sweden. Wallander stared at the note before the obvious question to ask the guy at the other end of the line struck him.

"Can you tell me your views on South Africa?" he asked.

"I can't see what that has to do with it," said Hans Jernberg.

"Answer the question," Wallander demanded impatiently. "Or else I'll have to call my colleagues in Göteborg."

The reply came after a short silence.

"I consider South Africa to be one of the best organized countries in the world," said Hans Jernberg. "I regard it as my duty to do all I can to support the whites living there."

"And you do that by renting out your house to Russian bandits who run errands for the South Africans, do you?" asked Wallander.

This time Hans Jernberg was genuinely surprised.

"I don't know what you're talking about."

"Oh yes you do," said Wallander. "But you can answer another question instead. Which of your friends has had access to the house during this last week? Think carefully before you answer. If there's the slightest sign of evasion I'll ask one of the Göteborg prosecutors to issue a warrant for your arrest. And that's what will happen, believe you me."

"Ove Westerberg," said Hans Jernberg. "He's an old friend of mine who runs a construction firm here in town."

"Address?" demanded Wallander, and received it.

It was all very confusing. But some effective work on the part of the CID in Göteborg threw some light on what had happened at the yellow house over the last few days. Ove Westerberg proved to be as good a friend of South Africa as Hans Jernberg. Through a series of contacts whose identities seemed shrouded in mist, he had received a query some weeks previously as to whether the house could be placed at the disposal of some South African guests, who would pay good money. As Hans Jernberg was abroad at the time, Ove Westerberg had not told him about it. Wallander also suspected the money had gone no further than Westerberg's pocket. But Westerberg had no idea who these guests from South Africa were. He did not even know they had been there. That was as far as Wallander got that day. It would be the job of the Kalmar police to delve further into contacts between Swedish neo-nazis and the representatives of apartheid in South Africa. It was still not clear who had been in the yellow house with Konovalenko. While neighbors, cab drivers, and bus conductors were being interrogated, Wallander made a thorough search of the house. He could see that two of the bedrooms had been used recently, and that the house had been vacated in a great hurry. It seemed to him Konovalenko must have left something behind this time. He had left the house, never to return. It was possible, of course, that the other visitor had taken Konovalenko's belongings with him. It was also possible that there was no limit to Konovalenko's caution. Maybe he anticipated the possibility of a burglary every night, and hid all his belongings before going to bed? Wallander summoned Blomstrand, who was busy searching the toolshed. Wallander wanted every available cop to search the house looking for a bag. He couldn't say what it looked like or how big it was.

"A bag with something in it," he said. "There must be one somewhere."

"What kind of things in it?" wondered Blomstrand.

"I don't know," said Wallander. "Papers, money, clothes. Maybe a gun. I just don't know."

The search began. Various bags and cases were carried down to where Wallander was waiting on the ground floor. He blew the dust off a leather briefcase containing old photos and letters, most of them starting with phrases like *Dearest Gunvor* or *My dear Herbert*. Another, just as dusty and unearthed in the attic, was crammed with exotic starfish and seashells. But Wallander waited patiently. He knew there would be traces of Konovalenko somewhere, and hence also perhaps his unknown companion. While he was waiting, he spoke with his daughter and Björk. News of what had happened that morning had spread all over the country. Wallander told his daughter he felt OK, and it was all over now. He would return home that night, and they could take the car and spend a few days in Copenhagen. He could tell by her voice she was not convinced he was well, or that it was all over. He thought afterward he had a daughter who could read him like a book. The conversation with Björk came to an end when Wallander lost his temper and slammed down the receiver. That had never happened in all the years he had worked with Björk. But Björk had begun to question Wallander's judgment because, without telling anybody, he had set out after Konovalenko on his own. Of course, Wallander could see there was a lot to be said for Björk's point of view. But what upset him was the fact that Björk started going on about that now, when he was in the middle of a critical stage of the investigation. As far as Björk was concerned, he regarded Wallander's furious outburst as an unfortunate sign that he was still mentally disturbed. "We'll have to keep an eye on Kurt," Björk told Martinson and Svedberg.

It was Blomstrand himself who finally found the right bag. Konovalenko had hidden it behind a stack of boots in a closet in the corridor between the kitchen and the dining room. It was a leather suitcase with a combination lock. Wallander wondered whether the lock might be booby-trapped. What would happen if they forced open the case? Blomstrand drove to Kalmar airport at high speed with it, and had it put through the x-ray machine. There was no indication it might blow up if anybody opened it. Wallander took a screwdriver and forced the lock. There was a number of papers in the case, tickets, several passports, and a large sum of money. There was also a small pistol, a Beretta. All the passports belonged to Konovalenko, and were issued in Sweden, Finland, and Poland. He had a different name in each passport. As a Finn he was called Konovalenko Mäkelä, and as a Pole he had the German-sounding name of Hausmann. There were forty-seven thousand Swedish kronor and eleven thousand U.S. dollars in the case. But what interested Wallander most was whether the other documents could indicate who the unknown traveling companion might be. To his great disappointment and annoyance, most of the notes were written in a foreign language, which he thought must be Russian. He could not understand a word. They seemed to be consecutive memos since there were dates in the margin.

Wallander turned to Blomstrand.

"We need somebody who speaks Russian," he said. "Somebody who can translate this on the spot."

"We could try my wife," said Blomstrand.

Wallander stared at him in surprise.

"She studied Russian," Blomstrand went on. "She's very interested in Russian culture. Especially nineteenth-century writers."

Wallander closed the suitcase and tucked it under his arm.

"Let's go see her," he said. "She'd only get nervous if we brought her to this circus."

Blomstrand lived in a row house north of Kalmar. His wife was an intelligent, straightforward woman, and Wallander took an immediate liking to her. While they were drinking coffee and eating sandwiches in the kitchen, she took the papers into her study and looked up a few words in the dictionary. It took her nearly an hour to translate the text and write it down. But then it was ready, and Wallander could read Konovalenko's memos. It was like reading about his own experiences from a different point of view, he thought. Many details of what had happened now became clear. The main thing was that the answer to the question of who had been Konovalenko's final and unknown companion, who had moreover managed to leave the yellow house without being seen, was quite different from what he had expected. South Africa had sent a substitute for Victor Mabasha. An African called Sikosi Tsiki. He had entered the country from Denmark. "His training is not perfect," Konovalenko wrote, "but sufficient. And his ruthlessness and mental resilience are greater than those of Victor Mabasha." Then Konovalenko referred to a man in South Africa by the name of Jan Kleyn. Wallander assumed he was an important go-between. There was no clue about the organization Wallander was now certain must be behind it all, and hence at the center of everything. He told Blomstrand what he had discovered.

"An African is in the process of leaving Sweden," said Wallander. "He was in the yellow house this morning. Somebody must have seen him, somebody must have driven him someplace. He can't have walked over the bridge. We can rule out the possibility he's still on Öland. There is a possibility that he might have had his own car. But more important is the fact that he's trying to leave Sweden. Where, we don't know; just that he is. We have to stop him."

"That won't be easy," said Blomstrand.

"Difficult, but not impossible," said Wallander. "After all, there must be only a limited number of black men passing through Swedish border controls every day."

Wallander thanked Blomstrand's wife. They returned to the police station. An hour later an APB went out on the unknown African. At about the same time the police found a cab driver who had picked up an African that morning from a parking lot at the end of Hemmansvägen. It was after the car burned up and the bridge was blocked. Wallander assumed the African had first hidden outside the house somewhere for an hour or two. The cab driver took him to the center of Kalmar. Then he paid, got out, and disappeared. The cab driver could not give a description. The guy was tall, muscular, dressed in light-colored pants, white shirt, and dark jacket. That was about all he could say. He spoke English with the cab driver.

It was late afternoon by now. There was no more Wallander could do in Kalmar. Once they picked up the fleeing African, the last piece of the puzzle could be fitted in with all the others.

They offered to drive him to Ystad, but he declined. He wanted to be on his own. Shortly after five in the afternoon he said goodbye to Blomstrand, apologized for shamelessly taking over command for a few hours in the middle of the day, and left Kalmar.

He had studied a map and come to the conclusion that the shortest way home was via Växjö. The forest seemed eternal. Everywhere was the same mood of silent detachment he had experienced inside himself. He stopped in Nybro for a meal. Although he would have preferred to forget all that had happened to him, he forced himself to call Kalmar and find out if the African had been traced yet. The reply was negative. He got back in the car and kept on driving through the endless forest. He got as far as Växjö and hesitated for a moment whether to take the Älmhult route or to go via Tingsryd. In the end he chose Tingsryd so that he could start driving southward right away.

It was when he had passed through Tingsryd and turned off toward Ronneby that a moose loomed up on the road. He had not noticed it in the gathering dusk. For one desperate moment, with the brakes screeching in his ears, he was convinced he had reacted too late. He would run straight into the enormous bull moose, and his safety belt was not even fastened. But all of a sudden the moose turned away, and without knowing how it happened, Wallander shot past and did not even touch it.

He stopped at the side of the road and sat there without moving. His heart was beating madly, his breath coming in pants, and he felt ill. When he had calmed down he got out of the car and stood motionless in the silent forest. A hair's breadth away from death yet again, he thought. I can't have any get-out-of-jail-free cards left. He wondered why he did not feel jubilant at having been miraculously saved from being crushed by the bull moose. What he did feel was more like a vague guilty conscience. The bottomless depression that had taken possession of him that morning as he sat drinking coffee returned. What he wanted most was to leave the car where it was, walk off into the forest and disappear without trace. Not to disappear for ever, but for long enough to recover his equilibrium, to combat the feeling of dizziness that had taken hold of him as a result of the previous week's events. But he got back into the car and kept on driving southward, now with his safety belt fastened. He came to the main road to Kristianstad, and turned off toward the west. At about nine he stopped at an all-night café and had a cup of coffee. Some long-distance truck drivers were sitting in silence at a table, and a group of youths were whooping it up around an electronic games machine. Wallander did not touch his coffee until it was cold. But he did drink it in the end, and went back to his car.

Shortly before midnight he turned into the courtyard outside his father's house. His daughter came out onto the steps to greet him. He smiled wearily and said everything was fine. Then he asked if there had been a telephone call from Kalmar. She shook her head. The only calls had been from journalists who had found out her father's telephone number.

"Your apartment has been repaired already," she said. "You can move back in."

"That's great," he said.

He wondered if he ought to call Kalmar. But he was too tired. He left it until the next day.

They sat up late that night, talking. But Wallander said nothing about the feeling of melancholy weighing down on him. For the moment, that was something he wanted to keep to himself.

Sikosi Tsiki took the express bus from Kalmar to Stockholm. He followed Konovalenko's emergency instructions, and got to Stockholm just after four in the afternoon. His flight to London would leave at seven o'clock. He got lost and could not find the airport bus, so he took a cab to Arlanda. The driver was suspicious of foreigners and demanded the fare in advance. He had handed over a thousand-kronor bill, then settled down in a corner of the back seat. Sikosi Tsiki had no idea every passport officer in Sweden was on the lookout for him. All he knew was that he should leave the country as a Swedish citizen, Leif Larson, a name he had very quickly learned to pronounce. He was completely calm, as he trusted Konovalenko. His cab had taken him over the bridge, and he could see something had happened. But he had no doubt Konovalenko would have disposed of the unknown man who had shown up in the yard that morning.

Sikosi Tsiki took his change when they got to Arlanda, shaking his head when asked if he wanted a receipt. He went into the departure hall, checked in, and stopped by a newspaper stand on the way to passport control to buy some English newspapers.

If he had not stopped by the newspaper stand, he would have been arrested at passport control. But during those very minutes he took choosing and paying for his newspapers, the passport officers changed shifts. One of the new ones went to the rest room. The other, a girl named Kerstin Anderson, happened to have arrived for work at Arlanda very late. There was something wrong with her car, and she turned up at the last moment. She was conscientious and ambitious and would normally have been early enough to read through all the notices that had arrived that day with lists of people to look out for, as well as the lists still current from previous days. As it was, she had no time to do so, and Sikosi Tsiki went through passport control with his Swedish passport and smiling face, no problem. The door closed behind him just as Kerstin Anderson's colleague came back from the rest room.

"Is there anything special to look out for this evening?" asked Kerstin Anderson.

"A black South African," replied her colleague.

She remembered the African who had just gone through. But he was Swedish. It was ten o'clock before the supervising officer came to check that all was in order.

"Don't forget that African," he said. "We have no idea what he's called, or what passport he'll be traveling on."

Kerstin Anderson could feel a sudden tightening of her stomach.

"He was a South African, surely?" she said to her colleague.

"Presumably," said the supervisor. "But that needn't indicate what nationality he'll claim when he leaves Sweden."

She told him immediately what had happened a few hours earlier. After some hectic activity, they established that the man with the Swedish passport had taken a British Airways flight to London at seven o'clock.

The airplane had taken off on time. It had already landed in London, and the passengers had been through customs. Sikosi Tsiki had used his time in London to tear up his Swedish passport and flush it down a toilet. From now on he was a Zambian citizen, Richard Motombwane. Since he was in transit, he had not been through passport control with either his Swedish or his Zambian passport. Moreover, he had two separate tickets. As he had no check-in baggage, the girl at the desk in Sweden had only seen his ticket to London. At the transit desk in Heathrow he showed his other ticket, the one to Lusaka. He had flushed away the first ticket together with the remains of his Swedish passport.

At half past eleven the Zambia Airways DC-10 Nkowazi took off for Lusaka. Tsiki arrived there at half past six on Saturday morning. He took a cab into town and paid for a South African Airways ticket for the afternoon flight to Johannesburg. It had been booked some time ago. This time he used his own name. He returned to Lusaka Airport, checked in, and had lunch in the departure hall restaurant. He boarded at three, and shortly before five his plane landed at Jan Smuts Airport outside Johannesburg. He was met by Malan, who drove him straight to Hammanskraal. He showed Sikosi Tsiki the deposit receipt for the half-million rand constituting the next to last part of the payout. Then he left him on his own, saying he would be back the next day. Meanwhile, Tsiki was not to leave the house and walled-in yard. When Sikosi Tsiki was alone, he took a bath. He was tired, but contented. The journey had passed without any problems. The only thing worrying him was what had happened to Konovalenko. On the other hand, he was not especially curious about the fact that he would soon know who he was being paid so much to shoot. Could any individual person be worth so much money, he asked himself. But he did not bother to answer. Before midnight struck he had settled down between cool sheets and fallen asleep.

On the morning of Saturday, May 23, two things happened more or less simultaneously. Jan Kleyn was set free in Johannesburg. Nevertheless, Scheepers informed him he could expect to be called in for further questioning.

He stood by a window, watching Jan Kleyn and his lawyer, Kritzinger, making their way to their cars. Scheepers had asked for him to be watched around the clock. He took it for granted Jan Kleyn was expecting that, but thought it would at least force him to be passive.

He had not managed to extract any information at all from Jan Kleyn to clarify the circumstances surrounding the Committee. On the other hand, Scheepers now felt certain the real scene of the intended assassination was to be Durban on July 3, and not Cape Town on June 12. Every time he had come back to the notebook Jan Kleyn displayed signs of nervousness, and Scheepers thought it was impossible for anybody to fake reactions such as sweating and shaking hands.

He yawned. He would be glad when it was all over. At the same time he could see the chances of Wervey being pleased about his efforts had now increased.

He suddenly thought about the white lioness lying by the river in the moonlight.

He would soon have time to visit her again.

At about the same time as Jan Kleyn was being released in the southern hemisphere, Kurt Wallander was back at his desk in the Ystad police station. He had received the congratulations and good wishes of those colleagues who were at work early that Saturday morning. He smiled his lopsided smile and mumbled something inaudible in response. When he got to his office he closed the door behind him and took the telephone off the hook. His whole body felt like he had been raving drunk the night before, even though he had not touched a drop of alcohol. He had feelings of remorse. His hands were shaking. He was also sweating. It took him nearly ten minutes to gather sufficient strength to call the Kalmar police station. Blomstrand answered the phone, and passed on the disappointing news that the African they were looking for had probably slipped out of the country the night before, at Arlanda.

"How is that possible?" asked Wallander indignantly.

"Carelessness and bad luck," said Blomstrand, explaining what had happened.

"Why the hell do we bother?" asked Wallander when Blomstrand had finished.

Wallander ended the conversation, but left the receiver off the hook. He opened the window and stood listening to a bird singing in a tree outside. It was going to be a hot day. It would soon be June 1. The whole month of May had passed by without him really noticing that the trees were now in leaf, flowers were starting to grow, and the scents of early summer were in the air.

He went back to his desk. There was something he could not postpone until the following week. He fed a sheet of paper into his typewriter, took down his English dictionary, and started slowly to write a brief report for his unknown colleagues in South Africa. He put down what he knew about the planned assassination and described in detail what had happened to Victor Mabasha. When he got to the end of Victor Mabasha's life, he inserted another sheet of paper into the typewriter. He continued typing for an hour, and finished with the most important information: that a man by the name of Sikosi Tsiki was Mabasha's replacement. Unfortunately he had managed to slip out of Sweden. It could be assumed he was on his way back to South Africa. He said who he was, found the telex number to the Swedish section of Interpol, and invited them to get back to him if they needed any more information. He gave the secretary instructions to send it urgently to South Africa that same day.

Then he went home. He crossed the threshold again for the first time since the explosion.

He felt like a stranger in his own apartment. The furniture that had been damaged by the smoke was stacked in a heap, covered by a plastic sheet. He pulled out a chair, and sat down.

The atmosphere was stifling.

He wondered how he was going to get over everything that had happened.

About then his telex message arrived in Stockholm. A stand-in not fully familiar with procedures was instructed to send the message to South Africa. Because of technical problems and careless checking, page two of Wallander's report was never sent. And so the South African police were informed that night, May 23, that a gunman by the name of Victor Mabasha was on his way to South Africa. The police in the Johannesburg section of Interpol were puzzled by this strange message. It was unsigned, and ended very abruptly. Nevertheless, they had been requested by Inspector Borstlap to send all telex messages from Sweden to his office immediately. As the telex arrived in Johannesburg late on Saturday evening, Borstlap did not receive it until the following Monday. He contacted Scheepers right away.

They now had confirmation of what was in the letter signed by the secretive Steve.

The man they were looking for was called Victor Mabasha.

Scheepers also thought the telex was strangely abrupt and was concerned that it was unsigned. But since it was merely a confirmation of something he already knew about, he let the matter rest.

From now on all resources were concentrated on the hunt for Victor Mabasha. Every border post was put on standby. They were ready.

Chapter Thirty-three

The day he was released by Georg Scheepers, Jan Kleyn called Franz Malan from his house in Pretoria. He was convinced his telephones were tapped. But he had another line nobody knew about, apart from the BOSS special intelligence officers in charge of security-sensitive communications centers throughout South Africa. There were several telephone lines that did not exist officially.

Franz Malan was surprised. He did not know Jan Kleyn had just been released. As there was every reason to suspect Malan's telephone was also tapped, Kleyn used an agreed code word to prevent Malan from saying anything that should not be mentioned on the telephone. The whole thing was camouflaged as a wrong number. Jan Kleyn asked for Horst, then apologized and rung off. Franz Malan looked up his special code list to check the meaning. Two hours after the call, he was to make contact from a specified public phone booth to another.

Jan Kleyn was extremely eager to find out immediately what had been happening while he was under arrest. Franz Malan must also be clear that he would continue to take main responsibility. Jan Kleyn did not doubt his own ability to shake off shadows. Even so it was too risky for him to make personal contact with Franz Malan or to visit Hammanskraal, where Sikosi Tsiki was presumably already in residence, or would soon arrive.

When Jan Kleyn drove out through his gate, it did not take him many minutes to locate the car tailing him. He knew there was also another car in front, but he did not worry about that for the moment. They would naturally be curious when he stopped to make a call from a public phone booth. It would be reported. But they would never find out what was said.

Jan Kleyn was surprised that Sikosi Tsiki had arrived already. He also wondered why there was no word from Konovalenko. In their master plan was an agreement to inform Konovalenko that Sikosi Tsiki had actually arrived. That check should be no later than three hours after the assumed arrival time. Jan Kleyn gave Franz Malan some brief instructions. They also agreed to call from two other specified phone booths the following day. Jan Kleyn tried to discern whether Franz Malan seemed worried at all on the telephone. But he could hear nothing apart from Malan's usual slightly nervous way of expressing himself.

When the call was over he went to have lunch at one of the most expensive restaurants in Pretoria. He was pleased at the thought of the horrified reaction when his shadow handed his expense report to Scheepers. He could see the man at a table at the other end of the dining room. Jan Kleyn had already decided that Scheepers was unworthy of continuing to live in a South Africa that, within a year or so, would be well organized and faithful to its old ideals, created and then defended forever by a close community of Boers.

But there were moments when Jan Kleyn was hit by the awful thought that the whole business was doomed. There was no turning back. The Boers had lost, their old territory would be governed by blacks who would no longer allow the whites to live their privileged lives. It was a sort of negative vision he had difficulty in fending off. But he soon recovered his self-control. It was just a brief moment of weakness, he told himself. I've allowed myself to be influenced by the constantly negative approach South Africans of British origin have toward us *boere*. They know the real soul of the country is to be found in us. We are the people chosen by God and history, not them, and so they cherish this unholy envy they cannot shake off.

He paid for his meal, smiled as he passed the table where his shadow was sitting, a small, overweight man sweating profusely, and then drove home. He could see in the rearview mirror that he had a new shadow. When he had put his car away in the garage, he continued his methodical analysis of who could possibly have betrayed him and provided Scheepers with information.

He poured himself a little glass of port and sat down in the living room. He drew the drapes and switched off all the lights apart from a discreet lamp illuminating a painting. He always thought best in a dimly lit room.

The days he had spent with Scheepers had made him hate the current regime more than ever. He could not get away from the feeling that it was humiliating for him, a superior, trusted, and loyal civil servant in the intelligence service, to be arrested under suspicion of subversive activities. What he was doing was the exact opposite of that. If it were not for what he and the Committee were doing in secret, the risk of national collapse would be real rather than imaginary. As he sat sipping his port, he became even more convinced that Nelson Mandela must die. He no longer regarded it as an assassination, but an execution in accordance with the unwritten constitution he represented.

There was another worrisome element that added to his irritation. It was clear to him from the moment his trusted security guard on the president's personal staff called him that somebody must have supplied Scheepers with information that should really have been impossible for him to obtain. Someone close to Jan Kleyn had quite frankly betrayed him. He had to find out who it was, and quickly. What made him even more worried was that Franz Malan could not be completely excluded. Neither he nor any other member of the Committee. Apart from these men there could possibly be two, or at most three, of his colleagues in BOSS who could have decided, for some unknown reason, to sell him down the river.

He sat in the darkness thinking about each of these men in turn, dredging his memory for clues; but he found none.

He worked from a mixture of intuition, facts, and elimination. He asked himself who had anything to gain by exposing him, who disliked him so much that revenge could be worth the risk of being found out. He reduced the group of possibilities from sixteen to eight. Then he started all over again, and every time there were fewer and fewer possible candidates left.

In the end, there was nobody. His question remained unanswered.

That was when he thought for the first time it might be Miranda. Only when there was no other possible culprit was he forced to accept that she too was a possibility. The very thought worried him. It was forbidden, impossible. Nevertheless, the suspicion was there, and he had no choice but to confront her with it. He assumed the suspicion was unjustified. As he was certain she could not lie to him without him noticing, it would be resolved the moment he spoke to her. He must shake off his shadows within the next few days and visit her and Matilda in Bezuidenhout. The answer was to be found among the people on the list he had just worked through. The problem was that he still had not found an answer. He put both his thoughts and his papers on one side, and devoted himself instead to his coin collection. Observing the beauty of the various coins and imagining their value always gave him a feeling of calm. He picked up an old, shiny, gold coin. It was an early Kruger rand, and had the same kind of timeless durability as the Afrikaner traditions. He held it up against the desk lamp and saw it had acquired a small, almost invisible stain. He took out his carefully folded polishing cloth and rubbed the golden surface carefully until the coin started to shine once again.

Three days later, late on Wednesday afternoon, he visited Miranda and Matilda in Bezuidenhout. As he did not want his shadows to follow him even as far as Johannesburg, he had decided to lose them while he was still in central Pretoria. A few simple maneuvers were sufficient to shake off Scheepers's men. Even though he had got rid of the shadows, he kept a close eye on the rearview mirror on the freeway to Johannesburg. He also did a few circuits of the business center in Johannesburg, just to make certain he was not mistaken. Only when he was sure did he turn into the streets that would take him to Bezuidenhout. It was very unusual for him to visit them in the middle of the week, and in addition, he had not given advance notice. It would be a surprise for them. Just before he got there, he stopped at a grocer's and bought food for a communal dinner. It was about half past five by the time he turned into the street where the house was situated.

At first he thought his eyes were deceiving him.

Then he saw the man who just came out onto the sidewalk had emerged from Miranda's and Matilda's gate.

A black man.

He stopped by the curb and watched the man walking towards him, but on the other side of the road. He lowered the sun visor on each side of the windshield so that he could not be seen. Then he observed him.

He suddenly recognized him. It was a man he had been keeping under observation for a long time. Although they had never managed to prove it, BOSS had no doubt he belonged to a group in the most radical faction of the ANC that was thought to be behind a number of bomb attacks on stores and restaurants. He used the aliases of Martin, Steve, or Richard.

Jan Kleyn watched the man walk past, then disappear.

He froze. His mind was in turmoil, and it took some time to recover. But there was no getting away from it: the suspicions he had refused to take seriously were now real. When he eliminated one after the other of his suspects and ended up with none at all, he had been on the right track. The only other possibility was Miranda. It was both true and inconceivable at the same time. For a brief moment he was overcome by sorrow. Then he turned ice-cold. The temperature inside him fell as his fury grew, or so it seemed. In the twinkling of an eye, love turned to hate. It was aimed at Miranda, not Matilda: he regarded her as innocent, another victim of her mother's treachery. He gripped the wheel tightly. He controlled his urge to drive up to the house, beat down the door, and look Miranda in the eye for the last time. He would not approach the house until he was completely calm. Uncontrolled anger was a sign of weakness. That was something he had no desire to display in front of Miranda or her daughter.

Jan Kleyn could not understand. What he did understand made him angry. He had dedicated his life to the fight against disorder. For him, disorder included everything that was unclear. What he did not understand must be fought against, just as all other causes of society's increasing confusion and decay must be fought.

He remained sitting in his car for a long time. Darkness fell. Only when he felt totally calm did he drive up to the front door. He noticed a slight movement behind the drapes in the big living room window. He picked up the bags of supplies, and opened the gate.

He smiled at her when she opened the door. There were moments, so short that he barely managed to notice them, when he wished it was all in the imagination. But now he knew what was true, and he wanted to know what lay behind it.

4 6 7

The darkness in the room made it difficult to distinguish her dark features.

"I've come to visit you," he said. "I thought I'd surprise you."

"You've never done this before," she said.

It seemed to him her voice was rough and strange. He wished he could see her more clearly. Did she suspect he had seen the guy leaving the house?

At that moment Matilda came out of her room. She looked at him without saying a word. She knows, he thought. She knows her mother has betrayed me. How will she be able to protect her except by staying silent?

He put down the bags of food and took off his jacket.

"I want you to leave," Miranda said.

At first he thought he had misheard her. He turned around, his jacket still in his hand.

"Are you asking me to go?" he asked.

"Yes."

He contemplated his jacket for a moment before letting it drop to the floor. Then he hit her, as hard as he could, right in the face. She lost her balance but not her consciousness. Before she could manage to scramble up off the floor, he grabbed her blouse and dragged her up on her feet.

"You are asking me to leave," he said breathing heavily. "If anybody is going to leave, it's you. But you aren't going anyplace."

He dragged her into the living room and flung her down onto the sofa. Matilda moved to help her mother, but he yelled at her to stay back.

He sat down on a chair right in front of her. The darkness in the room suddenly made him furious. He leapt to his feet and switched on every light he could find. Then he saw she was bleeding from both her nose and her mouth. He sat down again and stared at her.

"A man came out of your house," he said. "A black man. What was he doing here?"

She did not answer. She was not even looking at him. Nor did she pay any attention to the blood dripping from her face.

It all seemed to him a waste of time. Whatever she said or did, she had betrayed him. That was the end of the road. There was no going on. He did not know what he would do with her. He could not imagine a form of revenge that was harsh enough. He looked at

Matilda. She still had not moved. Her face bore an expression he had never seen before. He could not say what it was. That made him insecure as well. Then he saw Miranda was looking at him.

"I want you to go now," she said. "And I don't want you ever to come and visit me again. This is your house. You can stay, and we'll move out."

She's challenging me, he thought. How dare she? He felt his rage rising again. He forced himself not to beat her again.

"No one's leaving," he said. "I just want you to tell me what's going on."

"What do you want to know?"

"Who you've been talking to. About me. What you've said. And why."

She looked him straight in the eye. The blood under her nose and on her chin had already congealed.

"I've told them what I found in your pockets while you were sleeping here. I listened to what you said in your sleep, and I wrote it down. Maybe it was insignificant. But I hope it ruins you."

She spoke in that strange, rough voice. Now he realized that was her normal voice, and the one she had used all those years had been a sham. Everything had been a sham. He could no longer see any substance in their relationship.

"Where would you have been without me?" he asked.

"Maybe dead," she replied. "But maybe I'd have been happy."

"You'd have been living in the slums."

"Maybe we'd have helped to pull them down."

"You leave my daughter out of this."

"You are the father of a child, Jan Kleyn. But you don't have a daughter. You have nothing but your own ruin."

There was an ashtray on the table between them. Now that words were beyond him he grabbed it and flung it with all his might at her head. She managed to duck. The ashtray lay beside her on the sofa. He leapt up from his chair, shoved the table to one side, grabbed the ashtray, and held it over her head. At the same moment her heard a hissing noise, like from an animal. He looked at Matilda, who had moved forward from the background. She was hissing through clenched teeth. He could not make out what she was saying, but he could see she had a gun in her hand.

Then she fired. She hit him in the chest, and he lived only for a

469

minute after collapsing to the ground. They stood looking at him, he could see them although his vision was fading. He tried to say something, tried to hold onto his life as it ebbed away. But there was nothing to hold onto. There was nothing.

Miranda felt no relief, but neither did she feel any fear. She looked at her daughter, who had turned her back on the corpse. Miranda took the pistol from her hand. Then she went to call the man who had been to see them, the one called Scheepers. She had looked up his number earlier, and written it on a scrap of paper beside the telephone. Now she realized why she had done that.

A woman answered, giving her name as Judith. She shouted to her husband, who came straight to the telephone. He promised to come to Bezuidenhout right away, and asked her to do nothing until he got there.

He explained to Judith that dinner would have to be postponed. But he did not say why, and she suppressed her desire to ask. His special assignment would soon be over, he had explained the previous day. Then everything would return to normal, and they could go back to the Kruger and see if the white lioness was still there, and if they were still scared of her. He called Borstlap, trying various numbers before tracking him down. He gave him the address, but asked him not to go in until he got there himself.

When he arrived in Bezuidenhout, Borstlap was standing waiting by his car. Miranda opened the door. They went into the living room. Scheepers put his hand on Borstlap's shoulder.

"The man lying dead in there is Jan Kleyn," he said.

Borstlap stared at him in astonishment.

Jan Kleyn was dead. It was striking how pale he looked, and how thin his face seemed to be, almost skeleton-like. Scheepers tried to make up his mind whether what he was witnessing was the end of an evil story, or a tragic one. He did not yet know the answer.

"He hit me," said Miranda. "I shot him."

When she said that, Scheepers happened to have Matilda in eyeshot. He could see she was surprised to hear what her mother said. Scheepers realized she was the one who had killed him, had shot her father. He could see Miranda had been beaten from her bloodstained face. Did Jan Kleyn have time to realize what was happening, he wondered. That he was going to die, and it was his daughter who was holding the last gun that would ever be pointed at him.

He said nothing, but indicated to Borstlap he should accompany him into the kitchen. He shut the door behind them.

"I don't care how you do it," he said, "but I want you to get that body out of here and make it look like a suicide. Jan Kleyn has been arrested and interrogated. That hurt his pride. He defended his honor by committing suicide. That'll do as a motive. Covering up incidents involving the intelligence service doesn't usually seem to be all that difficult. I'd like you to take care of this right now, or at least before tomorrow morning."

"I'll be putting my job on the line," said Borstlap.

"I give you my word that you're not risking anything at all," said Scheepers.

Borstlap stared at him for what seemed like an eternity.

"Who are these women?" he asked.

"People you've never met," replied Scheepers.

"Of course, it's all about the security of South Africa," said Borstlap, and Scheepers appreciated his weary irony.

"Yes," he said. "Exactly."

"That's another lie." said Borstlap. "Our country is a production line for lies, twenty-four hours a day. What'll happen when the whole thing collapses?"

"Why are we trying to prevent an assassination?" said Scheepers. Borstlap nodded slowly.

"OK, I'll do it," he said.

"On your own."

"Nobody will see me. I'll leave the body somewhere out in the countryside. And I'll make sure I'm in charge of the investigation."

"I'll tell them," said Scheepers. "They'll open the door for you when you come back."

Borstlap left the house.

Miranda had spread a blanket over Jan Kleyn's body. Scheepers suddenly felt tired of all the lies surrounding him, lies that were partly within himself as well.

"I know it was your daughter who shot him," he said. "But that doesn't matter. Not as far as I'm concerned, at least. If it matters to you, I'm afraid that's something you'll have to deal with yourselves. But the body will disappear later tonight. The police officer who came here with me will pick it up. He's going to refer to it as suicide. Nobody will know what actually happened. I can guarantee that for you."

Scheepers detected a gleam of surprised gratitude in Miranda's eyes.

"In a sense, maybe it was suicide," he said. "A man who lives like him maybe shouldn't expect anything else."

"I can't even cry over him," said Miranda. "There's nothing there."

"I hated him," said Matilda suddenly.

Scheepers could see she was crying.

Killing a human being, he thought. However much you hate somebody, no matter how desperate you were, there will be a wound in your soul that will never heal. He was her father after all, the father she didn't choose, but couldn't get rid of.

He did not stay long, as he could see they needed each other more than anything else. But when Miranda asked him to return, he promised to do so.

"We're going to move out," she said.

"Where to?"

She threw her arms wide.

"That's something I can't decide alone. Maybe it's best if Matilda decides?"

Scheepers drove home for dinner. He was thoughtful and distant. When Judith asked how much longer this special assignment was going to go on, he felt guilty.

"It'll be over soon," he said.

Borstlap called just before midnight.

"I thought I'd better tell you Jan Kleyn has committed suicide," he said. "They'll find him tomorrow morning in a parking lot somewhere between Johannesburg and Pretoria."

Who is the strong man now, wondered Scheepers. Who will be directing the Committee now?

Inspector Borstlap lived in the suburb of Kensington, one of the oldest in Johannesburg. His wife was a nurse on permanent night duty at the big army camp in town. As their three children had left the nest, Borstlap spent most weekday evenings alone in the house.

He was generally so tired when he came home from work, he did not have the strength to do anything but watch television. He sometimes went down to a little hobby room he had made for himself in the basement. He cut out silhouettes. It was an art he had learned from his father, although he had never managed to be as skillful as he was. But it was a restful occupation, carefully but boldly cutting out faces in black paper. That particular evening, when he had transported Jan Kleyn to the dimly lit parking lot he knew about because there had been a murder there not long ago, he found it difficult to relax when he got back home. He was going to cut out silhouettes of his children, but he was also thinking about the work he had been doing these last few days with Scheepers. His first reaction was that he enjoyed working with the young lawyer. Scheepers was intelligent and energetic, and he had imagination to boot. He listened to what others had to say, and he did not hesitate to admit he was wrong when appropriate. But Borstlap wondered what his assignment really was. He realized it was something serious, a conspiracy, a threatened assassination of Nelson Mandela that had to be prevented. But apart from that, his knowledge was pretty scanty. He suspected there was a gigantic conspiracy, but the only one he knew was involved was Jan Kleyn. He sometimes had the impression he was taking part in an investigation with a blindfold on. He said that to Scheepers, who told him he understood. But there was nothing he could do to help. His hands were tied by the level of secrecy he was working under.

When the strange telex message from Sweden landed on his desk that Monday morning, Scheepers had immediately gone into high gear. After a couple of hours they tracked down Victor Mabasha in the register and felt the tension increase when it was established that he had frequently been suspected of being a professional killer engaged in contract murders. He had never been convicted. Reading between the lines of the case histories, it was clear that he was very intelligent and always went about his business with skillfully set-up camouflage and security arrangements. His most recent known address was the township of Ntibane just outside Umtata, not far from Durban. That had immediately increased the credibility of Durban, July 3, as the crucial setting. Borstlap had contacted his colleagues in Umtata without delay, and they confirmed that they kept an eye on Victor Mabasha all the time. That same afternoon Scheepers and

Borstlap drove there. They joined up with local detectives and raided Victor Mabasha's shack at dawn. It was empty. Scheepers had trouble in concealing his disappointment, and Borstlap wondered what they could do next. They returned to Johannesburg and mobilized all available resources to track him down. Scheepers and Borstlap agreed that the official excuse, for the moment, should be that Victor Mabasha was wanted for violent attacks on white women in the province of Transkei.

Strong warnings were also issued that no word of Victor Mabasha should reach the mass media. They were working around the clock now. But they still failed to find any trace of the man they were looking for. And now Jan Kleyn was dead.

Borstlap yawned, put down his scissors and stretched.

The following day they would have to start all over again, he thought. But there was still time, whether the crucial date was June 12 or July 3.

Borstlap was not as convinced as Scheepers that the evidence pointing to Cape Town was a red herring. It seemed to him he ought to act as devil's advocate with regard to Scheepers' conclusions, and keep a close eye on the trail leading to Cape Town.

On Thursday, May 28, Borstlap met Scheepers at eight in the morning.

"Jan Kleyn was found at just after six this morning," said Borstlap. "Some motorist stopped to take a leak. He informed the cops right away. I spoke to a patrol car that was first on the scene. They said it was obviously a suicide."

Scheepers nodded. He could see he had made a good choice when he asked for Inspector Borstlap as his assistant.

"There are two weeks to go before June 12," he said. "Just over a month to July 3. In other words, we still have time to track down Victor Mabasha. I'm not a cop, but I would think that gives us plenty of time."

"It all depends," said Borstlap. "Victor Mabasha is an experienced criminal. He can remain hidden for long periods. He could disappear in some township or other, and then we would never find him."

"We have to," objected Scheepers. "Don't forget that the authority

I've been given means I can demand practically unlimited resources."

"That's not the way to find him," said Borstlap. "You could get the army to besiege Soweto and then send in the paratroops, but you'd still never find him. On the other hand, you'd have a revolt to deal with."

"What do you think?" asked Scheepers.

"Announce discreetly a reward of fifty thousand rand," said Borstlap. "A similarly discreet message to the underworld that we'd be prepared to pay for information enabling us to nail Victor Mabasha. That'll give us a chance of tracking him down."

Scheepers eyed him doubtfully.

"Is that how the police go about their business?"

"Not often. But it happens, sometimes."

Scheepers shrugged.

"You're the one who knows about these things," he said. "I'll take care of the money."

"The word will be out tonight."

Scheepers turned his attention to Durban. As soon as possible they should take a look at the stadium where Nelson Mandela was due to address a large crowd. They must find out now what security measures the local police intended to take. They needed a strategy for how to proceed if they did not manage to find Victor Mabasha. Borstlap was worried that Scheepers was not taking the other alternative as seriously as Durban. He said nothing, but made up his mind to get in touch with a colleague in Cape Town and ask him to do some leg-work on his behalf.

That same night Borstlap contacted some of the police informers he regularly received more or less useful rumors from.

Fifty thousand rand was a lot of cash.

He knew the hunt for Victor Mabasha had now started in earnest.

Chapter Thirty-four

On Wednesday, June 10, Kurt Wallander was given sick leave, effective immediately. According to the doctor, who regarded Wallander as taciturn and very uptight, he was vague and not sure exactly what was pestering him. He talked about nightmares, insomnia, stomach pains, nocturnal panic attacks when he thought his heart was about to stop beating—in other words, all the well-known symptoms of stress that could easily lead to a breakdown. At this point, Wallander was seeing the doctor every other day. His symptoms varied, and on every visit he had a different opinion as to which ones were worst. He had also started having sudden bouts of violent sobbing. The doctor who finally ordered him to take sick leave on grounds of acute depression, and prescribed anti-depressants for him, had no reason to doubt the seriousness of the situation. Within a short space of time he had killed one human being and actively contributed to another being burned alive. Nor could he wash his hands of responsibility for the woman who died while helping his daughter to escape. But most of all he felt guilty about the death of Victor Mabasha. It was natural that the reaction should set in with the death of Konovalenko. There was no longer anyone to chase, and no one hunting him. Paradoxically, the onset of depression indicated that the pressure on Wallander had eased. Now he would have the time to set his own house in order, and so his melancholy broke through all the barriers he had managed to erect thus far. After a few months, many of his colleagues began to doubt whether he would ever return. Occasionally, when news reached the police station of his peculiar journeys to places near and far, to Denmark and the Caribbean islands, there were some who thought he ought to be granted early retirement. The very thought caused much gloom. But in fact, it did not happen. He did come back, even though it took a very long time.

Nevertheless, the day after he had been ordered to take sick leave was a hot, windless summer day in southern Skåne, and Wallander was sitting in his office. He still had some paperwork to attend to before he could clear his desk and go off in search of a cure for his depression. He felt a nagging sense of uncertainty, and wondered when he would be able to go back to work.

He had arrived at the office at six in the morning, after a sleepless night in his apartment. During the silent hours of the morning he had at last completed his comprehensive report on the murder of Louise Åkerblom and everything that followed in its wake. He read through what he had written, and it was like descending into the underworld yet again, repeating the journey he wished he had never needed to undertake. Moreover, he was about to submit a report that was in some respects untruthful. It was still a mystery to him why some parts of his strange disappearance and his secret collaboration with Victor Mabasha had not been exposed. His extremely weak and in some parts contradictory explanations of some of his remarkable behavior had not, as he expected, aroused widespread skepticism. He could only think it was because he was surrounded by sympathy mixed with a rather vague *esprit de corps*, because he had killed a fellow human being.

He put the fat report on his desk and opened the window. Somewhere out there he could hear a child laughing.

What about my own summary, he thought. I found myself in a situation where I had no control over what happened. I made every mistake a cop can make, and the worst of all was that I put my own daughter's life at risk. She has assured me she doesn't blame me for those horrific days when she was chained up in a cellar. But do I really have any right to believe her? Have I not caused her suffering which might only come to the surface sometime in the future, in the form of angst, nightmares, a ruined life? That's where my report has to begin, the one I'll never write. The one which ends today with me being so shattered that a doctor has put me on sick leave indefinitely.

He went back to his desk and flopped down onto his chair. He had not slept a wink all night, it was true, but his weariness came from somewhere else, from the depths of his depression. Could it be that his fatigue was in fact depression? He thought about what would happen to him now. The doctor had suggested he should immediately start confronting his experiences through counseling. Wallander had taken that as an order that had to be obeyed. But what would he actually be able to say?

In front of him was an invitation to his father's wedding. He did not know how many times he had read it since it came in the mail a few days before. His father was going to marry his home aide the day before Midsummer Eve. That was in ten days. He had talked several times to his sister, Kristina, who had come on a short visit some weeks earlier, when the chaos had been at its worst, and thought she had managed to put an end to the whole idea. Now Wallander had no more doubts about whether or not it would happen. Nor could he deny that his father was in a better mood now than he could ever remember, no matter how hard he tried. He had painted a gigantic backdrop in the studio, where the ceremony was to take place. To Wallander's amazement it was exactly the same motif as he had been painting all his life, the static, romantic woodland landscape. The only difference was that he had now reproduced it giant-sized. Wallander had also talked with Gertrud, the woman he was going to marry. It was actually she who had wanted to speak with him, and he realized she had a genuine affection for his father. He had felt quite touched, and said he was happy about what was going to happen.

His daughter had returned to Stockholm over a week ago. She would come back for the wedding, and then go straight to Italy. That had brought home to Wallander the frightening realization of his own solitude. Wherever he turned, things seemed to be just as bleak. The night after Konovalenko's death he visited Sten Widén and drank up nearly all his whiskey. He got very drunk, and started talking about the feeling of hopelessness that was getting him down. He thought it was something he shared with Sten Widén, even if his old friend had his stable girls to go to bed with occasionally, thus creating a superficial glimmer of what might be called companionship. Wallander hoped the renewed contact with Sten Widén would turn out to be lasting. He had no illusions about being able to return to the friendship they had shared in their youth. That was gone forever, and could not be resurrected.

His train of thought was interrupted by a knock at the door. He started. He had noticed last week at the police station that he was scared of being with people. The door opened and Svedberg looked in, hoping he wasn't disturbing him.

"I hear you're going away for a while," he said.

Wallander immediately felt a lump in his throat.

"It seems to be necessary," he said, blowing his nose.

Svedberg could see he was emotional. He changed the subject immediately.

"Do you remember those handcuffs you found in a drawer at Louise Åkerblom's house?" he asked. "You mentioned them once in passing. Do you remember?"

Wallander nodded. To him, the handcuffs had represented the mysterious side of everybody's character. Only the day before he had been wondering what his own invisible handcuffs were.

"I was clearing out a closet at home yesterday," said Svedberg. "There were lots of old magazines there I'd decided to get rid of. But you know how it is. I ended up sitting down and reading them. I happened to come across an article about variety artistes over the last thirty years. There was a picture of an escape artist, and he'd used the fanciful professional name of Houdini's Son. His real name was Davidsson, and he eventually stopped wriggling out of chains and metal boxes and the like. Do you know why he stopped?"

Wallander shook his head.

"He saw the light. He became a born-again Christian. Guess which denomination he joined."

"The Methodists," said Wallander thoughtfully.

"Exactly. I read the whole article. At the end it said he was happily married and had several children. Among them a daughter called Louise. Née Davidsson, later married to a man called Åkerblom."

"The handcuffs," said Wallander pensively.

"A souvenir of her father," said Svedberg. "It was as simple as that. I don't know what you thought. I have to admit a few thoughts I wouldn't repeat in front of children entered my head."

"Mine, too," said Wallander.

Svedberg got up. He paused in the doorway and turned round.

"There was one other thing," he said. "Do you remember Peter Hanson?"

"The thief?"

"That's the one. You may remember I asked him to keep his eyes open in case the things stolen from your apartment turned up on the market. He called me yesterday. Most of your stuff has no doubt been disposed of, I guess. You'll never see it again. But oddly enough he managed to get hold of a CD he claims is yours."

"Did he say which one it was?"

"I wrote it down."

Svedberg searched through his pockets and eventually came across a crumpled scrap of paper.

"*Rigoletto*," he read. "Verdi."

Wallander smiled.

"I've missed that," he said. "Send my regards to Peter Hanson, and thank him."

"He's a thief," said Svedberg. "You don't thank guys like that."

Svedberg left the room with a laugh. Wallander started going through the remaining stacks of paper. It was nearly eleven by now, and he hoped to be finished by twelve.

The telephone rang. At first he thought he would ignore it. Then he picked it up.

"There's a guy here who wants to talk with Chief Inspector Wallander," said a female voice he did not recognize. He assumed it was the stand-in for Ebba, who was on vacation.

"Transfer him to somebody else," said Wallander. "I'm not receiving visitors."

"He's very insistent," said the receptionist. "He's adamant he wants to talk with Chief Inspector Wallander. He says he has important information for you. He's Danish."

"Danish?" said Wallander in surprise. "What's it about?"

"He says it has something to do with an African."

Wallander thought for a moment.

"Send him in," he said.

The man who came into Wallander's office introduced himself as Paul Jørgensen, a fisherman from Dragør. He was very tall and powerfully built. When Wallander shook hands with him, it was like being gripped by an iron claw. He pointed to a chair. Jørgensen sat down and lit a cigar. Wallander was glad the window was open. He groped around in his drawers before finding an ashtray.

"I have something to tell you," said Jørgensen. "But I haven't yet made up my mind whether I'm going to or not."

Wallander raised his eyebrows.

"You should have made your mind up before coming here," he said.

In normal circumstances he would probably have been annoyed. Now he could hear that his voice was far from convincing.

"It depends whether you can overlook a minor breach of the law," said Jørgensen.

Wallander began to wonder whether the man was making a fool of him. If so, he had chosen a most unfortunate moment. He could see he had better get a grip on the conversation, which looked like it was going off course almost before it had begun.

"I was told you had something important to tell me about an African," he said. "If it really is important, I might be able to overlook any minor breach of the law. But I can't promise anything. You must make up your own mind. I have to ask you to do so right now, though."

Jørgensen screwed up he eyes and gazed at him from behind a cloud of smoke.

"I'll risk it," he said.

"I'm listening," said Wallander.

"I'm a fisherman on Dragør," Jørgensen began. "I make just about enough to pay for the boat, the house, and a beer in the evenings. But nobody turns down the chance for some extra income, if the opportunity arises. I take tourists out for little sea trips now and then, and that produces some pocket money. Sometimes I'm asked to take somebody over to Sweden. That doesn't happen often, just once or twice a year. It could be some passengers who have missed a ferry, for instance. A few weeks ago I did a trip over to Limhamn one afternoon. I had just one passenger on board."

He stopped abruptly, as if expecting a reaction from Wallander. But he had nothing to say. He nodded to Jørgensen, telling him to go on.

"It was a black guy," said Jørgensen. "He only spoke English. Very polite. He stood in the wheelhouse with me all the way. Maybe I should mention there was something special about this trip. It had been booked in advance. There was this Englishman who spoke Danish, and he came down to the harbor one morning and asked if I could do a little trip over the sound, with a passenger. I thought it sounded a bit suspicious, so I asked a pretty high fee in order to get rid of him. I asked for five thousand kronor. The funny thing was he took out the money right away and paid in advance."

Wallander was extremely interested by this. Just for a moment he forgot all about himself and concentrated exclusively on what Jørgensen had to say. He indicated he should continue.

"I went to sea as a young man," said Jørgensen. "I learned quite a bit of English. I asked the guy what he was going to do in Sweden. He said he was going to visit some friends. I asked how long he'd be staying, and he said he'd probably be going back to Africa in a month, at the latest. I suspected there was something fishy going on. He was probably trying to get into Sweden illegally. Since it's not possible to prove anything now that happened so long ago, I'm taking the risk of telling you."

Wallander raised his hand.

"Let's dig a little deeper," he said. "What day was this?"

Jørgensen leaned forward and studied Wallander's desk diary.

"Wednesday, May 13," he said. "About six in the evening."

That could fit, thought Wallander. It could have been Victor Mabasha's replacement.

"He said he would stay for about a month?"

"I guess."

"Guess?"

"I'm sure."

"Go on," said Wallander. "Don't leave out any details."

"We chatted about this and that," said Jørgensen. "He was open and friendly. But all the time I somehow felt he was on his guard. I can't really put it any better than that. We got to Limhamn. I docked, and he jumped ashore.

"Since I'd already been paid, I backed out again right away and turned back. I wouldn't have given it another thought if I hadn't happened to come across an old Swedish evening paper the other day. There was a photo on the front page of a guy I thought I recognized. A guy who got killed in a gun battle with the cops."

He paused briefly.

"With you," he said. "There was a picture of you as well."

"When was the paper from?" asked Wallander, although he already knew the answer.

"I guess it was a Thursday paper," said Jørgensen hesitantly. "It could have been the next day. May 14."

"Go on," said Wallander. "We can check up on that later if it's important."

"I recognized that photo," said Jørgensen. "But I couldn't place it. I didn't catch on to who it was until the day before yesterday. When I dropped that African off in Limhamn, there was a giant of a guy waiting for him on the quayside. He stayed in the background, as if he didn't want to be seen. But I have pretty good eyes. It was him. Then I started thinking about it all. I thought it might be important. So I took a day off and came here."

"You did the right thing," said Wallander. "I'm not going to pursue the fact that you were involved in illegal immigration into Sweden. But that assumes, of course, that you have nothing more to do with it."

"I've already packed it in," said Jørgensen.

"That African," said Wallander. "Describe him to me."

"About thirty," said Jørgensen. "Powerfully built, strong and supple."

"Nothing else?"

"Not that I can remember."

Wallander put down his pen.

"You did the right thing, reporting this," he said.

"Maybe it's not important," said Jørgensen.

"It's extremely important," said Wallander.

He stood up.

"Thanks for coming to tell me," he said.

"That's OK," said Jørgensen, leaving.

Wallander looked for the copy he had kept of the letter he sent to Interpol in South Africa by telex. He pondered for a moment. Then he called Swedish Interpol in Stockholm.

"Chief Inspector Wallander, Ystad," he said when they answered. "I sent a telex to Interpol in South Africa on Saturday, May 23. I wonder if there's been any response."

"If there had been, you'd have heard right away," came the reply.

"Look into it, would you, just to be on the safe side," Wallander requested.

He got an answer a few minutes later.

"A telex consisting of one page went to Interpol in Johannesburg in the evening of May 23. There has been no response beyond confirmation of receipt."

Wallander frowned.

"*One* page?" he queried. "I sent two pages."

"I have a copy in front of me right now. The thing does seem to stop in mid-air."

Wallander looked at his own copy on the desk in front of him.

If only the first page had been transmitted, the South African police would not know Victor Mabasha was dead, and that a replacement had probably been sent.

In addition, it could be assumed the assassination attempt would be made on June 12, as Sikosi Tsiki had told Jørgensen the latest date he would be going home.

Wallander could see the implications right away.

The cops in South Africa had spent two weeks searching for a man who was dead.

Today was Thursday, June 11. The assassination attempt would probably be made on June 12.

Tomorrow.

"How the hell is this possible?" he roared. "How come you only sent half my telex?"

"I have no idea," was the answer he received. "You'd better talk to whoever was in charge."

"Some other time," said Wallander. "I'll be sending another telex shortly. And this one must go to Johannesburg without delay."

"We send everything without delay."

Wallander slammed down the receiver. He could not understand how the hell such incompetence was possible.

He did not bother to try and invent some kind of response. Instead he just put a new sheet of paper into his typewriter and composed a brief message. *Victor Mabasha is no longer relevant. Look instead for a guy named Sikosi Tsiki. Thirty years of age, well-proportioned* (he looked the phrase up in the dictionary, and rejected "powerfully built"), *no other obvious peculiarities. This message replaces all previous ones. I repeat that Victor Mabasha is no longer relevant. Sikosi Tsiki is presumably his replacement. We have no photograph. Fingerprints will be investigated.*

He signed the message and took it to reception.

"This must go to Interpol in Stockholm immediately," he said. He did not recognize the receptionist.

He stood over her and watched her fax the message. Then he returned to his office. He thought it might be too late.

If he were not on sick leave, he would have demanded an immediate investigation into who was responsible for sending only half of his telex. But as things stood, he couldn't be bothered.

He continued to attack the stacks of paper on his desk. It was nearly one o'clock by the time he was done. He had cleared his desk. Without a backward glance, he left his office and closed the door behind him. He saw nobody in the corridor, and managed to get away from the station without being seen by anybody apart from the receptionist.

There was just one more thing he had to do. Once that was done, he was finished.

He walked down the hill, passed the hospital, and turned left. All the time he thought everybody he met was staring at him. He tried to make himself as invisible as possible. When he got as far as the square, he stopped by the optician's and bought a pair of sunglasses. Then he continued down Hamngatan, crossed over the Österled highway, and found himself in the dock district. There was a café that opened for the summer. About a year ago he had sat there and written a letter to Baiba Liepa in Riga. But he had never mailed it. He walked out onto the pier, ripped it into pieces, and watched as the scraps floated away over the harbor. Now he intended to make another attempt to write to her, and this time he would send it. He had paper and a stamped envelope in his inside pocket. He sat down at a table in a sheltered corner, ordered coffee, and thought back to that occasion a year ago. He had felt pretty gloomy then, too. But that was nothing compared to the situation he found himself in now. He started writing whatever came into his head. He described the café he was sitting in, the weather, the white fishing boat with the light-green nets moored not far from where he sat. He tried to describe the sea air. Then he started writing about how he felt. He had trouble finding the right words in English, but he persevered. He told her how he was on sick leave for an indefinite period, and that he was not sure whether he would ever return to his post. *I may well have concluded my last case*, he wrote. *And I solved it badly, or rather, not at all. I'm beginning to think I am unsuitable for the profession I have chosen. For a long time I thought the opposite was true. Now I'm not sure anymore.*

He read through what he had written, and decided he was not up to rewriting it, even if he was very dissatisfied with his writing, which seemed to him vague and unclear. He folded up the sheet of paper, sealed the envelope, and asked for his check. There was a mailbox in the nearby marina. He walked over and mailed his letter. Then he continued walking out onto the jetty, and sat down on one of the stone piles. A ferry from Poland was on its way into the harbor. The sea was steel gray, blue and green in turn. He suddenly remembered the bicycle he had found there that foggy night. It was still hidden behind the shed at his father's place. He decided to return it that same evening.

After half an hour he got to his feet and walked through the town to Mariagatan. He opened the door, then stood staring.

In the middle of the floor was a brand new stereo system. There was a card on top of the CD player.

Get well soon and hurry back. Your colleagues.

He remembered that Svedberg still had a spare key he had gotten so he could let in the workmen doing the repairs after the explosion. He sat down on the floor and gazed at the equipment. He was touched, and found it difficult to control himself. But he didn't think he deserved it.

That same day, Thursday, June 11, there was a fault in the telex lines between Sweden and southern Africa between noon and ten at night. Wallander's message was therefore delayed. It was half past ten before the night operator transmitted it to his colleagues in South Africa. It was received, registered, and placed in a basket of messages to be distributed the next day. But somebody remembered a memo from some prosecutor by the name of Scheepers about sending all copies of telexes from Sweden to his office immediately. The cop in the telex room could not remember what they should do if messages arrived late in the evening or in the middle of the night. They could not find Scheepers's memo either, although it ought to have been in the special file for running instructions. One of the men on duty thought it could wait until the next day, but the other was annoyed because the memo was missing. If only to keep himself awake, he started looking for it. Half an hour later, he found it—needless to say, filed away in the wrong place. Scheepers's memo stated clearly and categorically that late messages should be conveyed to him immediately by telephone, regardless of the time. By then it was nearly midnight. The sum total of all these mishaps and delays, most of which were due to human error or sheer incompetence, was that Scheepers was not telephoned until three minutes past midnight on Friday, June 12. Even though he had made up his mind the assassination attempt would be in Durban, he had difficulty in getting to sleep. His wife Judith was asleep, but he was still awake, tossing and turning in bed. He thought it was a pity he hadn't taken Borstlap with him to Cape Town after all. If nothing else it would have been an edifying experience. He was also worried that even Borstlap thought it was odd they had not received a single tip about where Victor Mabasha might be hiding, despite the big reward waiting to be collected. On several occasions Borstlap had said he thought there was something fishy about the total disappearance of Victor Mabasha. When Scheepers tried to pin him down, he just said it was a hunch, nothing based on fact. His wife groaned when the bedside telephone started ringing. Scheepers grabbed the receiver, as if he had been waiting for a call all the time. He listened to what the Interpol duty officer read out for him. He picked up a pen from the bedside table, asked to hear it one more time, then wrote two words on the back of his left hand.

Sikosi Tsiki.

He hung up and sat there motionless. Judith was awake by now, and wondered if anything had happened.

"Nothing of danger to us," he said. "But it could be dangerous for somebody else."

He dialed Borstlap's number.

"A new telex from Sweden," he said. "It's not Victor Mabasha, but a guy called Sikosi Tsiki. The assassination attempt will probably take place tomorrow."

"Goddammit!" said Borstlap.

They agreed to meet at Scheepers' office without delay.

Judith could see her husband was scared.

"What's happened?" she asked again.

"The worst that could possibly happen," he replied.

Then he went out into the darkness.

It was nineteen minutes past midnight.

Chapter Thirty-five

Friday, June 12, was a clear but somewhat cool day in Cape Town. In the morning a bank of fog had drifted into Three Anchor Bay from the sea, but it had dispersed by now. The cold season was approaching in the Southern Hemisphere. You could already see lots of Africans on their way to work, dressed in woollen hats and thick jackets.

Nelson Mandela had arrived in Cape Town the previous evening. When he woke up at dawn, he thought about the coming day. It was a custom he had grown used to during the many years he spent as a prisoner on Robben Island. He lapsed into thoughtful silence. So many memories, so many bitter moments, but such a great triumph in the end.

He was an old man now, more than seventy years old. His time was limited: he was no different from anybody else and would not live forever. But he ought to live a few more years at least. Together with President de Klerk, he had to steer his country along the difficult, painful, but also wonderful path that would eventually lead to South Africa ridding itself of the apartheid system forever. The last fortress of colonialism on the black continent would finally fall. Once they had achieved that goal, they could withdraw, even die if need be. But he still had a great lust for life. He wanted to see it all through, and enjoy the sight of the black population liberating itself from the many hundreds of years of subjugation and humiliation. It would be a difficult path, he was aware of that. The roots of oppression ran deep into the African soul.

Nelson Mandela realized he would be elected the first black president of South Africa. That was not something he was striving to achieve. But he would have no grounds for declining.

It is a long way, he thought to himself. A long way to go for a man who has spent almost half his adult life in captivity.

He smiled to himself at the thought. But then he grew serious again. He thought about what de Klerk told him when they last met, a week ago. A group of highly placed *boere* had formed a conspiracy to kill him in order to create chaos and drive the country to the brink of civil war.

Could that really be possible, he wondered. He knew there were fanatical *boere*. People who hated all blacks, regarded them as animals without souls. But did they really think they could prevent what was happening in the country by means of some desperate conspiracy? Could they really be so blinded by their hatred—or was it fear, perhaps—that they thought it was possible to return to the old South Africa? Could they not see they were a dwindling minority? Admittedly with widespread influence still. But even so? Were they really prepared to sacrifice the future on the altar of a bloodbath?

Nelson Mandela shook his head. He had difficulty in believing that was true. De Klerk must have been exaggerating or misreading the information he had received. He was not afraid of anything happening to him.

Sikosi Tsiki had also arrived in Cape Town on Thursday evening. But unlike Nelson Mandela, he arrived unnoticed. He came by bus from Johannesburg, and got off unobserved when they reached Cape Town, got his bag, and allowed himself to be swallowed up by the darkness.

He had spent the night in the open. He slept in a hidden corner of Trafalgar Park. At the break of dawn, roughly the same time as Nelson Mandela had woken up and stood at his window, he climbed up the hill as far as he needed to, and installed himself there. Everything was in accordance with the map and instructions he had received from Franz Malan at Hammanskraal. He was pleased that he was being backed by such good organizers. There was nobody around; the barren slope was not suitable for picnics. The path to the summit, 350 meters high, meandered upwards on the other side of the hill. He had never used an escape car. He always felt freer moving around on foot. When it was all over he would walk quickly down the hill and blend in with the furious crowds demanding revenge for the death of Nelson Mandela. Then he would leave Cape Town.

Now he knew it was Mandela he was going to kill. He realized that the day Franz Malan told him when and where the assassination was to take place. He had read in the papers that Nelson Mandela was due to speak at the Green Point Stadium in the afternoon of June 12. He contemplated the oval-shaped arena stretched out in front of him, some 700 meters away. The distance did not worry him. His telescopic sights and the long-range rifle satisfied his requirements of precision and power.

He had not reacted to the news that it was Nelson Mandela who was to be his target. His first thought was that he ought to have been able to work that out himself. If these crazy *boere* were to have the slightest chance of creating chaos in the country, they would have to get rid of Nelson Mandela first. As long as he continued to stand up and speak, the black masses would be able to keep their self-control. Without him everything was more uncertain. Mandela had no obvious successor.

As far as Sikosi Tsiki was personally concerned, it would be an opportunity to right a personal wrong. It was not actually Nelson Mandela who had kicked him out of the ANC. But as he was the overall leader, he could nevertheless be regarded as responsible.

Sikosi Tsiki looked at his watch.

All he had to do now was wait.

Georg Scheepers and Inspector Borstlap landed at Malan Airport on the outskirts of Cape Town just after ten on Friday morning. They were tired and washed out after being on the go since one in the morning, trying to find out about Sikosi Tsiki. Half-asleep detectives had been hauled out of bed, computer operators controlling various police registers had turned up in overcoats over pajamas, having been collected by patrol cars. But when it was time to go to the airport, the result was depressing. Sikosi Tsiki was not in any of the registers. Nor had anyone ever heard of him. He was totally unknown to everybody. By half past seven they were on their way to Jan Smuts airport, just outside Johannesburg. During the flight they had tried increasingly desperately to formulate a strategy. They could see their chances of stopping this man, Sikosi Tsiki, were extremely limited, practically nonexistent. They had no idea what he looked like, they knew absolutely nothing about him. As soon as they landed in Cape Town, Scheepers went off to call President de Klerk and tell him that if possible, he should try and persuade Nelson Mandela to cancel his appearance that afternoon. Only when he went through the roof and threatened to have every police officer at the airport arrested did he manage to convince them who he was, and they left him alone in a room. It took almost a quarter of an hour to contact President de Klerk. Georg Scheepers told him as briefly as possible what had happened during the night. But de Klerk had responded in ice-cold fashion to his suggestion, saying it would be pointless. Mandela would never agree to cancel his engagements. Besides, they had gotten the time and place wrong before. That could happen again. Mandela had agreed to increase his bodyguard. There was nothing more the president of the Republic could do at the moment. When the conversation was over, Scheepers again had the uncomfortable feeling that de Klerk was not prepared to go to any lengths to protect Nelson Mandela from assassination. Was that really possible, he wondered indignantly. Have I misunderstood his position? But he had no time to go on thinking about President de Klerk. He found Borstlap, who had meanwhile picked up the car the police had ordered from Johannesburg. They drove straight to Green Point Stadium, where Nelson Mandela was due to speak three hours later.

"Three hours is not long enough," said Borstlap. "What do you think we'll have time to do?"

"We have to succeed," said Scheepers. "Its as simple as that. We have to stop the man."

"Or stop Mandela," said Borstlap. "I can see no other possibility."

"That's just not possible," said Scheepers. "He'll be on the platform at two o'clock. De Klerk refused to plead with him."

They showed their IDs and were allowed into the stadium. The podium was already in place. ANC flags and colorful streamers were everywhere. Musicians and dancers were getting ready to perform. Soon the audience would start arriving from the various townships of Langa, Guguletu, and Nyanga. They would be greeted by music. For them, the political meeting was also a festival.

Scheepers and Borstlap stood on the podium and looked around.

"There's a crucial question we must face up to," said Borstlap. "Are we dealing with a suicide pilot, or somebody who will try to get away afterwards?"

"The latter," said Scheepers. "We can be sure about that. An assassin prepared to sacrifice his own life is dangerous because he's unpredictable. But there's also a big risk that he would miss the target. We are dealing with a man who is expecting to get away after shooting Mandela."

"How do we know he'll be using a gun?" asked Borstlap.

Scheepers stared at him with a mixture of surprise and irritation.

"What else could he do?" he asked. "A knife at close range would mean he'd be caught and lynched."

Borstlap nodded gloomily.

"Then he has lots of possibilities," he said. "Just look around. He could use the roof, or a deserted radio cabin. He could choose a spot outside the stadium."

Borstlap pointed to Signal Hill, which loomed up half a kilometer away from the stadium.

"He has lots of possibilities," he repeated. "Too many."

"We have to stop him even so," said Scheepers.

They could both see what this implied. They would be forced to choose, to take chances. It was simply impossible to investigate every possibility. Scheepers suspected they might have time to check about one in ten; Borstlap thought perhaps a few more.

"We have two hours and thirty-five minutes," said Scheepers. "If Mandela is on time, that's when he'll start speaking. I assume an assassin won't delay things any longer than necessary."

Scheepers had requested ten experienced police officers to assist him. They were under the command of a young sergeant.

"Our assignment is very simple," said Scheepers. "We have a couple of hours in which to turn this stadium inside out. We're searching for an armed man. He's black, and he's dangerous. He must be put out of action. If possible we should take him alive. If there's no other choice, he has to be killed."

"Is that all?" asked the young sergeant in surprise when Scheepers had finished. "Don't we have a description of the guy?"

"We don't have time for arguing," interrupted Borstlap. "Arrest anybody who seems to be acting at all strangely. Or is somewhere he shouldn't be. We can find out if we have the right person or not later."

"But there has to be some kind of description," insisted the sergeant, and was supported by murmurs from his ten officers.

"There has to be nothing of the kind," said Scheepers, noticing he was starting to get annoyed. "We'll divide the stadium into sections and get started right away."

They searched through cleaners' closets and abandoned storerooms, crept around on the roof and out onto girders. Scheepers left the stadium, crossed over Western Boulevard, the broad High Level, and then started climbing up the hill. He stopped after about two hundred meters. It seemed to him the distance was far too great. A potential assassin couldn't possibly pick a spot outside the stadium itself. He returned to Green Point soaked in sweat and short of breath.

Sikosi Tsiki had seen him from where he was hidden behind some bushes, and thought it was a security officer checking the area around the stadium. He was not surprised; he had expected something like this. What worried him was that they might use dogs to patrol the area. But the guy scrambling up the slope was on his own. Sikosi Tsiki crouched down low, a pistol with a silencer ready. When the man turned back without even going as far as the top, he knew nothing could go wrong. Nelson Mandela had just a couple of hours to live.

Crowds were already flocking into the stadium. Scheepers and Borstlap fought their way through the teeming mass of bodies. All around drums were beating, people were singing and dancing. Scheepers was terrified by the thought that they might fail. They just had to find the guy Jan Kleyn had hired to kill Nelson Mandela.

An hour later, thirty minutes before the meeting was due to begin with Mandela's arrival at the stadium, Scheepers was in a panic. Borstlap tried to calm him down.

"We haven't found the guy," said Borstlap. "We have very little time left to continue the search now. We have to ask ourselves what we might have missed."

He looked round. His eyes focused on the hill outside the stadium.

"I was there already," said Scheeper.

"What did you see?" asked Borstlap.

"Nothing," said Scheepers.

Borstlap nodded, lost in thought. He was beginning to think they would not find the assassin until it was too late.

They were pushed backwards and forwards by the massive crowds.

"I just don't get it," said Borstlap.

"It was too far away," said Scheepers.

Borstlap looked at him questioningly.

"What do you mean?" he asked. "Too far away?"

"Nobody could hit a target from that distance," said Scheepers angrily.

It was a while before Borstlap realized Scheepers was still talking about the hilltop outside the stadium. Then he suddenly became serious.

"Tell me exactly what you did," he said, pointing to the hilltop.

"I climbed up part way. Then I turned back."

"You didn't actually go to the summit of Signal Hill?"

"It's too far away, I told you!"

"It's not too far away at all," said Borstlap. "There are rifles that can shoot over a kilometer. And hit the target. That's only 800 meters away at most."

Scheepers stared at him in bewilderment. Just then an enormous cheer went up from the dancing crowd, followed by intense drumming. Nelson Mandela had arrived in the stadium. Scheepers caught a glimpse of his grayish-white hair, his smiling face, and his waving hand.

"Come on!" yelled Borstlap. "If he's here at all, he has to be somewhere on that hillside."

Through his powerful telescopic sights Sikosi Tsiki could see Nelson Mandela in close-up. He had removed the sights from the rifle and followed him from the moment he stepped out of his car at the stadium entrance. Sikosi Tsiki could see he had only a few bodyguards. There did not seem to be any noticeable alert or unrest around the white-haired man.

He remounted the sights on the rifle, checked the loading mechanism, and sat down in the position he had carefully selected.

He had rigged up a stand made of light metal. It was his own invention, and would give his arms the support he needed.

He glanced up at the sky. The sun was not going to cause him any unexpected problems. No shadows, no reflections, no glare. The hilltop was deserted. He was all alone with his gun and a few birds hopping around on the ground.

Five minutes to go. The cheering in the stadium hit him at full volume, even though he was over half a kilometer away.

Nobody would hear the shot, he thought.

He had two spare cartridges. They were lying on a handkerchief in front of him. But he did not expect to have to use them. He would save them as a souvenir. Maybe one day he would turn them into an amulet? That would bring him good luck for the rest of his life.

He avoided thinking about the money awaiting him. He had to carry out his mission first.

He raised his rifle, put his eye to the telescopic sight and watched Nelson Mandela coming to the podium. He had made up his mind to shoot at the first opportunity. There was no reason to delay. He put down the gun and tried to relax his shoulders, taking deep breaths at the same time. He felt his pulse. It was normal. Everything was normal. Then he raised the rifle again, placed the butt against his right cheek and closed his left eye. Nelson Mandela was standing just below the podium. He was partly shielded by other people. Then he broke away from the group and strode toward the microphone. He raised his arms over his head like a victor. His smile was very wide.

Sikosi Tsiki pulled the trigger.

But a fraction of a second before the bullet shot out of the barrel of the rifle at tremendous speed, he felt a thump on his shoulder. He couldn't stop his finger on the trigger. The shot rang out. But the thump had nudged him nearly five centimeters. That meant the bullet did not even hit the stadium, but landed on a parked car on a street a long way away.

Sikosi Tsiki turned around.

There were two men, breathing heavily and staring at him.

Both had pistols in their hands.

"Put down your gun," said Borstlap. "Slowly, carefully."

Sikosi Tsiki did as he was told. He had no choice. The two white men would not hesitate to shoot, he could see that.

What had gone wrong? Who were they?

"Place your hands on your head," said Borstlap, handing Scheepers a pair of handcuffs. He stepped forward and locked them around Sikosi Tsiki's wrists.

"Get up," said Scheepers.

Sikosi Tsiki stood up.

"Take him down to the car," said Scheepers. "I'll be there in a moment."

Borstlap led Sikosi Tsiki away.

Scheepers stood listening to the cheering from the stadium. He could hear Nelson Mandela's unmistakable voice over the loudspeakers. The sound seemed to come from very far away.

He was soaked in sweat. He could still feel traces of the horror he had felt when it seemed they wouldn't find the man they were looking for. The sense of relief had still not hit him.

It struck him that what had just happened was a historic moment. But it was a historic moment that nobody would ever know about. If they had not managed to get up the hill in time, if the stone he had thrown at the man in desperation had missed, another historic moment would have taken place. And that one would have been more than just a footnote in the pages of history. It could have sparked off a bloodbath.

I am an Afrikaner myself, he thought. I ought to be able to understand these crazy people. Even if I don't want it that way, they are my enemies today. Maybe they haven't really understood deep down that the future of South Africa will force them to reassess everything they've been used to. Many of them will never manage that. They would rather see the country destroyed in an explosion of blood and fire. But they will not succeed.

He gazed out over the sea. As he did so, he wondered what he was going to say to President de Klerk. Henrik Wervey was also expecting a report. In addition he had an important visit to make to a house in Bezuidenhout Park. He was looking forward to meeting the two women again.

What would happen to Sikosi Tsiki, he had no idea. That was Inspector Borstlap's problem. He put the rifle and the cartridges back into their case. He left the metal frame where it was.

*   *   *

Suddenly he thought of the white lioness lying on the river bank in the moonlight.

He would suggest to Judith they should pay another visit to the safari park soon.

Maybe the lioness would still be there.

He was deep in thought as he descended the hillside.

He had realized something that had not been clear to him before. At last he realized what the white lioness in the moonlight had meant to him.

First and foremost he was not an Afrikaner, a white man.

He was an African.

Epilogue

Parts of this story are set in South Africa, a country which has long been poised on the brink of chaos. The potential social upheaval and the internal human trauma have reached a point where many fail to see any possible outcome beyond an inevitable apocalyptic catastrophe. On the other hand, one cannot deny hopeful signs: the racist-controlled South African empire will collapse in the foreseeable future. At this writing, June 1993, a preliminary date has been fixed for the first free elections in South Africa: April 27, 1994. In Nelson Mandela's words: "a watershed has finally been reached. In the long term, the outcome can already be predicted, albeit with the natural reservations that apply to all political prophesies: the establishment of a democratic society based on the rule of law."

In the short term the outcome is less certain. The understandable impatience of the black majority and the active resistance of the white minority is leading to increased violence. No one can state with certainty that civil war is inevitable. Nor can anyone state that it can be avoided. It could be that uncertainty is the only certainty.

Many individuals have contributed—sometimes without realizing—to the South African sections of the novel. Had it not been for Iwor Wilkins and Hans Strydom's essential work in exposing the realities behind the Afrikaner secret society the Broederbond, its secrets would have been concealed from me as well. Reading Graham Leach's writings on Boer culture was also a veritable adventure. And to round things off, Thomas Mofololo's stories cast light on African customs, not least with regard to the spirit world.

There are many others whose personal testimony and experiences have been significant. I thank them all, without naming individuals.

This is a novel. That means the names of characters and places, and also the timing, are not always authentic.

The conclusions, and indeed the story as a whole, are my own responsibility. No one apart from myself, named or unnamed, should be blamed for any shortcomings.

Maputo, Mozambique, June 1993
Henning Mankell.